SHADOWS OF THE MOSS

KIM POOVEY

Shadows of the Moss

Published by Dickens Ghost Publishing, LLC.

Cover Design by Rena Violet.

Published in the United States of America.

ISBN: 978-0-9996219-4-3

1. Fiction-Historical

2. Fiction-General

Created with Vellum

Dedicated to God, my rock and my salvation,
and to all those who gave their lives in the pursuit of freedom.

PROLOGUE

APRIL 1848, PHILADELPHIA

Blood trickled from Maggie's nose as she traipsed along the frosted path to the cattle barn, her wounded frame shuddering in the cold. *How had things gone so wrong so quickly*? Defeated, she entered the stables where the low rumbling of cattle shifting on straw beds comforted her. Her head was still spinning from the battering as she looked for a place to rest when she spied the ladder to the loft. It seemed as good a place as any to spend the night.

A slight rise in the temperature accompanied each step although winter's icy fingers still held her in its grasp. Maggie walked to the far corner, pulled her shawl tightly around her and burrowed beneath a blanket of hay. Exhaustion weighted her limbs and pounded in her head like a hammer. At least her nose had stopped bleeding. Sleep toyed with her overwrought mind; her thoughts drifting back to the day she left her Irish home on a wild adventure to America. All of her expectations had been destroyed within a few months leaving her to ponder how to escape before it was too late.

PART I

1

SEPTEMBER 1847: THE HARTFORD SAILS FROM IRELAND TO PHILADELPHIA

Maggie fought to keep her stomach from emptying its contents as the sea rocked the ship's hull to and fro. To make matters worse, the old man several rows down continued to cough and sputter keeping everyone in steerage from sleep. *If only she could help him*, Maggie thought. She shifted on the lumpy pad of her bunk, her muscles inundated by exhaustion while her mind rebuffed the tranquility of slumber. When she closed her eyes she could see the old gent's face with his watery blue stare, bedraggled hair, and sallow skin tone that suggested he might not survive the journey. Despite the uncomfortable accommodations, Maggie focused on how wonderful things would be once she reached America.

Morning broke to the silence of the old gent's eternal rest. Unfortunately, strong winds and heavy rains prevented anyone from going on deck, leaving the body to putrefy for three days before it could be pitched overboard. Maggie felt pity for the man's kin, as they would never know what became of him, and no proper burial would be afforded such an affable bloke.

In order to maintain her sanity, Maggie dreamt of all the

wonderful things she would see and do in America, not to mention meeting her mother's brother and his family. With no surviving members on her father's side, and never knowing any of the English relatives on her mother's side, Maggie was excited at the prospect of enlarging her family circle. The thought of her father drew her mind back to the day she sailed from Ireland. She could still smell the slight odor of sulfur as smoke billowed from the stacks of the ship, the din of the crowd muffling her pleas to remain with him.

"It's for your own good m' dear. I'll not have m' daughter starvin' to death before m' very eyes. You're better off with your uncle in America than facin' the unknown here." His easy-going demeanor and composed countenance gave her the strength to go. "No need for frettin', it won't be forever," he said, touching her cheek.

The ship's horn roared, broadcasting the vessel's impending departure. Maggie embraced her father. "I love you, Da," she whispered in a thick Irish accent, rallying as much courage as she could muster.

Holding her at arm's length, her father warned, "Watch that accent. You're an educated young lady and I'll not have people thinking you've got no brains in that pretty head o' yours."

"Da, I'm proud to be half Irish. I'll never understand your constant need to whittle it out of me."

"Trust me on this lassie, I know what I'm talkin' about. Make me proud, and speak like an English lady, not an Irish peasant," he said with a wink.

"Not to worry, Da. I'll make you proud."

"Have you got the money hidden in a safe place?"

She patted the satchel over her shoulder. "It's right here along with my book of Byron's poetry."

"Don' let anybody know about it. Don' want nothin' happening to my lassie."

She hugged him once more, inhaling his special scent of

pipe tobacco and wool sweater. The ship bellowed another warning, ending their embrace.

"Goodbye, Da. I'll write often!"

"As will I, m' dear."

She'd hurried up the gangplank with the leather satchel across her shoulder and her travel bag filled with two dresses, three pairs of stockings, and an extra shawl. A silver locket hung on a ribbon beneath her bodice that housed a curl of her mother's hair on one side and a snippet of her father's hair on the other. Making her way through a throng of people, Maggie maneuvered to the railing and waved to her father as the ship slipped from the dock. Her arm numbed as she waved it in the air until her father's figure dissolved into the distance, loneliness enveloping her despite the crowds swirling around the deck.

After days of teetering and tottering within the belly of the ship, Maggie was thrilled when the storms subsided and she was able to spend more time on deck. Salt air whipped Maggie's auburn tresses against her face as the ship skirted over ocean waters forging towards her new home. Weeks on the open sea left Maggie's body cocooned in dirt and sweat, the sticky salt air sealing in the wretched odors of passengers crammed into tight quarters. The stench was overwhelming, making her miss the sweet scent of Ireland's sprawling fields. Food rations were meager and nearly inedible while water was its own form of putrid. Never would she have imagined such deplorable conditions. Regardless, she made the best of her circumstances taking advantage of time on deck to catch her breath and read a few lines from Byron.

Tensions augmented by cramped accommodations roused the anger of exasperated Irishmen, making daily brawls a common occurrence. Sadly, there was no escaping these escapades, which distressed onlookers, especially the children.

Sleep was a treasured commodity and difficult to obtain

amongst the filth, strong odors, and shifting of the hull. Considering the fighting, grumbling, and illness that spread as quickly as a plague of locusts, it seemed inconceivable that anyone would survive the journey, and all this to escape impending death from famine!

Following weeks at sea, Maggie was thrilled when the coastline of her new home came into view. The ship's horn wailed as the vessel maneuvered into the slip amongst a field of hankies and hands waving like wheat stalks in an autumn breeze. Maggie waited patiently for the throng of passengers to disembark, her stomach simmering with anticipation.

Chaos surrounded her as people shuffled about with bags and trunks, rushing to reunite with family members. With her satchel slung across her shoulder and the travel bag clutched in her hand, Maggie stood on her toes searching the crowd in an effort to find someone, anyone, who might be waiting for her. Apprehension prickled her nerves as the crowd thinned with only a few people remaining. In the distance, a statuesque gentleman lingered beside a gleaming ebony carriage. A duster coat, tan trousers tucked into knee-high leather boots, and a top hat perched upon his burnished mane of hair gave him an appearance of distinction. Surely, this was her uncle, or so she hoped.

Maggie's heart quickened with each step as she made her way toward the gentleman. With a curtsey, she spoke in her best English, "Good day. Might you be Mr. Stevenson?"

"I am," he replied, his arms crossed as he scrutinized her appearance.

"Nice to make your acquaintance. I'm your niece, Maggie McFarland."

"You definitely look Irish, although you don't sound like it," he huffed.

"My father has taken great pains to educate me in the English ways."

"Still doesn't take away the Irish."

Puzzled by his demeanor, Maggie's chest tightened at the awkward welcome. Having never known her mother or her maternal relatives, she'd no idea what to expect from this side of the family. Then again, it may have been the difference in culture that made the situation feel uncomfortable.

"Let's not squander any more time," he snapped. "I've already wasted an afternoon. You'll ride up there," he said, nodding toward the bench at the front of the carriage as he stepped into the cab and shut the door. Tears stung Maggie's eyes at the cold reception until she realized she must reek after the voyage. The driver, a stout, dark-skinned man with sympathetic eyes secured her travel bag to the boot of the carriage. With his help she clambered to the leather bench trying not to catch her skirt in the process. Once she was settled, the driver took his place beside her, launching the horses into action with a cluck and a tap of the reins.

Shades of burnt orange, gold, and bright reds clothed the trees as the carriage caromed over sun-dappled roads. Maggie took in the surroundings, her spirits buoyed by the crisp air and sprawling hills.

"I'm Maggie McFarland, Mr. Stevenson's niece," she said, uncomfortable with the silence.

The driver gave a sideways glance.

"I'm Milton."

"Pleasure to meet you."

"D' you always speak to the help, Miss?" he asked, raising his eyebrows.

"I speak to everyone. Is that not the way in this country?"

"We speak to our own kind. I'm a driver and don't associate with the family. Wouldn't be right."

"I don't understand."

"I be livin' over the livery stables, and you be livin' in the big house. We only see each other when I drive you somewhere," he said curtly. "And if you is family, why's you up here with me?"

"Perhaps my uncle wanted me to enjoy the scenery of my new country," she replied, sitting a bit straighter.

"You got lots to learn, Miss," Milton grumbled, shaking his head.

In an effort to calm her trepidation, Maggie convinced herself the odd greeting was nothing more than a difference between American and Irish culture and that the tension would dissipate once she settled into her new home. But her resolve crumbled as the carriage turned down a dirt drive, sending a chill bumping across her skin and an ominous feeling niggling at her nerves.

2

FIELDING HALL

Massive Elm trees lined the drive leading to a drab stone mansion with ivy snaking up its sides. Its gloomy façade intensified Maggie's unease as the carriage came to a halt at the base of marble stairs that dipped and cracked in places. Sections of shutters had gaps like missing teeth while rot ate away at window trims and eaves. The front door was faded and the landscape littered with weeds. The declining state of the home's exterior alluded to a once prosperous beginning now crumbling with neglect.

Milton alighted from the bench seat in one fluid movement, offered his hand, and helped Maggie to the ground. From there he hurried to convey his boss from the vehicle. Mr. Stevenson disembarked and strode toward the house, stopping when he reached the steps.

"Are you waiting for a parade? Get your things and come inside," he grumbled, marching up the stairs where a chocolate Labrador wagged his tail. Mr. Stevenson leaned over and scratched the dog's head.

"That's my good Jasper," he said, walking through the door, the dog trotting behind him.

"Good luck Miss," Milton said with a nod, handing Maggie her bag.

"Thank you," Maggie said softly. Her chest constricted as she watched him climb to the tufted leather seat and drive away.

Maggie hurried inside surprised to find the home's interior much more ostentatious than the unkempt exterior. A center staircase anchored the space with rooms running the length of the entryway on both sides. A gallery of oil paintings and ornate sconces adorned damask covered walls with a gilded chandelier crowning the area. Mesmerized, Maggie looked up and down as she padded along the hall taking in the general splendor. Her Irish cottage would fit in this section of her uncle's house.

"You're slower than a box turtle," Mr. Stevenson declared, interrupting Maggie's thoughts, his tone of voice dampening her spirits.

Not wanting to upset him further, Maggie followed him to one of the rooms where a Persian rug obscured gleaming heart pine floors and the windows were framed in layers of swagged draperies. Two women sat upon velvet covered chairs, stitching a canvas of colorful blooms on an embroidery frame. The younger one looked up with warm brown eyes and hair the color of dark chocolate while the older woman's stolid stare sent a chill through Maggie.

"Miss McFarland, this is my wife, Mrs. Stevenson, and my daughter, Miss Susannah Stevenson."

Curtseying, Maggie articulated her best English, "It's lovely to make your acquaintance."

Susannah glided over, the deep blue silk of her gown rustling like leaves in a fall breeze. Her complexion held a rosy glow as she smiled and took Maggie's hands in hers.

"It's ever so good to have you here, Cousin. I'm certain we'll become devoted friends."

Her warm reception released the anxiety holding Maggie's muscles captive. Finally, someone was kind.

Resuming her sewing, Mrs. Stevenson called to her daughter.

"Susannah, please show Miss McFarland to her quarters. She'll need to make herself presentable for dinner."

"Of course, Mother."

The two stepped into the hall when Mr. Stevenson called Maggie back.

"Miss McFarland, I believe there's the business of a stipend from your father?"

"I nearly forgot," a blush warmed her face. Maggie sifted through her satchel and produced a small leather pouch. She handed several bank notes to her uncle.

"Irish money? What am I to do with this?"

"It's all my father had," she responded, her fingers clutching her satchel.

"If a pittance of foreign currency is all your father plans to provide then you'll have to earn your keep around here. Don't believe for a moment you'll be permitted to laze around and be pampered."

"Yes, Uncle."

"What did you say?" Anger choked his words.

"I said yes, Uncle?" Baffled by his response, she queried, "Is that not appropriate?"

"It certainly is not!"

"Would you prefer Mr. Stevenson?"

"*Sir* will be fine."

"Sir?"

"That's what I said. You do understand English, do you not?"

"Yes, sir."

Tears hovered in the corners of Maggie's eyes. Like a convict facing the hangman, she stood before him her legs held captive by fear.

“Have you something else to say, Miss McFarland?” he blustered.

“No sir,” she whispered, looking down.

“Then go,” he grunted with a menacing gaze, his teeth clenched.

Maggie rushed from the room where her cousin waited in the hall.

“Is he upset about something?” Maggie whispered, her body still quaking from the discourse.

“Father can be gruff at times. So long as you do as you’re told and find meaningful occupation, all will be well.”

Maggie pondered her uncle’s coarse demeanor as she followed her cousin to the second-floor landing. A grand hallway in shades of soft blues and gold with ornately framed paintings and a garden of floral arrangements on marble topped plant stands sprawled before her.

“How lovely,” Maggie murmured.

“Father takes great pride in his home.”

“Are the bed chambers on this floor?” Maggie asked.

“My quarters are at the end of the hall across from my parent’s room. The room to your immediate left is for guests. Father’s private office is to the right.”

“What about the other door?”

“No one uses that room anymore,” she replied softly, sorrow veiling her expression. “Your accommodations are on the third floor.”

They climbed the stairs to the third story which was notably plainer than the lower levels. Their footsteps echoed down a narrow hallway with simple door trims and bare floors. Susannah stopped at the second room on the left and opened the door.

“You’re welcome to make any changes that suit your needs,”

Susannah declared as she stood aside for Maggie to enter. "Father likes people to take initiative."

The modestly furnished room boasted a rope bed, a washstand with ironstone pitcher and basin, and a three-drawer chest topped with a clouded mirror. Gauzy curtains flanked smudged windowpanes. The only means of warmth was a small hearth with a few sticks of kindling.

"Can I not stay in the guest room on the second floor with the rest of the family?"

"Father needs to reserve that room for special visitors. Nothing is too good for guests at Fielding Hall," Susannah said with a smile.

Apparently, everything was too good for Irish relatives, Maggie thought as a lump formed in her throat. "What about that other room?"

"As I said, it's no longer in use." Susannah's lips thinned and her eyes shifted to the floor.

"Does anyone else stay up here?"

"The house servants have quarters up here, but not to worry, I'm certain they won't disturb you," she replied, her welcoming demeanor returning. "I'll leave you to settle in. Dinner is at six o'clock," Susannah announced, closing the door behind her.

Dismayed, Maggie surveyed the room with its grimy walls and worn floors. It wasn't that she was opposed to her accommodations, after all, she'd never lived an extravagant lifestyle, but the obvious distinction between family and servant pained her.

Homesickness trickled across Maggie's cheeks. Perhaps with time things would get better. Obviously, Mr. Stevenson was uncertain about taking a stranger into his home for an undisclosed period of time. Maggie was convinced she could win his approval once he realized she wasn't a burden.

She tightened the woolen shawl about her shoulders and

started a fire. As the flames crackled to life, she curled up on the bed, and drifted off to dreamland where she was comforted by the visions of rolling hills, baying sheep, and the fragrant scents of the Irish countryside.

MAGGIE STIRRED, leaning up on her elbow to get her bearings. Embers smoldered in the small fireplace casting a gloomy veil over the room. Her back and shoulders were stiff. A thick layer of dust covered the mantel clock suggesting it hadn't been wound in some time. Not wanting to be late for the evening meal, she rose from bed, changed into a fresh, albeit wrinkled frock, and re-pinned her auburn tresses. Trepidation plucked at her heart as she took a deep breath and headed downstairs.

According to the tall clock at the base of the first-floor staircase, she was a quarter of an hour ahead of schedule. In an effort to calm the palpitations thrumming in her chest, she traipsed down the hall perusing the artwork. Two stately portraits of a lady and gent caught her attention. Salt and pepper hair crowned their heads and both exuded stern expressions although the lady's was particularly disturbing. There was a faint furrow to her brow and discontent glinted in her eyes. Most unsettling was the slight rise on the right side of her mouth as if animosity and anger were a pleasant emotion for her. Maggie shuddered beneath her stare.

Footfalls echoed from the stairs as Mr. Stevenson descended with Jasper toddling at his side. Mrs. Stevenson and Susannah followed a short distance behind. Maggie curtseyed as her uncle and aunt marched past as if she were a mere shadow. Susannah reached out and touched Maggie's hand, a smile curling her lips.

All took their places at the table, Jasper at Mr. Stevenson's feet. The delectable scents of roasted meat and bread wafted through the air making Maggie's stomach rumble. She'd not eaten all day. As if on cue, a host of servants entered the room serving food and pouring wine. The meal went on in complete silence heightening the tense atmosphere. Using her best table manners, Maggie ate as delicately as possible, careful to sit straight, take small bites, and not spill anything.

When the last of the dishes were cleared, Mr. Stevenson leaned back in his chair, swirling wine in his glass.

"Miss McFarland, it pains me to see how little effort you put into your appearance."

"My apologies, Unc...sir," she replied, her palms beginning to moisten.

"Father, she only arrived this afternoon and hasn't had an opportunity to settle in yet." Susannah offered, smiling at Maggie.

"Miss Stevenson, I don't recall asking for your opinion," he snapped.

Susannah's eyes dropped as she mumbled, "Sorry, Father."

He tossed his napkin on the table and rose, signaling all to follow. Maggie met her cousin's gaze as she walked past. The sorrowful expression in her eyes told Maggie her uncle's wrath knew no bounds, even with his own daughter.

Mr. and Mrs. Stevenson sat in plush parlor chairs on either side of the fireplace with Jasper snuggling at his master's feet. Susannah motioned for Maggie to join her at the embroidery loom.

"Do you embroider?" Susannah asked, speaking in a hushed tone.

"I had no one to instruct me," Maggie sighed.

"Then I'll do my best to teach you."

"I'd like that."

For the next hour, Susannah showed Maggie how to stitch the petals of a pink rose. When the clock chimed nine, Mr.

Stevenson announced it was time to retire. Maggie was relieved, her fingertips sore from working the tiny stitches.

Once in her room, Maggie roused the dying flames in the small hearth and sat upon the bed. With the satchel in her lap, she removed the book of poetry and placed it on the side table along with the silver locket from around her neck. Tears threatened to fall as she shivered in the chilly room far from her beloved Da and the pleasant existence she'd always known. In the flickering shadows of the oil lamp, she eased her head against the pillow. She read a few lines of Byron before succumbing to slumber's embrace, the book of poetry sliding shut along with her hopes.

3

Tossing and turning throughout the night, Maggie awoke with her chest tight and her head aching. The fire had died during the wee hours of the morning and frost licked the edges of the windowpanes. She wrapped the quilt tightly around her body and padded to the washstand where the water was splintered with icy crystals. Tears puddled in her eyes at the hopelessness of her situation. What was she to do? She couldn't go home. Wiping the sadness from her cheeks, she did her best to rub the wrinkles from her dress, fix her hair, and wipe down her face with the small amount of water in the basin.

She arrived downstairs just as the Stevensons were entering the dining room. The morning meal was a repeat of dinner except Mr. Stevenson spent much of the time behind a newspaper. The only sound was the clinking of flatware against china plates. When the dishes were taken away, Mrs. Stevenson spoke.

"Miss McFarland, did you sleep well?"

With a sideways glance toward her uncle, Maggie chose her words carefully, fearful he would find fault with her response.

“I did, thank you,” she replied. “Although, it would be nice to have a bit more wood for the fire.”

Maggie startled when Mr. Stevenson crumpled the paper.

“Complaining already?” he bellowed.

“No, sir. It’s just very cold and the fireplace is so small.”

“Mr. Stevenson, I see no problem providing a bit more wood to stoke her fire,” her aunt said with arched eyebrows.

“I’ll consider it.”

“Thank you, sir. I’m grateful for your consideration.”

“As you should be,” he replied, raising the paper and muttering, “Worthless Irish scamp.”

Maggie stared at the flickering flame of the candle in the center of the table, the wax dripping down the taper much like her hopes. Biting her lower lip, she bridled the Irish spirit raging to break free with a sharp response. Fury and fear battled within, moistening her eyes and shaking her limbs.

Regardless of her feelings, she needed to appease him. After all, she had no idea how long she’d be staying and this was the only home available to her. Her Da always said to repay meanness with kindness and good things would result. The thought of her beloved father seized her heart, adding a dash of sorrow to the emotional cyclone swirling within her chest. Her father’s love was a balm to her soul even if he was an ocean away, giving her the courage to try to win her uncle’s approval.

Mrs. Stevenson stood and summoned Susannah.

“Come my dear, we have bible study.”

Obediently, Susannah followed her mother glancing back at Maggie as she stepped from the room.

“Mother, perhaps Miss McFarland would like to join us?”

Mrs. Stevenson stopped. “If Miss McFarland would care to learn the ways of proper religion, she’s welcome to do so.”

“I’d be delighted to join you.” *Anything to avoid being alone with my uncle*, she thought.

"What church did you attend in Ireland?" Mrs. Stevenson queried.

"The Catholic church."

Mrs. Stevenson sniffed in derision. "I don't believe our bible study will benefit your particular beliefs. However, if you insist on joining us, we've no choice but to accept. Our religion requires us to welcome all, even those who worship inappropriately."

Susannah's smile faded and her eyes dropped at her mother's judgmental words.

Maggie overlooked the insult, hoping to appease her aunt. The bible seemed a good place to start. They read passages for an hour before dispersing to their own rooms for prayer and reflection. Maggie was certain her aunt would find favor with her, and hopefully convince Mr. Stevenson to do the same. It was her best chance.

Once in her room, Maggie gazed out the window rubbing the thin layer of moisture from the panes with the edge of her shawl. A blurred glimpse of the gardens below mirrored the barrenness she felt. Granted, she'd only be here for a limited period of time. When things improved at home, she could return to her da. Until then, she needed to make things tolerable, otherwise she'd go mad. At least Susannah seemed kind, making up for her aunt and uncle's apathy. How odd that two people could be so gruff, yet have such a gracious daughter. All the same, Maggie was determined to do her best to make her Da proud even if her efforts did little to alter her uncle's opinion.

MRS. STEVENSON CLIMBED the stairs and found her husband at his desk studying the accounts ledger.

"May I speak with you about Miss McFarland's request for more firewood?"

"Go on," he said not looking up.

"I believe we need to grant this request."

"Why?" Mr. Stevenson barked, leaning back in his chair, his lips pursed as he folded his arms across his chest.

"We must allow some provisions for her comfort. Freezing the girl could jeopardize future financial support."

"Don't tell me how things should be done in this house! Remember your place," he thundered. His tone was like barbs across her skin. Experience told her to proceed cautiously or she'd end up being the target. Years of reproach had schooled her well in self-preservation.

"I only want what is best for our family. What if she were to write her father about her circumstances? He might remove her *and* the financial support."

"Humph," he grunted, resuming his perusal of the ledgers. "Then make sure she doesn't write to him." Rubbing his forehead, he muttered, "If my son were alive, we'd not be in this situation. Instead, I'm cursed with a pathetic daughter and a nonsensical wife. Women have but two functions, neither of which serve any useful purpose in maintaining financial security."

"I'm sorry for troubling you," she replied, curtly.

"Don't even consider befriending that little scamp. The last thing I need is a harem of screeching harlots about the place." Mr. Stevenson reached down and scratched the dog's ear. "You're the only intelligent creature in this house, Jasper."

Mrs. Stevenson seethed with contempt but held her tongue, her lips pressed in a straight line. She left the room relieved that she'd escaped his wrath, this time.

~

In an effort to clear her mind, Maggie decided to stroll the grounds. Whenever she was stymied at home, a brisk walk always seemed to allay her troubles. She hurried down the back staircase and into the crisp autumn air, the dew-tipped grass sparkling beneath blue skies. She tightened the shawl around her torso, puffs of breath furling from her lips as she meandered down a dirt path.

Chickens squawked and scattered as she passed a substantial coop and followed the trail to a series of cottages cresting over the hill. Curiosity summoned her to the area where steam billowed from a large iron pot suspended from a tripod over an open fire. A wispy, dark-skinned woman with specks of gray tinting her hair, hauled a bucket over to a stout woman in a blue checked dress whose waist had dissolved into her chest and hips. Both women were sheathed in aprons splattered by whatever was heating in the cauldron.

As Maggie approached, the two women stood statuesque like deer in an open field.

"G'mornin'," Maggie called out, the Irish tinting her words.

The taller woman's eyebrows arched as she rested a hand on her hip.

"Who you be?"

Regret fingered Maggie's heart for being so forward with people she didn't know. Wringing her hands, Maggie introduced herself. "I'm Mr. Stevenson's niece, Maggie McFarland."

"Didn't know he had any other family. Thought they was all dead," the slender woman replied, wiping her hands on the apron covering a brown calico frock that blended with her coffee-colored complexion.

"Don't be so blunt, Letty. Can't you see you've made the poor girl nervous." A smile plumped the other woman's cheeks. "I's Willa and this here is Letty."

"Nice to meet you both."

"Is you needin' somethin'?" Letty asked, her ebony eyes glinting.

"Just walking around the farm. Reminds me a bit of my home in Ireland."

"Explains why you talk funny," Letty said, resuming her work.

A flush colored Maggie's cheeks. Willa scrunched her face, slapping Letty's arm as she passed. "Be nice, will ya?"

Turning to Maggie she asked, "How come you's here?"

"Things are bad at home, so my father sent me to stay with my uncle."

Willa and Letty gave each other a knowing glance, sending a shiver through Maggie. Why was everyone so guarded?

"What's so bad at home that he send you here?" Willa asked.

"Famine. There's barely enough food to feed one person more or less both of us. When things get better, I'll return home."

"And your father thought this was a good place for you?" Letty asked, raising her eyebrows.

"It was the only place for me. My father doesn't have any family left and my mother died shortly after I was born. I'd never known anyone from her side of the family until now."

"Humph," Letty crinkled her lips.

"I don't want to keep you from your work. Perhaps I'll see you again soon," Maggie said.

"Not likely if you is..."

Willa pinched Letty midsentence.

"We's always glad to have you visit," Willa smiled. "We hopes you like it here."

"I'm sure I will, once I get settled."

With a wave, Maggie followed the dirt path over the hill. The sun drifted higher in the sky as cows clustered in a sprawling pasture next to a red barn where a tall, lanky fellow hammered a loose board.

Curiosity drew her to the structure. The young man looked up, his dark eyes sparkling as a broad smile formed.

"Good mornin'," he said with a nod. "Can I help you with something?"

"Please don't let me keep you from your work. I was only exploring the grounds."

"You gots a funny way of talking," he said with a sideways glance.

"That's because I'm from Ireland," she chuckled. "I'm Maggie McFarland, Mr. Stevenson's niece. I'll be staying here for a while."

"Ireland? Where's that?" he asked.

"On the other side of the ocean," she replied.

"Why's you here?"

"Because of the famine. My father wanted me to be safe so he sent me here."

"How you like it so far?"

"I've not been here long enough to form an opinion." Maggie looked away, fighting back tears.

"Sounds more like an excuse than an answer," he said, resuming his work.

"May I ask you a question?"

"Go ahead," he said, resting his arm on his knee.

"Do you get along with Mr. Stevenson?"

"Why you think I don't get along with him?"

"I'm not inferring you don't," panic squeezed Maggie's heart. "I was only curious."

The young man seemed to know exactly what she was trying to ascertain. Obviously, he'd suffered under Mr. Stevenson's wrath.

"Mr. Stevenson is a hard man but he treat me fair 'nuff.

Long as I do my duties, he leaves me be. How bouts you? Does you get along with him?"

"He doesn't seem to like me."

Laughter rolled from his lips. "Don' take no offence at that. He don't like nobody."

Maggie gave a halfhearted chuckle, her stress beginning to evaporate. Something about the young man's countenance and direct manner of speaking was comforting.

"I'm sorry but I don't know your name," she said.

Shaking his head, he grinned. "You got me thinkin' bout Mr. Stevenson and I forgots to tell you. I'm Sellers."

"It's nice to meet you Mr. Sellers."

"Ain't no mister to it, just Sellers."

"It's good to make your acquaintance, but you'd best get back to work. I don't want to cause you any trouble."

With a nod and a smile, he continued hammering as Maggie walked away.

A slight wind tumbled across the open fields, billowing the auburn locks that had escaped the bun at the back of Maggie's neck. A shiver slithered across her skin making her pull the woolen shawl tighter. Despite the brisk conditions, she was beginning to relax, finding solace in her walk. The trail meandered past a milking shed and a smokehouse until it burrowed into the nearby woods. Studying the sun's position in the sky, Maggie figured it was probably nearing midday and she needed to get back before lunch was served.

By the time Maggie reached the house, the frosty air had flushed her nose and cheeks. Although rejuvenated by her morning explorations, she dreaded another disdainful encounter with her uncle. However, the workers seemed nice enough making her believe that with a little effort she'd eventually be accepted, or so she hoped.

. . .

Later that evening, everyone gathered in the parlor. Mr. and Mrs. Stevenson settled near the hearth while Maggie sat with Susannah at the loom.

"What did you do today, Miss McFarland?" Mr. Stevenson asked.

"I took a walk around the farm. It's quite lovely."

"How productive of you to spend your time eyeing my daughter's inheritance. Bear in mind you'll not get an acre of it," he growled.

"I was only complimenting your property, sir," Maggie stuttered. "I'd never assume to lay claims…"

Disgust contorted his expression as he leaned forward. "Keep it that way. You'll *never* have anything in this house or the farm. Do I make myself clear?"

"Yes, sir." Maggie swallowed the fear hovering in her throat. *So, this is why he's angry with me. He thinks I'm here to steal my cousin's inheritance.*

Now more than ever, she was determined to prove her loyalty. Once he realized she meant no harm he'd acknowledge her as part of the family.

At nine o'clock the family adjourned to their quarters. Maggie trudged up the stairs to her room where she changed for bed and snuggled beneath the quilt to read. A soft rap at the door sent her heart racing.

"Come in," she said, sitting up.

Susannah opened the door, padded across the floor, and sat on the edge of the bed.

"I wanted to apologize for father's outburst earlier. He can be intense at times."

"Why would he think I wanted your inheritance?"

"He's been obsessed with finances and legacies for years now. Ever since…" Susannah's eyes dropped and she wrung her hands before regaining a happier attitude. "Anyway, if you find some useful purpose here, things will be better for you."

"Have you any idea what that purpose might be?" Maggie asked, hoping for guidance. "It seems my presence aggravates him."

"Like I said, he can be brusque at times but he means well. Perhaps Mother could advise you."

Maggie's stomach flopped at the thought. Although not as mean as Mr. Stevenson, Maggie's aunt was intimidating in her own way.

"Maybe I'll speak with her after breakfast." Maggie yawned.

"It's rather late and I need to get back to my room before anyone discovers my absence. Goodnight, Cousin."

"Goodnight, Susannah."

The door squealed shut leaving Maggie in the flickering light of the oil lamp. She'd take Susannah's advice and ask her aunt for guidance and try to put forth a better effort to appease Mr. Stevenson.

4

Following the morning meal, Maggie caught up with her aunt in the hallway.

"Mrs. Stevenson, may I speak with you?"

"Yes?" she responded, her mouth forming a straight line.

Maggie glanced around to ensure Mr. Stevenson wasn't within earshot. "I was wondering if you had any suggestions of how I might pass my time in a suitable manner?"

"I'll consult with Mr. Stevenson and let you know what he says."

"Please, don't bother him with something so trivial. I don't wish to upset him," Maggie declared. The mention of her uncle's name sent a ripple of fear pulsing through her veins.

"You've asked a question and I intend to provide an answer," she replied with a sneer.

Mrs. Stevenson started down the hall, her skirts rustling against the polished floors. A wave of nausea crashed over Maggie. Somehow, she didn't think her question would bode well with her uncle's volatile temperament. Too nervous to find out, she decided a long walk would do her good, at least until lunchtime when she'd have to face her uncle's response.

~

Much to Maggie's relief, Mr. Stevenson was not at the midday meal. Regardless of his absence, the meal proceeded in silence as if he were there. Occasionally, Maggie's eyes met Susannah's gaze and they exchanged a quick grin. Maggie was growing fond of her cousin and relished the bond forming between them. If only she could forge a similar relationship with her aunt and uncle.

After luncheon, Maggie joined her cousin in the front parlor. Susannah continued her needlework tutorial as they sat side by side at the embroidery stand pulling colored floss up and down through the creamy cotton canvas.

"How did you pass your time in Ireland?" Susannah asked as she made another stitch.

"Most of my time was spent on my studies. Da was adamant about my education."

"To what point? You'll need sewing skills and good manners to make a proper match."

"Funny, Da never said anything about marriage. Only thing he cared about was my attending University. Something about a promise to my mother before she died."

"What would you study at University?" Susannah queried, resting her hand on the loom.

"I've never found anything outside of reading poetry that appealed to me. I'm only seventeen so I suppose I'll figure it out when the time comes." Maggie yelped when she pricked her finger with the needle. "I'm not very good at this."

"Not to worry, with a little practice I'm sure you'll master the technique," Susannah said, resuming her stitching.

Maggie glanced at her cousin's neat and even stitches that formed the delicate petals on a crimson rose.

"How long have you been embroidering?"

"Mother began instructing me at five," she replied, drawing

the needle down through the canvas. "I finished my first sampler by my sixth birthday."

"How lovely to have your mother to teach you." Maggie's mind imagined what it would be like to sit by her own mother as they pulled colorful strands through a linen background.

"Did you know your mother well?"

"I haven't any memory of her," Maggie sighed, "She died when I was a few months old."

"I'm sorry," Susannah said, her shoulders slumping.

"Once, Da tried to teach me how to do needlepoint after reading a lady's magazine, but his fingers were too clumsy and all that resulted was a knotted mess. At that moment, he declared that needlework was not to be in my repertoire and never made mention of it again," Maggie chuckled at the memory.

Susannah's eyebrows arched. "I cannot imagine my father picking up a needle."

"Da and I have a special relationship."

"In what way?"

"We only have each other. My father enjoys poetry and the classics so we'd read by the firelight every evening before bed. He'd sit across from me puffing on his pipe while I read." Her eyes moistened at the memory and she pricked her finger again.

"Sounds like a lovely way to live." Susannah's hand quivered a bit as she knotted the silk thread.

"How do you spend your time?" Maggie asked, sucking her fingertip.

"Bible study, embroidery, etiquette, things I'll need to run a household someday."

"Have you no other ambitions?"

"Children, of course. Surely you want the same," Susannah said, tilting her head.

"Someday, perhaps. After I finish at University, I plan on traveling abroad before settling down."

Susannah sat upright. "How progressive. I've never met anyone who wanted something so...daring."

"I don't know that I'd call it daring, I just want to live a little before I have a family of my own."

"That doesn't sound very ladylike," Susannah said, resuming her stitches.

"I'm sure a lot of the things I've done would be deemed unladylike by you."

"Like what?" Susannah asked, her eyes sparkling.

"Herding sheep, repairing fences, hunting duck. Sometimes Da needed my help."

"Extraordinary," she said, shaking her head. "I cannot fathom doing such things. What an interesting life you've led."

"Funny, your life seems charmed to me. You live in this beautiful home and wear lovely gowns. No doubt you've never been knee deep in mud trying to dislodge a sheep that wondered off or plucked the feathers off a duck for your supper."

Susannah wrinkled her nose, "Thankfully, no. I don't think I'd care for such tasks."

"Probably not. I can't say I enjoyed them either, but it was a matter of survival, and with Da by my side it wasn't so bad."

They chatted on, their bond strengthening with each stitch. Maggie enjoyed her cousin's company, which made up for the uncomfortable atmosphere created by her uncle's sour demeanor.

Fortunately, Mr. Stevenson was gone for a week on business, giving Maggie and Susannah plenty of time to forge a relationship. She was the sibling Maggie had always longed for. Each morning after breakfast, Maggie joined her aunt and Susannah for bible study, and then she strolled the grounds or spent time in the library. Fielding Hall housed an extensive book collection, one that would have astounded Maggie's father.

Once Mrs. Stevenson retired to her chambers, Susannah would sneak to Maggie's room. Maggie looked forward to her cousin's visits as it helped to quell her frazzled nerves and longing for home.

One evening, Susannah came to Maggie's room with a sly grin. I brought you something," she said, pulling a hair comb from her wrapper pocket.

"It's lovely. What's the occasion?" Maggie asked, studying the jeweled piece, its coral beads shimmering in the lamplight.

"I know father has been harsh about your appearance. Since I haven't any dresses to loan you, I thought the comb would be brilliant in your hair."

"I don't know what to say." A smile crinkled Maggie's cheeks as her eyes moistened.

Susannah leaned over and clutched Maggie's hand. "You needn't say anything. I'm happy to give it to you."

"What about your father? Won't he be upset that you've given me something so fine?"

"Not at all. It belonged to his mother, *our* grandmother. I think it's fitting you should have it."

Maggie studied the orangey beads and filigree gold setting. It had belonged to her grandmother, a woman she'd never known. Her heart warmed at the kind gesture. Susannah's friendship made everything else bearable.

"Thank you. It's one of the most beautiful things I've ever owned," she said, pulling her cousin into a hug.

They chatted and giggled about all sorts of things as Susannah swept Maggie's hair into a stylish twist and slid the comb into her auburn swirls. When yawns began to stifle the laughter, Susannah bid goodnight, leaving Maggie filled with hope that things were improving, and that life in her new home could only get better.

The following morning, Maggie arranged her reddish locks into an elegant coiffure and snuggled the comb at the top. She checked her image in the clouded mirror before padding down the stairs to join her aunt and Susannah for breakfast. Shock radiated through her body when she entered the dining room to find her uncle in attendance. Reaching to her upswept hair, she readjusted the comb before taking her seat at the table.

Thankfully, the meal passed uneventfully until Maggie followed Mrs. Stevenson and Susannah for bible study. As she reached the doorway, a hand gripped her arm and yanked her back.

"Miss McFarland, a word please," her uncle growled.

"I have bible study with..."

His eyes narrowed as he leaned close to her face. "You dare to contradict me?"

"No sir," she breathed, her breakfast churning in her stomach.

Tightening his grasp, he squeezed a yelp from her.

"You little thief. I knew you'd be a problem."

"Sir, I don't know what you're talking about. I haven't stolen anything," she replied, her voice trembling.

"And a liar too." In one swift motion, he yanked the comb from her hair taking several strands with it.

"Ow!" she hollered, grabbing her head.

His hand slid from her arm, latching onto a clump of her hair. Whimpering beneath his grasp, Maggie leaned back as far as she could to relieve the pressure from his hold.

"You stole this from my daughter, you little tramp. If I discover anything else missing in this house, I'll deal with you in a manner befitting your kind."

"I didn't take it sir, Susannah..."

Yanking her head back, he clenched his teeth and snarled, "Don't you ever refer to my daughter so informally. She is above you in station and breeding. You will address her as Miss Stevenson."

Barely able to speak, due to the angle at which he held her head backwards, she managed to croak out, "Yes, sir."

Releasing her hair, he shoved her into the sideboard, and stormed from the room with the comb clutched in his hand.

Maggie's knees wobbled as she leaned against the wall trying to steady her quaking body. Tears fell as she rubbed her neck and lamented the loss of the lovely gift from her cousin. Not wanting to encounter her uncle's animosity again, Maggie hurried to her room. She sat upon the floor before the hearth and sobbed, her body shaking with each gasp until there were no more tears to shed.

Emotionally numb, she sat before the fire wondering what her Da was doing and how she might get home to him. Right now, all she wanted to do was escape the evil residing at Fielding Hall.

ANNOYED by the fact he was forced to take in his wretched niece and lamenting the catastrophic losses of his last card game, Mr. Stevenson collected the mail and lumbered upstairs to his study with Jasper trailing on his heels. His ability to join another game depended upon his cash flow, which had all but dried up. The mounting IOUs were hindering his ability to join poker games not to mention the back and forth writing of checks between two banks to keep his accounts afloat. He needed to find the funds to continue.

The leather chair moaned as he sat at his desk taking a moment to scratch Jasper's velvety ears, the dog's sympathetic soft eyes gazing up at him. Mr. Stevenson grinned at the dog and patted his head before sorting through his correspondences. As he flipped through the mail an Irish postmark caught his eye. Tearing into the envelope, he unfolded the parchment and read.

Mr. Stevenson,

I regret to inform you that things have worsened here and I've been evicted from the farm. I do not have a permanent address at this time and am traveling to the next county in search of work. Rest assured, when I am able to send more money for Maggie's support, I shall do so. Thank you again for taking in my darling daughter. I shall write as soon as I've settled and have news to share. I've enclosed a separate letter for Maggie. Please do not share my misfortune with her, as I don't wish to burden her with my plight.

Gratefully,

Gerald McFarland

Fury shook his hands as Mr. Stevenson read the letter for Maggie. A series of well wishes and adoration from Mr. McFarland to his daughter filled the page. Crumpling the letter, Mr. Stevenson threw it across the room. *Typical Irishman, taking advantage of me*, he stewed.

Mr. Stevenson stormed downstairs to the kitchen with Jasper trailing on his heels. McFarland might think him a fool by pawning off his worthless daughter on him, he thought, but he'd remedy the situation and get his money out of her, one way or another. in one form or another.

Maggie sat in her room penning a letter to her father. She glanced at the silver locket housing snippets of her parents' hair, and wrote of the glorious autumn colors tinting the trees and the cool breezes that danced across hills. She avoided mentioning her uncle's ruthless nature, instead focusing on the relationship with her cousin. The last thing she wanted to do was burden her father. A tear spattered onto the parchment as she signed her name before sliding the letter into the envelope. Treading downstairs, she found her aunt in the formal parlor.

"Good afternoon, Mrs. Stevenson."

"What do you want?" she asked, her nose tilting upwards.

"Would you please mail this letter to my Da?"

Her upper lip curled into a sneer. "Da is such a vulgar term, is it not?"

"I've always called him Da," Maggie said, her cheeks flushing.

"Give it to me," she said.

"Thank you," Maggie muttered, placing the envelope in her aunt's outstretched hand.

Leaving the room, Maggie felt a sense of relief, as if the letter somehow connected her to home. Unbeknownst to her, Mrs. Stevenson turned the envelope over in her hand several times, satisfaction curling her lips as she tossed it into the hearth and watched the flames devour it.

Maggie made her way to the cottages enjoying the crisp autumn air, her soprano voice floating through the atmosphere as she hummed an Irish melody.

"Hello," Maggie called out as she approached Letty and Willa.

"You's back?" Letty said, pursing her lips.

"I hope that's alright."

"Do as you please, just don't know why you'd wanna come round here."

Maggie felt a twinge of discomfort, wondering if she was a burden to them.

"I don't mean to disturb you," she muttered.

"You ain't disturbin' nothing," Willa chimed in. "Letty's only wonderin' why you'd want to spend time with us instead of staying at the big house."

Maggie's eyes shifted to the ground as she bit her lower lip and scuffed the dirt with the toe of her boot. She fought back tears until a sob escaped her lips.

Willa rushed to Maggie's side, draped her arm about her shoulders, and led her to one of the large logs that served as a seat.

"Sit down and tell us what's got you in such a state," Willa said.

"I don't understand why he hates me so." The dam of Maggie's emotions broke free, flooding her face with days of pent-up anguish. "No matter what I say or do, he berates me." Her shoulders shook as she buried her face in her hands.

Willa sent Letty for a cup of coffee while she sat by the sobbing girl.

"Why you think he don't like you?" she queried, even though she suspected she knew the answer.

Maggie shared the disdain her uncle had exhibited, as well as the frigid reception she'd received since arriving and her confusion as to why he would think so poorly of her.

"Don' mind him. He's not one to show affection to anyone," Willa said, trying to sooth Maggie.

"What would make a person so bitter?" she asked, wiping her eyes with her sleeves and sniffling.

"Things happen in life that shape who we be. Mr. Stevenson faced lots of bad things," Letty said, handing Maggie a steaming cup.

"Like what?"

"That don' matter right now. Drink that coffee and calm down. No sense lettin' him see you cryin'. He won't like that at all."

Letty's words struck her with the force of a hammer. He'd be angry because of her tears? Surely, he'd understand she was far from home and missing her Da. Why would he fault her for that? Once more, Maggie swiped her eyes and sipped the bitter brew Letty had given her.

When the flush from Maggie's cheeks began to fade, Willa smiled. "You feelin' better now?"

"Yes, ma'am."

Willa bolted upright with her hands planted on her hips. "Don' be callin' me ma'am. I's just plain Willa."

A smile broke through the sorrow on Maggie's face. "Thank you, both," she said. Rejuvenated, and wanting to change the subject, Maggie asked, "What are you making?"

"Remedy for diarrhea, Willa replied."

"What's in it?" she queried, her curiosity roused.

"We gots some boxwood, black cherry, and prickly ash bark we gonna mix with dandelion root and butternut bark." Maggie approached the workbench scanning all of the ingredients.

"I's getting ready to mix it up if you wants to help," Willa offered.

"I'd like that."

Letty handed Maggie an apron and the three of them mixed several batches of the concoction until the sun shifted in the sky alerting Maggie that the dinner hour was fast approaching.

"I'd better get back to the house. I don't want to be late for supper," she said, untying the apron and draping it across the table. "Would it be alright if I came back tomorrow?"

"You's welcome here anytime, so long as you think Mr. Stevenson approves."

"I think he'll be pleased to know I've found *meaningful occupation*."

Maggie bid adieu and hurried up the path excited that she had something productive to report to her uncle. The entire process of mixing the ingredients and processing the remedies fascinated her and she looked forward to doing more the following day.

Upon entering the house, she smoothed her dress as best she could and went to the dining room. The family had yet to arrive giving Maggie a chance to contemplate what she'd say to her uncle if he asked about her day. Her stomach fluttered with excitement, as she was certain he'd be pleased with her productivity.

Minutes later, she heard the familiar tramping of his boots upon the stairs accompanied by the swishing of her aunt's and cousin's skirts. Maggie rose from her chair as they came into the room taking their respective places at the table.

Initially, Mr. Stevenson's presence stifled Maggie's enthusiasm causing her courage to dwindle as she contemplated how to broach the subject of her day's activities. She ate her food slowly, her nerves prickling with anxiety.

Disappointment took over when the dishes were cleared and her uncle had yet to utter a word. Mrs. Stevenson and Susannah scooted through the door while Mr. Stevenson stopped in the doorway.

"Miss McFarland, our family is going to the parlor. You will go to your room."

"Sir?" she asked, her heart racing.

"You have an early morning and need to get your rest." His eyes narrowed as a sneer crimped his upper lip.

"What will I be doing in the morning?"

"Working with the kitchen staff."

Her mouth went dry as the moisture raced to her eyelids.

"Why am I to work in the kitchen, sir?"

His hot breath brushed the tip of her nose as he leaned in. "Because I won't tolerate your lazy ways. You'll make yourself useful and earn your keep. I can't be expected to spend my money on an Irish peasant."

His words cut through her like a knife sawing through bread, tearing at her very soul. Shaken by the scene, Maggie scurried up the stairs to her room. She changed for bed and slid beneath the quilt, clutching the silver locket in her hand.

Burying her face in the stale pillow, she sobbed. She cried for her situation, she cried for her Da, and she cried for the misery plaguing her existence. Somehow starvation seemed a better lot than what she currently faced. At least she'd be loved.

All her life she'd longed for this unknown family and now that she knew them, she wished she'd never met them. Furthermore, she was beginning to understand why her Da had shielded her from their existence.

5

After a restless night, Maggie dressed, and headed downstairs. She'd convinced herself the women in the kitchen were probably much like Willa and Letty, giving her the courage to face the day.

Maggie stepped into the kitchen where a suffocating heat radiated from a hearth spanning the far wall. Three ladies worked on various tasks, one baking biscuits, another cooking ham slices in an iron skillet, and the other grinding coffee beans. Forcing the corners of her lips to curl, she swallowed the fear rising in her throat.

"Good morning. I'm Maggie."

All eyes glared at her.

"I'm here to help with breakfast," she said meekly.

"Why you think we needs your help?" the woman patting out biscuits declared. Her hair was wrapped in a scarf and her dark eyes seared a hole through Maggie's hopes for comradery.

"My uncle sent me."

"Get an apron from the back of the door and gather some eggs from the coop. Then you can help Patty," the older woman said, nodding toward the girl cooking ham.

"Miss Alma, why's I got to have her with me? I does jes' fine on my own!" the spindly girl whined, her small stature and smooth brown skin suggesting she was young, maybe fourteen or fifteen.

"Cause I said so and this be my kitchen," the older woman said, shaking a wooden spoon in the girl's direction. Miss Alma's broad shoulders and stern countenance suggested she wasn't one to be defied.

Over the course of the morning, Maggie scrambled eggs, cooked ham, and prepared coffee. The food was arranged in silver vessels. Three other ladies clad in black dresses with crisp white aprons, took the food into the dining room. Maggie recognized them from the meals she'd taken with the family.

Hours later, when the dishes were washed and put away, Maggie rubbed her neck trying to release the cramp holding it hostage. She started to remove her apron when Alma's voice thundered,

"What you doin'?"

"I was going to go upstairs and rest a bit before lunch."

Alma raised one eyebrow and planted a hand on her hip. "Ain't no rest in this kitchen. It time to start the midday meal. Grab a fresh apron and start chopping the vegetables in the basket over there." Under her breath she mumbled, "Take a rest. Where she think she is?"

Tears stung Maggie's eyes as the other girls snickered. The day passed with the swiftness of a snail climbing up a hill. They were permitted a brief respite at one o'clock to eat before beginning dinner preparations.

She skipped the evening meal, instead choosing to retire for the night. On her way to her quarters, Maggie hovered at the second-floor landing wondering if Susannah was asleep. Not wanting to risk an encounter with her uncle, she trudged up the last flight of stairs and fell into bed as the hall clock chimed ten.

. . .

DAYS LATER, during her lunch break, Maggie sat on the edge of the bed leaning over the night table to write a letter. She removed the lid from the inkbottle, dipped the pen, and began writing. The words were slow at first and then flowed across the page. When she finished, her hand was stained with ink and splotches stippled the parchment where her tears had rendered the script illegible. Maggie took in a deep breath. Why distress her father? He was already struggling to survive, and what could he possibly do to help? If the workers on the farm had learned to cope with Mr. Stevenson's callousness, so could she.

Maggie crumpled the letter and tossed it into the hearth watching it dissolve into a sooty mound beneath the flames. Not everything here was awful. She was getting closer with Susannah as well as Willa and Letty. With a bit more time and effort, things would be better so long as she could avoid upsetting her uncle. Eventually, she'd look back on all of this as nothing more than a difficult adjustment to a new family in an unfamiliar country.

She penned a new note telling her father about the beautiful countryside and her joy over having something akin to a sister. Maggie waited for the ink to dry, folded the letter into an envelope, and sealed it with a kiss. Scurrying downstairs, she found her aunt in the ladies' parlor perched gracefully at the walnut secretary scripting her daily correspondence, the room bathed in soft shadows.

"Mrs. Stevenson?"

"What?" she responded, looking up.

Maggie walked across the room and handed her the letter. "I was wondering if you could post this for me?"

With a nod, she took the envelope and studied the address. "Of course."

"Have there been any letters for me?"

"I don't believe so."

"Thank you, Mrs. Stevenson," Maggie gave a quick curtsey and returned to the kitchen.

Once Maggie was out of sight, Mrs. Stevenson tossed the envelope into the hearth, shaking her head as she returned to her task.

Over the next few days, Maggie fell into a routine in the kitchen and managed to forge a tolerable relationship with the others. The two younger girls always glared at her as if she was an insult to their existence but she kept her comments to a minimum, only speaking when necessary. They made it abundantly clear she was *not* one of them. She worked hard, hoping to win them over but their wall of distrust would take a while to break through.

She'd not spoken to Susannah since she started work in the kitchen and Maggie was beginning to feel the isolation of her situation. Never in her life could she have imagined being so alone when surrounded by so many.

DECEMBER BROUGHT the first snowfall of the season, blanketing the landscape in a layer of iridescent white. Maggie finally had a day off and decided to visit Willa and Letty. She loved the snow and was grateful for the fresh air as crystal fragments crunched beneath her feet.

"How are things going at the big house?" Letty asked, pouring a cup of coffee and handing it to Maggie.

"Alright, I suppose. I've been working in the kitchen."

"You been workin with Alma?"

Maggie nodded. "She's hard driven but fair. I was afraid of her at first but when the other girls were mean to me, she stepped in."

"Them girls ain't nothin' but trouble," Letty declared with a smirk.

"Letty's right about that. They think they so much better than the rest of us 'til they need something for a burn or a cough, then we's important enough."

"Can't say that I love the work, but it's tolerable," Maggie said before she sipped the steaming coffee.

"Why you workin' at all? You's family."

Maggie stared at her coffee cup and shrugged. "I don't understand it myself. My Da sent money for my expenses."

"Your father sent money to Mr. Stevenson?" Willa asked.

"He sent what money he could spare with an assurance he'd send more as he was able."

Willa and Letty glanced at each other.

"What's the matter?" Maggie asked, cradling the warm cup in her chilled hands.

Willa's chest rose as she took in a deep breath. "Probably shouldn't tell you this but Mr. Stevenson ain't the most responsible person when it comes to money."

"What do you mean?" Maggie set the cup down.

"He's been known to play at cards. Sadly, he ain't too good and loses more than he gains. One time he gambled away our pay."

"He gambles on cards?"

"Uh-huh. It gots real bad after his son died," Willa said, shaking her head.

"Mr. Stevenson had a son?"

"He doted on that boy. When the child got the fever, we concocted all the remedies the doctor called for. Then Miss Susannah took ill. Mr. Stevenson spent all his money trying to get his son well. But it was his daughter who survived. The boy didn't have her spirit. Somethin' snap in Mr. Stevenson after that and he gots meaner than before, especially to Miss Susannah."

"So, he's always been like this?"

"Oh my, yes," Letty declared, slapping her hands against her thighs.

"If he's so terrible, why do you stay?" Maggie queried, stunned that anyone would work for such an odious man.

"Where's we gonna go? We is safe here."

"Wouldn't you be safe anywhere?"

"There be people that could snatch us up and sell us south as slaves. So long as we's here and do our jobs, Mr. Stevenson give us what we need and leave us be."

"How did you learn about his gambling?"

"We talks with Miss Mabel. She in charge of the house."

Maggie contemplated everything they'd said as she drained her cup. "I'd better get back. Hopefully, I'll be able to visit next week, if that's ok."

"We's always happy to see you," Willa said, a smile rounding her cheeks.

As Maggie scurried off, Willa looked at Letty and shook her head. "I don't like what's happenin' with that girl."

"Ain't good, that for sure."

THE CLOCK STRUCK ten o'clock when Susannah snuck up to Maggie's room.

"How have you been?" she asked, sitting on the edge of the bed. "It feels much warmer since father had more wood sent up."

"I'm thankful for it. With the early mornings it's much easier to get ready when the wash basin isn't frozen."

Recalling Willa's explanation of what Susannah had endured, Maggie's heart softened. She and her cousin shared Mr. Stevenson's disdain and somehow this made Maggie feel a stronger connection to her.

"Is the kitchen work dreadful?"

"At first, but now that I'm in a routine, it's not so bad," Maggie said with a grin.

Susannah's eyebrows furrowed. "Don't tell me you enjoy it?"

"I'm learning a lot about cooking. Da always said that knowledge in any form is a good thing."

"Your father sounds like such a nice man," Susannah replied, blowing a breath across her lips.

Maggie's demeanor lightened as she sat straighter. "My Da is the kindest man in the world. He's never spoken ill to me nor struck me, even when I accidently left the gate open and the sheep escaped down the lane. Took him half the day to herd them back to the pasture."

Susannah's eyes dropped to her lap where she fidgeted with her dress. Immediately, Maggie regretted her words, reaching for her cousin's hand. "I didn't mean to upset you. I'm certain your father is quite proud of you."

"Nothing I do meets his expectations. I've never heard a kind word in all my years, only how I'm not good enough or how he wished I were..." She choked back a sob.

"Dear Cousin, please don't fret. It can't be all that bad," Even though Maggie knew the truth, she desperately wanted to comfort her cousin.

"My brother was everything to him. When Edgar died, Father didn't leave his study for days. The servants had to leave his meals outside the door. Nobody saw him, not even my mother, except for Jasper who was always at his side."

"How awful for your mother."

"What about me?" she exclaimed, the pain of her loss pooling in her eyes. "I adored Edgar. He was the only one who ever showed me an ounce of affection. My father loves that dog more than he does me!"

"I'm so sorry. But we have each other now," Maggie said softly, grasping her cousin's hand.

"We do and I'm thankful for you." Susannah met Maggie's gaze, tears streaking across her cheeks when footfalls from below caught their attention. The two bolted upright, holding their breath.

"I'd better get back to my room," Susannah whispered. "Sometimes Father goes to his office to work when he can't sleep."

"Be careful."

Susannah squeezed Maggie's hand and opened the door slowly, peeking into the hallway. She gave a nod to Maggie and padded down the hall as stealthily as a mouse.

SUSANNAH CREPT DOWN THE STAIRS, careful to tread lightly. A sliver of light beamed across the floor from her father's office. He was up. Taking a deep breath, she tiptoed toward her chambers, mindful not to step on the creaky floorboard near her brother's old room. With each step, her heart pounded a bit harder. Just beyond her father's office door she released the breath she'd been holding when a stern voice bellowed.

"Miss Stevenson, come in here."

Terror gripped her muscles as she forced her legs to move into the dimly lit room where her father sat in the chair near the hearth.

"Where have you been?"

Susannah's head dropped as her fingers began to fidget. "I was..."

"Out with it!"

"I was visiting my cousin."

He leaned back, his face as stone cold as a statue. The sneer of his upper lip and the deadpan gaze of his eyes divulged a man with no heart whatsoever.

"How often do you *visit* her?"

"Not often," Susannah said, swallowing hard.

Mr. Stevenson walked to his desk, sat down, and removed the coral comb from his desk draw. He slammed it onto the desktop splintering one of the prongs.

"Often enough to give her gifts?"

"My apologies, father, I wasn't thinking," she mumbled, her heart thumping.

"Why are you affiliating with someone below your station?"

"I only wanted to check on her. She's had a difficult time since she arrived."

"Was she complaining?" he asked, the chair leather whining as he shifted forward.

"Actually, she's quite content considering her circumstances."

"What circumstances?"

The bluster of his tone sent a tremor through Susannah as she tightened the grip on her restless fingers. "She's far from home and now she's working in the kitchen, so I thought..."

"*You thought*? he mocked. "As if you were capable of producing an intelligent idea." He sat back in his chair. "What did she say?"

"That she enjoys the work now that she's settled into a routine. Apparently, she likes learning new things."

Mr. Stevenson rubbed his jaw as he stared at the flames flickering in the hearth. His silence usually meant he was plotting which was more terrifying than anything he could say.

"You may leave," he announced.

Relief washed over Susannah as she gave a quick curtsey and fled her father's study. She rushed to her room, wiping away tears when her mother appeared.

"My dear, might I have a word?"

"Mother, if you please, I'm not feeling well and would like to retire for the evening."

"This cannot wait." Her mother's words were stern, letting her know there'd be no avoiding the lecture.

Flustered, Susannah entered her parent's bedchambers. Candlelight washed the room in a warm glow, shadowing the faces of elegant ancestors staring from gilded frames. Mrs. Stevenson's demeanor instantly transformed from soft spoken to rabid tigress. Susannah was met with a hard slap across the face, stinging her tear-stained skin.

"Why did you strike me?" Susannah exclaimed, grabbing her cheek.

"You foolish girl! Is it not enough I make excuses for your shortcomings? Befriending that Irish tramp is indefensible!" She strode across the room, the silk train of her wrapper swishing with each step. "I'll not have you stirring up trouble with your father. You know his expectations when it comes to propriety."

"I was only being hospitable. Maggie *is* my cousin," she muttered, still stunned by her mother's tirade.

"Put that ridiculous notion out of your head," her mother snapped. "There's a good reason the family disowned her mother for soiling the family line by marrying an Irishman. They never forgave her infraction, and neither shall we!"

"I don't understand why you dislike her so."

"Because she's Irish."

"What has that got to do with anything?"

"They're coming to our country in droves to take everything we've worked for. They'll steal our land, our money, and desecrate good society with their filthy ways."

"Mother, they're coming here to escape starvation."

"You stupid girl. They could remain in their own country and work the land, but instead they come here to take all we've worked for. It's not our responsibility to feed and clothe them. They're like locusts, devouring our prosperity and leaving us with nothing."

"If we hate them so much, why is Maggie here?"

Mrs. Stevenson's tone softened.

"My dear child, how little you understand of the world. Her presence is accompanied by financial support."

"Are we in trouble?" Fear plucked at Susannah.

"Our lifestyle does not come cheaply and times are hard. Without your brother to help run the business, we need to make money where we can. His death was very hard on your father."

Susannah sighed at the mention of her deceased brother. It seemed his memory would haunt her forever, a constant reminder that she was nothing more than a useless girl, bringing shame and disgrace.

"Mother, if her presence benefits us, why be cruel?"

"We're not being cruel. We're merely exercising our good standing over that of a lower-class citizen. It's much like the servants on the farm. We'd never associate with them socially."

"But we're kind to the workers. Maggie is family. Doesn't she warrant more consideration?"

With a deep breath, Mrs. Stevenson pursed her lips at her daughter's ignorance.

"She's Irish. They're lazy, worthless creatures, lowering the standards of good people. I'll not have you tainted by the likes of an Irish woman." Sensing her daughter's angst, Mrs. Stevenson purred in a motherly tone, "My darling, the lessons of life can be painful. Better you learn them from me than a harsh and unforgiving world. I have your best interest at heart."

Susannah tried to absorb all her mother was saying; however, the absurdity of it was overpowering.

Mrs. Stevenson continued, "You shall marry well and live a respectable life, as have I. You owe that to your family, especially in light of your brother's death. It's your responsibility to make a suitable match that will maintain our lifestyle. If your brother were here, he would've saved us from financial ruin, preventing us from having to play boarding house to your cousin. Mark my words, a tramp like Miss McFarland will lure away your prospects, leaving you a hopeless old woman with no one to love you."

Mrs. Stevenson kissed her daughter's cheek. "Don't fret, my dear, all will work out as it should."

Susannah stepped into the hallway, trying to process her mother's words. The idea that her parents only accepted Maggie into their home for financial gain wrenched her heart, not to mention the constant reminders of her own inadequacies as a female. Nothing she did would ever fulfill her parents' expectations. Suffocating beneath the weight of hopelessness, Susannah shivered as if she'd been struck with fever. Sometimes, she wished the influenza had taken her instead of her brother.

Changing into her nightdress, Susannah crawled into bed, her limbs weak from the vitriolic words her parents had spewed and her face stinging from her mother's strike. She lay in bed trying to figure out how to pacify her parents while remaining true to the only person, aside from her brother, who'd ever treated her with kindness.

6

On her way to breakfast, Susannah still felt the abashment of the previous night's attack from her parents. Hopelessness enveloped her in turmoil and regret. She envied the relationship Maggie had with her father. If only she could experience compassion from either of her parents, she'd be content.

Shortly after the morning meal, Susannah headed for her room in a haze of melancholy. She'd hardly touched her breakfast and her head ached. Trudging down the hall towards her chambers, Susannah froze at the sound of her father's voice calling her. *Now what*, she thought, preparing for a hostile encounter.

Devoid of emotion, she entered his office, hopelessness saturating her soul. He sat in the same chair as the night before, his expression softer than she'd seen in years.

"Father," she said with a slight curtsey, her gaze diverted to the rug.

"There's something I need to discuss with you."

"I've not seen Miss McFarland this morning, I promise."

Her stomach churned, threatening to expunge the few bites she'd consumed at breakfast.

"Actually, that's what I wish to discuss. Your relationship with her may be of benefit after all."

"I don't understand," she muttered, cocking her head.

"Sit with me and we'll discuss it."

Terror raced through her body. It was a ploy. She'd get closer and he'd beat her as he'd done when she was four and spilled her milk at the dining room table. Her breath caught at the memory of her brother racing to her side, blocking her father from enacting further punishment. It was the only time she ever saw her father direct his rage at her brother. Nevertheless, the assault ended and he never struck her in Edgar's presence again, using words to inflict pain instead.

Reluctantly, she padded to the chair next to him and perched on the edge, prepared to flee if need be.

"I believe we can make use of the few talents you possess. This is your opportunity to contribute to the betterment of our family."

Susannah shifted in her seat. Her father was acting in a decent manner and she'd no idea how to respond.

"What would you have me do?"

"Continue your evening visits to Miss McFarland's room. Find out how she's faring in the kitchen and report back to me."

Susannah mulled over his request, her fingers twisting in her lap. He was asking her to do something for him. No insults, no violence, just a simple request. Best of all she'd be able to spend time with Maggie.

"I'd be happy to oblige."

"Very well. I'll expect a full report each evening."

Susannah stood and started for the door.

"Susannah?"

"Yes."

"Let's not discuss this arrangement with anyone else. It will be our secret."

Susannah nodded. "Of course, Father."

She scurried to her room where she crumpled onto the bed and cried. But these were joyful tears. In her seventeen years, he'd never uttered a single word of kindness or asked her to do something for him. And she couldn't recall ever hearing him address her so informally. She desperately wanted to believe he was being sincere but history made her doubt. For now, she would accept his kindness, and hope that things were finally getting better.

SUSANNAH WENT to Maggie's room after her mother retired to her chambers. In the dimness of the firelight, Susannah settled at the foot of her cousin's bed, her eyes alight with anticipation.

"My goodness Susannah, you're beaming. Has something happened?"

Susannah's eyes dropped to the quilt, a smile parting her lips like the early morning sun breaking free from the horizon.

"Nothing in particular, just a good day. Speaking of which, how was your day?"

"Tiresome, but productive."

"Tell me more about it."

"Most of the morning was spent kneading dough and chopping vegetables for the midday stew." Maggie rubbed one of her shoulders. "Funny, we don't think of cooking as a strenuous activity until our muscles cry out from chopping and stirring."

"I'm sorry your day was unpleasant."

"It wasn't bad. I learned how to make hollandaise sauce and braze carrots. I'm beginning to feel like a first class cook," she said, lifting her chin.

"Did you cook much in Ireland?"

"Not often. When I did cook, it was something simple like eggs, bacon, and potatoes. Mrs. Driscoll prepared lunch and dinner. Da wanted me to focus on my studies."

"Who is Mrs. Driscoll?"

"Our housekeeper. She'd worked for my Da since I was a wee tyke but he had to let her go when the famine took hold. Before that, our farm was rather prosperous. Da saved every penny for my education. Told me he'd promised my mother I'd be well schooled. She felt education was the key to a good future."

"Where did you go to school?"

"I had a tutor, Mrs. Connolly. She came to our house three times a week to instruct me."

"Sounds expensive."

"Da bartered when he could with wool from the sheep, including Mrs. Driscoll's services. She spun the most beautiful yarn." Maggie lifted the corner of the shawl draped across her shoulders. "She knitted this for me."

"It's lovely."

Woefulness clouded Maggie's expression. "It's like being wrapped in all the things I love. Wool from our farm, my Da, and knitted by the nearest thing to a mother I've ever known." She snuggled it tighter and yawned.

"I'd better let you get some rest. No doubt, you've an early start."

"Indeed." Maggie reached for Susannah's hand and squeezed. "Thank you for your visit. I enjoy your company."

"I'll sneak up again tomorrow evening, if that's acceptable?"

"You're always welcome."

"Goodnight, Maggie."

"G'night, Cousin," Maggie said, a bit of Irish seasoning her words as she blew out the lamp and curled beneath the covers.

~

SUSANNAH HURRIED down the stairs and rapped on her father's office door.

"Come in," he bellowed.

"Good evening, Father. I've just come from Magg...I mean Miss McFarland's room."

A sneer crumpled Mr. Stevenson's lips, sending a chill up Susannah's spine.

"And?"

"She said she learned how to make hollandaise sauce and braze carrots. She seemed rather proud of it."

"Anything else?"

"She said her father employed a woman to keep house and a tutor for her education."

"So, he does have money. I knew this was a scam," he said, rubbing his chin. "Well done, Susannah."

"She did say they released the housekeeper due to the famine."

"Not likely. You may go now," he said, making a notation in his journal.

Susannah hurried to her chambers, pride welling in her chest at her father's sudden acceptance. Finally, he was treating her with dignity and respect, and she was reveling in it.

THE FOLLOWING MORNING, Maggie traipsed down the stairs, delighting in the quietude of the early hour. The house was dimly lit at this time of the morning and the only signs of life were ghost-like servants lighting oil lamps and preparing things for the family's awakening. The kitchen was the only place in the house fully awake with the clanging of pots and pans and the bustle of kitchen staff. Maggie secured an apron around her waist and retrieved the large tin of flour to start mixing biscuits.

"Miss Maggie, let Gracie do the biscuits. I needs you to restack the flour in the pantry."

"Don't you need me to help with breakfast first?"

"Just move all the flour sacks to the other side of the pantry. It'll take most the morning so you best get started."

A flush tinted Maggie's cheeks as Gracie and Patty glared at her. When she walked into the pantry, everything was organized with a wall of flour sacks on one side and canned goods on the other. It made no sense to rearrange the room since it worked efficiently as it was. She started to ask Miss Alma why she was doing this but thought better of it, not wanting to endure the mocking glances and snickers from the girls.

Her arms and back strained from the weight of the flour sacks as sweat trickled down her back and across her forehead. Between the laborious nature of the task and the heat from the kitchen, Maggie felt as if she'd been hauling hay in the height of summer. Emerging from the small room, she swept a sleeve across her brow and joined the others for lunch. Famished, Maggie ate with the appetite of a ravenous lion. Her hand quivered with each spoonful of the stew, her muscles protesting the morning's vigorous activity. It had been months since she'd engaged in anything so strenuous, and her body was reprimanding her for it.

After lunch, Miss Alma had her scouring pans that hadn't been used in ages and hauling water from the pump to clean all the utensils not in use. It seemed a useless occupation as the items were clean already, but she didn't dare question Miss Alma's authority.

By the end of the day, Maggie trudged to her room, her back aching and her shoulders tight, making the stairs feel twice as steep. After washing up and stoking the fire, she crawled into bed, relieved for the rest. Fatigue tugged at her eyelids as she drifted off to sleep.

Moments later, Susannah rapped at the door.

"Come in," she croaked, leaning up on her elbow.

"My goodness, you look exhausted," Susannah said, plunking down on the edge of the bed.

"It was a rough day. I fear I may not be good company this evening."

"I'm sorry things were disagreeable."

"Not really disagreeable, just different. It's been a while since I've done any heavy lifting."

"Heavy lifting? In the kitchen?"

"Miss Alma had me restack all the flour sacks. I'd hoped to write a letter to my Da, but my hand is too stiff to hold the pen."

"How unfortunate. Do you write to him often?"

"I try to write a little something every day and post it at the end of the week."

Susannah nodded as she picked at a thread on the quilt.

"Do you know if any letters have come for me?" Maggie asked.

"No, but I'll check with mother in the morning."

Alarm raised Maggie's eyelids. "No need. I'm sure your mother would have told me if something had arrived."

"I should let you get some rest. I'll see you tomorrow," Susannah said, patting Maggie's arm.

"Goodnight," Maggie replied, slumping back against the pillow.

Susannah left the room, closing the door gently behind her. Maggie shifted in the bed trying to find a comfortable position, too tired to read Byron. Instead, she recited his words in her head until she drifted off to sleep.

~

"WHAT HAVE you to tell me this evening?" Mr. Stevenson asked, eager to hear his daughter's report.

"Poor thing was exhausted. She barely had the strength to sit up. Apparently, she had to move flour sacks."

A crooked smile split his lips. "Anything else?"

"She asked if she'd received any letters from her father."

"She acts like I'm some sort of postal service," he huffed, drumming his fingers on the desk. "You've done well, Susannah. Perhaps you and your mother can ride to town tomorrow. It's been some time since you've had a new dress."

Exhilaration energized her. "Oh father, that would be lovely. Thank you."

"You may go now." He returned to the ledgers as Susannah gamboled down the hall, her heart aflutter at her good fortune.

Susannah's confidence grew with each passing day under her father's approval. She relished the attention and found her outlook greatly altered. Throughout her life she'd dreamed of a loving relationship with him, and now it was happening. For a moment, Susannah worried how the information she shared with her father would impact her relationship with Maggie, but quickly dismissed it. It wasn't as if she were sharing dark secrets, just Maggie's daily activities.

Only days before, she'd wished to be dead. Now there was a bounce in her step and a carefree attitude lifting her spirit. Finally, she had purpose and meaning in her life.

Once the dinner dishes were washed and put away, Maggie retired to her room to write a few lines to her Da. Wanting to shield him from any unpleasantness; she reported things as positively as she could without outright lying. After sealing the envelope, she set it on her nightstand for Mrs. Stevenson to post with the morning correspondence.

A short time later, Susannah swaggered into the room, her countenance lighter and her smile exuberant.

"You're absolutely radiant. Has something happened?" Maggie asked.

"Nothing of great importance. Mother took me to town today to purchase a new dress. Then we had tea at a lovely little café before stopping at the milliners for a bonnet to go with my dress. It was such a wonderful day and Mother was so attentive."

"That does sound wonderful," Maggie replied, fingering the edge of the quilt.

"And how was your day?"

"Not as enjoyable as yours. First, I scrubbed all of the baking pans and then chased a chicken for thirty minutes that had escaped," Maggie chuckled. "In all my years on a farm, I've never encountered such a crazy bird."

"You've chased chickens before?"

"A few times. They may not be the brightest creatures, but they have a keen ability to get away from the most secure coops."

Susannah glanced around the room trying to find something else to talk about when she spied the letter on Maggie's night table.

"Would you like me to post that for you?"

"Could you? It would save me from having to search for your mother in the morning."

Maggie handed Susannah the envelope and hugged her. "Thank you for your visits. Your friendship means the world to me."

"I feel the same, dear cousin," she replied before leaving the room.

~

SUSANNAH KNOCKED on her father's office door and popped her head inside.

"Hello father."

"Come in," he replied, closing the ledger on his desk. "What news do you have this evening?"

"Not much I'm afraid. She scrubbed some pans and chased a chicken."

"Was she upset about it?"

"Not at all. In fact, she seemed amused by the chicken incident."

"Would you say she's enjoying the work?" Mr. Stevenson asked, leaning back in his chair.

"I don't know that she enjoys it but she seems content. She's the type of person who tries to find the joy in things. I admire that about her."

A sharp look from her father sent a shudder through Susannah's body.

"Sorry Father," she mumbled.

Mr. Stevenson ran his fingers through his hair when he noticed the envelope in his daughter's hand.

"What's that?"

"Maggie asked me to post this for her."

"Give it to me."

Susannah handed him the letter.

"Humph," he snorted. "A letter to her father. She's probably complaining about us." He tore the envelope open and withdrew the letters.

"Father, you can't read those, they're personal." Susannah's eyes widened as she sucked in a breath.

"Miss Stevenson, this is my house and I'll do as I please." The dark tone of his voice warned her not to argue further.

"Of course, Father," Susannah replied, ducking her head at his gruff use of her formal name.

He scanned the letters and smiled. "Well done, Susannah. You may leave."

She hurried from the room, her stomach churning with guilt. Maggie had trusted her to mail the letters and she desperately wanted to maintain that trust, but Susannah knew contradicting her father was dangerous. His recent kindness toward her had been unexpected and pleasurable, and she didn't want to lose that connection. The internal struggle between wanting to please her father and preserve her relationship with Maggie clamored on the battlefield of her mind, making for restless sleep. In an effort to sooth her frazzled conscience, Susannah convinced herself he would reseal the letters and post them the following morning.

TEMPERATURES DROPPED as winter extinguished autumn's mild weather with barren trees and overcast skies. Each morning, it was harder for Maggie to leave the warmth of her woolen shawl and quilted bed for the rigorous tasks of the kitchen. Miss Alma had her gathering eggs and hauling water from the pump. Once she completed these tasks, she helped with meal preparations unless Miss Alma had something else for her to do. While the other girls weren't as mean as they'd been that first day, they still didn't speak much or include her in their whispered exchanges.

Every day, Maggie made it a habit to check the mail basket near the back door hoping to find a letter from her father, but it was always empty. Chances were that Mr. Stevenson had already collected the mail. Maggie made a mental note to ask Susannah about it.

"Has there been any mail for me?" Maggie asked when Susannah arrived that evening.

"None that I'm aware of, but I'll check again tomorrow."

"He probably hasn't had time to write," Maggie consoled herself, trying to keep her worry at bay. "At least he'll receive my letters."

Susannah cast her eyes toward the quilt on the bed. Her stomach lurched at the memory of her father opening Maggie's letter.

"Did you do anything special today?" Maggie asked.

"Nothing out of the ordinary, just bible study with mother and some embroidery. I've made great progress on the panel you helped me with."

"Wish I could join you," Maggie's voice trailed off.

"Perhaps you'll have an opportunity soon," Susannah suggested, trying to break the discomfort hovering in the room.

"I don't believe I'll have any free time unless your father has a change of heart," Maggie said, slumping against the headboard.

"Well, I should go," Susannah announced. "See you tomorrow evening."

"Goodnight, Cousin."

"Goodnight, Maggie."

~

SUSANNAH DESCENDED THE STAIRS, ruminating over Maggie's situation. Remorse saturated her conscience as she knocked on her father's door.

"Enter."

"Hello Father. I've just been to see Miss McFarland."

"Did she say anything about the day's work?"

"No."

"She's not complained for several days. Perhaps the work is too simple and it's time to challenge her," he mumbled, drumming his fingers on the desk. "I'm quite pleased with your loyalty to this family, Susannah. You've proven yourself worthy."

"Thank you, Father,"

"That will be all."

"Goodnight, Father."

Susannah padded down the hall to her room where her new bonnet perched on the hat stand. She fingered the fluffy ostrich feathers and pondered her father's words. He'd never complimented her so sincerely. It seemed her life was finally getting better, but at what cost?

7

When Maggie reached the kitchen the following morning, she was told to go to the cattle barn.

"The cattle barn?" Maggie asked, catching sight of Gracie and Patty who had stopped what they were doing to stare at her.

"That what he say," Miss Alma replied.

Gracie snickered.

"What you makin' a fuss for?" Miss Alma snapped. "If you ain't gots enough to do I can give you extra work."

The grin melted from the girl's face as she ducked her head and continued chopping potatoes.

Miss Alma walked over and patted Maggie's shoulder. "No use sulkin' over it. I's gonna miss having you here. You's a good worker and don't cause no trouble." She raised her voice at the last sentence, looking over her shoulder to make sure the girls heard what she'd said.

"Thank you, Miss Alma. Perhaps it's only temporary."

"'Fraid not darlin'."

Maggie raced up the stairs to retrieve her shawl, tears streaming down her cheeks. Why was she being sent to the cattle barn? Wrapping the shawl about her shoulders, she criss-crossed it over her stomach and tied the ends behind her waist to hold it in place as she hurried down the stairs and out the door. Frigid air slapped her face as she buried her hands beneath the woolen wrap to shield them from the cold. By the time she arrived at the cattle barn, her cheeks were frost kissed and her toes tingled.

Sellers was at the other end of the barn, tossing flakes of hay into the stalls, his sleeves rolled to his elbows and bits of hay clinging to his trousers and hair.

"What you doin' here?" he asked, rolling his sleeves back down.

"Mr. Stevenson left word that I was to work here today." Maggie's teeth chattered as she looked around the barn.

Sellers stopped what he was doing, scratched his head, and asked, "You sure 'bout that? He said he was sendin' help but I didn't think it'd be family."

Trying to hide her shame, Maggie averted her gaze and muttered. "I'm only doing what I was told to do."

"Ain't no help when you shiverin' so hard you can't move." He hurried to the feed room and emerged with a wool sack coat and handed it to her. "Wear this, it'll keep you warm."

"Thank you," she murmured as she slid her arms into the coat sleeves, relishing the warmth. Her spirits lifted a bit at his kindness. "Tell me what to do."

"Not sure there's much you can do, being you's a girl. This is hard work."

Maggie's shoulders stiffened as her stature straightened. "I'll have you know I used to help my Da with the sheep and I'm perfectly capable of doing anything you can do." She punctuated the statement by crossing her arms over her chest, the extra length of sleeve flopping over her hands.

Sellers planted his hands on his hips. "You think so? Then

fill that hay wagon and cart it to the far pasture. I be turnin' the cows out when they's done with they grain."

Maggie steered the wagon to the stacks of hay at the back of the barn and loaded it as full as she could without blocking her ability to see over the top. The wagon swayed and shifted as she tried to maneuver it down the aisle without capsizing it. Maggie stopped, took a deep breath, gripped the handles, and lifted. With a quick glance over her shoulder to make sure Sellers wasn't watching, she started pushing. Thankfully, Sellers was busy scooping grain into feed bins and didn't notice how the wagon wobbled as she strained to push it. It had been a while since she'd helped her father on the farm, but all of the water hauling and flour sack moving had strengthened her muscles and at this moment she was glad of it. Her Irish pride wouldn't let Sellers know that she was struggling.

She wobbled along the stony pathway to the far pasture where she parked the wagon and opened the gate. As she rolled it forward the wheel hit a rock yanking the handles from her grasp, sending the hay bales plummeting across the ground. Quickly, she glanced back to make sure Sellers hadn't seen it before she proceeded to spread the hay around in stacks.

She wheeled the wagon back into the barn and planted it at Sellers' feet. "Now what?" she said, her chin lifted in satisfaction.

"I gots to move the herd to the pasture so you can start muckin' out the stalls."

She walked to the tool shed, grabbed a wheelbarrow and pitchfork, and started working. By lunchtime, blisters speckled her palms and her shoulders were tight as a drum.

"Let's get lunch," Sellers said as he finished sweeping the aisle.

Maggie brushed the dust from her skirt, following him out of the barn and down the path.

"Where are we going?" Maggie asked.

"To Willa's and Letty's. That's where we eat our meals."

"Do all the workers eat lunch there?"

"The others only eat there for special occasions. Work days it's just me, Letty, and Willa. I share my rations, fix things at they cottages, and haul milk across the hill for them and they do all the cookin'. Works out good for us, we's like a family that way."

They traipsed along the hard ground until the roofs of the small buildings came into view. Sellers walked into the first brick cottage with Maggie at his heels.

"Brought a guest with me."

The two women stared at Maggie, making her feel self-conscious about being there without an invitation.

"Why's you here with Sellers?" Letty asked.

"I work at the cattle barn now," she replied sheepishly.

Letty grunted. "Nothing that man do surprise me anymore."

"Don' mind her, we's happy to have you," Willa said, patting Maggie's ice-cold hand. "Lawd chil' your hand is cold as death. Why you not wearing gloves?"

"I haven't any. I didn't think I'd need them," she stifled a sob, tears stinging her eyes.

"Come now, no use frettin' over it. I'll give you a pair of mine before you leave."

Maggie sucked in a breath trying to hold back the sorrow threatening to flood her cheeks while her stomach rumbled. With the shock of the morning's revelations, she'd completely forgotten she'd not had breakfast. Willa served up bowls of steaming vegetable beef stew, corn muffins, and coffee. Maggie was famished, gulping down the stew and eating three muffins.

"You gots a healthy appetite for such a little thing," Letty said, refilling her coffee cup.

"She a hard worker too, for a girl," Sellers winked.

"I can outwork you any day," Maggie teased, nudging his arm with her elbow. She let out a yelp when her shoulder seized at the movement. Rubbing it, she moaned, "It's been a while since I've done this sort of work."

Willa got up from the chair, searched through the pantry and removed a jar. "Take this with you and rub it on your shoulders before bed."

Maggie turned the jar in her hand. "What is it?"

"Ointment for stiff muscles. Don't smell so great but it'll fix you right up."

"Thank you."

Willa gave Maggie a pair of gloves that were a bit large but they were better than lifting with frost bitten, blistered hands. She shoved the jar into her coat pocket and walked back to the barn with Sellers.

Several hours later, the sun began its descent in a flurry of deep orange and purple. Maggie took off the coat as she prepared to leave. "Thank you for lending this to me."

Sellers shook his head. "Keep it, I gots another one."

"I don't want to take your things."

"I told you, I got another one so keep it for now."

She slipped back into it, thankful for the warmth it provided.

"You better get going or you be late for supper at the big house."

Maggie froze. She'd been eating with the kitchen workers but suspected that was no longer an option and dinner with the family was out of the question. Not knowing what to say, she shrugged her shoulders as tears welled.

"What's wrong?"

"I no longer dine with the family. Until today I was taking my meals with the kitchen staff."

"Have supper with us. There'll be plenty."

A tear trickled down her face. "I don't know what to say."

"No time to think about what to say. Just come to dinner. We gots an early mornin' so we gots to eat early."

When the meal with Willa and Letty was over Sellers walked with Maggie toward the main house, the darkness magnifying the cold. After a delicious meal filled with lively discussion and good humor, Maggie felt rejuvenated.

"Tell me why you's really here," Sellers asked.

"I already told you, people at home are starving so my Da sent me to live with my uncle."

"And he thinks this is better?"

Maggie's heart skipped. Even Sellers could see something was amiss.

"He didn't know my uncle before this. Mr. Stevenson is my mother's brother. For some reason, they lost touch after my mother married my father."

"Where your mama now?"

"She died a few months after I was born."

A cold breeze rumpled her coat sending a shiver through her body as they walked.

"Sorry 'bout that."

"What about you?" Maggie asked. "Where's your family?"

"They's all gone."

His words were sharp telling Maggie not to query further. As the house loomed ahead, Maggie stopped.

"You should go home. I don't want to cause you any trouble."

He nodded. "See you in the mornin'."

"Goodnight, Sellers. And thank you for everything."

He strode back down the trail, his long legs adding a swagger to his gait. Maggie stared at the house with its windows glowing in the darkness like the eyes of a skull. Emptiness pervaded her soul as if all emotion had been gutted from her body leaving an empty shell. Although her day had been filled with hard work, it had been pleasant. Being far from her uncle was the best thing she'd experienced since arriving, outside of

Susannah. The thought of her cousin gave her the courage to go inside.

Stepping through the back door, she heard the sound of dishes being cleared from the dining room. A flicker of anger sparked her Irish flame. She was part of the family and ought to be dining with them. She should be retiring to a room on the second floor and attending to her studies but instead she'd been cast aside with no more consideration than an old shoe. Her hands shook and her jaw tightened and for a brief moment she considered confronting her uncle. The grandfather clock chimed breaking the spell, sending her bolting up the stairs to her room.

Much to Maggie's surprise, Susannah didn't visit that evening for which she was relieved. Bed called to her aching muscles and stiff back. She longed to know if any letters had arrived but was too exhausted to check. After rubbing the ointment on her shoulders and upper arms, she changed for bed and slid under the quilt. Maggie fingered the silver locket on the night table calming her weary soul, her mind drifting back to her Da. Within minutes she fell asleep, escaping the drudgery of her new life.

IN THE DARKNESS OF MORNING, Maggie crunched over frosty fields, her breath furling from her lips as she made her way to the cattle barn. She feared her uncle might move her elsewhere so she'd risen a bit early just in case she had to make a change. When she approached the barn, she could hear Sellers filling the grain wagon.

"G'morning, Sellers," Maggie called out.

"You's up early."

"Wasn't sure if I'd have to go elsewhere today so I thought it best to get here ahead of the expected time." She took a deep breath. "Have you heard from Mr. Stevenson?"

"Nope. Suppose that means I'm stuck with you again today," he said with a wink.

"Indeed," she replied, a smile lifting her cheeks and her spirits.

Maggie loaded the hay cart and wheeled it to the pasture despite the protests from her sore muscles. The ointment she'd used the night before had helped although Willa was right about the odor.

Sellers was putting the grain cart away when she returned to the barn.

"What's next?"

"Breakfast," he said, brushing off his shirt.

Maggie walked past him with the hay cart and began refilling it. When she turned around, he was staring at her.

"What's wrong?"

"You're keeping me from my morning meal," he replied with his hands on his hips. "Put that up and come on."

She did as she was told and walked with Sellers to the cottages where the scent of bacon wafted through the air as smoke streamed from the chimney of Willa's cottage. They stepped into the warm embrace of the cabin to the aroma of freshly baked biscuits and coffee.

"Good morning," Willa said, handing Maggie a cup of coffee.

"Good morning, Willa, Letty."

Letty grunted a greeting and continued cooking eggs.

Maggie leaned over to Willa. "Have I upset her?"

"Don' mind old Letty, she ain't a morning person. She be back to her regular *sweet* self after her coffee," Willa smirked.

Letty shot a look over her shoulder and rolled her eyes at Willa's sarcasm.

Over breakfast they chatted about the cows and the state of the harvest when Willa asked, "How'd that ointment work for you?"

"Very well. I feel much better this morning."

"You's such a girl," Sellers snorted.

"Sellers don't you be acting all high and mighty. We done give you that same ointment more than once when you worked a long day," Letty retorted with squinted eyes.

His cheeks raised in a broad smile as he winked at Maggie who nudged his arm with her shoulder. "Who you callin' a girl?"

"You, weakling."

"Both of you cut it out and gets to work. Letty and me gots some remedies to mix before the weather get too cold."

"Remedies?" Maggie queried.

"We keeps the cupboard full of things for the workers in case they gets hurt or sick."

"Sounds interesting."

"If Sellers can spare you this afternoon you can help us."

Sellers grinned. "She better off doin' girls work then getting under my feet."

"Hey," Maggie replied, sticking her tongue out at him.

Maggie and Sellers bid the ladies goodbye and stepped into the frigid morning air. When they reached the top of the hill Maggie looked at Sellers, the right side of her mouth rising. "Bet I can outrun you."

"Not likely with them short little legs."

Maggie took off at a full run with Sellers close on her heels. Cold air filled her lungs as her auburn strands whipped against her face. When they reached the barn door, Maggie scooted through and declared triumphantly, "Ha, beat you!"

Huffing, Sellers bent over resting his hands on his knees. "Darn, you's fast. Who'd thought them short legs could fly?"

She laughed and patted his shoulder. "I'll give you another chance to beat me later. Let's get these cows hayed."

When the sun hovered in the midday sky, Maggie joined Willa and Letty to help with the remedy preparations. Maggie was intrigued by the concoctions and their uses at the same time repulsed by some of the pungent odors resulting from the process. Nevertheless, she enjoyed the work and found herself craving more of the knowledge affiliated with it.

Despite the friendships she was forming with Sellers, Willa, and Letty, she longed for home and the comfort of her father's voice and warm embrace. Why hadn't he written her yet? She'd sent several letters and knew he'd not neglect writing her back. Fear squeezed her heart, making her thankful for the long, busy days distracting her from her worries.

MAGGIE WASHED UP, changed into her nightdress, and began braiding her hair when a knock at the door announced Susannah's arrival.

"Come in."

"Good evening, Maggie. My goodness, you look refreshed."

"I feel refreshed," she chuckled pulling a piece of straw from her hair. "And how was your day?"

"Pleasant enough. Mother and I had our bible study in the morning and then spent the afternoon working on new embroidery panels for a set of chair cushions. It's one of the loveliest designs I've ever stitched."

"That sounds nice," Maggie replied, glancing at the floor.

"My apologies, I didn't mean to dwell on my good fortune when you've spent the day in that dreadful barn." Susannah wrinkled her nose.

"It wasn't so bad. Sellers is a nice fellow and Willa and Letty always make me smile."

"Who are Willa and Letty?"

"They grow the vegetables and herbs, make all of the remedies, and launder the clothes for the workers."

"And you find these people acceptable companions?"

"Wouldn't you?"

"Not at all. They're workers and not up to our status," Susannah said with a huff.

Maggie bit her lower lip and averted her gaze in an effort to hide her discontent with her cousin's views. After all, she was a worker too. Susannah reached out and took Maggie's hand.

"Please forgive my impertinence, sometimes I don't consider my words," she chuckled. "I'd better let you get some sleep." She leaned over kissing Maggie's cheek. "I'll see you tomorrow evening."

Maggie sat in the shadowy light of the oil lamp contemplating her cousin's sentiments. It seemed out of character for Susannah to be so cavalier. Then again, Maggie was probably being too sensitive, making more of Susannah's comments than she should.

RUSHING DOWNSTAIRS, Susannah knocked on her father's door.

"Enter."

Susannah darted into the room with a quick curtsey.

"Have you spoken with Miss McFarland?"

"Yes, father."

"And what has she to say?"

Rolling her eyes, she huffed, "She's enjoying it. Although I can't imagine how she could find pleasure in something so...undignified."

A sly smile creased his face. "Of course, you feel that way. You're a lady and would never be expected to partake of such demeaning activities."

Susannah stood a bit straighter, basking in his praise. It was the most generous compliment he'd ever given her.

"You've done well, Susannah."

"Thank you, Father."

"You may leave now."

With a bounce in her step, she gamboled to her room, her heart swelling with joy. *So, this is what it's like to be loved*, she thought. One thing was certain; she enjoyed her father's praise and was determined to do what was necessary to maintain his affection.

8

When the workload at the cattle barn was light, Maggie assisted Willa and Letty with herbal remedies and cooking. One afternoon over a kettle of stew, the topic of Mr. Stevenson arose.

"It's beyond me why he's such a hard soul. His cruelty to his own daughter is contemptible," Maggie said, aromatic steam puffing from the pot as she stirred the bubbling stew.

"That's cause she still here," Letty replied.

"Where would she go?" Maggie asked, baffled by the comment.

"Mr. Stevenson never got over his son's death, especially since his daughter survived."

"Susannah mentioned her brother but didn't elaborate on what happened to him."

"Edgar was a good boy but when he died from the fever and Miss Susannah recovered, it do something to Mr. Stevenson." Willa shook her head. "I believe he resent her for surviving. That's when he took up gambling. Was gone most every night. There was times he didn't have no money for our pay so he'd gamble some more to try to fix things."

"How do you know all of this?"

"Miss Mabel hear everything and tell us," Willa said, with a nod.

"Was he ever nice, I mean before his son's death?"

"That man been mean for a long time. Ain't no wonder. Forgive me for speakin' ill of the dead, but his mama, the late Mrs. Stevenson, was said to be a cruel woman," Willa responded. "Supposedly, she favored his sister who ran off and got married. Rumor say they have to move here to escape the shame of it all."

Maggie absorbed all she was hearing when a revelation registered in her head. *No wonder he hates me so*, she thought. *His mother punished him for my mum marrying my father.* Suddenly, her Da's reluctance to speak of Maggie's maternal grandparents as well as her uncle's hatred of the Irish made sense.

"Mr. Stevenson done the same thing as his mama. He favored his son and picked on Susannah. I remember him slapping her face so hard it leave a mark. She weren't but a little thing."

"I feel badly for her," Maggie said.

"Be careful of that one. His blood run through her veins and that mean she capable of anything," Letty added.

"There's no need for concern on Susannah's part." Maggie smiled. "We're quite close."

"I'd keep my distance if I's you," Willa said, shaking her finger.

Willa and Letty's words stalked Maggie's conscience. *Why would her grandmother be cruel to her own son because her daughter ran off to marry the kindest, dearest man Maggie had ever known?* Tears crested in her eyes. All she'd imagined of her unknown relatives was dissolving like sugar in a teacup, leaving her feeling empty and confused.

At least her cousin was kind. Considering all Susannah had

endured, Maggie was glad they had each other. If nothing else, Mr. Stevenson's contempt had forged a bond between them.

When Maggie returned to the cattle barn, she found Sellers sitting on a bale of hay with a knife and a small chunk of wood.

"What're you doing?"

"Whittlin'."

She sat next to him watching as he made quick, scraping motions with the blade forming a curved point in the wood. Within minutes, the nimble strokes of the knife molded a bill and then two eyes.

"It's a duck!" Maggie declared.

A smile spread across his face as he carved more details into the piece.

"Where'd you learn to do that?"

"Used to be an old man here on the farm, Mr. Gillespie. He worked in the livery stables with Milton. He carved all kinds of things. One day I asked him to teach me."

Maggie watched in amazement, as the duck head grew more lifelike with each swipe of the blade.

Their respite lasted a few minutes more when Sellers rose to his feet, slipping the duck head into his pocket and sheathing the knife.

"Probably best we gets back to work. Almost feedin' time."

Several days later, the temperatures dropped to well below freezing leaving everything frozen solid. Maggie helped Sellers with one of the water troughs as the afternoon sun shimmered across the glassy surface of the pond nearby.

"Does anyone ever go for a slide on the pond?

"Slide? Is that like skatin?"

"Yes, but without skates."

"Heavens no!" Sellers grumbled, astounded by the suggestion.

"Why not?"

"We could fall through the ice and freeze to death!" Sellers replied.

"Don't be so melodramatic. Come on," Maggie goaded, holding out her hand.

"Whatcha mean, come on? You's crazy if you thinks I's gonna break my neck out there."

Maggie traipsed to the edge of the pond rubbing the worn tip of her leather boot over the slick expanse.

"I think it'll hold. It's been frozen for a week now."

Gently, Maggie stepped onto the ice and in one graceful motion glided across the surface toward the center. Giggling, she twirled awkwardly before skimming back to the edge where Sellers stood with hands planted on his hips.

"Ain' no way I's going out there!"

"Aye, are ye afraid of taking a spill and hurting your bum, wimpy young man?" Her Irish brogue swirled around each word.

"I's not afraid, I's smart!"

Without warning, Maggie grabbed Sellers' hand and pulled him onto the gleaming surface, his legs as wobbly as a newborn foal. She left him standing near the center as she circled around him.

"See, it's not so hard. Now you give it a try," she taunted.

His long legs slipped and skidded in different directions as he tried to get his bearings, but to no avail. He crashed to the ice with a thud. Maggie slid backwards a few feet, chuckling at his predicament.

Sellers pushed up on his arm in order to regain a vertical

stature only to catapult forward onto the ice, sending Maggie into a fit of giggles.

"Doggone it! Get over here and help me!" he hollered.

Maggie slid over to him in a graceful pirouette and offered her hand. He grabbed it but instead of getting up, he yanked her down, bringing her colliding to the frosty veneer.

"Ooo, not so funny now, is you?" he jested.

Sprawled across the frozen surface like an open fan, Maggie laughed until tears formed in her eyes.

"We're going to have to work together. I'll stand up but don't tug on me; otherwise, I'll fall again. Once I'm standing, you push up slowly and I'll help you balance."

Maggie got to her feet, offered her hand, and grabbed Sellers' elbow to steady him. With great effort and concentration, he managed to straighten to a standing position.

"I did it!" he declared, throwing his arms in the air, which knocked him off balance. He crashed to the glassy surface taking Maggie with him. Laughter exploded once more as they struggled to right themselves.

"Let's try again but this time don't move once you're on your feet. Wait for me to guide you," Maggie cautioned.

They repeated the process with Sellers rising to his feet, his lanky frame quivering to stay upright. Once he got his balance, he looked to Maggie for guidance.

"Now, take tiny steps forward and if you start to fall, stop and steady yourself before moving on."

He nodded as he slid each foot forward. Maggie mirrored each step until Sellers was able to follow her around the pond in jerky, uneven movements.

"You're doing it!"

"I reckon." His concentration was intense as he maneuvered across the slippery plane with his eyes glued to his feet and his arms floating out from his sides.

"Told you it was fun!" she declared, dashing past him.

"Speak for yourself!"

With hands on her hips Maggie stopped, scrunching up her face.

"You're no fun. I should leave you out here."

"Oh no you don't!"

"Quit if you like, but I'll not help you back." Maggie whizzed past, her nose in the air.

Sellers' competitive nature took over. In his attempt to chase her he lost his footing, propelling him into a bank of snow at the edge of the pond.

"Doggone you!" he said, tottering to an upright stance.

"Don't be sore. You'll get better with practice." She whirled across the ice, her arms outstretched toward the sky and her red locks billowing in the wintry air. Circling around, she slid to the embankment where Sellers sat.

"Shall we get back to work?" Maggie queried, offering her hand.

"Certainly."

Sellers grabbed her hand and gave a sharp tug catapulting her into the snow bank before he jumped up, laughing as his willowy legs trudged across the snow.

"You're gonna pay for that!" she hollered. Maggie leapt to her feet, grabbed a handful of snow, and lobbed it at Sellers who retaliated in kind. The two chased and lobbed snowballs until they were out of breath and covered in a dusting of snow. Maggie's flushed cheeks glowed in the wintery air, her chest heaving from their escapades.

They returned to the barn to feed and bed down the cattle for the night. Although her situation seemed hopeless at times, Maggie was thankful for Sellers, Willa, and Letty. If it hadn't been for them, and Susannah, she'd have gone mad.

When they'd finished the evening meal and said goodnight, Maggie traipsed back to the main house, her hand resting on the doorknob. She hadn't realized how paralyzing her situation had become until that moment. Fearful of encountering Mr. Stevenson, she slipped in the door, shut it gently, and scurried up the back stairs to her room. Despite its impersonal atmosphere, her quarters were fast becoming a haven in the sense that Mr. Stevenson never ventured to the third floor.

After an exhausting, yet fulfilling day at the cattle barn, Maggie stoked the fire and hung her outer garments on the hearth to dry. Rubbing her hands together over the flames she reminisced on the day's antics, chuckling at the image of Sellers sprawled across the ice like a giraffe.

Susannah's visits had dwindled as of late but Maggie knew their clandestine meetings depended upon her cousin's ability to sneak past her parents' room.

As the nip dissolved from her fingertips, she wrapped the shawl tightly around her shoulders and penned a quick note to her father. For a moment, she stared at the flames flickering in the hearth, her mind wandering back to home. *What's Da doing right now*, she thought, a tear threatening to fall. She'd been at the farm for weeks now and hadn't received a single letter from him. A burning sensation eked up her throat at the idea that something terrible may have had happened to him when a rapping at the door chased the thoughts from her head.

"Maggie, are you there?"

"Come in," Maggie replied.

Susannah stepped inside wearing a lovely frock of emerald green silk with gold trim scrolling along the hemline. The matching shawl cascaded delicately over her shoulders accentuating her tiny waist and delicate features, her coffee-colored tresses highlighting her porcelain complexion.

"Sorry that it's been a few days since my last visit but Mother and I made a trip to town for silk and then the following day to the dressmaker for measurements. Father said I needed another dress so that I might attend some of the upcoming Christmas socials. He feels certain I can make a good match if I conduct myself properly. What do you think?" she asked, twirling.

"It's lovely." Maggie admired the glimmering sheen of the fabric and the delicate handiwork of the trim.

"And how did you pass the day?"

"I helped herd a cow that got loose, prepared an elixir for coughs, and then Sellers and I went for a slide on the pond."

"Who is Sellers, again?"

"He works at the cattle barn. We had fun," she giggled. "You should try it some time."

"Father would be furious if I were to engage in such unladylike behavior. He's very strict regarding my endeavors."

Maggie bit her lower lip diverting her gaze to the fire blazing in the hearth. Susannah patted her cousin's hand, "Poor Maggie. I didn't mean to make you feel badly. I should be more attentive to my words. It's only fitting you should spend your day sliding on the pond with the workers."

Holding her tongue, Maggie pondered how to respond. It was an odd statement for her cousin to make.

"I'd better leave you to rest," Susannah said, sauntering across the room. "Goodnight, cousin."

"G'night."

Susannah shut the door behind her, leaving Maggie in the wavering shadows of the oil lamp. For a moment she felt debased by Susannah's comments but quickly dismissed it as nothing more than her own insecurity over her current situation. Outside of the workers, Susannah was her truest ally. Weariness took hold as Maggie lay on the lumpy straw mattress, the crackling fire in the hearth lulling her to sleep.

IT HAD BEEN NEARLY a week since Susannah's last visit, so Maggie was thrilled when her cousin arrived wearing a lovely wool wrapper trimmed with lace that swept the worn floorboards as she sashayed across the room and sat on the edge of the bed.

"Did you have a pleasant day, Cousin?"

"It was a splendid day."

"A splendid day working at the cattle barn?" Susannah sniffed.

"It's physically challenging but I find the activity gratifying. *Idle hands make for an idle mind*, my Da always said."

"Wise words from a wise man, no doubt," Susannah said, her expression sullen as she tugged at the edge of her wrapper.

"How did you pass the time?" Maggie asked.

"Reading mostly."

"Anything of interest?"

"Just some ladies' journals. Mother said it's important that I know how to maintain a household once I'm married."

"Have you a suitor?" Maggie asked, sitting a bit straighter.

"I've met some nice gentlemen recently but father doesn't approve of them."

Maggie cocked her head. "Why not?"

Susannah inhaled as she fingered the ruffle on her sleeve. "I'm not sure. Phillip Landon is a lovely young man who works for his father at the bank. He's been sweet on me for some time. Then there's Joseph Cunningham. His family owns the general store and the bakery in town. He's quite handsome and dances beautifully."

"Both sound like wonderful matches."

"Father means to leave the family business and property to a man. My brother," her voice broke, "would have taken that position had he survived. Since he's no longer with us, the property and business interests will need to be handled by someone my father deems worthy, not necessarily someone of my choosing."

"And you accept that?"

"Do you actually think I have a say in the matter?" Susannah shrugged her shoulders.

"Perhaps if you spoke with your mother she could help."

"Not likely. I've attended several soirees in the past week and all my father can say is to choose better."

"What's the sudden interest in finding you a husband? You're only seventeen."

"I don't know. But my father is determined to marry me off as soon as possible."

An uncomfortable pause lingered before Susannah stood.

"I'd better return to my room. I fear I'm not very good company this evening. Until tomorrow," she said, scooting out the door.

Maggie leaned back against the headboard troubled by her cousin's confession. It seemed poor Susannah was always caught in an emotional web when it came to her parents. Despite Susannah's revelations, Maggie sensed there was something more to her melancholy state than just finding a suitable husband to please her parents.

MR. STEVENSON OPENED the ledger on his desk where the bank balances were pitifully low after his last poker game. Massaging his temples, he mulled over his options. If he could join the game in Philly next month on New Year's Eve, he was certain he'd win back his losses and then some. But the amount to enter was substantial and he didn't have it. Of course, he could be rid of an expense while potentially gaining financial relief if he could marry off his idiot daughter. Sadly, she kept attaching herself to men without the means he deemed viable for his needs. He'd already drained what little money he had to buy her dresses to catch the eye of someone suitable. Instead, she bungled her prospects with her foolish notion of finding love instead of security. *Why had he been left with such a worthless heir*?

To make matters worse, no matter where he placed that wretched Irish tramp, she found some way to enjoy it. But that was a thought for another time. Right now, he needed to find some capital and fast. Somehow, he'd get the money needed to earn a seat at the next game and win big. Mr. Stevenson rubbed the shimmering gold pocket watch dangling from his waistcoat. It had been in the family for generations and was the most valuable thing he owned. But he'd never part with it. There had to be another way. He could muddle through until then; after all, he'd always been resourceful in these situations.

9

The days of December passed with the speed of a racehorse. Maggie stood before the washstand in her room splashing cold water on her face and neck, wiping away a layer of grime with a linen towel. Her dresses were beginning to wear and without means to sew a new one, or the courage to ask for another, she resigned herself to brushing the dust from her skirts with a hairbrush.

Pausing, she studied her surroundings. The bowl of the pitcher set was cracked, making for a slow leak, and the hairbrush had more empty space than bristles. Tears crested but refused to fall as she admonished herself for the self-pity. Inhaling deeply, she closed her eyes and thought of home. She reached for the silver locket, popped it open, and stared at the locks of her parent's hair beneath the crystals. While this usually calmed her, it only intensified her anguish regarding her current circumstances. With a soft *click*, she closed the locket, placed it on the night table, and snuggled beneath the covers. Tears stained her cheeks as she questioned whether she'd ever feel loved again.

The next day she sat with Willa and Letty mixing cough

syrup. With all the work and worry infiltrating Maggie's existence she'd not given any thought to the approaching holiday.

"You's gonna spend Christmas Day with us, ain't ya?" Willa asked, holding a jug while Maggie ladled the sticky mixture into it.

"I hadn't thought about it," Maggie huffed. "I seriously doubt Mr. Stevenson will want me around."

"Then it's settled. When you and Sellers get done with the cows you gonna join us for the evening feast."

"Sounds wonderful," she said, looking forward to the celebration. She needed something to quell the melancholy state of her heart that yearned to be home with her Da.

CHRISTMAS DAY BEGAN like any other, with the feeding and turning out of cattle, followed by breakfast, and then chores. The only notable difference was the passing of Christmas greetings amongst the workers. Most duties were suspended for the day except for essential ones that involved the care of animals. After lunch, Maggie and Sellers sat on the edge of the hayloft chatting.

"How did you celebrate Christmas growing up?" Maggie asked, leaning back on her elbows as her feet dangled over the edge of the loft.

"I didn't."

"Why not?"

"Don't like to talk about my early years," he responded, staring off.

"I've told you about my past, I'd like to know about yours," she said, sitting up and wrapping a piece of straw around her finger.

He looked away and considered her request. "I can tell you but you gots to swear on your life you'll not tell nobody, not even Willa and Letty," his eyes glimmered revealing the serious nature of his statement.

"Promise," Maggie replied with a nod.

Sellers sat straight facing the edge of the hayloft as he began his tale. "My mama was a slave in Georgia. When the massa decided to sell me to a plantation in Louisiana, we ran away."

Maggie was familiar with the barbaric institution of slavery but had never encountered it firsthand.

"We hid in all sorts of places and stay still as death when we hear the dogs comin' for us. Sometimes we went days with nothing to eat. It were hard but my mama was strong and determined to make us free."

"What happened to your father?" Maggie asked, sitting straighter.

"Don't know nothing 'bout him, 'cept he was from a neighboring plantation. He was sold off shortly after I was born. Mama never talked about him cause it made her so sad."

"How old were you when you escaped?" Maggie said, folding her hands in her lap.

"About fifteen. We almost got caught in Maryland when a farmer came into the barn where we was hidin'. His dogs must've picked up our scent and started carrying on. We barely made it to the river.

"By the time we gots to Pennsylvania mama started looking for work. A free negro told her 'bout Mr. Stevenson needin' a cook. He agreed to take me on too and put me to work here in the cattle barn. That's what I done in Georgia. People always said I got a way with cows."

"Mr. Stevenson never questioned where you came from?"

"Once he tasted my mama's cookin' I don't think he care one bit how we got here," Sellers said with a huff, staring at the floor below.

"What happened to your mother?"

"She come down with the fever when Mr. Edgar got sick. She died a week after he did."

"I'm so sorry," she muttered, reaching for his hand.

"Mr. Stevenson was so sad over his boy, he didn't even acknowledge my mama's death," Sellers muttered, looking at Maggie, his eyes glistening.

"I'm surprised you didn't leave."

"Where's I gonna go? I's a runaway. And Willa and Letty been real good to me, almost good as my mama. I couldn't leave them."

Sellers rolled up the sleeve on his left forearm revealing a scar forming the crude letters, LP. "That be my brand. I was five when the massa do this to me. I wailed so loud when that red-hot iron touch my arm. Feel like somebody peeling my skin off with a knife. When he done, he beat me for screaming. That why I always wear long sleeves to cover up where I come from."

"How awful," she mumbled, nauseated by the tale.

The two sat quietly, meditating on their respective backgrounds when Sellers spoke, "I never told nobody about this," he said, rolling his sleeve back down and fastening the button.

Sitting straighter, Maggie crossed her heart with her hand. "I'll never tell another living soul. Promise."

"I trusts you, even if you is a girl," he winked.

His demeanor lightened as he gave Maggie a slight shove with his shoulder, which she returned before leaning her head against him. "You might not have your mama anymore but you've got a sister who cares about you."

Sellers wrapped his arm around her shoulder and squeezed. "I suppose it's better than nothing." A sly smile spread across his face.

Maggie pinched his arm causing him to yelp. He leapt up, tossing a handful of hay her direction. She lobbed another handful back. They chased each other around the hayloft throwing hay until they were both breathless from laughter and covered in sprigs of straw. Dust danced in the rays of light sneaking through the slats of the roof as Sellers bent over with his hands on his knees shaking his head.

"We best get those cows in. Don't wanna be late for Christmas dinner."

"Last one down the ladder has to bring in old Casey!"

They scurried for the ladder, neither wanting to spend the extra time walking the geriatric cow into the barn. Maggie managed to slip in front of Sellers and scale down the ladder when his lanky frame hopped from the third rung down to the floor below.

With hands on his hips, he looked up with a triumphant smile.

"That's not fair!" she hollered.

"Don't remember you saying how we's supposed to get down the ladder."

Pursing her lips, Maggie shook her head as she started down the aisle, "Next time I'll make sure to state the rules more clearly!"

Maggie loved that Sellers found joy in everyday things, choosing to focus on the positive aspects of his life, not the ones beyond his control. He gave her hope that someday she too would escape the burden of her oppression and once again find happiness.

ONCE THE COWS were fed and bedded for the night, Maggie and Sellers answered the call of the dinner bell and gathered with the other workers for Christmas supper. The feast was more abundant than usual including ham, a side of beef, and a goose. A smorgasbord of cakes and pies, all lovingly prepared earlier in the week, were served after dinner. By the close of the meal, Maggie's stomach was stretched to capacity.

Several of the men built a large bon fire that crackled and sparked in the darkened sky. Sitting on logs, the group surrounded the blaze each provided with a cup that Milton filled with fermented cider. A toast to Christmas was made, the cups drained of the stinging elixir, and hymns sung. Maggie's lilting soprano voice sparkled amongst the others. When yawns spread through the group like a north wind, many returned to their cottages leaving Sellers, Maggie, Letty, and Willa. The four sat around the flickering flames, contentedly stuffed and a tiny bit tipsy.

"Did you have a good day?" Willa asked Maggie.

"It's been wonderful, thanks to you all," she said, rubbing her stomach.

"We're glad you enjoyed yourself," Letty replied.

"I'm sorry I wasn't able to help with the preparations."

"Chil', you needed a break and we was happy to give it to you. Consider it a Christmas gift."

"Thank you." Warmth spread through Maggie's body at the love they showered upon her but then again it may have been the cider.

Sellers reached behind the log on which he sat and produced a large paper sack.

"I gots a treat for everyone."

The three women leaned over to peer in the bag as Sellers opened it.

"Chestnuts!" they all squealed in unison.

"Got these from Arthur at the Butler's place."

Willa waddled to the cottage returning with a large grate to place the nuts on for roasting. Fire licked the edge of the grate as the nuts roasted. Contentment enveloped Maggie, bringing a smile to her lips.

"What you grinning for?" Willa asked.

"I was just thinking about Christmas Eve in front of the hearth with my Da."

"What you all do on Christmas Eve?"

"We'd sit before the fire after Mass and Da would tell me a story, the same one every year about the Christmas fairies."

"Tell us 'bout them fairies," Willa said with a nod.

All eyes were trained on Maggie as she sat up straight and began the tale, allowing a bit of Irish to tint her words.

"It were a wee bit of a chilly Christmas Eve and the fairies had assembled for their annual feast. Franny, queen of the fairies, had been gatherin' all sorts of treasures from the weed ridden gardens of villagers. Fairies were generally known for their mischief, but with most villagers spending their days indoors due to the cold it was difficult for the fairies to do what they did best, wreak havoc. Franny had been training the newest fairy, Felicity, in the ways of vexing villagers. But Felicity was a failure in every sense of the word. Instead of knocking things about, she'd put them right. When others were pluckin' the fruit from the vines of hard-working farmers, Felicity was harvesting berries from the woodland, leaving them in small piles on cottage doorsteps. No matter how hard Franny tried to indoctrinate Felicity in the way of fairies, she failed, leaving the fairy queen no choice but to eradicate the good-hearted imp. Perusing the ancient book of spells, Franny found a recipe for a special brew of tea concocted of hemlock and chamomile.

"This particular brew was legendary. Its origins were centuries old beginning with the story of a highly moral farmer whose goal was to thwart fairy activities for which he was quite successful. The queen fairy sought revenge on the old man, tainting his tea with the hemlock and chamomile mixture. After partaking of the tea, his heart was darkened and he shriveled into a gnome, joining the ranks of the menacing little fairies.

"Determined to exact the same results, Franny brewed the potion and slipped it into Felicity's teacup for the Christmas Eve toast. A speech was made by the winged leader and the fairies emptied their cups. With great anticipation, the queen watched for Felicity to fall into a deep sleep while the hemlock melted the goodness from her heart thus transforming her kind ways into roguish ones. Unbeknownst to the fairy queen, hemlock's effect on a pure heart has a much different outcome. Felicity began to radiate a bright purplish aura that spread like the perfume of a thousand roses. As it intermixed with the irksome creatures, an unexpected result occurred. The fairies began to shrink and shrivel into figs, until only Felicity remained. Instead of altering Felicity's heart, the tea intermingled with her amiable spirit and diffused an aura of love infecting all of the fairies in her presence.

"Shocked by the sudden shriveling of her fellow fairies, Felicity did what any good-hearted fairy would do, she gave them a proper burial. But come spring, the figgy fairies began to sprout and bloom, creating a whole new population of fairies. Figgy fairies are the first bloom on the trees planted with fairy figs. Initially, the blooms were a luscious pink and purple. When the sun shone upon them, their wings sparkled as the newly formed fairies took flight into the world. But these fairies weren't the menacing type; they had big hearts and kind thoughts. They helped villagers by carrying pollen to and from flowers and plants, making the village a spectacular sight in the spring and producing an abundant harvest in the fall. The fairy village became well known for its bounty and charity.

"Felicity, now queen of the fairies, ruled with kindness, leaving joy in her wake. In honor of Felicity, and her troupe of figgy fairies, fig pudding is always served on Christmas Eve. It's said, if you partake of figgy pudding on Christmas Eve, the impish fairies will be repelled allowing the altruistic ones to remain for an abundant and profitable harvest in the coming year."

Perched on the edge of their seats, everyone listened to the tale, their eyes glimmering in the firelight.

"And that's how figgy pudding became a Christmas tradition," Maggie said, slapping her hands against her knees followed by applause from her audience.

"You ever seen one of them fairies, Miss Maggie?" Willa asked in amazement.

"Once in the vegetable garden behind our cottage." Maggie's eyes were wide as she leaned toward Willa.

"Oh my," she replied her plump hand resting on her heart.

The group broke into hearty laughter while Sellers pulled the chestnuts from the fire to cool.

"You reckon you can make some figgy pudding next Christmas?" Sellers asked.

The question tethered Maggie's heart. She hadn't considered being here another year but now that she faced the possibility it made her chest ache. She loved them all but longed to be home with her Da.

"I'd love to but I'm certain I'll be home by this time next year," she replied in a whisper.

Willa, Letty and Sellers exchanged sorrowful glances. In an effort to ease the tension, Seller refilled everyone's glasses. They enjoyed another round of cider as they partook of the warm chestnuts. When the cups were emptied and the fire fizzled to embers, Willa and Letty returned to their cottages while Maggie and Sellers walked side by side towards the cattle barn.

"I gots something for you," Sellers said, reaching into his pocket.

"Oh no, I wish you hadn't. I've nothing for you."

"It ain't much," he said, handing her a small wooden heart. "I carved it for you. We's family and you got more heart than anyone I knowed since my mama."

Turning it over in her hand, Maggie studied the detailed carving. The flickering light from the lantern highlighted the little swirls rippling across the surface. It was truly a piece of art.

"It's beautiful, I'll treasure it always."

"I know you ain't gonna stay here," he blurted out. "This way you always gonna know someone love you and you won't forget old Sellers."

She gazed at him in the shadowy lamplight, tears clinging to her eyelids.

"I'd never forget you. Merry Christmas, Sellers."

"Merry Christmas, Maggie."

The two embraced before heading in opposite directions to their respective homes.

MAGGIE ROSE at her usual time to white-rimmed windowpanes and a frigid room. Peeking out the window, she beheld a coverlet of white flowing over every surface. She'd always loved a fresh snowfall and decided to take a stroll. She placed the carved wooden heart from Sellers next to the silver locket, dressed in her warmest attire, and hurried down the back stairs.

The brisk air tinted her cheeks as the ground crunched beneath each step. Something about watching the sunrise sparkle across pearlescent snow banks ignited the thrill of winter's exuberance.

Rounding the hill, Maggie heard Sellers whistling. Quickly, she scooted behind a towering maple as he plundered through the deep tundra. Mischief tickled her thoughts as she formed a handful of snow into an icy sphere. When Sellers was within a reasonable distance, she lobbed the snowball his direction smacking the side of his head in a burst of snowy fragments.

Stunned, Sellers cried out, "Who did that?"

Maggie stifled a laugh and tossed another snowball, this time hitting his shoulder.

"You is in for it now!" he declared, grabbing a large ball of snow and running toward the maple tree.

Maggie darted from behind, swooping down to gather another handful of snow, hurling it his direction as she ran. This one missed its target. Sellers threw a snowball making contact with Maggie's back. She volleyed another attack and the two rambled along, hiding behind trees and bushes while launching snowballs back and forth. Most of Maggie's efforts hit the target while Sellers' aim was not as accurate. Thirty minutes later the two were breathless and stiff.

Doubled over, Sellers asked, "Where'd you learn to throw?"

"Da and I used to do battle across the back hedge. I learned to duck and dart pretty quick if I wanted a chance at victory."

"I ain't seen no girl throw like that," he said, rubbing his head where the last snowball had hit.

"Rematch tomorrow?" she queried sheepishly.

"Don't think so. I might not be the best snowball fighter, but I's smart enough to know when to call it quits."

"So, you're saying you got beat by a girl?" Maggie taunted.

"That's exactly what I's saying. You ain't gonna trick me into another battle. Those things hurt," he replied with hands on his hips.

Work was harder in the snow, the cold air frosting Maggie's breath and freezing her lungs when she inhaled. Maggie's fingers stung after breaking up the ice in the water troughs. Lunch and supper were welcome respites as they huddled round Willa's hearth melting the stiffness from their frostbitten fingers. Sunset waltzed with the moonrise amidst a royal blue sky that shimmered across a glowing carpet of white. Sellers walked with Maggie to the split in the lane between the house and his cottage. Pensively, Maggie looked toward the mansion.

Sensing her woe, Sellers patted her shoulder.

"Don' be sad, I'm sure things'll get better real soon."

"Liar," she replied with a smirk.

"G'night, Maggie."

"Goodnight, Sellers," she said stepping back.

Maggie watched Sellers saunter toward his cottage, pondering the unfairness of her situation while dreading the cold, unwelcoming room waiting on the third floor.

MR. STEVENSON SAT at his desk with his head in his hands, stewing over the message that the poker game had been postponed until spring. Farris, the wretched man hosting the event, had decided to take his family on a grand tour of Europe and wouldn't return until April. He'd been counting on this game to pay the expenses he'd accrued for the holiday festivities, especially the wardrobe purchases to make his pathetic daughter attractive to men of distinction.

Why couldn't she settle on a man with financial means? Instead, she focused on love as if that held any meaning for a lasting match. He needed her to think with her head, not her heart. Leaning over, he patted Jasper's silky brown fur, thankful he had such a loyal companion.

If only he could find the money to cover expenses until the poker game. He was convinced he could win a fortune against this Farris character. Then he wouldn't have to rely on his idiotic daughter for financial salvation. In the meantime, he'd continue writing checks between the two banks. Thus far, he'd been able to stay ahead of the checks and was certain he could continue a little while longer.

If only that good-for-nothing Irishman hadn't ruined all his plans by shirking his responsibility to provide funds for his worthless daughter's upkeep. One thing was certain, he'd get every penny out of her, even if it meant working her day and night. At least making her miserable was a pleasurable distraction from his troubles.

10

APRIL 1848

Winter's bitter days faded into spring's rebirth with barren trees sporting tiny buds promising an array of glorious blooms. It had been weeks since Maggie had seen or heard from her uncle, making her believe he'd finally written her off. Sadly, Susannah hadn't been to visit since before Christmas.

Maggie reveled in the fresh air, putting a bounce in her step as she made her way to the cottages. The sun crested over the horizon flooding the pasture in waves of mango and gold. Hard work gave her purpose and a distraction from the cruelty of her circumstances, not to mention worry for her Da. Although she'd survived the harshness of winter's grasp, the warmer temperatures prodded her need to return home. Disappointed that she'd not received any letters from her father, she reminded herself that he was busy with the farm and hadn't time to write. She took comfort knowing he'd been receiving her letters.

After Sellers and Maggie fed the cows and turned them out, they made their way to the cottages. Reaching the top of the hill, they were met by the aroma of sizzling eggs and ham.

Maggie's mouth watered as they hurried down the dew moistened path.

"Mornin'," Willa called out.

"Good morning," Maggie responded, ambling up the steps and accepting a cup of coffee from Letty while Sellers leaned against the door jam.

"Gonna be fishin' later," he announced.

"Bring us whatever you catch and we'll make a good stew," Willa said with a nod.

"I've never been fishing before," Maggie said, taking a sip of her coffee.

"What you be wantin' to fish for? You's a girl."

"Maybe I'd like to learn," she replied, tilting up her chin. "Or maybe you're just scared I'll catch more fish than you."

"No, I isn't! Besides, girls ain't meant to fish."

"Girls don't usually work with cattle, but I do."

"That's cause Mr. Stevenson don't like you."

His words struck like a punch to the gut. Realizing he'd wounded her, Sellers tried to mend the situation.

"Maggie, I's sorry. I didn't mean..."

"There's no need to apologize. What you said is true." Maggie looked away, her demeanor sullen.

"How 'bout I show you how to fish after we's done with the cows?"

"I'd like that very much, but are we allowed?" Maggie asked, her eyebrows raised.

"We's got most everything done since I gots you to help. We can take a little time to do some fishing. Mr. Stevenson don' mind so long as we done what we supposed to do," Sellers replied with a wink.

After lunch, Sellers gathered the fishing tackle and walked with Maggie to the same pond they'd skated across only months before. Standing on the small dock, Sellers began his tutorial.

"First you gots to put the worm on the hook."

Maggie sneered as he demonstrated the vulgar act.

"That's disgusting!"

"Not if you wants to eat."

Maggie scrunched her face and turned her head slightly to the left. She sucked in a breath simultaneously spiking the wriggling worm onto the hook before exhaling.

"Now what?" she asked with a scowl.

"We cast the line and wait."

Maggie mimicked his actions reeling the line smoothly across the water on her first attempt.

"You's sure you never done this before?" he asked, skeptically.

"Quite sure," she giggled.

They stood on the small wooden dock in silence waiting for something to happen when Maggie's line bobbed followed by a slight tug.

"I think I've got something!" she declared.

"Don't panic. Ease it in real slow."

Sellers stood close, directing her every move. A sizable fish popped from the water, waffling and wavering at the end of the line, its scales shimmering in the late afternoon sunlight.

Grabbing the net, Sellers caught the gyrating creature and wrestled it into the bucket.

"Not bad for a first catch," he declared.

"That should make for some good eating."

"If we gets a few more of these, Willa will make fish stew. It's a mighty good meal for sure."

Over the course of an hour, they caught five large fish and several smaller ones, all of which found a temporary home in the tin bucket. When they'd caught enough for supper, Sellers pulled out a knife and started to clean the fish as Maggie plunked down on the edge of the dock, her feet dangling above the water.

"What're you doing?"

"Taking a break."

"You ain't done."

"I believe I am," she replied, her forehead wrinkling.

"No, you ain't. You gots to clean and gut 'em now."

"I'll pass," she replied, wrinkling her nose.

"A tough Irish girl like you can't handle a bit of fish guts? You's weak," he chided.

"I'm not weak, just a bit squeamish about guts and stuff," she said, crinkling her upper lip.

"You wanted to learn how to fish and this is part of it. Get over here."

Reluctantly, she trudged to his side. He proceeded to gut the fish, slopping entrails into a small bucket.

Maggie's stomach turned at the sight, but determination kept her from heaving.

"Here," he said, handing her a fish and the knife.

Maggie took a deep breath, grasped the fish, made the cut, and pulled the innards out, quickly depositing them in the bucket.

"Ha! I thought you was gonna faint," he laughed. "You's such a girl."

Maggie's eyes narrowed as she grasped a glob of entrails and slapped them across his face.

"You's gonna pay for that!" he exclaimed, grabbing fish heads and tossing them at her, hitting his target.

In disgust, Maggie brushed the fishy residue from her dress before grabbing the bucket of fish parts and dumping it over Sellers' head. With a scandalous grin, he walked towards her, mischief blazing in his eyes.

Backing away, she hollered, "I'm sorry, I didn't mean to..."

He chased her off the dock along the embankment when he caught her by the waist, lifting her in one smooth motion and depositing her into the murky waters of the pond. Soaked, she waded from the muddy depths shaking her head.

"You're in for it now!"

She ran after him, his long legs outrunning her with ease.

"I gives up!" he announced, throwing his hands in the air.

Maggie fell to the ground huffing from the chase and chuckling with each gasp. They returned to the pond to rinse the putrid remnants of fish guts from their clothes before cleaning the rest of the fish.

"We best get these to Willa if she gonna cook 'em up for supper."

Proudly, they made their way to the cottages with their clothes dripping from their escapades. Sellers presented the bucket of fish to Willa.

"Those be some fine lookin' fish. I be able to make a good stew with these." Willa declared, taking the bucket and lumbering over to the table by the cooking pot. Crinkling her nose, she asked, "Ooo…somethin' be stinkin' pretty bad."

"Sellers started whistling and gazed toward the sky while Maggie lowered her head and chewed her lower lip.

Willa's eyes narrowed. "Don't know what kinda mischief you gots into but you's gonna clean up before supper. Ain't gonna have half drowned rats stinkin' up the dinner table." With a nod of affirmation, she waddled to the table to chop the day's catch.

THE STEW WAS EVEN BETTER than Sellers had described. After eating two bowls, along with a large slice of corn bread slathered in butter, Maggie was ready to retire for the evening. Bidding the group goodnight, she and Sellers meandered down the path.

"Told you the stew was good."

"I don't remember the last time I ate so much," she said, rubbing her stomach.

They walked along the path in silence, content with full bellies and each other's company when Maggie started humming.

"What you in such a good mood 'bout?"

"The wonderful dinner and the warmer weather," she spun in a circle with her face tilted toward the sky. "Makes me feel like I might find my way home."

"Honestly, I don' want you to leave. I know that selfish but you's my family now."

Maggie glanced at the pasture stretching across the hilly expanse. "It's not selfish." A tear christened her eye. "I'd miss you too, but I want to go home. I don't care about the lack of food. I can make a little go a long way." Her voice trailed off, stymied by the lump forming in her throat. "It's so unfair. My Da is fighting to survive and I'm here with plenty to eat. I'd gladly do without just to be near him again."

"Life ain't fair, we both knows that. Neither one of us can have what we wants."

"At least we don't have to do it alone," she said, nudging his arm with her elbow.

"They say misery loves company. Sounds like you and me is a perfect match."

"I suppose we are," she answered, her spirits lifting as they shuffled along the path arm in arm.

MR. STEVENSON STARED at the recent notice from the bank threatening to place a lien against the house. His property was the most important thing in his life and he'd not relinquish it, no matter what happened. The desk chair squeaked as he shifted his weight and rubbed his forehead. His losses at the last poker game were substantial with an IOU hanging around his neck like a noose. He'd drained the accounts and the business was long gone. Somehow, he had to find some cash, and fast. He realized where he'd made his mistake at the last game and was certain his luck would change with the next. Mr. Farris had returned from his European tour and was scheduled to play the following week. Farris's reputation of having more money than sense made this the perfect situation for Stevenson to win big. But he needed money to secure a seat at the table and he'd tapped out all of his resources. *If I could find the money to secure a seat in the game, I know I could turn my luck around this time. After all, no one could suffer a permanent run of bad luck,* Stevenson thought.

He remembered the diamond necklace his wife had inherited after his mother's death and considered pawning it. In a sense, it rightfully belonged to him and she rarely wore the thing so no harm would be done. He could retrieve the necklace with his winnings without her ever knowing it was gone. Pawning things was below him but desperation could drive a man to do dishonorable things.

If only his stupid sister hadn't been so selfish to run off with McFarland. He was a farmer for goodness sake, not to mention Irish! Their mother had arranged a perfectly acceptable marriage that would have benefitted the family both in title and finances. Instead, she fell for the seduction of a conniving Irishman, no doubt interested only in her wealth. His mother never spoke his sister's name again. Yet her wrath toward him increased tenfold as if he was to blame for his older sister's indiscretions.

Recollecting all he'd endured after his sister's disappearance, he decided pawning the necklace was a fitting way to enact revenge on his mother's memory. *Wicked thing,* he thought. *She'd roll over in her grave if she knew what I was about to do.* He'd endured her torment most of his life and was relishing his revenge.

His upper lip crinkled as he rose from his chair and made his way to the bedchamber where he searched his wife's jewelry casket. Pulling the sparkling strand from its velvet cocoon, he held it to the light admiring the glinting prisms. Yes, this would bring the money he needed while smiting his mother's memory. It was a glorious plan and one he'd enjoy carrying out. He dropped the necklace into his coat pocket and headed downstairs.

11

Sweat beaded across Maggie's forehead as she pummeled and crushed herbs in the mortar.

"What gots you so worked up? You's pounding them herbs like they you worst enemy."

Maggie looked up, wiping her sleeve across her brow. "I'm frustrated. I've not heard a word from my Da since I arrived and I'm terrified he's..." a sob burst from her lips as she buried her face in her hands. Willa rushed to her side and led her to the chair.

"What you scared of?"

"That he's dead," Maggie gasped. "I've not received a single letter."

"Has you checked the mail yourself?" Letty asked, one hand planted on her hip.

"No, Miss Mabel collects the mail and leaves it in my uncle's office."

Letty looked at her with eyebrows arched and lips pursed. "I thinks you figured out the mystery." She returned to the salve she'd been stirring in the iron pot.

A shiver ran up Maggie's spine, prickling the nape of her neck.

Of course, she thought, *he's been keeping my Da's letters from me.*

Shaking her head, Maggie rethought the idea. "I know he's a cruel man, but do you think he'd do something so wicked?"

"You need to ask that question?"

Maggie exhaled. "At least my Da has been getting letters from me."

"Who been sending your letters?" Letty asked.

"I gave a few to Mrs. Stevenson to post, but lately Susannah's been taking them."

"Tsk, tsk, tsk. That ain't good."

"What do you mean?"

"Cause the missus be as devious as Mr. Stevenson, and she daughter too."

Heat rose in Maggie's chest coloring her cheeks. Surely, she hadn't misjudged Susannah, they'd grown so close. They shared the bond of suffering beneath Mr. Stevenson's vitriolic speech so there was no reason for her to side with him.

"What you thinkin' chil'?" Willa asked, dread straightening her back.

Wildness clouded Maggie's eyes as she looked at the two women. "I'm going to get my Da's letters," she stated firmly. Untying her apron, she flung it across the stump when Willa grabbed her by the wrist.

"You can't just barge into that house and start demanding things. You don't even know if he has those letters. Letty was just asking if you checked 'em yourself."

"What other explanation could there be? My uncle knows how much those letters mean to me." Tears extinguished the fury as she leaned into Willa's ample frame soaking her shoulder with months of pent-up anger and sorrow.

"Sit down and let's talk 'bout this before you do something you's gonna regret."

Maggie sat down. Letty placed a cup of coffee next to her as Willa spoke.

"You gots to let this go. If you upset Mr. Stevenson, he could get violent."

Maggie took a sip of coffee and nodded. "You're right. I need to ask Miss Mabel about the letters."

"Ain't no point in that either. She know her place and ain't gonna go against Mr. Stevenson's wishes."

"What am I supposed to do?" she asked. Her shoulders slouched as she stared into the coffee cup.

"Ain't nothing can be done. He in control and nobody gonna stand up to him. Not ever."

Maggie looked up at Willa, her eyes blurry with tears as hopelessness coursed through her veins. "You're right, but it's so unfair. Maybe if I..."

"Stop trying to make this fair. Life don' work that way," Willa declared. "Things ain't so bad for you here and in time you find a way to get back home. But confronting Mr. Stevenson only gonna get you hurt."

Setting the cup on the table, Maggie sniffled. "I should probably get to the barn. It's almost time to bring in the cows."

"That's a good girl, now you's being sensible 'bout this whole thing."

Maggie started toward the cattle barn, her thoughts steeped in Willa's wisdom. As she crested the hill, she glanced in the direction of the house. Her heart burned with the anger she'd fought to suppress for so many months and her Irish spirit took hold. Instead of returning to the barn, she marched along the trail to the house. Her uncle was usually gone this time of day, and Susannah and her mother would be in the front parlor for tea, which meant she could sneak inside and search his office for the letters. This way she'd find out if her father had been writing to her with little risk on her part.

Reaching the back door, she stood for a moment, her hand resting on the brass nob. The courage that had driven her there was beginning to wane. What if her uncle was home and questioned her presence this early in the day? Then again, if he wasn't home and she timed it right, she could slip into his study without notice.

Determined to find answers, she inhaled and crept inside and shut the door as quietly as possible. Sounds from the kitchen rattled through the back hall as preparations for the evening meal were underway. The thudding of her heart beat in her ears making it difficult to concentrate. With a deep breath, she scurried up the back stairs to the second-floor landing and down to her uncle's study.

The stale scent of tobacco and brandy assaulted her nose as she slipped into the room. A stack of mail sat upon the desk catching her attention. Thumbing through the correspondence, Maggie's heart seized when she noticed an Irish postmark. Her Da *had* written. Fury burned in her gut as Willa's words echoed in her mind, reminding her that her suspicions were just that, speculation. Perhaps this was the first letter he'd sent. Lost in thought, she startled when footsteps thudded in the hall. She shoved the letter into her pocket as she scooted behind one of the silken drapery panels, adrenaline rattling her body so hard she feared the shuddering curtains would give her away. With all her might she commanded her body to stay still as she held her breath and waited as the door opened and closed.

The chair creaked beneath the weight of her uncle as he rummaged through the desk, opening drawers and slamming them shut. She exhaled when she heard him exit the room and waited momentarily to make sure he was gone. Maggie hurried from behind the curtain toward the door when something on the desk caught her attention. Wisdom told her to get out of there as quickly as possible, but curiosity stifled its cries when she saw the ledger lying open on his desk. Glancing down the page, she noticed discrepancies in the balances. She turned back several pages to find many of the accounts in red. One entry in particular seized her heart. The date was a few days after her arrival in the amount her father had sent. The wretched man had spent all of her father's money and none of it was for her upkeep! All this time she'd been working from dawn to dusk to offset her expenses.

Rage drummed against her chest as her heart thrummed to the beat of revenge. Despite her fear, she was going to confront her uncle about his scandalous ways and demand he return the money so she could go home. No doubt, he'd be pleased at her departure.

Maggie's plotting rendered her unconscious of the figure shadowing the doorway. Before she could react, a hand landed against her cheek, knocking her to the ground. Blood trickled from her nose across her lip.

"Filthy Irish Trash! What are you doing in my private office?" His words seeped through gritted teeth in a low growl.

She started to rise when his boot slammed into her side knocking the breath from her lungs and sending a sharp pain skittering through her stomach. Blood dripped onto the rug as she tried to catch her breath when he yanked her up by the arm.

"Why are you in my study?" he thundered.

Before she could respond he slapped the side of her head, sending sparks of light across her field of vision. Self-preservation clamped her mouth shut as she tried to come up with an excuse to pacify his rage.

"I meant no harm, please let me go."

He tightened his grip on her upper arm causing her to cry out.

"Why are you here?" The spittle from his words moistened her face as he leaned over her.

"Only to ask if I'd received a letter from my Da," she muttered, her eyes cast down hoping he'd accept the explanation.

"Why would he bother to write such a loathsome excuse of a daughter? You're lazy, ugly, and worthless which is why he sent you here. Obviously, he wanted to be rid of you. Can't say I blame him. I only wish he'd have been more responsible with the funds. You're not worth the pittance he provided, then again, an Irishman isn't worth much himself."

His last phrase hit the target, but instead of silencing Maggie it loosened her tongue.

"How dare you speak of my Da in that manner after you stole his money and banished me to work in the cattle barn! He's more of a man and a provider than you've ever been!"

Regret squeezed her throat as soon as the words fell from her lips. The rage in her uncle's eyes magnified a hate so deep it rendered him unrecognizable. His face contorted and his lips curled into a snarl like a rabid dog.

His fist landed in the center of her gut, slamming her against the wall with the ease of a ragdoll. She struggled to get to her feet when his boot landed against her stomach with such force that she gasped for air. Pulling her from the floor by her arm, he landed another slap across her face before back-handing her back to the ground. The taste of iron filled her mouth as blood seeped from her nose and lip, her left eye beginning to swell. He reached down, clutched her arm in a vice grip, and drug her across the floor into the hall, slamming his office door behind him.

He's going to kill me, and I'll never see my Da again, she thought, salty tears mixing with her bloody lip.

He leaned over, his hot breath caressing her ear. "Get your worthless Irish carcass out of my sight. If I ever see you in this area of the house again, I won't be responsible for the consequences. And if you utter one word about what you saw in that room, I will finish you. Do you understand?"

Maggie nodded, still unable to catch her breath when he punctuated his sentiments with another kick to her ribs.

"And get off my rug, I'll not have you soiling it with your blood," he grumbled, stomping away with Jasper at his heels.

With all the strength she could muster, Maggie got onto her hands and knees when a wave of nausea squeezed her stomach. Her hand flew to her mouth as she swallowed the bile in an effort to prevent further soiling of the rug. With a few deep breaths, she braced herself against the wall and struggled to her feet, her head spinning. Carefully, she maneuvered the staircase to the third floor, gripping the balustrade to steady her wobbling knees.

Inside the sanctity of her modest room, she collapsed to the floor in a heap of sobs. Her gut lurched as drool slithered over her swollen lip and her body quaked with the force of the ocean. How had things gone so wrong so quickly? As her sobs subsided into hiccupped gasps, she unfolded her quavering legs from beneath her, grasped the footboard of the bed, and pulled herself to a standing position. She felt as weak as a newborn calf, nearly falling to the ground as she staggered along the edge of the bed.

With shaking hands, she splashed cold water on her face and dried it with the towel. Glancing in the mirror, she noticed her puffy lip and a bruise beginning to darken her cheek where the first strike landed. Another gasp of sorrow erupted as she sat on the edge of the bed when something in her pocket poked her hip. In the mêlée she'd forgotten about the letter from her father.

She ripped the envelope open, pulled the letter from within, and did her best to steady her hands as she read.

. . .

My dearest Maggie,

I hope you are doing well with your studies and spending time in the fresh air. Please do not fret over my circumstances as I am doing well where I am and have enough for now. When I get settled somewhere more permanent, I'll let you know. My only peace is knowing that you're safely ensconced with your uncle in America where you're far from the hunger and poverty ravaging our beloved country. All will be well in time and I pray you do not worry for my sake. I'm a resourceful bloke and hold onto the day when we will be together again.

Your loving Da

Maggie's mind rustled like autumn leaves caught in a gust of wind. *Relocate? Somewhere more permanent? Where was her Da and what happened to the farm?*

Grabbing the envelope, she searched for a return address but found none. Something was wrong, terribly wrong and she needed to get home. No matter what it took, she was leaving this place.

Daylight faded into darkness as she plotted her escape. She couldn't let anyone know of her plans for fear they would try to discourage her and she hadn't the fortitude to stand up to their objections. Thankfully, her uncle hadn't returned since the beating. For a brief moment she thought he might feel badly for what he'd done; however, Maggie knew that was wishful thinking on her part. At one time she may have been naïve enough to believe that all people were good in some manner but life at Fielding Hall had taught her otherwise. Her uncle had no heart, no conscience, and cared only for himself and his dog. He'd have no regrets for his attack and would likely do worse the next time, and she was certain there would be a next time. If she were going to go, she needed to do it without delay.

Maggie peered out the window watching night squeeze the

life from the last of day's light in shades of deep blue and orange. Gathering her few belongings, she shoved them into her satchel. When she reached for the silver locket, she popped it open and gazed at the locks of her parents' hair bringing fresh tears to her puffy eyes. She clicked it shut and stuffed it into the satchel along with the wooden heart from Sellers and her worn copy of Byron's poetry.

12

The carriage rocked to and fro over the road to Philadelphia. Mr. Stevenson had pawned the diamond necklace and felt more confident with the wad of cash tucked inside his coat pocket. He could feel his luck changing with each lurch of the carriage. Tonight, he'd win enough cash to stave off the creditors a while longer. A smile parted his lips as he thought of his future winnings. Nothing could stop him.

When he arrived at the brownstone in downtown Philly, he sent Milton on his way with instructions to come back at midnight. Stevenson bounded up the brick steps and rapped the brass knocker against the gleaming oak door. A butler led him to the parlor where Mr. Farris and three other men huddled around a game table with stacks of coins, a pile of bills, and half empty whiskey glasses while cigar smoke swirled through the air.

"Sir, a Mr. Stevenson wishes to join the game."

The owner of the establishment, Lawrence James, walked over with a cigar gripped between his lips puffing like a steam engine as he offered his hand.

"Good to see you Stevenson. We were hoping you'd join us this evening. Mr. Farris has been keeping the game lively." He laughed, the cigar bobbing between his lips.

"Sorry I'm late but I had to make a stop along the way."

"No apologies necessary," he said, patting Stevenson's shoulder. "Have a seat, my good fellow."

He called for the butler to bring a whiskey and a cigar for the newest member of the group while another gent shuffled the cards and dealt each man a hand.

"I believe there's the business of an entry fee?" Mr. James asked.

"Of course." Stevenson pulled one hundred dollars from his frock coat and handed it to him.

"Welcome to the game Mr. Stevenson, and good luck."

MAGGIE OPENED the door and was startled to see Susannah standing there. Suddenly self-conscious of her appearance, Maggie ducked her head to the side hoping to hide her bruised cheek and fat lip.

"Whatever happened to you dear cousin?" she asked sarcastically, stepping into the room.

"I had a little accident at the cattle barn this afternoon and tumbled from the hay loft ladder." Embarrassed by her circumstances, Maggie couldn't bring herself to tell Susannah about the horrible beating Mr. Stevenson had inflicted.

"Liar," she replied, her voice curt. "Father was enraged when he got downstairs and left without saying where he was going. What did you do?"

Stunned by the question, and the innuendo tainting it, Maggie assured herself her mind was too foggy to think clearly and that she was imagining any indignation from her cousin.

"Why would you doubt my word after what your father did?"

"Leave my father out of this!"

The abrupt nature of her declaration caught Maggie off guard.

"Susannah, what's the matter? Have I done something to offend you?"

Susannah's eyebrows arched at the question. "Your presence is the only offense."

Her cousin's vicious words and manner of speaking mimicked Mr. Stevenson in every aspect. Astounded, Maggie shook her head, Willa's words resonating in her mind.

"How did I *not* know?" Maggie whispered.

Despite the obvious nature of the situation, Maggie clung to the hope that she hadn't been a complete fool regarding Susannah.

Like the sunrise cutting through early morning fog, the reality of her relationship with her cousin became clear. Mr. Stevenson's negative responses and changes in her daily assignments, he knew it all because Susannah had told him. An ominous sensation pulsed through Maggie's veins making her head throb and her stomach flutter with a thousand butterflies. How could she have been so gullible?

Unable to form a response, Maggie looked at Susannah who stood with head high and eyes glaring. A sinister smile lifted Susannah's porcelain cheeks, and for the first time, Maggie saw her cousin for the fiend she was.

"You betrayed me," Maggie whispered. "I thought you were my confidant, but you've been play-acting. I trusted you."

"My father is a respectable man. I was more than proud to keep him informed of your devious ways."

Tears pooled in Maggie's eyes, threatening to flood her flushed complexion. "How can you be so cruel? Your father has treated you harshly. Have you learned nothing from his example?"

Susannah's insolence was steeped in the bitter leaves of hatred, chilling Maggie to the core.

"Have you any idea what it's like to live in the shadow of a dead sibling? The brother who would have saved the family line, a real Stevenson, not a worthless bit of fluff such as myself." She stepped closer. "Then you arrive with stories of a loving father who dotes on your every breath."

"I don't deserve this," Maggie said.

"You deserve whatever fate befalls you. For the first time in my life, Father finds favor with me. Delivering information about you has created a bond between us that can't be severed and I'll not apologize for it!"

Susannah's coldness numbed Maggie as if someone had stabbed her in the heart with an icicle. She was caught in a web of turmoil by the venom of a woman whose soul was so unfeeling it would wilt any love that tried to grow in its presence.

"My father raised me to be a fair and honest lass," Maggie said, straightening her stature.

"Your precious father. You drone on and on about how wonderful he is and how much he cares for you. If he loves you so, why did he send you halfway around the world? Why not find relatives in your own country?"

"I've told you his reasons for sending me here. And how could you believe I was engaged in anything deceitful when I work so hard?" Maggie still couldn't accept what was unraveling before her.

"Because the Irish act as if they're honest, hardworking people when they're actually lazy thieves. Your kind has denigrated our society far too long by cheating Americans out of opportunities for honest work."

"I'm not what you proclaim, Cousin. I never have been, nor will I ever be." Maggie's Irish spirit began to surface.

"Let us understand each other. We are *not* cousins, we are *not* equals, and you are *not* honest. Americans should never allow your kind to cross our borders. Then again, we do need people to empty chamber pots and launder clothes." Wickedness curled her lips into a smile.

"You're despicable!"

"Trust me, you're the one in the wrong, not I. There's a reason your mother was disowned for sullying the family name with Irish filth. My grandmother was devastated by your mother's folly and I dare say it probably ended her life prematurely."

"She was my grandmother too," Maggie replied, shocked by the change in Susannah's attitude and the nasty things she was spewing.

"She would have been sickened by your very presence. Why don't you return to your precious *Da* and leave us be?"

"You know I can't do that."

"Of course, you can't because you know he doesn't want you either."

"You're lying! My Da loves me!" Maggie knew better.

"May you rot Miss McFarland, like the Irish filth you are," Susannah growled as she charged from the room and down the stairs.

Willa and Letty were right; Susannah was no different than her father. Maggie chided herself for trusting someone like that. But she'd garnered an important piece of information from the horrible encounter. Mr. Stevenson was gone from the house. Now was her chance to get away unnoticed.

Maggie waited until the dinner hour to slip down the back stairs when she knew Susannah and her mother would be dining. Stepping into the cool night air, she inhaled deeply. Her head throbbed and her body ached. She realized she'd not make it far in the dark and pondered what to do next when her gaze settled on the cattle barn that crested over the hill like a beacon. She'd sleep in the hayloft tonight and rise before dawn. If she timed it right, she'd be well on her way when Sellers arrived to feed the cows and no one would miss her until she was far from Fielding Hall. She couldn't stand the thought of leaving without saying goodbye but she knew it was better this way. Mr. Stevenson would question them and the less they knew, the safer they'd be.

The plan gave her some peace as she entered the darkened barn. The sounds of cows shifting on straw bedding and munching hay comforted her. Maggie had grown fond of the gentle creatures, even old Casey. She climbed the ladder and nestled in the far corner of the hayloft where she rested her head on the satchel, pulled her shawl around her, and willed herself to sleep.

MR. STEVENSON'S forehead glistened in the candlelight as he considered his hand. A beautiful suit of Five, Six, Seven, Eight, Nine, all of Diamonds, gleamed before him. Finally, he'd gotten a nearly unbeatable hand and he could feel his luck shifting. That miserable Farris had outplayed him all night and now he was about to win back every last penny and then some. His palms dampened as he strained to hide his joy at the impending win. He wanted to make Farris sweat and suffer. Savoring the moment, he gave a sly smile before revealing his hand.

"Straight flush," he said, fanning the cards on the table.

"Well played Stevenson," Farris replied, downing the last gulp of whiskey and spreading his cards on the table. "But not good enough. Royal flush." He leaned back in his chair, a smile lifting the ends of his mustache.

Mr. Stevenson's jaw clenched, his blood turning to ice as he stared at the cards; Ten, Jack, Queen, King, Ace of Spades. His heart thundered in his ears. Something was wrong. Farris had a reputation of consistently losing. Stevenson glanced around at the other men. Not one of them was familiar to him. His gut churned. He'd heard about these gambling rings and now wondered if he'd been made out as a fool. He had been so focused on the game he hadn't noticed that the other players were strangers. Only the host was familiar.

"I'm done for the night," one of the men said, standing in a stretch and offering his hand to Farris. "You played well."

"Indeed," Farris said, returning the handshake. The other two men followed suit until only Farris and Mr. Stevenson remained.

"Don't look so down, my friend. It wasn't your night." Farris counted the money as Stevenson stewed, trying to figure out where he went wrong. His strategy was foolproof. There's no way he could lose, of that he was convinced.

"There seems to be a shortage. With that last hand, you owe me a thousand bucks."

Stevenson's eyes shot up meeting his debtor's gaze. "That can't be correct," he muttered, staring at the pile of cash.

"If you doubt my integrity, you're welcome to count it yourself," he said, puffing his cigar and motioning toward the money.

"No need," he said, swallowing hard. "I haven't the funds with me this evening. I'll have to write an IOU."

"Hmmm, that is a problem. You see Mr. Stevenson; the rules of this game were abundantly clear. All debts must be paid in full at the close of the evening. But I'm not an unreasonable man. Bartering can be arranged, say for the gold watch chain dangling from your waistcoat?"

Stevenson glanced down at the glittering chain attached to his pocket watch. The heirloom had belonged to his grandfather, the only person in his life who had treated him with kindness. It had been passed down to his father and then to him. Had his son Edgar survived he'd have inherited the piece. No matter his circumstances, he'd not part with something so valuable.

"That's unacceptable, Mr. Farris." Stevenson thought for a moment. "I have a substantial number of livestock on my farm if you'd be willing..."

Shaking his head, Farris frowned, "Afraid I don't deal in farm implements or livestock. I'm a city man. Never had much use for the countryside."

"I've a fine set of horses and a carriage that might appeal to you."

"Already got that. What I am in need of is a good housekeeper. Last one, pretty little thing, found herself in the family way and the wife demanded I send her off. Don't suppose you could spare a housekeeper, preferably something with a pretty face?" His eyes glimmered as the corner of his mouth curled.

Mr. Stevenson shifted in his seat. "I may have the perfect solution. How would you feel about a young lady who isn't opposed to hard labor?"

"Tell me more about her," he said, leaning forward and resting his elbows on the table, the cigar clenched between his teeth. "How old is she?"

"Around eighteen. Strong back, hard worker, red hair."

Farris's eyes widened, "A red head. Never had one of those." He smoothed the whiskers on his chin. "She sounds intriguing."

"I can bring her tomorrow if you wish. She can work off the debt."

"Is she a *willing* worker?"

"She'll do as she's told."

Farris sat back, puffing the cigar, tapping his fingers on the table as he considered the offer. "And you can spare her until the debt is paid?"

"Keep her as long as necessary to pay what I owe."

He reached into his coat pocket and handed Stevenson a card. "Here's the address. Bring her tomorrow and drop her at the back of the house. Nice doing business with you Mr. Stevenson," he said, rising from the table, his hand outstretched.

Mr. Stevenson returned the handshake. "See you tomorrow."

13

By the time Mr. Stevenson arrived home it was well after two in the morning. Jasper waited at the front door, his tail wagging as Mr. Stevenson reached down to scratch his ear. Exhausted, he trudged up the stairs to his study where he locked the pawn receipt in his desk drawer. His shoulders were tight and his head ached. It wasn't the result he'd hoped for but at least he'd not lost more than a diamond necklace, ironically with a suit of diamonds.

The only positive part of the evening was that he'd finally be rid of that pathetic Irish scamp. His lips parted in a sneer. *Farris will fix her rebellious ways and calm her sharp tongue*, he thought. Rubbing his forehead, he decided to stay in his study instead of retiring to bed. He needed to catch Miss McFarland before she left for the cattle barn in a few hours. Now if he could marry off his ridiculous daughter, there'd be one less burden on his finances. *Maybe Farris has a son*, he thought, and poured a shot of brandy.

. . .

Mr. Stevenson startled awake, his neck stiff from sleeping in the chair. The half-empty bottle of brandy sat on his desk and Jasper snoozed at his feet. Rubbing his temples, he looked at the mantel clock which read quarter past four.

His sleep had been heavier than usual and for a moment he worried that he'd missed his niece. He decided to clean up and then go to her room.

After changing clothes, he shaved the stubble from his chin and returned to his study where he poured a shot of brandy and downed it in one gulp. Opening the desk drawer, he removed a pistol and snuggled it into his coat pocket in case she put up resistance to his demands. He couldn't let anything interfere with this transaction.

He tramped up the stairs and banged on Maggie's door. Silence. *Lazy creature is still asleep*, he thought. A sneer wrinkled his lips as he barged into the room. His eyes darted about the dimly lit space but no one was there and the bed was made. Gritting his teeth, he turned on his heel and headed out the door. Apparently, she'd already gone to the cattle barn.

Mr. Stevenson drew in a long breath. Hopefully she wouldn't put up a fuss when he told her to accompany him back to the house and pack her things. Too much was at stake.

The sound of mooing nudged Maggie from her slumber. Leaning up on one elbow, she tried to get her bearings as she scanned the hayloft when she heard Sellers rummaging through the feed room below. The realization that she'd overslept electrified her body sending her to her feet.

Blasted, she thought, *how am I to get away now?*

Careful not to make any noise, she slung the satchel strap across her chest, crawled to the edge of the hayloft, and peered over the edge. If she was cautious, she could slip away while

Sellers was at the other end of the barn. For a moment she considered telling him of her plans but quickly squashed the idea. He'd try to talk her out of it and her confidence was already beginning to waver. As desperately as she wanted to say goodbye, she knew it would be better if she left without speaking to him.

Her heart ached at the thought of leaving him, as well as Willa and Letty. They'd been her family and she loved them. But Sellers was special, he'd been as loyal as a brother, not deceitful like her cousin. Susannah's words ripped through Maggie's memory, deepening the scars left by Mr. Stevenson. Still, Maggie couldn't bring herself to hate Susannah. With her upbringing, it was no wonder she behaved as she did. Maggie could forgive her for that.

But Sellers was different. She'd never been so close to a person outside of her Da. Maybe someday she'd write when she was far from this miserable place. Then again, all the mail passed through Mr. Stevenson and would probably never make into Sellers' hands. She wasn't even sure he could read.

For a moment, she considered asking him to come with her until she remembered Willa and Letty's words. If they left the farm they could be captured and sold into slavery. She couldn't ask him to take that risk.

When the hay wagon squeaked down the aisle, Maggie darted for the ladder. She started down each rung as quickly as she could, holding her breath as her heart hammered against her chest. Once on the ground, she scurried to the hay bales stacked against the far wall when Sellers emerged from a stall.

He whistled in rhythm with the screeching of the cart's wheels as he made his way back to the feed room. She'd have to wait until he turned the cows out before she could scoot out the back door and head for the woods. Taking a few deep breaths to calm her racing heart, she leaned against the wall of hay and waited.

Each minute felt like an hour making her realize how much faster the morning routine went when two people worked. Guilt peppered her heart when Mr. Stevenson's voice shattered the morning quietude causing her knees to buckle.

"Sellers!" he bellowed.

"Yes sir?"

"Where's Miss McFarland?"

"Sir?"

"McFarland! Where is she?"

"I've not seen her this mornin' Mr. Stevenson," Sellers replied, slinging another bale of hay onto the wagon.

Maggie's body began to quake with only a wall of hay separating her from them.

"What do you mean you've not seen her? This is her time, is it not?"

Sellers stood upright, his six-foot stature meeting Mr. Stevenson's angry gaze.

"She usually comes in when I start hayin'."

"I don't believe you."

"Sir, I promise I've not seen her this morning."

Mr. Stevenson grabbed Sellers by the arm, "You ignorant darkie. Where is she?"

"Sir, she's not here." Although his words were steady, there was a doubtful edge to his voice.

Maggie considered calling out, but terror choked back her words.

"Is she in the hayloft?" The fury in Mr. Stevenson's voice rose with each utterance like mercury in a thermometer.

"Don' know where she be, sir," Sellers repeated.

Mr. Stevenson marched across the dirt floor toward the loft ladder, Maggie jolting each time his boot landed on a rung.

Sellers went to grab another bale of hay when he caught sight of Maggie crouching in the shadows. Holding his finger to his lips, he winked, reassuring her he'd not reveal her location.

He positioned his body so that Mr. Stevenson wouldn't see behind the stack of hay.

Moments later, Mr. Stevenson's voice echoed from the loft, "Cursed little tramp has taken off!"

He climbed back down the ladder, his anger stirring the dust as he stormed over to Sellers.

"You think I'm a fool, don't you?" Mr. Stevenson snarled. "You'd better tell me where she went!"

"Sir, I already told you I didn't see her when I gots here this mornin'."

Maggie peeked from the shadows, her heart pounding so hard she felt certain it would reveal her location. Conjuring as much bravado as possible, she forced herself to stay calm and let Sellers handle the situation. So much hinged on her escape, she couldn't lose her nerve now.

"Where is she?" he asked, pointing a pistol at Seller's head.

"Sir, please put the gun away," Sellers' voice escalated an octave as his hands went up in front of him.

Maggie's breath came in short puffs as terror gripped her lungs. Panicked, she tried to stand but her legs wouldn't respond.

"I'll give you one more chance to tell me where she is," Mr. Stevenson said, dropping the pistol to his side.

Sellers lowered his hands and exhaled. "Sir, I's sorry but I can't tell you what I don't know."

"Then I suppose this conversation is over."

In one fluid motion, Mr. Stevenson raised the gun and pulled the trigger. The sound cracked through the barn shattering the last bit of innocence residing in Maggie's soul. Sellers crumpled to the ground, his life flowing from his head in a crimson waterfall.

Maggie clasped both hands over her mouth to suppress the scream clamoring to escape. She waited for Sellers to say something, anything, to let her know he was OK. Her uncle was a monster but he wasn't a murderer. It was probably just a warning shot to instill fear.

The silence that followed was nauseating as she willed Sellers to speak. At that moment, everything slowed. It wasn't until a stream of blood trickled across the dirt floor to the edge of the hay where she crouched that she realized the gravity of her situation. Survival mode set in, keeping her perfectly still as she swallowed hard to control the bile flooding up her throat into her mouth.

Still unconvinced she wasn't nearby, Mr. Stevenson roared,

"Are you happy? Sellers is dead because of your cowardice! If you don't want to end up like him, I suggest you come here this minute!"

Paralyzed, Maggie cowered behind the hay bales, praying he didn't find her.

"I'll hunt you to the ends of the earth!" he bellowed. "You can't escape me. I'll not stop until I find you and when I do, you'll rue the day you ever met me!"

Mr. Stevenson loitered a few minutes more. After what seemed an eternity, she heard him walk away swearing as he went. Inhaling, she peered from behind the bales where a red halo rimmed Sellers' head letting her know there was nothing to be done. Tears sprang from her eyes at the sight of his lifeless figure. If she didn't run now, she'd miss her opportunity and most likely end up like Sellers.

Tiptoeing to the side door of the barn, she cracked it open, the whining hinges threatening to expose her location. She sucked in a breath and peeked through the opening searching for any sign of movement. Nothing. She bolted towards the woods, her will to survive pumping adrenaline through her limbs giving her the strength to flee.

Branches and underbrush grabbed at her clothes and swiped her face as she ran through the trees. Too panicked to stop, she kept her gaze focused ahead, her lungs burning as she heaved in air. Once she reached the other side of the wooded area, Maggie lurched over to catch her breath, a sob wrenching free from her gut followed by a waterfall of grief.

Frightened that her uncle might be close behind; Maggie hoisted herself to an upright position, wiped her cheeks, and looked both ways down the dirt road. Which was the safest route? *He'd likely follow the road to town,* she thought. She scampered across the dirt road and headed into another heavily wooded area, hoping to avoid detection.

Trudging through the dense thicket, Maggie cried for Sellers. Her uncle was right about one thing; Sellers' death was her fault. If she'd come forward when he'd called, Sellers would still be alive. Shame buckled her knees as she grabbed the trunk of a towering oak to steady herself. She had to keep going, not only for her own sake but to honor Sellers. He gave his life for her and she was determined to make his sacrifice worthwhile. One thing was certain, she had to get far away from her uncle's farm or she'd meet the same fate as the man she'd loved as a brother.

14

After miles of travel, the soles of Maggie's feet throbbed and her shoulders ached. She perched on a downed tree to rest, trying to force the image of Sellers' bloody body from her mind. Her eyes were gritty from the early spring pollen sticking to her tear-soaked lashes as she took in the serenity of her surroundings. She pondered how there could be so much beauty and peace in the world while others suffered and died needlessly.

The sun leaked through the canopy of trees, dripping slivers of light across the moss-carpeted forest as birds serenaded and squirrels scurried about. Judging by the angle of the sun in the sky, she figured it was midmorning.

Maggie rose to her feet and started walking when a trickling noise caught her attention. She honed in on the sound of running water and realized how truly parched she was. Determined to find the source, she followed the sound until she came upon a shallow creek fed by a small waterfall. Had her circumstances been pleasanter, she'd have delighted in the natural beauty of the scene, but for now she could only think of getting a drink and moving on.

Plopping down on the embankment, she slipped off her boots and stockings, and submersed her aching feet in the coolness of the rippling current. The flowing water tickled her blistered heels soothing the tender skin like a balm. When the ache subsided, she patted her feet dry with the hem of her dress and tugged her stockings and boots back on. She leaned over scooping handfuls of water into her mouth not caring that she soaked the front of her bodice in the process. Propriety was the furthest thing from her mind. Slightly refreshed, she resumed her trek, following the sun as it arched across the sky.

When daylight succumbed to evening tide, Maggie sought a place to stay for the night. She scanned the area wondering where she was. Hungry and emotionally drained, she noticed a barn cresting over the horizon and trudged toward the dilapidated building. With the final rays of sun settling beyond the horizon, Maggie peered into the abandoned structure where darkness enveloped the interior space.

Stepping inside, she squinted in an effort to make out her surroundings. Rusty tools stood in one corner next to a plow. Cobwebs as thick as cotton shielded every corner of the roof. Unlike the cattle barn, this one lacked stalls and must have been used for storage of implements and hay instead of housing animals. Fatigue coiled around her aching joints and throbbing muscles. She slumped onto a pile of loose hay, her eyes dry and her stomach protesting its empty state. Between the lack of sustenance and sheer exhaustion, she felt completely hopeless and alone. Unable to hold her eyelids open, she lay her head on her satchel where the memories of the day's events haunted her until sleep took hold.

A ROOSTER'S crow roused Maggie from her restless slumber, her stomach complaining of its vacant condition. Rising to her feet, Maggie's legs wobbled beneath the weight of her misery.

When her stomach groaned once more, she realized she'd not eaten for more than twenty-four hours and needed to find food. She gathered her satchel and stepped into the crisp morning air when she heard the rooster cackle once more. Maggie followed the sound to a hen house and peeked inside. Chickens squawked at her intrusion as she scooped up a couple of eggs.

Thrilled with her find, she scurried away to a wooded area nearby with the speckled orbs when she realized she hadn't any cooking utensils and building a fire would alert people to her presence. Tears wet her cheeks as she contemplated what to do. She needed to eat. Desperation drove her to crack each egg and dump the contents in her mouth. The slimy globs trickled down her throat as she fought to keep it all from reemerging. A shiver of disgust rattled her body before she started through the woods for another day of travel. Hopefully by nightfall, she'd find something more to sustain her.

Maggie's feet burned with blisters as the sun hovered overhead, soaking her body with sweat. Weariness numbed her senses and she felt as if she had fifty-pound weights cinched to her ankles. After nearly two days of walking, she found herself at the edge of a bustling township. Perhaps she could earn a few dollars and find some food.

Carriages transporting a variety of goods from milk containers to boxes of produce, clattered past in a whirlwind of dust. Shopkeepers tidied storefronts, with dazzling displays of the wares offered within. A two-story building with a broad front porch sported a mercantile sign and seemed a good place to seek temporary employment. At this point she'd gladly work for food.

Maggie peered through the sprawling bowed window at shelves of candies and canned goods. Smoothing her skirt, she stepped inside where the musky scent of tobacco caused her to sneeze, instantly catching the attention of the shop owner. A lanky gent with thick glasses and a crooked nose started towards her, the smile on his face fading as he scrutinized her appearance.

"Yes?" he said curtly.

"Good afternoon. I'd like to inquire about possibly doing a little work..."

Before she could finish her sentence, the man held up his hand.

"We don't need help."

With a nod, Maggie stepped from the store, surprised by the cold reception until she studied her appearance in the reflection of the glass door. Her boots were caked with mud, her dress was splotched with dirt, and the hem was frayed in places. No wonder he acted as he did. She looked like a vagabond. Across the street was a seamstress shop. Even though her sewing skills left much to be desired, Maggie was a quick study and willing to learn.

Stepping inside the modest one-story building, Maggie was mesmerized by the kaleidoscopic of fabric and trims neatly stacked on floor to ceiling shelves. In the far corner, a scrawny woman stitched the sleeve of a silky plum colored frock. Wisps of gray hair fell about her sculpted cheeks as she hunched over the dress. At the clanging of the bell, the woman stood.

"How may I be of assistance?" she queried before her demeanor soured. "What do you want?"

"I was hoping to find work in exchange for food, and possibly a place to spend the night."

"Can you read?"

"Yes ma'am, quite well."

The wooden floors creaked beneath her rapid footfalls as she scampered to the front window. Pulling a placard from the corner, she held it up for Maggie to see.

"Experienced seamstress needed. Irish need not apply."

"What makes you think I'm Irish?"

A sneer wrinkled the woman's upper lip. "The accent, not to mention the stench."

"I don't understand," Maggie responded, her hopes sinking.

"It means Irish aren't welcome!" The woman's dark eyes flared with repulsion, her bony hands resting on her hips.

Maggie couldn't process what she was hearing. Why would anyone be opposed to the Irish? She thought her uncle's hatred of the culture stemmed from a family resentment and yet here she was miles from him and the animosity was standing before her.

"But why?"

"Because you're worthless and lazy, that's why. I'll not give a perfectly good job to an Irish vagrant when there are decent folk in need of work."

"I'm only asking to do some odd jobs for food." Desperation clung to Maggie's words.

"Leave the premises or I'll be forced to call the constable!" she screeched.

Perplexed, Maggie exited, contemplating how her circumstances had gone from bad to worse to impossible. She'd been proud to be Irish; it never occurred to her that she'd be shunned because of her heritage, especially in America. It was supposed to be a land of opportunity and dreams. For her it was a nightmare.

As she neared the edge of town, Maggie eyed a small bakery. A woman of measurable girth, wearing a green calico dress sheathed beneath an apron dappled with flour, swept the front stoop. Dread tangled Maggie's gut when the woman looked her direction and called out to her.

"Hello there."

Maggie dropped her head.

The woman stood upright, resting her hand on the broomstick. "You look like you could use a cup of tea. Care to join me?"

Confused, Maggie hesitated before shuffling to the porch. She followed the woman inside where she was greeted by the scent of fresh baked bread intermingling with cinnamon and sugar. Maggie's stomach rumbled, sending a blush across her cheeks. The woman was probably playing some sort of cruel trick by inviting her in. Drowned by hunger, dark thoughts swam through Maggie's head. She could barely walk more or less think clearly.

The woman's rotund figure waddled behind the counter and prepared a tray of tea with sliced pound cake and cookies. "Come on back, we'll sit for a spell."

The sight of the food made Maggie's mouth water and her swollen eyes moisten. *Now that she's tempted me with food, she'll throw me out, and I'll starve to death.* At that moment, Maggie realized she'd perish and no one would ever know what became of her.

"Would you like to wash up before you eat?" The woman's soft brown eyes sparkled with kindness, easing the trepidation coursing through Maggie's veins.

"Yes, please."

The woman directed her guest to a small washstand in the far corner where Maggie washed her hands and face, making her feel more like herself. She sat at the small table as the woman poured a cup of tea and doled out the sweets.

"You look as if you could use some nourishment," she said, setting the plate and cup in front of Maggie.

"Thank you," Maggie responded, fighting back tears and the temptation to ravish the delicacies before her.

"I'm Rosalie."

"I'm Maggie. It's very nice to meet you," she replied.

Maggie sipped the tea and bit into the moist cake, closing her eyes in delight as the lemony substance melted across her tongue.

"You like the pound cake?" A smile plumped Rosalie's cheeks, obviously pleased by her guest's reaction.

"I believe it's the most delicious cake I've ever tasted," Maggie replied, draining the teacup as she washed down another bite of cake.

"What brings you to town?"

Maggie glanced down at the table. She hadn't considered what to say if asked about her background.

"I'm in need of employment."

"Of course, you are. A nice girl like you wouldn't be running from anything," she said, raising an eyebrow while refilling both cups. "How'd you come to get the black eye and bruised cheek?"

Unable to swallow the lump of cake, Maggie replied with a muffled, "I fell down." Managing to get the wad of cake down her throat, Maggie asked, "Why would you think I'm running away?"

"A famished young lady in rags with bruises and a black eye? What else am I to think?" Rosalie reached across the table to pat Maggie's hand. "Don't worry, I'll not give your secret away. You seem like a nice girl. Whatever he did, I'm sure you had good reason to leave him."

"Why are you being so nice to me?"

"I've no reason to be cruel."

"But the others..."

"Don't mind those bitter old hypocrites. They hate everybody, even themselves," Rosalie chuckled, taking a sip of tea.

"One lady practically chased me from her store."

"Ah, Gertrude. Pay no attention to her, or the others for that matter."

"Why do they hate the Irish?"

"Because they take jobs at lower wages. No one will give them fair pay so they work for whatever they can get. Then the locals can't find jobs and they blame the Irish for it. They've only themselves to blame. Residents buy the goods at lower prices but then complain because they can't get better paying jobs."

"What makes you think I'm Irish?" Maggie asked.

"My dear girl, if the accent didn't reveal your ancestry, the red hair surely would."

"No disrespect, but why are you talking to me if everyone hates the Irish?"

"Because I know what it's like to be shunned."

"How so?"

Her pudgy finger pointed to the Star of David hanging behind the counter.

"You're Jewish," Maggie said with a nod.

"It took some time to find a place where I could have a business without persecution."

"And the people here welcomed you?"

"Accepted would be a more accurate description. They weren't thrilled about my presence until they tried my apple cake. Suddenly, everyone loved me." Her chin waffled as she giggled. "Do you have someplace to stay tonight?"

"No ma'am."

"You can stay here. We'll have some supper and talk more about your situation."

"I haven't any money," Maggie croaked, a tear streaming across her cheek.

"Consider yourself a guest in my home."

"I appreciate your generosity but I'd feel better if I could do something in return."

"How about sweeping the floors once we close?"

Maggie smiled. For the first time in days, she felt comfortable. But as much as she liked her new friend, Maggie knew she couldn't stay for any length of time. She had no idea where her uncle would search and couldn't risk being found.

Rosalie's living quarters were at the back of the bakery.

Maggie settled in the attic for the night, snuggling beneath a patchwork quilt on a straw stuffed mattress. Her exhaustion, as well as the throbbing in her legs, made sleep a welcome respite.

THE FOLLOWING MORN, Maggie was greeted by the scents of baking bread and eggs frying as she made her way downstairs.

"Good morning. Did you sleep well?" Rosalie queried, pushing scrambled eggs around in an iron skillet.

"It's been a while since I've slept so soundly."

"Breakfast is nearly ready."

"Is there anything I can do to help?

"You can set the table."

Maggie placed utensils and plates on the table, along with a water pitcher, and a pot of coffee. Taking their seats, the two women conversed about baking, the condition of the roads, and spring's warming temperatures.

"What brings you to this country?" Rosalie asked.

"My father sent me here to escape the famine. Things are bad at home right now." Maggie shifted the topic in an effort to avoid discussing more of her past. "Do you have any family?"

"I have a brother and a sister. My brother is a barrister in New York and my sister lives in Boston with her husband and five children."

"What brought you here?"

"A simple lifestyle has always appealed to me. I was never enamored with all the debutante balls and social gatherings. I loved to read and to bake which didn't settle well with my parents. I decided at a young age that I had no desire to marry. That decision nearly drove my mother to her limits. When I found this place, I used the money from my father's estate to buy it. In the beginning things were rough. People weren't happy about having a Jewess in town but once they tasted my baked goods their prejudices dissolved. Funny how feeding the stomach softens the soul." Rosalie winked. "People travel miles for my apple cake."

Maggie admired Rosalie's fortitude to defy family expectations as well as societal convention. Once the breakfast dishes were washed, Maggie swept the floors while Rosalie finished preparing the day's offerings, including a basket of warm biscuits, a tray of oatmeal cookies, three cakes, and a variety of fruit pies, all displayed on tiered shelves encased by glass.

As much as Maggie longed to stay, she knew it was only a matter of time before Mr. Stevenson's search led him here. For her sake, and Rosalie's safety, Maggie decided it was best to move on.

"Thank you for your generosity," she said, slinging the satchel over her shoulder.

"Are you sure you wouldn't like to stay on for a while? I'd enjoy the company and there's plenty to do here."

"I really must go."

"You never told me what you're running from."

"Wish I could," Maggie replied, tears dangling from her lashes.

"I understand. Wait here a minute."

Rosalie hurried behind the counter where she packed a loaf of bread, half a pound cake, and a few biscuits for Maggie's journey.

"Take good care of yourself. And if you ever pass this way again, know that you have a friend who'd be glad to have your company."

Maggie threw her arms around her hostess, thanking her for the lodging and food, before resuming her journey to the unknown.

Refreshed by Rosalie's kindness, a full belly, and a good night's sleep, Maggie traversed dusty roads, stopping at dusk to sleep in an old shed. The sun dipped beneath the horizon, taking Maggie's prospects and expectations with it. When

Maggie unwrapped the cake from Rosalie, a few coins tumbled to her lap bringing fresh tears to her eyes. With all of the unkindness and animosity she'd endured, Rosalie's compassion filled her with hope. She rationed her food, eating a meager amount before resting her head on the satchel. But when she closed her eyes, images of Sellers' lifeless body haunted her dreams, chasing away steady sleep. It seemed her entire existence had morphed into a living nightmare from which she couldn't wake.

Male voices and a barking dog startled Maggie from her slumber. Jumping to her feet, she grabbed the satchel and peered through one of the slats in the wall where she saw two men walking her direction. She tried to breath but her lungs refused to take in air until the men turned down a different path. Once they were a safe distance from the shed, Maggie slipped out the door, looking around before running the opposite direction as hard and fast as her legs would move.

As the sun crested over the horizon, she made her way along a creek through a wooded area. Water gurgled across stony mounds, drawing Maggie to the edge. She leaned over and cupped the cool liquid in her hands, drinking for several minutes. After that, she splashed water on her face before moving on. She spent the remainder of the morning dodging all manner of limbs and underbrush.

For two days she traveled, sleeping in the woods at night and rising with the sun. After devouring the last of the bread, she started on the road, the soles of her boots beginning to thin. She trudged along, wondering where she was and where she was heading. Hours later, a harvest of hope took hold when a township dawned in the distance. She needed to find work and some nourishment soon since her food rations from Rosalie were gone.

Maggie plodded into town, the midday light glimmering off the windows of a general store. Stepping through the double doors, she glanced around the large expanse of canned goods, sewing notions, bootlaces, and other items of necessity. To the left was a sprawling display of confectionary delights. Her mouth watered. It had been a long time since she'd had candy. Maggie mulled over the selection, bracing herself for a curt reception when a portly gentleman approached, his smile revealing a sparse collection of f teeth.

"Good afternoon young lady. What may I get for you today?"

Not wanting to invoke a negative response, Maggie masked her accent as best she could.

"I'd like a portion of bread, a slice of the cured ham, and three of the peppermint candies, please."

He wrapped the bread and ham before depositing the candies in a paper sack.

"That will be seventy-five cents."

Maggie rummaged through her satchel for the coins, her hands trembling as she pushed her Da's letter, the wooden heart, the locket, and the book of poetry aside trying to locate the money. Not there. Frantically, she emptied the contents on the counter looking for them. Nothing.

"I seem to have forgotten my money," she muttered, swallowing the lump forming in her throat.

"You forgot your money, eh?"

"I'm sorry to have troubled you."

Clasping the satchel in her hands, she started for the door as footsteps echoed behind her. She winced when the merchant's hand rested on her shoulder.

"You can pay next time you come in," he said, handing her the bagged items.

Maggie stared in disbelief.

"I can't take this without paying."

"I insist."

"But I..."

"Please, take it."

"Thank you," she uttered, fighting back tears. "I promise to repay you when I can."

"No need," he replied, a slight smile lifting his mustache.

Ashamed of what had transpired, she rushed through the front doors wondering where and when she'd lost the money Rosalie had gifted her. She walked to the far side of town and settled beneath a parasol shaped oak, its branches sprawling several feet from its trunk. Maggie nibbled the bread and ham, thankful for the kindness of a stranger. She searched the satchel once more but found nothing. The coins were gone. They must have fallen out somewhere along her route. Now more than ever, she needed to earn some cash. Wearily, she started down the road to the unknown, leaving the town and its kind merchant behind.

After hours of walking, she came across a lean-to overlooking a pond. A glowing moonrise reflected off the still water inviting her to sit. Maggie removed her tattered shoes, sat on the edge of the pond, and lowered her swollen feet into the cool water while nibbling the rest of the bread and ham. Images of the pond at her uncle's farm flooded her thoughts with memories of Sellers sprawled across the ice trying to get his bearings, and later when he taught her to fish. The pond had brought them such joy. She reached into the satchel and grasped the wooden heart Sellers had given her. Lowering her head, she cried a river of regret over all that had happened. Guilt for causing his death would imprison her for the rest of her days.

Depleted of energy and emotionally wrought, Maggie settled beneath the tin roofed structure and cried herself to sleep.

15

Each day Maggie traveled as many miles as her legs could handle. The soles of her shoes were paper-thin and her feet had developed callouses as tough as leather. She'd long since eaten the loaf and ham and again found herself weak with hunger. Lacking the means to purchase any food, she was fearful starvation would be the end of her. How odd that she came to this country to avoid starvation and now she faced it head on. The thought of dying in some lonely place and never seeing her father again crippled her fortitude. But she reminded herself she couldn't give up now.

Self-pity began taunting her when a township appeared in the distance. If she could make it there, perhaps she could find temporary work, get some food, and purchase a new pair of shoes.

Hungry and disheveled, she drifted through the streets of town in a haze of wakeful delirium, the numbness in her feet making it difficult to walk. Never would she have imagined being homeless, hungry, and hopeless. Having lost all track of time, Maggie was unaware how many days she'd been walking or even the day of the week. But her Irish spirit refused to surrender.

As she strolled along the street, Maggie stumbled when the toe of her boot dislodged from the sole. Regaining her balance, she gazed at a whitewashed structure, the front porch brimming with baskets of fresh produce. She considered going in when two women stepped from the building. One of them scrutinized her appearance, a sneer wrinkling her lip as she steered her friend in the other direction. Angry tears crested in Maggie's eyes. Why were people so cruel? Couldn't they see she was in need?

Maggie wiped a stray tear from her cheek with the ragged sleeve of her dress. Looking up, she stared at a rectangular sign on the roofline that read Campbell's General Store in bold green lettering. A sturdy man with snowcapped hair, bright eyes, and an apron tied around his waist, arranged plump red tomatoes in rows. Perhaps she could do some odd jobs at the store in exchange for food and new shoes.

She entered the double front doors where a balding man in a striped cotton shirt, linen waistcoat, and wire glasses handed a paper sack to a petite lady in a cornflower blue dress. His eyes sparkled as he glanced over his spectacles at Maggie and exclaimed, "G'morning, Miss. Welcome to Campbell's."

He returned to his customer while Maggie rambled down the aisle studying the various goods available. She needed to find work but this shop looked fully staffed with employees at various locations throughout the store. Rows of jars filled with an array of foodstuffs tempted her. *If she could slip a few into her satchel without notice...*

Chiding herself for contemplating theft, Maggie's attention shifted to her rumbling stomach, screaming for her to reconsider. Perhaps if she waited for the employees to be distracted, she could grab one of the jars from the shelf undetected.

The only unoccupied employee, a man of stout proportions with a shiny forehead protruding from a faltering hairline, approached a young mulatto woman as she fingered through a selection of fabric with the grace of a swan.

"Hello Miss Milner. What can I get for you today?"

"I've come for some cloth. Mama needs to stitch a few dresses before she's overrun with baking pies for the church bazaar next month."

His thin lips curved into a grin. "I do love your mother's pies. My mouth is watering at the thought."

The young lady smiled, revealing a set of pearlescent teeth that glimmered against her tan skin. Engrossed in the various choices before her, she finally decided upon a pale blue calico print as well as a brown plaid.

"I'll take five yards of the blue and ten yards of the brown please."

Reaching for the scissors, the man measured out the lengths while Miss Milner meandered about the store filling her basket with thread, a package of needles, and a tin of butterscotch candies. She returned to the fabric table and popped one of the candies in her mouth, grinning as the sugary substance dissolved over her tongue. The idea of something as insignificant as a piece of candy made Maggie's stomach grumble.

The merchant folded the fabric neatly and tied the bundle with string.

"Here you go Miss. Milner. Will there be anything else for you today?"

"Nothing, thank you. Please put this on Papa's bill."

"Of course," he replied, scribbling the purchases onto a receipt pad.

Miss Milner started toward the door, glancing at Maggie with a grin. Her infectious smile was punctuated with dimples and her dark eyes radiated joy. Maggie found herself envying this stranger in what she could only imagine was a happy existence.

Maggie turned away, her body trembling. Instead of continuing out the door the young woman paused, concern ironing the dimples from her cheeks.

"Are you alright, miss?" she queried.

"Yes," Maggie replied, looking at the floor. She didn't want to draw attention and regretted having lingered for so long. *Leave me be*, she thought, worried the young woman was getting ready to demean her in some manner.

Instead, her gaze traveled from Maggie's worn dress to the ragged shoes clinging to her feet.

"I don't believe I know you. Are you new in town?"

"Just passing through," Maggie replied curtly, her legs beginning to wobble. She reached for the counter to steady herself but collapsed to the floor. The young woman set her packages down and rushed to Maggie's side.

"Mr. Campbell, please bring a cup of tea!"

The white-haired gent rushed to the back and returned moments later with a steaming cup.

"Let me help you. I can see you're in need," she said softly, helping Maggie to a chair.

Something in Miss Milner's eyes touched Maggie's heart until memories of her misplaced trust in Susannah resurfaced.

"I really must go." Maggie tried to stand, but her trembling legs wouldn't allow her.

The young woman smiled, apparently sensing Maggie's anxiety.

"I mean you no harm." She handed the tea to Maggie. "Drink this, you'll feel better."

Mr. Campbell brought another chair for the young woman to sit on. She perched gracefully on the seat, watching Maggie drain the cup.

"I'm Annalissa Milner."

"I'm Maggie McFarland." Blood rushed to her head in a dizzying wave when she realized she'd given her real name.

"Where are you from?"

"I must be on my way." Maggie rose, her legs wobbling as she placed the cup on the counter.

Annalissa gently grabbed her arm.

"Why don't you come with me? Whatever is troubling you, I assure you my family can help."

Mr. Campbell smiled at Maggie and nodded his head.

At this point, she hadn't a choice in the matter; she'd not make it much further in her current state. With all the energy she could muster, Maggie thanked Mr. Campbell for the tea and walked with Annalissa down the street like a lost kitten. When they reached the carriage, a slender dark-skinned man tipped his hat before taking Miss Milner's packages.

"Ellis, this is my friend, Miss McFarland, who has agreed to come home with me. Miss McFarland, this is Ellis, our driver."

Ellis gave a nod as he helped the two women into the carriage. Alighting to the bench seat, he cued the horses with a tap of the reins and a cluck of his teeth.

As they rocked to and fro, Miss Milner chattered on about her family's farm and life in the countryside, her eyes twinkling when she spoke of her mother and father. Her hair was neatly contained beneath a simple, yet fashionable bonnet, and her skin was the color of coffee with cream. Everything about her was lovely, right down to her charismatic countenance.

Maggie peered out the window as they turned down a long drive, halting in front of a two-story stone house surrounded by a grove of apple trees. Ellis climbed down, helped the ladies from the carriage, and carried the packages inside. Miss Milner looped her arm through Maggie's and leaned in.

"You're going to love my parents," she whispered.

Caught between wanting to believe Miss Milner's benevolence and the dread of being cruelly treated again, Maggie fought to keep her emotions intact. But hunger pilfered the last of her strength, making her limbs feeble and her mind foggy.

Stepping through a bright red door, Maggie was taken aback by the comfortable feel of the modest space. Wide plank floors blanketed in braided rugs anchored a narrow staircase with a strip of carpeting running up the center. Maggie traipsed down the hall behind Annalissa. She noticed an informal parlor to the right that hosted shelves of books around an oak mantel while the space across the hall was more formal with a velvet covered parlor set, layered window treatments, and a large rug with fringed edges.

The scent of apples and cinnamon saturated the air. Miss Milner escorted Maggie to the kitchen where a willowy woman, wearing an indigo frock, stoked the fire in an expansive stone hearth on the far wall.

"I'm home Mama," Annalissa called out.

"Hello my dear. Were you able to get...?" She stopped when she saw there was a guest. "Who is this?" she queried, wiping her hands on her apron.

"Mama, this is Maggie McFarland. We met in town."

Gentleness emanated from the woman's deep brown eyes as she offered her hand.

"Welcome to our home, Miss McFarland."

"It's nice to make your acquaintance, ma'am," Maggie replied with a slight curtsey.

"There's no need for formalities here. You may call me Mrs. Milner, or Beth if you prefer."

Maggie tried to process the conviviality of the situation while pondering the connection between Miss Milner and her mother. Obviously, their relationship was not a biological one as her mother was fair skinned with a sculpted nose, high cheekbones, and glossy brown locks pulled into a bun. Then again, Miss Milner might resemble her father.

"I was getting ready to serve lunch. Are you hungry?"

Maggie was well past hungry, bordering on being famished. "Yes ma'am, I mean Mrs. Milner."

"Annalissa, take Miss McFarland to wash up while I finish the stew."

Maggie followed her new friend to a small room off the kitchen where they rinsed their hands in an ironstone bowl.

"You'll love Mama's cooking. She makes the best beef stew in the world." Handing the linen towel to Maggie, she continued. "Papa won't be home until later."

Maggie blotted the water from her hands and hung the towel on the wooden dowel. Miss Milner stopped in the doorway.

"Is there anything you need before we sit for lunch?"

"No, thank you, Miss Milner."

"Call me Annalissa," she said. "May I call you Maggie?"

Maggie nodded as they sat at the harvest table near the hearth. Steam erupted from a Dutch oven dangling over an open flame, the tantalizing aroma causing Maggie's mouth to water. Once everyone's bowls were filled, Mrs. Milner asked her daughter to say grace.

"Dear Heavenly Father, we thank you for the delicious meal we are about to receive. Please bless our family and thank you for our new friend, Maggie. May her days be filled with your blessings. Amen."

Maggie swallowed hard, overcome by the Milner's compassion. *Is it so hard to believe there's good in the world,* she thought? Scooping a spoonful of stew into her mouth, she closed her eyes, savoring the delectable flavors of beef, onions, and potatoes. Annalissa was correct; Mrs. Milner was an excellent cook.

"Where are you from, Miss McFarland?" Mrs. Milner asked handing her a basket of sliced bread.

Maggie froze. Distracted by her hunger, she hadn't prepared for that question. Obviously sensing her unease, Mrs. Milner reached across the table and took Maggie's hand.

"There's no need to say anything until you're ready, but please don't be afraid. You're amongst friends here."

A sob burst from Maggie's lips with such power it shook her entire body. She desperately wanted to compose herself but months of abuse and fear crashed forth in waves from the depths of her weary soul. Annalissa held Maggie's shoulders as she released all of the terror and anger in a waterfall of sorrow.

Minutes later, Maggie wiped her flushed cheeks and looked at the two women who waited to hear her story. Despite all she'd endured, something in the Milner's manner kindled a spark of trust, which Maggie quickly extinguished. She'd not be taken in by kind words and false promises again.

"My apologies for my outburst. I'm just tired from the journey."

"Would you like to lie down?" Mrs. Milner asked.

"The stew is delicious and I'd like to finish, if I may."

"Of course, we can talk later."

They ate their meal in silence, the air thick with tension. Once she finished eating, Maggie carried dishes to a washbasin where Mrs. Milner began rinsing them.

"Thank you, Maggie. I'll finish this. Annalissa will get you settled."

"Let me show you to your room," Annalissa offered.

"I don't want to impose," Maggie blurted out. "You've already been so kind and I really should be on my..."

Mrs. Milner held up her hand, stopping her.

"You're in no condition to travel," she said, glancing at Maggie's attire. "Please let us help you." The gentle firmness in her voice quieted Maggie's distrust. Resting in a safe place wouldn't be a bad thing.

Annalissa led her up a steep staircase at the back of the kitchen to a modestly furnished room with a poster bed, oval rug, small hearth, and pine dresser. Books lined a set of shelves in the opposite corner, giving the space a cozy feel.

"I hope this will suffice."

"It's lovely," Maggie whispered, amazed by the generosity of strangers. It was much more than she'd been given at her uncle's home.

"Holler if you need anything." Annalissa turned to leave when Maggie grasped her hand.

"Thank you for everything. I haven't any money but I'll find a way to repay my expenses. I promise."

"Don't concern yourself with such things. For now, get some rest." Annalissa stepped into the hallway, closing the door behind her.

After days of walking, a full stomach, and the emotional chaos she'd endured, Maggie's eyelids felt as heavy as anchors. Peeling the remnants of her shoes from her aching feet, she climbed into bed, snuggled beneath the patchwork quilt, and fell asleep.

PART II

16

Maggie stirred from her nap, slightly dazed. Sitting up, she studied the darkening room in an effort to verify her location. Relief washed over her when she realized she was far from Fielding Hall. She winced when her feet hit the floor, her soles still raw from days of walking. A homespun dress was draped across the foot of the bed along with a crisp white petticoat, and stockings. Maggie still couldn't understand why complete strangers were being so gracious.

She hobbled to the washstand and splashed water on her face as *what if*s bounced around her head. A knock on the door startled her from the circus of feelings juggling her nerves.

"Maggie, may I come in?"

"Yes."

Annalissa's head popped in the door. "Dinner is almost ready. Forgive me for entering your room earlier, but I thought you might like a change of clothes."

"Thank you. It's a lovely dress."

"Once you're ready, join us downstairs. Papa will be home any minute."

Maggie nodded. She examined her dress with its tattered

hemline caked with dirt. Even the seam on the right arm had come lose. A layer of dust had transformed the once bright green plaid to a dull brownish color. Unbuttoning the front, she let the worn frock fall to the floor. The condition of her undergarments wasn't much better. Slipping on the new undergarments and dress, she was shocked at how well they fit, as if they'd been custom made for her. Maggie fastened the buttons and stood back to study her image in the looking glass, amazed at how something as simple as a change of clothes could lift the spirits and make one feel more at ease. A new pair of brown lace up boots rested at the foot of the bed.

Maggie braided her hair and wondered if the red color would be a beacon for her uncle's search. Unsure how far she'd traveled, Maggie decided it was best if she left as soon as possible. It was only a matter of time before he was able to track her down and she couldn't risk the Milner's safety. Once she settled elsewhere and found work, she'd send them money to repay their generosity.

Plodding down the back stairs to the kitchen, Maggie found Mrs. Milner preparing supper. An older woman with salt and pepper hair tucked neatly in a bun and blue eyes that glimmered when she smiled, was assisting her.

"May I be of assistance?" Maggie queried.

Mrs. Milner smiled. "Thank you, but Darla and I have things under control. Annalissa is in the front parlor if you'd like to join her."

Maggie gave a nod and sauntered down the hall where her new friend read by the window.

"How refreshed you look. The dress fits well," Annalissa said, closing the book.

"You have a good eye."

"It's my job to know these things. Come sit with me," she said, patting the chair beside her.

"What is your job?" Maggie asked, taking a seat.

"Wanderers often seek refuge at Papa's church so we keep spare garments for them. It's important that I'm able to fit them correctly."

"What about your studies?"

"There's plenty of time for that. Mother instructs me here at the house. When my lessons are done for the day, I usually sew, run errands, that sort of thing. How do you pass the time?"

Maggie shifted in her seat, avoiding Annalissa's gaze. Thankfully, she changed the topic.

"Do you like to read?"

Maggie perked at the question, a grin dawning on her face. "I do. Poetry mostly."

"I can't be without a book, I'm completely forlorn without one," Annalissa said with a giggle.

"Da taught me to read at a young age. Said it would expand my opportunities. He was determined to make me into a lady." Her words dropped off as her mind leapt from the cliff of reality to the valley of the past.

"Sounds like he had great plans for your future. Is he still alive?"

"Yes, but I haven't seen him in a while."

"And your mother?"

"She died when I was very young."

"I'm sorry." Annalissa reached for Maggie's hand. "But you're with us now," she declared, her dimples reappearing.

Before Maggie could respond, the sound of carriage wheels rattled down the drive. "Papa's home!" Annalissa announced, her dimples returning.

A gentleman stepped inside, his eyes glinting as he greeted his daughter with a hug. "How's my darling girl this fine afternoon?"

"Quite well," she replied, leading him to the parlor. "Papa, we have a guest."

"Already? I wasn't expecting his arrival until tomorrow evening."

"Not *him*," she said, with a stern look.

The hairs on the back of Maggie's neck rippled at their guarded conversation. They were expecting a man tomorrow and it was apparent they wanted his identity to remain secret. What if her uncle had advertised her escape in neighboring townships and the Milners were scheming to turn her over? It would explain their extreme generosity. Perhaps her uncle was offering a reward and they sought to collect.

Her thoughts raced as she contemplated what to do. Should she run now or wait until early morning to leave? She decided to eat another good meal before sneaking away in the middle of the night. After all, the mysterious man wouldn't arrive until tomorrow evening. By then Maggie would be far from this place with a full stomach, and new clothes.

"Miss McFarland, may I introduce my father, Reverend Milner. Papa, this is Maggie McFarland."

"It's a pleasure to meet you," he responded, offering his hand.

"Your family has been exceptionally gracious, sir."

"I'm pleased to know it." His broad smile and dark hair coupled with the black suit and white collar alluded to his ecclesiastical manner. And yet, Maggie was afraid to trust him.

"I look forward to knowing you better, Miss McFarland. Excuse me while I wash up for supper." With a slight bow, he left the room.

Annalissa beamed with pride. "My father is a remarkable man. Whatever your circumstances, he'll be able to help you."

Maggie desperately wanted to tell Annalissa everything but held back. If she couldn't trust her own cousin, how could she possibly trust complete strangers? No, she'd not allow herself to fall prey to another family, no matter how benevolent they seemed.

A short while later, Maggie gathered with the Milner's at the dining table amongst a cacophony of chatter and flatware clinking against dishes. It had been such a long time since she'd been at a meal where people conversed that it felt foreign to her.

"Where are you from, Miss McFarland?" Mr. Milner asked.

"Please call me Maggie," she replied, her heart quickening at his question.

"Very well, Maggie. How did you come to be in Bradford?"

Maggie chewed her lower lip while she pushed food around her plate.

"Mr. Milner, you've made her uncomfortable," his wife chided. Turning to Maggie, she smiled, "My dear, there's no need to discuss anything unpleasant. We're happy to have you with us."

"My apologies, I didn't mean to pry," he said, a flush spreading across his cheeks.

Maggie smiled meekly before switching the topic. "Mrs. Milner, the meal is delicious."

"I'm glad you're enjoying it."

The conversation altered as Rev. Milner shared an incident from earlier in the day about a cantankerous lady in town.

"And if the horse running away wasn't bad enough, the latch of the carriage door broke loose! Thankfully, Mrs. Germaine was prevented serious injury when she landed in the thorny hedge at the cemetery fence. Although she was fine physically, the silk of her dress was not as fortunate."

Mrs. Milner stifled a laugh. "Oh my, I don't mean to chuckle but to see her amongst the brambles is almost poetic."

"Not half as poetic as her best bonnet covered in thickets."

Annalissa whispered in Maggie's ear. "Mrs. Germaine has a propensity for gossip, causing a great deal of division amongst the parishioners. She criticizes anyone who doesn't dress as finely as she. Even worse, she says colored folks are undignified and ignorant. The only reason she's civil to me is because Papa is the reverend."

Her response confirmed Maggie's suspicion that Annalissa was not the biological offspring of her parents. Her caramel colored skin and tight curls suggested a mixed ethnic background, not the discernable European features of her parents.

Once dinner was over and the dishes cleared, the family retired to the front parlor. Mr. Milner read from the Bible while the ladies gathered at a small round table near the front window where a lantern burned brightly. A series of candles and two oil lamps cast shards of light across the interior of the room as Mrs. Milner doled out thread and needles.

"Miss McFarland, do you sew?" Mrs. Milner asked, arranging fabric scraps and sewing tools on the table.

"A little, but I confess, I'd starve if I had to depend upon my sewing abilities to earn a living."

Everyone chuckled, momentarily easing Maggie's trepidation. Until she escaped, she'd be convivial and do her best to fit in.

"Perhaps you could cut these scraps into smaller squares." Mrs. Milner handed Maggie a few cotton remnants and a pair of scissors.

"What are we making?" Maggie asked.

"We're patching clothes for some of our workers."

"Do you employ many people at your farm?" Maggie queried, glancing at the basket of worn clothing.

"A few," she said without looking up from her sewing. "We also mend clothing for the parishioners. These are hard times for many and we seek to offer relief."

Guilt fingered Maggie's chest over her negative thoughts about a family that seemed so charitable. But money would go a long way to help those they cared for, and no doubt her uncle would give a respectable sum to locate her. The old Maggie wanted desperately to believe in the Milners' charity but the new Maggie wouldn't allow it.

As the evening wore on and the light from the candles wilted, the Reverend announced it was time to retire. Maggie handed the stack of patches to Mrs. Milner.

"Thank you for your help this evening. It's greatly appreciated." Mrs. Milner said, placing the scraps into the basket.

Tears pressed against the back of Maggie's eyes, demanding to be let loose. Her heart swelled as she longed to reveal everything to the Milners and beg they reconsider surrendering her to her uncle. Despite these urges, she remained silent.

Annalissa looped her arm through Maggie's as they climbed the stairs.

"I think mama likes you very much."

"She's a delightful lady," Maggie responded.

Approaching Maggie's room, Annalissa spoke softly.

"I'm very glad to have you here."

Maggie nodded and stepped into the room.

"Maggie?"

"Yes?"

"Whatever is troubling you, please know you can talk to me about it. I assure you our farm is a safe haven for all."

Annalissa flashed a smile before disappearing down the hall, leaving Maggie to her tortured reality. These people were so kind, why would they turn her over to such a horrible man for money? Then again, her uncle may have been deceptive in his efforts to find her, suggesting that he cared about her welfare. How she longed to tell Annalissa everything and beg for help, but she resolved to stay silent. Her life depended on it.

17

Slumber eluded Maggie as she feared oversleeping and missing the opportunity to slip away. Unable to settle, Maggie peeked out the window of her room. It was still dark but an orange glow splintered the horizon. She dressed, gathered her satchel, and peeked into the darkened hallway for signs of movement. Seeing no one was about, she meandered to the back staircase and made her way to the kitchen, her eyes darting in the shadows for any indication of early risers. A small fire burned in the hearth and a candle flickered on the table but no one was around. She exhaled and reached for the doorknob of the back door when a voice sent her heart racing.

"Miss McFarland, where are you going at such an hour?" Darla asked, stepping from the pantry.

Maggie froze, fumbling for an explanation.

"I was only, um, I'm going..." She felt like a trapped animal facing the hunter's rifle. Should she run and risk being pursued or stay and try to make her escape when no one was around? Panic cascaded down her cheeks.

Darla ran to Maggie, placing an arm around her shoulders and guiding her to a chair.

"What's troubling you?" she asked, sitting beside her.

"It's not safe for me to stay," Maggie muttered, dizziness swirling behind her eyes.

"My dear, this is the safest place in the world."

"Not for me. I can't say anything more, but I must leave." Maggie knotted her hands in her lap.

Reassurance glimmered in Darla's faded blue eyes as she patted Maggie's shoulder.

"You needn't tell me anything, but know you're protected here."

"I want to believe you but I'm aware of..."

"Aware of what?"

"The *visitor* that's supposed to arrive this evening."

Darla sat up straight, her eyes narrowing. "What do you know about a visitor?"

There was no going back now. She'd already said too much. Like water breaking through a dam, the words fell from her lips in sobs.

"I heard the Milners speaking about a visitor arriving this evening. I fear it may be my uncle who's anxious to find me."

Darla took hold of Maggie's trembling hands. "Don't know nothing about your uncle but I assure you he's not the person they're expecting."

"How can you be so sure?"

"Cause I know who's coming."

"Who is it?"

"There are things I'm not at liberty to speak about. What I can tell you is that the Milners are special people who would never cause any harm. They're in the business of helping others, not hurting them."

"But I..."

"Whatever happened to bring you here is irrelevant. Furthermore, you need to tell the Reverend the truth. He can help you. You have to trust me on this." Darla gave Maggie's hands a firm squeeze.

Darla's expression was stern, her lips forming a hard line as her brows furrowed, magnifying the conviction of her words. Maggie couldn't explain it, but somehow her wounded heart saw the truth reflecting in this woman's eyes.

"Alright, I'll speak with him," she muttered.

"That's a good girl." Slapping her hands against her thighs, Darla stood. "Since you're here, you may as well help. No sense squandering your time."

Maggie did as she was told and worked her fears and frustration out as she kneaded dough. A short time later, footfalls sounded on the stairs announcing Mrs. Milner's arrival.

"Good morning," she said, pouring a cup of coffee. "Maggie, there was no need for you to rise so early. You're a guest in our home."

"I couldn't sleep," Maggie replied.

Darla shot a knowing glance at Mrs. Milner alerting her that something was awry.

Mrs. Milner gave a nod and approached Maggie, resting a hand upon her shoulder. "We're glad to have your company this morning."

Mrs. Milner fell into step with the morning routine when the sound of Annalissa's shoes scuffling down the steps echoed through the room. Her entrance was like a ray of sunshine piercing through an overcast sky.

"Good morning, all!" she declared giving Maggie a hug. "I hope you rested well last night." From there she peeked over her mother's shoulder.

"Mmm...are we having flap jacks this morning?"

"Indeed, we are. Could you fetch the syrup from the pantry?"

Annalissa pulled a jar of syrup from the shelf and filled a small pitcher. Bacon crackled in an iron skillet as Darla whisked eggs in a large bowl. The work rhythm in the kitchen was like a symphony, each performing their duties harmoniously.

Once breakfast was prepared, everyone assembled at the harvest table. The Reverend said grace and all partook of the morning meal amidst lively conversation. When the last scrap of bacon was eaten, and the table cleared, the Reverend left the room. On his way out, he reminded Mrs. Milner of the appointment later that evening, his declaration sending a shudder through Maggie's body.

Sipping her coffee, Maggie waffled between staying and going. For a brief moment, she'd trusted Darla but now she felt a strong impulse to run.

"Mrs. Milner, may I take a walk around the property?" Maggie asked.

"That's a splendid idea. Annalissa, why don't you show Maggie around the farm?"

"I don't want to keep you from your responsibilities," Maggie said, hoping to deter her from coming along.

"I'd love to go with you," Annalissa declared.

"I appreciate the offer, but I need some time to myself, if you don't mind." Maggie scrambled for any reason to get away unencumbered.

Darla rushed to Maggie's side. "Miss McFarland, perhaps you should speak with the Reverend and Mrs. Milner first. Trust me, please."

Darla's plea caught Mrs. Milner's attention.

"Is there a problem?" Mrs. Milner asked, wiping her hands on a cotton towel.

"Miss McFarland?" Darla's eyebrows arched, her eyes imploring Maggie to disclose her secret.

Annalissa looked at Maggie and smiled. "Whatever's distressing you, rest assured you can share it with us."

"Darla, please prepare a pot of tea. Annalissa, get your

father." Mrs. Milner spoke softly to Maggie. "I don't know what's wrong but I feel certain we can help. The reverend is a very resourceful man."

Maggie's inner voice screamed for her to run, while her heart beseeched her to tell them everything. Maybe they'd take pity on her and not turn her over to her uncle. Moments later the reverend returned, sitting next to his wife as Darla set the pot of tea along with cups and saucers on the table. She filled each cup and went about her daily duties. Annalissa sat beside Maggie.

"Miss McFarland, Annalissa tells me you're worried about something," Rev. Milner said, folding his hands on the table.

"I'm not sure what to say," she muttered.

"Start at the beginning. There's no rush."

Maggie took in a deep breath. She couldn't explain it, but something about the Milners gave her a sense of peace making her believe she could trust them. After all, she was alone in this country and running from her uncle. She needed to trust someone and the Milners seemed to be the best choice.

Wringing her hands, she blew out a breath and shared her story beginning in Ireland with the famine, her father's need to send her away, and meeting her uncle for the first time. Her voice trembled and tears cascaded across her cheeks as she described how her long held dream of meeting her estranged family members quickly turned into a nightmare. All the while, the Milners sat quietly, attending to Maggie's every word.

"Then things took a terrible turn when he knocked me to the ground and beat me. That's when I ran. After days of travel, I arrived in Bradford where I met Annalissa, and you know the rest."

"That's quite a story, Miss McFarland," Rev. Milner said, shifting in his seat.

"He won't stop searching until he finds me," she whispered. "He hates me so."

"No wonder you've been skittish." Mrs. Milner offered. "But you're safe now."

"And he shan't find you," Annalissa added.

Maggie smiled. "Thank you. I'm overwhelmed by your willingness to help someone you hardly know."

"I know you're a child of God and that's enough to make you part of our family." Rev. Milner professed.

"If my uncle discovers you've hidden me, he'll take action. Before I ran away, he made it abundantly clear he would hunt me down and kill me." Maggie wiped a tear from her cheek. "When I heard you talking about a visitor this evening, I assumed my uncle had found me. I'm sorry to have doubted your intentions."

"We know how to deal with people like him," the reverend stated. "You've nothing to fear. We've dealt with much worse."

For the first time since leaving her uncle's farm, Maggie felt a sliver of hope and a shadow of her old self, the one who saw the good in others.

MAGGIE NEVER DISCOVERED the identity of the mysterious visitor from her first day at the farm, and she didn't ask, not wanting to come across as nosey. She settled into the daily routine, helping with every chore she could. The work was fulfilling and appreciated by all.

Maggie shared some of her knowledge about mixing liniments, balms, and salves with Darla and Mrs. Milner. Intrigued, they asked if she would be willing to make some for the parishioners at the reverend's church. She readily agreed, happy to be repaying their kindness. Finally, she had a sense of purpose and it felt good.

Evenings were spent in the front parlor, chatting about the day, sewing, and listening to the reverend read. Still, Maggie feared being discovered by her uncle. Thankfully, the Milners' farm was far from the township with little traffic in its rural location.

A few weeks later, after a long day of preparing remedies, Maggie fell into bed, her muscles stiff and her back aching. Her dreams were filled with scenes of Ireland and the baying of sheep as her father herded them to the pasture. All of a sudden, the dream shifted to her uncle standing over her, pointing a gun at her head.

Bolting upright in the bed, Maggie gasped, her gown soaked and her body quivering. Unable to calm her shattered nerves, she padded to the window and looked out over mist-covered pastures as the sun began to crest. Movement at the edge of the woods startled her. She focused on the area where she saw a man camouflaging himself in the woods. Terror swept through her body, weakening her knees and flooding her mouth with bile. Her dream seemed to be materializing before her very eyes. He'd found her.

Maggie grabbed her wrapper and scurried down the stairs to the kitchen where Darla and Mrs. Milner were preparing the morning meal.

"Good morning, Maggie. My goodness, what's happened? You're pale as a ghost." Mrs. Milner wrapped her arm around Maggie's quivering shoulders.

"There's a man in the woods, I saw him. I think my uncle has found me," she replied, her words coming in short breaths.

Mrs. Milner's calm countenance faded into seriousness. "Darla, can you see to this?"

"No! He's dangerous; you don't know what he's capable of! Please don't go out there!" Maggie hollered.

"Calm down, I can handle myself just fine," Darla said confidently, removing her apron and heading out the door.

Mrs. Milner filled a cup with coffee. "Drink this."

"But he's..."

"Don't trouble yourself. Let us handle this."

Maggie settled on a chair, her limbs prickling with nervous energy and coffee sloshing over the edge of the cup as she raised it to her lips.

Darla came back in with a forced smile. "Nothing to be concerned about, just some stragglers who lost their way. They're hungry so I'm going to take them something to eat."

The two women exchanged guarded glances when Annalissa entered the room breaking through the tension with her bright demeanor.

"Good morning, all," she said before stopping abruptly, her gaze resting on Maggie's tear-stained face.

"Has something happened?" she asked, sitting next to Maggie and draping her arm about her shoulders.

"She was spooked by some travelers who've lost their way. Darla and I will tend to them. Why don't you stay here with Maggie, she's had a shock this morning."

Annalissa nodded as her mother and Darla gathered food and a jug of water. When the door closed behind them, Annalissa rubbed Maggie's hand.

"Everything will be fine, I promise."

"I feel so foolish for causing such a stir. I thought it was my uncle."

"Think nothing more of it." Annalissa rose and tied an apron around her waist. "I'd better see to breakfast; they might be a while."

"What can I do?"

"Finish your coffee."

"I'd feel better if I could do something," Maggie said, standing up.

"In that case, grab an apron and start the eggs," Annalissa replied, pointing toward the egg basket.

The two young ladies scrambled eggs, cooked ham, and set the table. By the time Darla and Mrs. Milner returned, breakfast was being served.

"You girls didn't need to do all this," Darla said, her hand on her chest.

"Don't be silly. Maggie and I were happy to help."

Annalissa gave a dimpled smile as Maggie nodded, her heart finally returning to a normal pace. The work distracted her from the situation in the woods and she was feeling better. No doubt, her nightmare had sparked her imagination.

"Does this happen often?" Maggie asked.

"Every once in a while, people lose their way and end up in our woods. It's not the first time, nor will it be the last," Mrs. Milner said, slathering jelly on her toast.

"It seems a long way from town for people to lose their way."

When she didn't elaborate and no one else offered further explanation, Maggie dropped the subject, sensing there was something more than they were willing to disclose. Despite their generosity, it seemed the Milners had a secret of their own.

18

Later that evening, a lantern burned brightly in the front window as they gathered in the parlor, the ladies mending clothing while the reverend read.

"It seems your workers go through a lot of clothing," Maggie said, patching a pair of trousers.

Annalissa glanced at her father, raising an eyebrow questioningly. Rev. Milner placed his Bible upon the small table and took in a deep breath.

"Maggie, for several weeks we've discussed how we might broach this subject with you and now seems as good a time as any. What I am about to tell you cannot be shared with anyone outside of this room. Do I have your word?"

"Of course, sir." Maggie placed the sewing on the table and sat straighter, giving her full attention.

"As you're aware, we believe all God's people are created equal, regardless of their appearance, religious affiliation, or ethnic background. Would you agree?"

Maggie nodded.

"Furthermore, we know our God promotes love, not bondage or hate. However, it's not enough to hold these beliefs, one must do God's work, and that means actively helping those in need."

He paused, considering his words.

"With that being said, we're part of a network of people helping to free those held in bondage. While an incredibly dangerous endeavor, and sadly an illegal one, we feel it's our duty to guide these people to freedom."

Maggie listened intently, intrigued by what he was saying. Her mind returned to what Letty, Willa, and Sellers had shared about their reason for remaining at Fielding Hall. It wasn't safe for them to go out on their own. They were fearful of being captured and sold into slavery. Although they were technically free, there was an unspoken standard of enslavement by those who sought financial gain from the sale of their flesh. Even the hatred and discrimination she'd endured under her uncle's wrath couldn't compare with the horror of being sold off like cattle. If she could help others avoid the cruelty she'd suffered, her life would have meaning, one that would make her Da proud.

"I want to help," she blurted out.

Annalissa beamed as she reached for Maggie's hand. "I never doubted your heart." Looking at her parents, she declared, "I told you we could rely on her."

"With my uncle searching for me, I may be more of a liability than I'm worth."

"You've already been a boon to our organization. All of the sewing you've done and the herbal remedies you've prepared have helped dozens of passengers."

Maggie glanced down, her heart swelling at the idea she'd helped others. The entire scenario began to make sense. The clothes and medicinal work weren't for the farm workers or parishioners, they were for the escapees.

"So, I can do my part anonymously?"

"It's all anonymous," the reverend replied. "We're one of the stops on the road to freedom. We house runaways regularly. Once they arrive, we provide shelter, clothing, and food. They travel at night, usually by way of rivers or the woods, and hide in different places during the day. The lantern in the front window designates us as a safe house. Sometimes passengers shelter in our house or in the barn. One group was forced to stay several days so we dispersed them amongst our farm hands and they blended right in.

"With your contributions, we've been able to address some of the medical issues arising from their means of travel. Many are forced to hide in snake-infested swamps while others are inflicted with wounds from improper foot wear, welts from bug bites, or being forced to climb trees to escape detection. Occasionally, we have some who arrive with dog bites."

"Dog bites?" Maggie gasped.

"Hunters use dogs to track them and on occasion the escapees are attacked."

"Were the people in the woods this morning running away?"

The reverend nodded. "They weren't scheduled to stop here. Sometimes groups run without the assistance of our organization but they hear about safe houses along the way and find refuge."

Mrs. Milner spoke softly, "Please don't feel obligated to commit. This is a hazardous undertaking and should not be entered into lightly. Perhaps you'd like to pray about it before deciding. No one would fault you if you chose not to take part."

"I don't need time to consider. It's horrible to be abused and belittled," Maggie said, sitting straighter. "The people who were supposed to love and protect me treated me with contempt and cruelty. I don't wish that on anyone. As for the risk involved, I've survived a great deal these past months and I'm changed by it." Her heartbeat hastened as the anger she felt toward her uncle and Susannah intermingled with the rush of adrenaline over the prospect of helping others escape such a despicable fate.

The mantel clock announced the nine o'clock hour.

"It's rather late. We can discuss this in more detail over breakfast. A group is scheduled to arrive tomorrow evening. They've traveled from Georgia and will probably be in need of medical attention. They'll be with us for a short period before going to the next stop at Reverend Stevens' church."

Rev. Milner rose from his chair in a stretch. "Let's get some sleep. We have a busy day tomorrow."

"I'll tell you more when we get upstairs," Annalissa whispered, looping her hand through Maggie's arm.

"Not too late girls," the reverend called out as Maggie and Annalissa sauntered from the room, giggling as they went.

"My father knows me too well."

For the next hour, Annalissa shared details of their role with the Underground Railroad from sheltering people, to financial support, to sending communications between sites. Maggie shook her head in disbelief.

"You do all this for people you don't know?"

"Papa said it's our duty to help those who are less fortunate."

"I admire your fortitude. I don't know that I could've been so brave." Maggie fidgeted with her fingers.

"I disagree. You were courageous enough to run from your uncle despite being hungry and in an unfamiliar land, yet you persevered. What we do is no different. There's something to be said about the human spirit when freedom is at the forefront."

"But these are the lives of strangers, not your own."

"It was my own."

Maggie stiffened. "You're an escapee?"

"In a sense. My mother was killed trying to carry me to freedom."

"How old were you?"

"Three." She fingered the petals of a small garnet brooch affixed to her collar. "The people who brought me here told my parents what happened. Supposedly, my mother was traveling northward with them when they heard people in the distance. She convinced the others to run with me while she distracted whoever was approaching. She was supposed to catch up with them but never did. By the time they found their way here, I was sickly. They said I had a keen sense for danger. If I went quiet there were hunters nearby. Otherwise, I was fussy," she giggled.

"Anyway, since my health was failing, they left me here. Mama said she fell in love the first time she laid eyes on me. Papa said I was a gift from God and that they honored Him by adopting me."

Annalissa glanced down at her collar. "This is all I have of my mother. The escapees said she pinned it to my dress before she sent them away."

"Do the people in town know your story?" Maggie queried, fascinated by the tale.

Annalissa's eyes widened. "Gracious, no! My parents told people I was an orphan from Ohio, born of a washer woman who died in my aunt's hometown."

"Does your aunt still reside in Ohio?"

"She doesn't exist," Annalissa chuckled. "The story was concocted to keep me safe."

"Has there been any resistance to your adoption?"

"Papa preaches at a small church. Occasionally, I get a few side glances but most seem to feel papa is doing his Christian duty by helping a poor orphaned mulatto girl."

"You seemed well accepted at Mr. Campbell's store."

"I am, but I have to be careful where I go and who I befriend," Annalissa said, furrowing her brow.

"But you took me in and didn't know me at all," Maggie replied.

"Like I said, I have a sense for people, at least that's what the escapees told my parents when they brought me here. How many babies do you know who go silent when danger is near?"

"People used to say I was too trusting, and they were right." Maggie looked down and chewed her lower lip.

"You've been through a terrible ordeal. It's only natural to doubt yourself and those around you. Not to worry, you have a true heart and in time you'll learn to trust again," Annalissa said boldly, patting Maggie's hand.

"Maybe someday," Maggie said with a yawn as the clock at the end of the hall chimed ten.

"I should get to bed. Papa warned us not to stay up too late," Annalissa said, embracing Maggie. "I may have been born an only child but now I feel like I have a sister."

Maggie fought back tears. She'd felt the same way about Susannah once. Her experience at the Milner's home was completely different than what she'd known at her uncle's farm. The thought of her uncle made her skin prickle. As long as she remained with the Milners, she was safe. Or so she hoped.

19

The following morning, Maggie hovered over the iron pot in the hearth, swiping a loose strand of hair from her eyes as she hummed.

"You've a lovely voice." Mrs. Milner said as she scooped preserves into a bowl.

A blush tinted Maggie's cheeks. "Thank you." Her mind went back to the conversation with Annalissa the previous night, arousing her curiosity. "Mrs. Milner, may I ask a personal question?"

"Go ahead."

"How did you come to be involved with freeing slaves?"

"My uncle lives in Lancaster and met Thaddeus Stevens who has been an abolitionist for some time and rallies for the freedom and equal treatment of the Negroes. His work with the Underground Railroad is admirable. He even adapted the cistern in his home to conceal runaways on their way north. When he discovered my uncle's views on slavery, they became instant allies. From there, my uncle enlisted the help of my husband and you know the rest."

"How many have you assisted to freedom?"

"It's hard to say, hundreds, I'm sure. Sadly, not every mission is successful. We've lost so many." A cloud shrouded Mrs. Milner's expression momentarily before her happy demeanor returned. "Although we've lost some, we have to focus on the individuals we've freed who are living happy and productive lives."

Maggie tingled with anticipation. She'd never been part of anything so meaningful yet so dangerous, and it thrilled her. "I'm excited to be of help. Thank you for believing in me."

Mrs. Milner walked to the pantry, patting Maggie's shoulder as she passed by. Maggie continued stirring the oatmeal, humming an old Irish tune, her lilting soprano voice floating through the air.

THE FOLLOWING day was Sunday and Maggie was invited to attend church with Annalissa. Mrs. Milner didn't attend in order to prepare for the *passengers* who were scheduled to arrive later in the evening. Enough time had passed that Maggie felt comfortable going out in public, as it seemed her uncle had ceased his search. The parishioners were gracious and kind, although she noticed a few sideways glances making her pause as to whether they were offended by her heritage or merely curious about the stranger residing in the Milner's home.

Nevertheless, she reveled in the bliss of her surrogate family. In all her life, she'd never imagined having a sister as dear to her as Annalissa. They shared a troubled past with a hopeful future thanks to the compassion of the Milners. Rev. Milner's voice echoed across the sanctuary as he read the Beatitudes from the Bible followed by an impassioned sermon. After the last hymn, the reverend issued the benediction.

"When you leave these doors, you leave the sanctuary of safety. Guard your heart and your mind with the veil of Christ's love. It's the only way we can survive. We are children of God, of the Beatitudes. Do not let His words falter in your heart. We must go into a world bombarded by societal pressure to partake of self-worth and wealth. But Beatitudes people live in a different way. We live to serve, to love, and to bring justice to the persecuted and the abandoned. As God's people, we must show mercy or we descend to the depths of hate as so many others have done. We are showered in the Lord's mercy and we must show that mercy to others. The world cannot grow otherwise."

The congregation herded from the church, pausing in the narthex to speak with Rev. Milner on their way out. Maggie and Annalissa waited in the sanctuary. Once the parishioners were gone, the reverend closed the doors and headed directly for the side entrance. A dark-skinned woman dressed in a brightly colored calico frock with her hair swathed in a kerchief entered carrying a mop, bucket, and several rags.

"Good day, Miss Taylor," Rev. Milner said with a nod.

"Afternoon, Reverend."

Her ample figure lumbered to a nearby pew and sat. Annalissa tugged Maggie's sleeve.

"That's Miss Taylor. She's a formidable, but kind soul."

"She's a washer woman?"

"No, silly. She has to appear that way so no one questions her reason for being here," Annalissa said, leading Maggie down the aisle.

"Miss Milner, it's good to see you," the woman grinned.

"And you. May I introduce Maggie McFarland. She's staying with us."

Miss Taylor arched an eyebrow and pursed her lips as she scrutinized Maggie.

"This is the young lady I mentioned," Rev. Milner said. "She's been quite an asset to our cause."

"I suppose if the reverend has placed his trust in you, I should do likewise."

"I hope to be of service to the Milners and those they seek to help," Maggie stated more forcefully than she meant to do.

A sly smile lifted one corner of Miss Taylor's mouth. "You got spirit, I like that."

"Girls, we've some business to discuss. Take the carriage home and tell Mrs. Milner I'll be along shortly."

"Yes, Papa."

The two girls hurried from the sanctuary and settled into the carriage. As it tottered along, Annalissa grinned. "I think Miss Taylor likes you."

"How can you tell?"

"I have a sense for these things, and I'm never wrong."

20

Up to this point, Maggie's role with the escapees had been indirect. She'd mended clothing and mixed batches of salves and other compounds, but had yet to interact with actual passengers.

Following Annalissa to the basement, Maggie surveyed the dank space with its cold tomblike walls and eerie shadows. Jars of canned goods filled shelves on one side while dried herbs dangled from rafters. Along the back wall was a large pine hutch, its shelves barren.

"Help me with this," Annalissa said, positioning herself beside the hutch.

Maggie stood on the other side and scooted the piece several inches from the stonewall, revealing a hidden room. Annalissa tugged the rickety door open, blackness spilling from within.

"What's back there?" Maggie asked, craning her head to look inside.

"This is where our visitors stay until they move on to the next station."

"In that cramped little space?" She held the lantern up illuminating a few quilts and a ticking mattress.

"These people travel through woods and swamps in all sorts of weather conditions. It's a treacherous journey with little food, constant risk of capture, and the possibility of being returned to enraged slave owners. Their trek is harsh." Annalissa's expression was solemn. "This is a respite compared to the circumstances in which our passengers find themselves along the route."

"But it's so cramped and there's no ventilation."

"It's sufficient for small numbers. Sometimes when we have larger groups, we disguise them as workers and have them stay on the third floor of the house. Generally, they aren't here for more than a night. But persistent masters are relentless, forcing us to take extreme measures to keep escapees safe," Annalissa explained. "Sadly, the group we're housing this evening has a high bounty for their capture so we have to hide them down here."

"And these *masters* have the right to reclaim them from a free state?"

"When money is involved a person's life is measured in dollars, not humanity."

"Forgive me, I find the concept of owning someone unfathomable."

"It's a deplorable act which is still legal in many parts of this country."

"And if the escapees are captured?"

"Many are sold into circumstances much worse than those they were running from, while others are whipped and beaten."

"Whipped?" Maggie gasped.

"I remember one family making it as far as the Canadian border when they were captured and sent back to their slave owner in South Carolina. The father was whipped to death, the mother and young children sold off for field work, and the baby dashed against a rock while the other slaves looked on."

Maggie's knees gave way. Annalissa rushed to her side and helped her to a small ladder back chair.

"I'm sorry to upset you, but these are some of the tales you'll hear. I shouldn't have shocked you with such vivid accounts. If I've discouraged your willingness to participate, no one would blame you."

"No," Maggie whispered, "it'll keep me focused." Rising, Maggie took a deep breath. "Where do we begin?"

A broad smile dimpled Annalissa's cheeks. "From the moment I saw you, I knew you were special. We're going to do great things together."

Annalissa tasked Maggie with making the hidden room as comfortable as possible while she gathered food and water. A short time later the room was ready for its guests.

"Is there anything else to be done?" Maggie asked, her spirits lifted by her efforts.

"Not until they arrive."

"And when will that be?"

"Well after midnight. We never know the exact time. The less we know, the better," Annalissa said. "Mr. Greer will escort them for the last leg of the journey. We'll stow them until tomorrow evening when another conductor will take them to the next station."

"You keep referring to stations."

"Havens along the route to freedom are referred to as stations, much like those on a railway system. My father is a stationmaster."

"This is all so complicated. How do you manage it?"

"Our network is broad. We have a point of contact in Ohio, Mr. Coffin, and another in Philadelphia, Mr. Stills. Both men have been involved with this organization for some time and are well acquainted with the ins and outs of its workings."

Annalissa glanced at her pocket watch. "We should wash up, it's nearly time for dinner."

They started for the stairs when Annalissa stopped. "One more thing, we don't discuss any of this in front of the servants or the workers."

"They're unaware of what goes on here?"

"They don't know, for their safety as well as ours. Only Darla is aware."

For the first time since arriving, Maggie saw urgency shroud Annalissa's jovial countenance. "It's imperative you only discuss things with me or my parents."

"Of course."

Annalissa's cheerful demeanor returned as they climbed the steps and prepared for dinner.

THE EVENING PASSED in the usual manner with Annalissa and Maggie sewing while the Reverend read. Mrs. Milner worked in the kitchen overseeing meal preparations for the following day.

"My stomach feels like a rumbling volcano," Maggie said, trying to steady her trembling fingers as she stitched a pair of trousers.

"The fear percolating in your gut is survival. It's what keeps us alert."

Shortly after midnight, wagon wheels rattled down the drive growing louder with each hoof beat.

"They're here," Annalissa whispered, her eyes bright with anticipation.

Reverend Milner motioned for the girls to follow him to the back of the house when he realized the carriage was stopping out front.

"That's odd," he said, opening the front door. They stood on the stoop, the crisp night air twining around them as the reverend walked to the carriage. The driver made no effort to disembark, tipping his hat as Rev. Milner approached.

"Good evenin', Reverend."

"Good evening, Mr. Greer. What news of our delivery?"

"No delivery this evening sir."

The reverend's shoulders dropped, his sigh misting the night air.

"What happened?"

"Wolves, sir. Got 'em before they crossed the border."

"Any survivors?"

"No, sir. All shot through the head."

"Thank you, Mr. Greer." The reverend handed the man a small pouch and bid him goodnight.

Mr. Greer smacked the reins against the horses' haunches and traveled down the drive into obscurity. Stepping into the warm embrace of the house, Maggie whispered to Annalissa, "Wolves?"

"Another term for hunters. They're ruthless."

Mrs. Milner met them in the hall.

"Where is Mr. Greer going?"

The reverend shook his head. "Wolves."

Her eyes closed as her hand rested on her lips, "May the Lord bless them."

Rev. and Mrs. Milner headed for the kitchen while Annalissa and Maggie hastened to the parlor.

"I don't understand," Maggie said. "What's happened?"

"Our wards have a labyrinth of trials to survive in order to make it here. One of the deadliest things they face are slave hunters who are paid high prices for the return of escapees. The master's instructions dictate whether deadly force can be used."

"If the reason for hunting the escapees is financial restitution, why kill them?"

"For some, power and cruelty are more intoxicating than

money. Sometimes the slave owners kill escapees as a means of preventing others from fleeing. By using deadly force, they instill fear and can maintain control."

"Seems a hopeless venture for the escapees." Maggie said, rubbing her upper arms.

"For many, death is better than bondage. They'd rather perish trying to escape than remain under the lash of the slave owner's whip."

"Why not abolish slavery altogether?"

"Many are advocating for it. Until it's stricken from our land, we'll have to continue our efforts. I know it seems a futile endeavor, but freeing even one person makes it worthwhile."

Maggie nodded while trying to absorb all that was happening around her. Although not as horrific, her life under the suffocating shroud of indignity at her uncle's farm made her appreciate the plight of those fleeing to freedom. Now more than ever, Maggie was ready to face any obstacle to help them.

VISIONS of the murdered passengers haunted Maggie's slumber, except it was Sellers' face on the bodies. She bolted upright in bed, her body sticky with sweat as she glanced about the room in an effort to regain her senses. Unable to sleep, she treaded down the back stairs to the kitchen where she found Mrs. Milner sipping tea. Apparently, Maggie wasn't alone in her late-night wanderings.

"Is everything alright?" Mrs. Milner asked.

"Couldn't sleep."

"Let me get you a cup of tea."

Maggie settled at the pine table, the candle in the center casting ghostly images against the wall. Mrs. Milner filled a cup and handed it to her.

"What's troubling you?"

Maggie gazed into the steaming cup. "I can't stop thinking about the people who were supposed to arrive this evening."

"We've mourned a great many passengers whose journeys ended prematurely. Our world is not always a righteous one." Mrs. Milner set her cup on the table. "It's important to focus on the work. We're accomplishing extraordinary things. Much like tossing a pebble in a pond results in a series of ripples, we are freeing many who have yet to be born."

"Never thought of it that way."

"The same is true for you. You've escaped a dreadful situation, one that could have cost you your future. But now you have hope and a purpose, and more importantly, a family."

Mrs. Milner reached across the table and took hold of Maggie's hand. Her gentle touch and soft brown eyes melted Maggie's unease after a night of vivid dreams. *This must be what it's like to have a mother's comfort*, she thought. One thing was certain; Mrs. Milner had a huge heart, large enough to mother dozens of children and Maggie was proud to be a part of her world.

"Let's talk about a more pleasant subject. Tell me about your home in Ireland."

Maggie shifted in her seat, the corners of her lips curling as she thought of her Da.

"My father is a sheep herder and my mother died when I was a few months old. I feel as if I've always known her with all the stories my Da has shared, yet he never mentioned her family. Now I know why," Maggie sighed. "My father did his best to teach me how to cook and mend. Sadly, he's not astute at ladies' work. He tried to learn knitting so he could instruct me, but always fumbled with the needles resulting in a knotted mess. Then after reading the instructions in one of the ladies' manuals, he tried to teach me needlepoint. Poor dear, he had more holes in his fingertips than the canvas." Maggie's eyes misted at the memory.

"He sounds like a wonderful man."

"He's the best person I know."

"How is he faring?"

"Last I heard, he'd moved on from the farm. I don't know what happened or where he is," Maggie whispered, wiping a tear from her cheek."

"Perhaps if you send a letter to his former address, it will find him."

"I hadn't thought of that."

"Don't give up hope. Where there's love there's always an answer," Mrs. Milner smiled. "By the way, if you're interested in learning how to knit, Darla can instruct you. She knits a great deal."

"I'd like that very much."

The grandfather clock at the end of the hall chimed twice.

"We should probably get some sleep. Tomorrow promises to be a busy day."

"Thank you for the tea," Maggie said, rising from the chair with a stretch.

"I often have difficulty sleeping and find a cup of tea and quiet to be the perfect remedy." Mrs. Milner's eyes sparkled in the candlelight. "You're always welcome to join me."

Maggie gave a nod before traipsing up the steps to her room. Cuddling beneath the patchwork quilt, she closed her eyes and drifted off to sleep, warmed by the tea and Mrs. Milner's words.

21

After months at the Milner's farm, Maggie functioned as one of the family. Although she missed her father terribly, the Milners were everything she'd hoped her uncle's family would have been. Still, it seemed odd that complete strangers could be more accepting than her own kin. Each morning after the breakfast dishes were washed, Darla instructed Maggie in knitting. Unlike the previous Christmas, Maggie was looking forward to the festivities of the season. Her heart still ached for Sellers and she missed Willa and Letty's daily wisdom, but at least she was safe and had a purpose.

Following Mrs. Milner's advice, she sent a letter to her old address hoping it would find its way to her Da. If only she could be certain he was safe, she could relax a bit. In an effort to quell her anxiety about his welfare, she stayed as busy as possible. *Busy hands calm a busy mind*, her Da always said when she was worried about something. And he was right. She threw herself into the work for the Milners, which offered a gentle distraction from her fears. Meanwhile, her copy of Byron's poems provided comfort each night before bed. She often lulled herself to sleep reading its tattered pages while gently caressing the wooden heart Sellers had carved for her.

When possible, Maggie snuck to her room and knitted gifts for the family. She was pleased with the results and felt certain everyone would appreciate her endeavors. A twinge of sorrow squeezed her heart as her mind drifted to her da. How was he celebrating the holiday? She fingered the scarf she was knitting and thought how proud he'd be to wear one. Maggie swiped a tear from her cheek and resumed her needlework. Staying busy would help distract her from the melancholy rising in her chest.

On the morning of Christmas Eve, Maggie was roused by the light of day peeking through the frosted panes of her bedroom window. Rising from bed in an elongated stretch, Maggie wrapped her robe about her, padded across the room, and peered at the snowy tundra below. A smile lifted her lips and a childish excitement fluttered in her chest. Even though she'd experienced snow before, there was something thrilling about this particular snowfall, and it called to her.

Dressing in a flannel petticoat and wool dress, she slipped on her gloves, and wrapped her shawl about her shoulders before scurrying down the stairs and out the back door. Maggie's boots crunched across the freshly formed snow banks, her breath crystalizing with each step. The chilly atmosphere was invigorating, quickening her pace. As she continued her stroll, a barn rose over the horizon, its red plank walls glowing against the fresh drifts of white. She trudged on, her spirit soaring with each step as the sun crashed through the horizon in a wake of orange and gold. The picturesque scene was reminiscent of a well-painted landscape, this one being God's work on the canvas of life.

Out of nowhere, a frosty orb struck the back of her head, nearly knocking her to the ground. Maggie spun around but saw no one there. Not wanting to be targeted again, Maggie scooped a handful of snow into her gloved hands and took refuge behind a large maple, ready for retaliation. Whoever had started this arctic war was obviously familiar with the terrain. She scanned the landscape for any sign of movement, but all was quiet. Too quiet. Maggie stepped from behind the tree when another snowball whizzed past her head, dashing against the sapling behind her. A giggle bounced across the air.

"Annalissa! I know it's you! Come out and fight like a girl!" Maggie hollered, her fingers beginning to numb as the snowball's icy temperature bit through her gloves.

Accepting the challenge, Annalissa darted from behind a large oak, lobbing several snowballs at Maggie, giggling all the way. Maggie ran forward, tossing a snowball before scooping another handful of snow and forming the next sphere.

"Come out if you dare!" Maggie exclaimed, her lungs heaving in the frigid morning air.

Annalissa emerged, pelting Maggie with a series of snowballs all the while dodging the ones Maggie tossed her way. Unexpectedly, a snowball zipped past Maggie's nose, hitting the base of the tree where Annalissa hid. The two women glanced at each other, puzzled by the onslaught of another winter warrior. Rev. Milner dashed across the yard to the side of the barn. Before long, several of the farm hands joined the fray, creating a frosty war zone amongst the trees and barnyard. All were coated in pebbles of snow by the time the breakfast bell clanged, sending them to their respective homes for the morning meal.

With ruddy cheeks and noses, Maggie, Annalissa, and the Reverend stepped through the back door where they were greeted by the sultry breath of freshly brewed coffee.

"My gracious, what have you been doing? You're a mess!" Mrs. Milner exclaimed, stirring a sizable pot of oatmeal.

"We took an early morning stroll," Annalissa huffed, mischief glinting in her eyes as her dimples deepened.

"I don't suppose there were snowballs involved in this stroll?" Mrs. Milner gave a knowing glance.

"Perhaps one or two," the Reverend replied, kissing his wife's cheek.

Maggie glanced at the floor, stifling a chuckle.

Annalissa poured three cups of coffee, handing one to Maggie who cradled the warm vessel in her chilled hands.

"It's going to be a busy day ladies, so you'd best eat a good breakfast."

Annalissa and Maggie exchanged glances. The time for play had drifted back to the responsibilities of the real world where fun and games were nothing more than a fleeting amusement.

CHRISTMAS MORNING ARRIVED with the promise of a joyful day. After breakfast, the family congregated in the front parlor to exchange gifts. Mrs. Milner handed Maggie a box wrapped in bright red paper. Tearing off the wrapping, she lifted a lovely leather-bound Bible from the box.

"I know you've been wanting your own copy," Mrs. Milner said.

"It's lovely," Maggie replied, paging through the tissue thin pages. "I'll treasure it always."

Maggie reveled as each of the Milner's unwrapped her gifts and proudly modeled their new scarves. A rush of 'thank yous' and 'when did you find the time to knit these?' tickled Maggie's ears, bringing a genuine smile to her lips. She'd not felt this much love since leaving Ireland, except for Sellers. But she couldn't think about him right now, otherwise she'd crumble into a sobbing heap filled by the guilt of her role in his demise.

Much of the day was spent in glorious relaxation, including a walk across the property with Annalissa, time to read, a sumptuous evening meal, and a game of charades after supper.

Before bedtime, they gathered around a roaring fire in the front parlor, sipping steaming cups of hot chocolate while the reverend read the Christmas story from his well-worn Bible. It was a simple, yet meaningful celebration, and the most perfect of days.

WINTER THAWED to spring in an explosion of rebirth. Tiny beads of life sprouted from the tips of every tree and bush. The frigid weather hadn't slowed Railroad activities, leaving Maggie busily preparing cough and fever remedies as well as knitting scarves and shawls for passengers during the brutally cold days. She'd become quite adept with the knitting needles and able to produce items quickly and efficiently. Needless to say, warmer weather was a welcome respite from winter's brutal temperatures.

A clap of thunder rattled windows and floors as rain pelted against the roof in an orchestral clatter, rousing Maggie from her slumber. She slid from bed and traipsed to the window, staring at the steely gray cloud cover. A bolt of light flared across the sky illuminating everything in its wake, including a shadowy figure near the tree line at the edge of the woods. Maggie's body trembled as if the lighting had struck her directly. Adrenaline rushed through her veins as she scrambled downstairs.

"I saw something in the woods. I didn't think we had passengers scheduled so I thought I'd better let you know," Maggie declared as she bolted into the kitchen.

"We're aware. Go upstairs and change, and then you can help," Mrs. Milner replied.

Darla was already in the pantry gathering supplies when Mrs. Milner called out to her, "Be sure to take some blankets. This rain will chill them and we don't want anyone taking ill."

Maggie turned to go back upstairs when Annalissa rushed into the room. "Mama there are…"

"We're working on it now."

Maggie dressed and headed back to the kitchen to help Mrs. Milner with breakfast. A short time later, Darla came in the back door, shaking the raindrops from her shawl.

"Were you able to help them?" Mrs. Milner asked.

"Yes. They're ever so thankful for the food. One of them said they hadn't eaten since yesterday morning and apologized for any inconvenience. I told them it was no trouble and they were welcome to more comfortable accommodations in the barn."

"How many are in their party?"

"Four; three ladies and one man. They've traveled from Florida in hopes of reaching New York, but will wait to resume their journey after nightfall."

"Did you give them guidance for the safest route?"

"I did. It's a good thing too or they'd have headed directly into the wolves' den. One woman has the most dreadful scar across her right cheek. There'd be no denying her identity if she were caught," Darla said, shaking her head. "I've brought the gentleman's coat, it's in terrible need of mending.

"May I patch the coat?" Maggie offered.

"That would be a great help. Looks like it's going to be a hectic day after all," Mrs. Milner replied.

"Good morning," Rev. Milner called out, entering the kitchen and pouring a cup of coffee. "You ladies seem especially busy this morning."

"We've visitors in the woods," Annalissa chimed in.

The coffee cup hovered at his lips, a serious expression clouding his face. "Are they well?"

"Darla already tended to them. They're settled in the old barn for now and plan on resuming their journey after nightfall," Mrs. Milner said. "We'll put together some provisions for their journey after we eat."

Once the breakfast dishes were cleared, Darla and Annalissa prepared a basket for the escapees while Maggie mended the man's coat.

"What are their chances of making it to New York without a conductor?" Maggie asked.

"Traveling without a guide can be precarious," Mrs. Milner replied.

Maggie's eyes dropped. "My situation was deplorable, but I can't say it was as dismal as what they've endured. No one owned me."

"Don't diminish what you've suffered. It's not a contest. Many runaways have told of fair treatment from their masters and claimed great affection for them, but the call to freedom is more powerful than all the kindness and good intentions in the world."

Maggie huffed. "Seems odd to think of a slave holder as being kind."

"Some masters make arrangements in their wills for slaves to be freed. I think it makes them feel justified for enslaving people. Sadly, many descendants retract the provisions of the will by keeping the slaves or selling them off."

"Even if it's in writing?"

"Unfortunately, the enslaved have no rights. We've a great deal of repentance to achieve in this country, beginning with equal treatment for all of God's children."

22

Maggie had been with the Milners for a year now and had settled in comfortably. Her efforts to help escapees in their quest for freedom had given her a sense of purpose while helping to quell the angst of worrying about her Da. She'd exhausted all efforts to locate him and was beginning to lose hope that she ever would.

Annalissa and Maggie sat in the parlor mending clothes when the rumbling of carriage wheels echoed through the open windows.

"That's strange, we aren't expecting any deliveries today," Annalissa said, peering out the window. "Oh, it's Miss Taylor," she declared, placing the sewing on the table. "She must have news of an upcoming mission."

Annalissa rushed to the front door. "Mama, Miss Taylor is here," she called out.

Maggie peered through the window, watching the robust figure emerge from the carriage and make her way to the front stoop.

"Good day Miss Milner," Miss Taylor huffed as she lumbered through the door. "Is your mother here?"

"She's coming. Please join us in the parlor."

Miss Taylor settled her ample figure onto the wing chair, fidgeting with her bag when Mrs. Milner entered the parlor.

"Miss Taylor, how kind of you to pay us a visit. To what do we owe this unexpected pleasure?"

"I fear my visit is not one of good tidings."

"Oh dear, what's happened?" Mrs. Milner asked, plunking onto the settee.

Glancing at Maggie and Annalissa, Miss Taylor arched her eyebrows. "Perhaps we should discuss this in private."

"Why don't you girls take a break and have some tea?"

"Yes ma'am," Annalissa responded. She and Maggie retreated from the room.

"What could be so serious that we can't hear?" Maggie whispered as they headed down the hall.

"It's probably Railroad business. They often chat in private when devising plans for a mission," Annalissa replied. "Although Miss Taylor did seem out of sorts. Must be a serious case."

They settled at the kitchen table and chatted over a cup of tea. A short time later, Mrs. Milner entered the room.

"Girls, would you please join us?" Mrs. Milner's tone of voice was serious and her expression sullen.

They looked at one another before rising from the table and following Mrs. Milner to the parlor where Miss Taylor's subdued demeanor remained unaltered.

"Miss McFarland, the time has come for you to make a major contribution to the Railroad. I've made arrangements for you to accompany me to one of the safe houses in the coastal region of South Carolina. Your service will continue there until the danger here has passed," Miss Taylor said, her stalwart stare and serious tone penetrating Maggie's heart.

"Why do you need me to escort you?"

"Because I'm a Negro and the area where we'll be traveling

is not receptive to the color of my skin."

Confused, Maggie queried further. "But I thought you could travel wherever you like."

"Not in a location where I'm at high risk of being captured and sold off. That's why you'll be traveling as my slave owner."

"I could never do such a thing!" Maggie protested, squaring her shoulders.

"You most certainly can and will. Your life and the lives of others depend upon it."

"How can I possibly portray a slave owner? The idea sickens me." Maggie slouched in her seat.

"You'll be making our passage safe by doing this. It's not as if you actually own me."

Despite her revulsion to the idea, Maggie was resigned to repay the Milners for all they'd done for her. She'd come to love them in the months she'd lived there and the idea of leaving weighted her chest. However, her need to support the Milner's efforts pushed her to put on a strong face. The last thing she wanted to do was upset them or seem ungrateful.

"I'll help any way I can," she said, trying to force a smile.

"A carriage will arrive at midnight. Here are the passes and other necessary documents for the trip. You'll act as a slave owner traveling with her personal maid to visit family in South Carolina. It's imperative you conceal your accent as it's a sure sign you're not from America."

"You said my life depends upon this too?" Maggie asked, her eyebrows furrowed.

"There's another obstacle."

"What is it?"

"I received word earlier today that a gentleman was in town inquiring about a missing person."

"Was it a slave owner?"

"An uncle."

A chill bumped across Maggie's skin. All of her fears resurfaced, squeezing the air from her lungs. He'd finally found her. So much time had lapsed, she'd assumed he'd given up the search but now he was close and she was in danger. Even worse, those she'd come to love and call family were in danger too.

"I've got to leave this instant," Maggie mumbled, "I won't put you all at risk." She tried to stand but panic paralyzed her trembling legs, causing her to crumble back to the chair.

Annalissa ran to Maggie's side.

"We won't let him find you."

"You've no idea how dangerous he is. I have to go, it's the only way to insure everyone's safety."

"She's right," Miss Taylor replied. "Her presence here is a danger to us all and to our mission. We cannot risk someone as corrosive as this man jeopardizing what we do."

Maggie looked at her dearest friend. "We always knew if my uncle found me, I'd have to leave this place. He's a wicked man." Maggie sucked in a sob, her chest aching with sorrow.

Tears trickled across Annalissa's cheeks, dissolving her dimples as she looked to her mother. "What will Papa say?"

"Miss Taylor spoke with him before coming here. He's aware of the situation and agrees with this plan. This mission has been in the works for some time, making it the perfect opportunity to help escapees while also providing sanctuary for Maggie. Consider it Divine intervention."

"You're the sister I've always longed for, and now you're leaving." Annalissa's words tapered off in a whisper as she stared out the double paned window. "I cannot imagine life without you."

"We can write," Maggie muttered.

"I'm afraid that's not possible," Miss Taylor said. "All Railroad communication is done discreetly through safe channels. If anyone intercepted the mail, it could compromise our work."

Despair swelled in Maggie's heart like a river after days of rain. Her teeth clenched as anger intermingled with the anguish of her situation. She'd managed to escape her wretched uncle and start fresh only to be hunted down by him. While she couldn't remedy the situation at present, she vowed one day to see Mr. Stevenson pay for his cruel interference in her life.

"I must get back and prepare for tomorrow's trip," Miss Taylor announced, walking to the door with Mrs. Milner at her side.

Annalissa grasped Maggie's hand. "We may be apart for a while but fate will reunite us, of that I'm certain. I have a sense for these things," she said with a slight smile.

Maggie's head dropped, a sob shaking her shoulders. The two embraced in a storm of tears when Mrs. Milner reentered.

"Girls, please come with me. We've much to discuss."

With hands clasped, Maggie and Annalissa trudged behind Mrs. Milner in silence to the kitchen where they gathered at the harvest table.

"Maggie, let me begin by saying how much we love you and wish you could stay. It's no surprise that this day has arrived, although we'd all hoped it wouldn't. Since your uncle is close to discovering your whereabouts, we feel it's best to change your name for this mission from McFarland to Milner. Should you meet people along the way, this could safeguard you from discovery, especially since we don't know if he's advertised in papers outside of the area."

Maggie and Ananlissa nodded, their eyes wet with tears.

"I realize this is difficult for both of you but know it's in service of others. Maggie you're about to embark on a treacherous venture that will require all of your wit and stamina.

"You'll be traveling to Rose Hall, one of the safe houses on the May River in South Carolina. Dr. Polk's family has been an active part of the Railroad system for many years. Currently, they're harboring a family from Georgia. Due to the high profile of the escapees, they've been unable to travel northward easily. They've been rerouted several times already. Mrs. Tubman is otherwise engaged so Miss Taylor has been working with Mr. Stills on the situation, which is where you come in."

Maggie leaned forward listening to the complex tale. She would travel south with Miss Taylor to deliver papers and money to fund the transport. Once Maggie was settled at Rose Hall, Miss Taylor would escort the escapees north in a labyrinth of routes and stops. Maggie would remain with the Polks until her uncle's search ended. When it was safe for her to return, she was welcome to do so.

While her heart was heavy, she knew this was for the best. But the idea of separating from the only loving family she'd known since arriving in America turned her stomach. Regardless, she trusted the Milners and knew they were acting in her best interest. Still, she couldn't bear the thought of leaving Annalissa. Their bond was as strong as the chains they sought to break for those seeking freedom.

STEPPING INTO HER ROOM, Maggie looked around, absorbing the comfortable space that had been her safe haven. How she wished she could stay.

Stop it, she thought, rebuking herself in an effort to quell the wooziness swirling in her stomach. Annalissa peeked in the room.

"May I help you pack?"

"I'd like that very much."

"Mama suggested we spend as much time together as possible before you go."

"I'm not even sure what to pack," Maggie mumbled, fighting back another wave of tears. She'd arrived with the rags on her back and worn-out boots. Now she had a modest wardrobe and all because of the Milner's generosity. Conflicted, she pondered whether she should take what they'd given her when so many others were in need.

"Mama said to use the trunk at the foot of the bed and take anything you deem necessary. The weather is considerably warmer there so they'll provide you with clothing suitable to the climate."

"Do you know these people?"

"No, but Miss Taylor does."

"How is it Miss Taylor can travel but you can't?"

"She's a master of disguise. Her repertoire of personas ranges from that of a slave to an educated preacher's wife, all by altering her demeanor, dialect, and stature. It's the secret to her success. But she always has to take a white person with her for safety."

Maggie nodded, her mood sinking with each item placed in the trunk. She clutched her Bible to her chest, closing her eyes to hold back the flood of tears threatening to fall. Annalissa got up from the bed, removed the garnet brooch from her collar, and affixed it to Maggie's.

"Take this," she said softly, the corners of her mouth curling.

"I couldn't possibly, it's all you have of your mother."

"Consider it a loan. This is a reminder of the sister you left behind. When we meet again, you can return it."

Fresh tears trickled across Maggie's flushed cheeks as she lamented her departure. She took Annalissa's hands in hers and forced her lips to curl.

"I'll return it as soon as I can."

They embraced for a moment before Annalissa stepped back and straightened up.

"As Miss Taylor would say, *enough of this blubbering, we've got a job to do*!" She mimicked the woman's stern tone, her hands swiping at her tears. "Let's get you packed."

. . .

THE CONVERSATION at dinner was strained as no one dared address Maggie's pending departure for fear the floodgates of sorrow would pour forth with no hope of damming them up. Once supper was cleared away, Maggie joined the family in the front parlor where Rev. Milner read from the bible before offering a prayer for traveling mercies for Maggie and Miss Taylor. When the grandfather clock chimed nine, the reverend suggested Maggie try to rest for a few hours before her departure.

Everything was packed and the trunk waited by the front door. Not wanting to lose Annalissa's brooch, or have to answer questions about its origin, she pinned it to the neckline of her chemise so that it would be close to her heart. Maggie sat on the edge of the bed in the darkness, which mirrored the heaviness of her soul. She slumped upon the quilted coverlet, her tears wetting the pillow as her burdens seeped from her eyes, lulling her to a restless sleep.

Not long after, she awoke to the sound of carriage wheels caroming down the drive. Leaning up on her elbow, she chased the haze from her mind and rose from bed. All she had to do was grab her shawl and go downstairs.

With oil lamp in hand, Maggie maneuvered the staircase to the entryway where a small gathering of well-wishers waited. Miss Taylor's appearance was quite transformed, her attire consisting of a calico frock, crocheted shawl, and straw bonnet.

"You ready?" she asked.

Maggie nodded.

"Have you got the papers?"

"They're in my satchel."

"Good, you'll need them if we're stopped along the way."

Mrs. Milner wrapped her arms around Maggie.

"Blessings for a safe journey, my dear." Her melodious voice plucked at Maggie's heart.

"I shan't forget your kindness," she replied, the Irish tinting her words.

"Watch that accent," Miss Taylor chimed.

Maggie took Annalissa's hands into hers, "We'll see each other soon," she said, forcing a slight smile.

"Indeed, we will."

"May the Lord bless you in your endeavors," Rev. Milner said, as Maggie released Annalissa's hands.

She hugged her benefactor close and thought of the last time she embraced her father before boarding the ship to America. It felt as if her heart might explode with the pain of it all.

"Miss McFarland, we must be on our way."

Miss Taylor escorted Maggie to the carriage. Once the door was shut, Rev. Milner whacked the side of the carriage three times as Annalissa and Mrs. Milner looked on from the shadowy light of the front stoop.

Mr. Greer clucked to the horses, propelling them forward. Maggie's nerves bobbled between fear and nervous excitement as the carriage staggered down the dirt drive into the mantle of darkness.

With each hoof beat, Maggie's heart thumped a bit harder. Now that the trip was underway, she was beginning to lose her nerve. *What if they were caught? What if her uncle found them? What if the new family hated her?* All of the scenarios paraded through her mind, whirling her emotions into a frenzied state.

Apparently sensing her discomfort, Miss Taylor reached over and patted Maggie's hand.

"Take comfort. You're doing God's work and he'll not fail you."

The anguish over leaving the Milner's was more powerful than her fear of the future. Despite the potential dangers that lingered, Maggie trusted Miss Taylor. No doubt, her indomitable spirit and resourceful nature would make the journey as safe as possible.

23

As the carriage jostled over rugged roadways, Miss Taylor passed the time instructing Maggie on what to do should they run into unfriendly folks.

"Don't say anything unless asked, and only reveal trivial bits of information. Trust your instincts. There's evil on this route and we'll be in constant danger of encountering it."

"Is there anything else I should know?" she asked, looking away to hide the tears clinging to her lashes.

"More than anything, you must remain calm. Pretend you're travelling at your leisure. And be confident. Any hesitation could lead to trouble. If we're stopped, have the papers ready. Do you understand?"

"Yes ma'am. I'm to present the documentation showing you're my slave and we're traveling south should anyone ask." Maggie nearly choked on the word *slave*.

"You need to say it with conviction. Any reluctance on your part could jeopardize our mission."

Maggie nodded.

"And the reason for your southern expedition?" Miss Taylor asked.

"My cousin from South Carolina sent word that my grandfather is not expected to survive the week and I must hurry if I'm to take leave of him before he passes."

"Don't waver. Sometimes the wolves along the route can be intimidating."

"I've heard that term before. Is it hunter or wolf?"

"You must be able to use these terms interchangeably. Warnings sometimes come with different phrases; therefore, you need to understand them all."

"Like passengers and cargo?"

"Exactly." Miss Taylor continued. "Slave hunters have gotten rather wary of our cargo over the past few months with rising suspicions of Railroad activity. They can be rather aggressive with their inquiries. The more confident your response and its delivery, the better our chances of getting through unscathed."

Nodding, Maggie wondered if she'd be able to remember everything if confronted.

"Lives are in peril. We need to secure funds and supplies for the railway stops in the south to be successful. There's more need than resources so every contribution is vital. You're traveling with a good deal of money. Don't let it fall into the hands of the enemy. Maintain your composure. I cannot stress this enough.

"Of course."

An hour into the journey, Maggie yawned, her back aching from sitting in one position for so long.

"We'll be stopping soon to rest the horses. You'll feel better once you walk about." Miss Taylor seemed to sense every discomfort even though Maggie hadn't uttered a word. The reason for her success was evident.

After traveling for another hour, the carriage slowed to a stop where a dilapidated shack fronted by a water trough came into view. Apparently, Mr. Greer and Miss Taylor had been here before as it was indistinct and off the main thoroughfare.

Mr. Greer opened the carriage door, handing the ladies out of the cramped compartment. Maggie felt as if she'd been riding in a canoe on the open seas during a storm, much like her journey from Ireland. Her back ached and her legs tingled as she stretched in an effort to liven the numbness in her joints.

"I'm not used to sitting for so long."

"Wish I could tell you it gets easier, but it doesn't. These journeys are often long and uncomfortable. After you've made a few trips, you'll adjust."

"Please don't think me ungrateful, but I wasn't aware I'd be making any other trips."

"First, we need to get you out of harm's way, but once you're settled you may be needed for future missions."

Maggie nodded as she meandered beneath a legion of stars twinkling against a canopy of black.

Once the horses had rested, Mr. Greer helped Maggie and Miss Taylor back into the carriage. They resumed the expedition, Miss Taylor pitching with the swing of the carriage, seemingly unaffected by her circumstances or the looming dangers. Maggie envied her fortitude. Careful not to show her true emotional state, Maggie stared out the carriage window as the landscape whizzed past in a formless display of shadows until weariness took hold, lulling her to sleep.

MAGGIE STRUGGLED with the routine of traveling at night and taking refuge at safe houses during the day. Throughout the excursion, Miss Taylor's strength was resolute. She was able to sleep in the carriage regardless of the road conditions and rest contentedly at each stop. Although she'd been advised to rest during the day, Maggie couldn't get her body to comply. All she longed to do was go back to the Milner's home.

By the third day of travel, Maggie found herself exhausted and cranky. She tried to sleep once the sun went down but her mind wouldn't quiet. After a couple hours of traversing solitary roads, Mr. Greer slowed the carriage. In the distance a blazing light flickered catching Miss Taylor's attention. She lowered the window and asked,

"What's the problem, Mr. Greer?"

"Could be trouble up yonder."

Miss Taylor rummaged through her basket.

"Is everything all right?" Maggie asked.

"Get the papers, this may be nothing or it could be trouble."

As the carriage slowed to a halt, adrenaline pulsed through Maggie's body. She fumbled for the papers, her hands quivering like a fly caught in a web.

"Respond only to questions posed and say nothing else. The briefer your statements, the less likely you are to divulge anything of a sensitive nature," she whispered.

With a nod, Maggie prepared for what waited outside the safety of the carriage.

From the side window, Maggie watched as a couple of torches bounced toward them from the center of the narrow roadway. In the shadowy dimness, two bearded men materialized from a curtain of darkness. Both were disheveled in appearance, sporting ragged attire and straw hats. A feeling of dread washed over Maggie in disquieted waves when she heard the shorter man inquire of Mr. Greer.

"Where you headin' darkie?"

"We be traveling south, sir. Got to get my Missus to she cousin's home 'fore she grandpa passes."

"You got papers to be in these parts?"

"Yes sir. De Missus gots all de proper doc'ments." The change in Mr. Greer's dialog shocked Maggie.

"Documents is a pretty big word for a dimwitted darkie.

Sure you ain't one of them escaped slaves tryin' to act smart?" the man taunted.

"No sir. I's owned by Miss Maggie."

"And who is Miss Maggie?"

"She in de carriage."

The taller fellow opened the door and peered inside.

"You must be *Miss Maggie*," he said insolently.

"I am indeed. May I ask why you've stopped my carriage?" Maggie was stunned at the calmness in her voice despite the fear knotting her tongue.

A devious grin spread across his face, revealing gaps where teeth should have been. He leered at Maggie as if she was a side of bacon.

"Why don't you ladies step out the carriage?"

"We haven't time to spare. Please allow us to resume our journey." Maggie's voice began to waver.

Mr. Greer started to intervene but halted when the short man aimed a pistol at him. "Sit back down darkie unless you want to get shot."

Mr. Greer lowered himself back onto the seat.

"Who's the darkie you got in there with you?" the taller man demanded.

"She's my maid. I must insist..."

"Insist on what? You're in our territory. Didn't nobody tell you it ain't safe to travel without an escort?" He hocked up a wad of spittle, spewing it on the ground. "Franklin, looks like we got us a couple of dates for tonight."

Maggie's insides swirled while Miss Taylor was astoundingly composed. In a staunch effort to appear brave, Maggie sat a bit straighter, attempting to steady her crumbling composure. But the man was unmoved. He stepped into the carriage, a sinister countenance veiling his weathered visage as he reached for Maggie's arm. Before he could grab hold of her, a shot rang out. Startled, the man stumbled backwards, managing to stay upright as he grabbed hold of the carriage door.

Scanning the darkness, Maggie noticed a dark figure on horseback a few feet away, a puff of smoke lingering from the barrel of his pistol.

"May I ask why you've stopped this carriage?" a steady voice echoed through the stagnant air.

"What business is it of yours?" the man grunted, reaching for his side arm.

"Remove your hand from that weapon or you'll end up with a nub," the mysterious rider said, his gun fixed on the target.

The tall fellow lowered his hand slowly. Unfazed by the encounter, the smaller miscreant turned his gun toward the man on horseback.

"You didn't answer his question. What business you got here?" he demanded.

"My business is that you've unlawfully detained my sister, and I strongly suggest you lower that weapon."

"Ain't but one of you and two of us."

"What makes you think I'm traveling alone?" the man on horseback replied, his voice steady and his stare locked on the man.

The smirk melted from the face of the offender, his eyes darting about as he lowered his weapon. The stranger's steadfast attitude suggested the two men dare not question the presence of others nearby.

"Sorry sir, we don't mean no harm," his once nefarious stature wilting into one of cowardice.

"Then you won't mind if we resume our journey."

The hoodlums nodded their heads and stepped aside as the gentleman on horseback spoke to the driver.

"Mr. Greer, are you ready?"

"Yes, sir."

The carriage tottered forward, the mysterious man riding

alongside. As the horses picked up speed, Maggie took a deep breath.

"Who is that?"

Miss Taylor grinned. "The Ghost. He works with the Railroad and has an uncanny talent for arriving at the most opportune moments."

"So it would seem," Maggie said, leaning against the tufted seat, her heart regaining a steady rhythm as the carriage bumped along. Her nerves were raw as she clasped her trembling hands together trying to steady them.

"I'm surprised those men gave up so easily," Maggie commented, still shaken from the encounter.

"Those men were ignorant cowards. They act as if they're tough, but they scare easily. It doesn't take much to call their bluff."

"Tell me more about the Ghost," Maggie said, anxious to know more about their rescuer.

"His name is Seth Daniels. Don't know much more than that. His background is as mysterious as his ability to show up at the exact moment he's needed. What's truly amazing is his horse, Phantom. He can slow his gate to a mere whisper. One wouldn't believe such a large beast could be invisible, and yet he is."

"Where does he live?"

"He lives at the plantation where you'll be staying, but spends a good deal of time conducting passengers."

Maggie mused over the nondescript tale of Mr. Daniels and his alliance with the Railroad, making her wonder if he had the ability to thwart her uncle's pursuits as well.

Too rattled to sleep, Maggie watched Mr. Daniels slip in and out of the shadows cast by the carriage lanterns as they resumed their journey south.

. . .

A BRILLIANT SUNRISE tickled Maggie's slumbering eyelids as the carriage rattled along. She sat up trying to rub the crick from her neck.

"Where are we?" she croaked.

"In North Carolina. How are you feeling this morning?"

"A bit stiff."

"You did well last night."

"I almost faltered."

"This work isn't for the weak of heart. It's turbulent and unpredictable. You did well for your first confrontation. You'll get bolder with each encounter."

After two more nights of travel, Maggie felt as if she'd go mad from the confinement. Her only respite was the occasional stop to rest the horses or have a meal. Watching for signs of Mr. Daniels, who appeared and disappeared intermittently, was her only means of entertainment. Something about him intrigued her. Whether it was the mystery of his past or his innate ability to show up when needed remained to be seen, but she was determined to learn more about this unusual man.

Following a night of rain and rutted roads, Maggie's joints ached and her body felt as if she'd been pummeled with a battering ram. A bright morning sun sparkled across the blue sky that harbored a few lingering clouds from the previous night's storms. Mr. Greer brought the carriage to a halt outside of a two-story clapboard farmhouse bordered by pastures of grazing cattle. He helped the two women from the carriage, a great relief to Maggie after jouncing about for several hours. Much to her surprise, she noticed Mr. Daniels's ebony horse grazing near the front porch.

"Good morning, glad to see you all made it," Mr. Daniels said, the words tumbling from his lips in a spirited tone. Maggie regarded his steely eyes, tanned complexion, and flaxen curls peeking from beneath a worn hat. He strutted down the stairs and offered his hand. "We haven't officially been introduced. I'm Seth Daniels."

Her hand fit comfortably within his, her fingertips tingling at his touch.

"Nice to meet you, I'm Maggie Milner. Thank you for your assistance the other night."

"Happy to be of service." A grin creased his sculpted cheeks, making Maggie's heart flutter like freshly laundered sheets floating on summer breezes.

The screen door smacked in the doorframe as a young woman appeared, her golden hair pinned back highlighting her plump cheeks and full lips.

"Hello!" she hollered from the porch. "Won't you all come in?"

The group followed the young lady inside to the parlor where scuffed pine floors evidenced countless visitors over the years. Miss Taylor and Maggie settled on the settee whilst Seth reclined in a rocker as if this was his home.

"Mother will be here in a moment," the young lady said with a smile. Offering her hand to Maggie, she introduced herself, "I'm Jolene Higgins."

"I'm Maggie, and this is Miss Taylor."

"We're well acquainted with Miss Taylor *and* Mr. Daniels," Joline giggled, her eyes sparkling when she said his name.

An older woman entered, carrying a tray with a teapot and five ironstone cups.

"It's good to see you again, Miss Taylor. I hope your trip was pleasant."

Miss Taylor grinned. "It's much better now that we're here."

Handing a cup to Maggie, the woman smiled. "I don't believe we've met. I'm Mrs. Higgins."

"I'm Maggie Milner. Thank you for the tea."

"You're most welcome." With a sideways glance at Mr.

Daniels, she arched one eyebrow. "She's a pretty one, is she not?"

A blush tinted his cheeks as his gaze shifted to the floor. Maggie detected a long scar running down his jawline that she'd not noticed before.

"I've embarrassed you, Mr. Daniels. I apologize." She winked at Maggie before taking a seat near her daughter.

Too tired to think about the implications of Mrs. Higgins' statement, Maggie sipped her tea. She attempted to follow the conversation as it zigged and zagged from one topic to another until exhaustion strong-armed her alertness, tugging at her eyelids in tandem with a few yawns.

"Miss Milner, may I show you to your room? You look as though you could use a nap," Jolene said with a smile.

"That would be wonderful, thank you. And please call me Maggie."

Jolene led her upstairs to a small room complete with a rope bed, washstand, and three-drawer chest crowned by a clouded mirror. Although the home was plain, it was hospitable.

"I hope the room is suitable. Please let us know if you need anything else. Lunch will be at noon."

"If you don't mind, I'd rather skip the midday meal. I'm not at all hungry and would prefer to sleep."

"Of course. If you change your mind, feel free to join us."

Maggie listened to Jolene's footfalls echo through the hall as she descended the stairs. Hopefully, Mrs. Higgins wouldn't take offense. The ragged state of Maggie's body after days of travel overshadowed her need to eat.

She crumpled onto the mattress, her body still cramped from a long night in the carriage. Of all the places they'd stayed, this was the most comfortable. Whether it was the presence of Mr. Daniels or the remote location of the farm, Maggie felt safe. Reaching into her satchel, she grasped the wooden heart, her mind drifting to the day Sellers had presented her with the precious gift. She curled the treasure into her hand and held it against her chest, running her thumb across the scrolled surface until she fell asleep. In spite of the overwhelming fatigue, her dreams were haunted by her uncle's fiery temper, robbing her of the rest she desperately craved.

Afternoon's hot breath billowed the curtains, prodding Maggie from her troubled sleep. Rising from bed, she fixed her hair and straightened her dress before padding down the narrow staircase to the kitchen where sunlight splashed across the beadboard walls. Jolene sat at the table sipping tea and reading a newspaper. Her eyes sparkled as she greeted her guest.

"How are you feeling? I hope you were able to sleep."

"Caught a few winks." The Irish speckled her words dragging her eyes to the floor as her hand covered her mouth.

"Your accent is lovely. I didn't notice it earlier. Would you like something to eat?"

Shaking her head, Maggie sat at the table and glanced around the space. It was plainer than the Milner's place with a brick hearth, shelves of cooking utensils, and a few jugs. The rug was faded from years of sunlight peering through the large window across the room. "Where is everyone?"

"Mother and Miss Taylor are surveying some of the buildings where our *cargo* is stored. One of the roofs has a terrible leak and we'll need some help repairing it."

"What about Mr. Daniels?"

Jolene's cheeks flushed. "Out scouting. He's not one to be sedentary. Not to worry, he'll be here for supper. He wouldn't miss Mama's cooking."

"He seems quite dedicated to this cause."

"That's saying it mildly. I recall the first time I met him. He'd escorted a group of passengers here from south Georgia. They'd endured terrible rainstorms with hunters close at hand.

The passengers spoke of his ingenuity and fearlessness for the two days they stayed with us. Once they were settled, Seth headed back out to reroute the hunters. It was one of the few times he sustained a serious injury in the process."

"The scar running down the right side of his face?"

"No, he's had that since I've known him. He broke his arm when Phantom slipped in the mud and unseated him."

"What about his past?" Maggie hoped Jolene knew more than Miss Taylor.

"Don't know much about that. I was only ten when I first met him." A sheepish grin raised her rosy cheeks. "You've got a shine for him, don't you?"

"Not at all, I was only curious," she said, looking away in an effort to hide the deception of her words.

"I should start preparations for supper. Mama will be back soon," Jolene announced, standing up.

"You don't have a cook?"

"Gracious, no. Mama wouldn't let anyone near her kitchen except me."

"And your father?

"He passed years ago. He was a staunch abolitionist and got his start on the Railroad long before I was born. When his rheumatism worsened, he started sheltering passengers instead of transporting them. My older brother, Harry, travels between Ohio and the Canadian border as a conductor."

Jolene's passion mirrored that of the Milners, endearing her to Maggie in a profound way. The kindness she'd encountered from members of the Railroad far outweighed the evil she'd experienced with her uncle, making Maggie proud to be a part of it.

DINNER CONSISTED OF ROASTED BEEF, carrots, mashed potatoes, and blackberry cobbler for dessert. The conversation was lively, roaming from the condition of the roads to the corn crop to Railroad activities.

"At our farm, we provide shelter and food for passengers. If they stay with us for an extended period, we teach them what we can," Mrs. Higgins said, scooping mashed potatoes onto her plate.

"Do you have many long-term guests?"

"Our location is remote, allowing passengers to spend days, sometimes weeks. We do our best to prepare them for their new lives. Reading and writing is an integral part of their assimilation into free society. Education is the key to true freedom."

Mrs. Higgins's words sparked something within Maggie, electrifying her motivation to do more. But for now, she had to be patient. Her purpose on this trip was as much about escape as helping those in need. Once she was free of her uncle's pursuits, Maggie could delve into the Railroad operations with every ounce of energy she possessed.

After dinner, they prepared to resume the journey. Mrs. Higgins provided a basket of biscuits, salted ham, and fruit so they could travel through to their destination. After a series of farewells and thanks, Maggie and Miss Taylor settled into the carriage. Seth mounted Phantom, tipped his hat to Mrs. Higgins and Jolene, and rode alongside the carriage as it caromed down the drive toward the coastal region of South Carolina and Maggie's new home.

DAWN CRASHED across the horizon in waves of color, waking Maggie. She tried stretching in the cramped space but was unable to relieve her stiff neck and aching back. She peered out the window, taking in the change of landscape.

"I don't see Mr. Daniels," she mumbled.

"He took a different route."

"What if we run into trouble again?"

"He's never far off. As I told you, he has impeccable timing."

Miss Taylor's confidence reassured Maggie.

"Will we be stopping soon?"

"In a bit to rest the horses."

Hours floated by like dandelion seeds on a spring breeze. The landscape altered from pine forests and red dirt to sandy roads lined with sprawling oaks and palmetto trees. Expansive waterways with tufts of swaying grasses bordered the roadway. Maggie lowered the upper panel of the carriage window, wrinkling her nose as she inhaled the pungent breath of the marsh. Miss Taylor grinned slyly at Maggie's reaction to the aromatic Lowcountry air. Closing the window, she sat back and shut her eyes, pondering what her new home would be like.

"How much longer before we arrive?" Maggie queried.

"We're nearly there."

24

Sunbeams dappled the winding drive as the carriage bounced across the sandy earth. An alabaster manse loomed from behind moss draped live oak trees. A calm cascaded over Maggie, her lips curling into a smile as tears crested in her eyes. The setting was akin to a scene from a fairy tale. Elaborately detailed arches supported a soaring roofline giving the house an ecclesiastical feel. Rockers on the front porch swayed in marsh breezes, welcoming all to sit a spell and enjoy the resplendent views. Never in all her days had Maggie beheld such a magnificent place.

Halting the horses, Mr. Greer climbed down from the driver's seat, opened the carriage door, and helped the ladies out. A young woman clad in a green cotton dress hurried down the brick walkway, her rosy cheeks glowing beneath coffee brown eyes. Something about her put Maggie at ease, as if they'd known each other for years.

"Miss Taylor, it's ever so good to see you again." They grasped hands before she turned to Maggie. "Good afternoon, I'm Elora Polk."

Maggie accepted her outstretched hand. "I'm Maggie

Milner. It's nice to make your acquaintance, Miss Polk." Using the Milner's surname comforted Maggie, making her feel as if she was still part of their lives.

"Please, call me Elora."

"Only if you call me Maggie."

Secretly she wanted to embrace the Polks, but her trepidation wouldn't allow it. Doubt prevented her from believing she'd be lucky enough to find a second family as wonderful as the Milners.

"Your timing is impeccable; tea is being served in the parlor."

Elora escorted them through the double front doors into an entryway befitting the elaborate façade. A winding mahogany staircase swirled beneath a massive crystal chandelier that dangled from a stained-glass dome, splashing shards of light across the floor in a kaleidoscope of hues.

They followed Elora into a parlor awash in the soft glow of afternoon.

"Mother will join us momentarily," Elora said, motioning her guests to sit. Miss Taylor settled on the ivory brocade settee while Maggie perched upon a red velvet chair. A slender woman with silky brown hair, porcelain complexion, and sparkling blue eyes, entered the room.

"Good day ladies, I'm so glad you've arrived safely."

Miss Taylor greeted the woman in a warm embrace.

"Mrs. Polk, may I introduce Maggie Milner."

"We're thrilled to have you with us and hope you'll feel at home here," she said, wrapping Maggie's hand gently between both of hers.

Anxiety released its grip from Maggie's shoulders at the kind welcome. A small part of her was beginning to believe all would be well.

A middle-aged, dark-skinned woman wheeled a teacart into

the room sporting a silver tea service and a plate of scones with strawberries.

"Anything else, Mrs. Polk?"

"No, thank you Clara."

With a quick bob, the woman disappeared. The scent of freshly baked scones mingled with the sweet strawberries making Maggie's taste buds tingle.

"Milk or sugar?" Elora asked, pouring the tea.

"Neither, thank you," Maggie replied, accepting the cup.

Elora passed a cup to Miss Taylor, and then to her mother before pouring her own.

"Please help yourself to some scones and strawberries," Mrs. Polk said, lifting the cup to her rose petal lips.

"How was your journey?" Elora queried.

"Long. We had one incident, but Mr. Daniels handled the situation."

"I'm glad to hear Seth was able to assist you."

Maggie noticed the glint in Elora's eye at the mention of Seth's name, and the informal manner in which she referred to him. Despite her obvious good upbringing and wealthy status, Elora was surprisingly carefree.

Miss Taylor shared a few more stories before directing the conversation to the mission at hand. "I've brought funds and papers to aid in the transport of the passengers coming from Georgia."

The mantel clock chimed four, alerting Elora to the hour. "Gracious, Father has yet to join us. He gets wrapped up in his work and loses all track of time. It's not healthy for him." With a chuckle, she continued. "Remarkable that I must remind a physician to care for his own well-being." She started for the door when a tall man with a well-trimmed beard and mustache appeared.

"I apologize for my tardiness but I had to finish some paperwork." His demeanor had a comforting aura to it.

"Papa, this is Miss Milner."

Elora presented her father with a cup of tea, which he sipped liberally before speaking to Maggie.

"We're glad you've joined us. I hope you'll find everything to your liking."

"It's a lovely place. Miss Polk, I mean Elora, has been quite hospitable."

"We want you to feel at home here. You're welcome to wander the grounds at your leisure."

His words unlocked the fear in the recesses of Maggie's mind, sending a twinge fluttering through her chest at the memory of her uncle's reaction when she explored his property. *Stop it,* she thought, *these are good people.*

After tea, Elora showed Miss Taylor and Maggie to their quarters. The accommodations were more elaborate than those at the Milner's home. Maggie's room sported a towering wardrobe, canopy bed, and marble-topped dresser. The room's window provided sweeping views of the marsh. Never in her life had she experienced such finery and opulence as the interiors of Rose Hall.

Dinner was a sumptuous spread of southern cuisine served on fine china with lively conversation. After the dishes were cleared, Maggie excused herself as she was weary from days of travel.

Once in her room, Maggie washed up and changed for bed. Reaching for her satchel, she removed the tattered copy of Byron's work. She rubbed her hand over the faded letters, her mind drifting back to her father's face as he read in the flickering light of the hearth. Tears crept from her eyes, cleansing her cheeks. She missed him so, and wondered what he was doing at that moment. Was he safe? Healthy? Missing her?

A sob erupted from her lips, opening the floodgates of suppressed worry. She cried in gulping torrents over her father, homesickness for the Milners, Sellers' bloody image, and the innocence she'd lost. It would haunt her for the rest of her life. When her tears ceased to fall, she placed the treasured tome on the night table with the silver locket upon it, and grabbed the wooden heart before blowing out the candle. Nestling beneath the cottony covers, she held the wooden heart to her chest as exhaustion wrapped its sinewy fingers around her, slowing her breath until she drifted to a place where the world was unfettered by the woes of reality.

THE MORNING MEAL followed the same formality as dinner the night before. Steaming bowls of eggs, ham, biscuits, and an odd substance called grits, with a texture befitting the name, were served.

Once the dishes were cleared, Mrs. Polk and Miss Taylor retired to the ladies' parlor to discuss business while Elora showed Maggie through the house. As they were crossing the center hall, the front door opened and Seth appeared.

"We were wondering what had become of you," Elora said with hands planted on her hips.

"Sorry for the delay, but Phantom had a loose shoe." Seth placed a kiss on Elora's forehead and smiled. "So, you missed me, huh?"

"Not at all," she replied, turning her nose in the air and swirling around with her back to him. He tickled her neck, sending her into a fit of giggles before nodding at Maggie.

"How are you today, Miss Milner?"

"Very well, thank you, Mr. Daniels."

Elora wrinkled her nose. "What's with all this formality? Her name is Maggie. And you can call him Seth, or anything else you can think of when he misbehaves, which is all the time."

"Don't be so sassy or I'll toss you in the river," he said, grabbing at her sides like he was going to lift her from the ground and carry her off.

"I'd like to see you try," she taunted, sticking out her tongue.

Their casual flirtation caused a pang in Maggie's chest, although she couldn't understand why. She hardly knew Mr. Daniels and it was none of her concern how he behaved.

"Maggie, would you like to take a walk around the grounds before lunch?" Elora offered.

"I'd like that very much."

"Mr. Daniel's, perhaps you'd accompany us?" Elora said with an air of propriety.

Seth replied with a sweeping bow. "I'd be delighted, m'lady."

They strolled along a sandy path with Maggie on one side of Elora and Seth on the other as she shared some of the plantation's history.

"My mother fell in love with the Gothic style while touring Europe. Poor Papa never had a say, he gave her complete control of the project. My brother, William, was to inherit the property, but he's made his home in Charleston, which means the house will come to me someday." She glanced back at the structure with such affection, one would have thought it was prince charming holding her gaze.

"Has your brother been away long?"

"Only two years, but we miss him terribly."

"Does he visit often?"

"Not as frequently as mother would like, but he writes every week. He did come for my seventeenth birthday last month," she grinned. "How old are you, if you don't mind my asking?"

"Nineteen on the twenty-sixth of May."

"We'll have to celebrate. I do love a party," she said with a sideways glance and a smile as broad as the river they walked beside.

The pathway jaunted around a clump of live oaks as the trio traipsed along the water's edge, Elora continuing her dialog.

"My grandfather, James Polk, purchased the land over fifty years ago. He was quite successful with the cultivation of Sea Island cotton, indigo, and rice, but Papa had issues with the slave labor used for daily operations. When my parents received the land as a wedding gift, they set about changing that aspect."

"How did they accomplish that?"

"They focused more on Papa's medical practice and less on crops. When they discovered folks were willing to work for fair wages, they began hiring free blacks. Of course, they don't advertise that," she said, giving a knowing glance. "Then one day, an older Negro man showed up, half-starved and in poor health. Papa was moved by his plight. When his master showed up looking for him, Papa hid him until he could find a way to get him somewhere safer. Fortunately, the old man knew of a conductor for the Underground Railroad. Papa made the arrangements and was able to get the man to freedom. And that's how Rose Hall became one of the safe houses."

"That's an amazing story."

"Later we met Seth. His story is rather amazing too," Elora declared with a coquettish grin.

Seth's brow furrowed as he looked away, obviously uncomfortable by the praise.

"How did you become acquainted with the Railroad?" Maggie asked.

"It's a rather a long story and I need to check on Phantom. He was a bit off yesterday and I want to make sure it's nothing more serious than a loose shoe."

"By all means, go tend to him. Maggie and I shall make our way about the property unescorted," Elora replied mockingly.

Resuming his charming demeanor, Seth removed his hat,

swinging it downward in a dramatic bow. "Until we meet again, ladies."

Elora rolled her eyes. "Only if you promise to behave yourself and act like a proper gentleman," she replied, pursing her lips.

Seth winked and placed the hat upon his head before starting toward the barn.

Maggie and Elora continued down the path.

"You seem quite fond of him," Maggie said once they were out of earshot.

"I adore him and miss him terribly when he's away."

"Is he much older than you?"

"Perhaps in years, but not maturity," Elora giggled.

As they rounded the curve of the river, a row of cottages sprouted from the horizon like a queue of neatly planted flowers.

Unlike Letty and Willa's brick structures, these cottages were slightly larger and clad in white washed siding. Stopping at the first one, Elora rapped on the door.

"You're going to love Miss Olive. She's a character," she whispered over her shoulder.

"I's a comin'," a raspy voice called out.

The paneled door creaked in protest as Miss Olive swung it open. Before them stood a wispy woman with ebony eyes blazing from beneath an indigo scarf wrapped about her head.

"Oh Lawd, trouble dun come a knockin' and she brought a friend!"

At first Maggie wasn't sure how to take the greeting until a smile creased the woman's weathered face, letting her know it was in jest.

"Come on in. You's just in time to help wid de bread."

Elora's shoulders dropped. "Please tell me it's already baked. You know how I hate to knead."

"Stop all that whinin'! I knows you don't like to knead. Take those loaves outta the pans and put 'em on the cooling rack."

Elora scurried to do as she was instructed.

"Who's your friend?"

"This is Maggie Milner. She's come to stay for a while," Elora said, carrying a steaming loaf to the worktable.

"She a bit scrawny, but I suppose she'll do," Miss Olive added, looking Maggie up and down.

"Well Miss Olive, I guess you're going to have to bake a whole batch of sugar cookies to fatten her up."

"I's gonna have to bake more than cookies. Might have to make a cake too!"

Maggie chuckled. Glancing down at her dress, she realized she was a bit thin. Even though she had plenty to eat at the Milner's, it would seem she'd dropped a few pounds on the trip.

Miss Olive looked up from the breadbasket she was preparing and shot Maggie a stern look.

"Chil' don' stand there, get an apron and help that little rascal you dun showed up with," she said with a huff.

Maggie tied one of the aprons around her waist, pinned the top to her bodice, and helped Elora arrange loaves on a large cooling rack. After the bread was stored and two baskets filled, Miss Olive plopped down at the pine table.

"Time for a break," she said, pulling a small flask from her apron pocket and taking a long draw. She offered it to Maggie.

"No, thank you."

Miss Olive replaced the cap and stashed it back in her pocket.

"You don' sound like you's from around here."

Maggie looked at Elora for guidance. She still wasn't sure how to handle questions about her past.

"Maggie came to us from up north." Elora volunteered.

While Miss Olive was bold with her remarks, she obviously sensed Maggie's hesitation and didn't ask any more questions.

No doubt, having to avoid extracting too much information from those who took refuge at Rose Hall was a common practice. After a brief chat, Elora announced she was taking Maggie to meet some of the others.

"I promise we'll visit again soon."

"I'll believe it when I sees it. You always say you gonna help poor Miss Olive, but you never does." She smirked, sending Elora into a fit of giggles.

"We have to come back. Don't forget, you've got to put some meat on poor Maggie's carcass."

"Dat's true. Now get out both of you 'fore I puts you back to work."

The two scuttled from the cottage into the heat of the afternoon. The blazing sun mixed with the sticky air, making it feel like the inside of an oven.

Maggie gathered her courage and asked, "Am I really too thin?"

"Not at all. Miss Olive likes to tease. She says what she thinks and stands by her word, so you should be expecting a dozen or more cookies and a cake very soon."

"And Miss Olive is a free woman?"

"Everyone here is free."

"And the neighbors accept it?"

"As I said earlier, they know nothing about it. All of our workers are provided housing, a salary, and are free to leave whenever they like. But most are dedicated to the work. They pretend to be enslaved as a guise, in order to keep our operations secret. Fortunately, Father is the only physician in this part of the county, so people don't harass our workers when they go to town or to neighboring plantations. Except for the Houstons who do their best to cause trouble whenever they can." Elora rolled her eyes.

"Who are they?"

"Let's not speak about *them* right now. It's a glorious day and too lovely to dwell on such loathsome people as the Houstons."

They spent the remainder of the afternoon visiting and making introductions. Maggie found several of the workers fascinating, especially Miss Heddy who held a multitude of jobs to include canning food, prepping supplies for passengers, and helping with injuries. Her breadth of knowledge on remedies was remarkable, instantly putting Maggie at ease. They spent a good deal of time discussing different salves. A smile curled Elora's lips as she watched the bond forming between them.

25

Early the next morning, Maggie ambled downstairs where Mrs. Polk and Miss Taylor conversed by the front door.

"Miss Taylor is leaving," Mrs. Polk announced.

Maggie offered her hand to Miss Taylor. "It was a pleasure traveling with you. I only hope in time I can be as effective."

Leaning toward Maggie, Miss Taylor pursed her lips.

"Stop worrying so much."

"What if I make a mistake and trust the wrong person. My record isn't very good in that respect."

"All you gotta do is listen with your soul and you'll do just fine."

A smile plumped Miss Taylor's cheeks as she gave a nod and walked through the doors to the end of the brick path. She wedged her broad figure into the carriage and closed the door. Maggie and Mrs. Polk watched Mr. Greer cue the horses into action, an emptiness engulfing Maggie as she watched the carriage disappear in a cloud of dust. A warm breeze ruffled her hair as she pondered how life would be in this unfamiliar place with her new family. Elora bounced down the stairs, her chipper demeanor emanating with each step.

"Good morning, Maggie. How did you sleep last night?"

"Very well, thank you."

"Let's have some breakfast and then we can meet the rest of the workers," she said, looping her arm through Maggie's.

When the last of the coffee was drained and the dishes cleared, Maggie and Elora walked to another section of the plantation.

"I want you to meet Miss Bertie and Hatch today," Elora said as they strolled along a tree-lined path dappled with sunlight.

They approached a cottage trellised by morning glories and an assembly of blooms lining the front.

"Miss Bertie teaches the children on the estate. Of course, it's illegal to educate Negroes, so don't mention it outside of our plantation. She also helps with mending things for the passengers that pass through."

Maggie inhaled the delicate fragrance of the gardens as Elora rapped on the door.

"Come in," a voice echoed.

They stepped into the neat little space with everything in its place, lacey curtains on the windows, and shelves filled with books and bric-a-brac. A brightly colored quilt graced the settee, catching Maggie's attention with its vibrant hues of gold, orange, and purple.

"I was wondering when I might get some help around here," a dark-skinned woman called from a long pine table covered in thread and fabric scraps. Ebony curls framed her visage and a smile accentuated her high cheek bones.

"What are you working on?" Elora queried.

"Making dolls for the little ones. I'm surprised to see you this morning, Miss Elora," she said, arching her eyebrows.

"Why would you say such a thing?" Elora asked, her lips

puckering into a pout.

"Because you only come when Dr. Polk sends you, otherwise you're with Olive. You're going to make me believe you don't like me," she said with a smirk.

"It's not you," Elora huffed. "I'm just not fond of mending clothes."

"You're not fond of baking either."

"Yes, but I get to sample the finished product at Miss Olive's," she replied with a sly grin. "Miss Bertie, this is Maggie Milner. She's come to stay with us for a while."

"It's nice to meet you, Miss Milner."

"Likewise."

"You girls have a seat and I'll bring some tea."

Bertie walked into the kitchen and began preparing refreshments.

"Her manner of speaking is so...proper," Maggie whispered to Elora.

"That's because I was born free and schooled in reading, writing, and arithmetic. I'm also well versed in three languages and play the piano," Bertie declared from the other room. Moments later, she returned, placing a tray with three cups of tea before them.

"My apologies," Maggie stammered. "I didn't mean any disrespect, it's only..."

"You've never heard a Negro use good English?"

"Yes ma'am." Maggie's gaze shifted to the floor.

"Don't be bashful, it's a legitimate observation. My life was one of comfort and privilege before I chose to come here."

"Forgive my impertinence, but why would you give all that up?"

"My mother always told me that those who have been given much, much will be expected. I've been disgusted by the plight of the enslaved my entire life. And then I met Henrietta Taylor. She told me they needed an educated person to help in the southern regions. My role is to teach the workers and their families. They in turn will pass that knowledge down to others, allowing the learning cycle to continue. When I'm not teaching, I sew."

"Isn't it difficult to live in an area where you're considered less than others?"

"I know I'm equal to any white person," she stated, her eyes flashing. "It's my moral obligation as a child of God, to do what's necessary to help them. In God's eyes, we're all worthy."

A pang of guilt gripped Maggie's chest as she considered all that Bertie and Miss Taylor had sacrificed, until Mrs. Milner's wisdom resurfaced. *Don't diminish what you've suffered. It's not a contest.*

After tea and a stimulating conversation, Elora took Maggie to the stables to meet Hatch. They walked to the barn where a large man with a jagged scar running down the back of his left arm cleaned stalls. Maggie tried not to focus on his disfigurement, but it was difficult to dismiss.

"Hello, Miss Polk," he greeted. "What bring you to de stables today?"

"I wanted to introduce Maggie Milner. She's staying with us."

"Nice to meet you, Miss," he said, a broad smile spanning his face.

"And you," Maggie replied.

The clopping of hooves reverberated as Seth emerged from the end of the aisle leading Phantom outside.

"Ladies," he said, walking past with a dip of his head.

"How's Phantom?" Elora queried.

"Fine. It was just a loose shoe." His sea-blue eyes glimmered as he addressed them. "I'm taking him out for a little jaunt. See you ladies this evening."

Alighting to the saddle, Seth took up the reins and trotted off. Maggie's heart thrummed against her rib cage and her palms moistened. *What is wrong with me*, she thought as they started back to the house for the midday meal.

"What happened to Hatch's arm?" Maggie asked, trying to shift her thoughts to something else.

"Hatch came to us shortly after his master sliced his arm while whipping him. He was only seventeen at the time. Papa was appalled when his master said he was going to sell Hatch into field work as a punishment."

"Is that bad?"

"Field work is the worst labor a slave can endure. They toil in the heat for hours with little sustenance. To make matters worse, if they don't achieve the harvesting goal, the overseers whip or starve them. I won't even mention what they do to the women." Elora shuddered.

"How did he end up staying here?"

"Papa has a way of making things happen. When Hatch's master was unable to pay for the medical services, Papa offered to take the slave in exchange for services rendered. Otherwise, Papa had no choice but to file legal charges for compensation. Not wanting anyone to know of his financial strains, the man agreed to the terms. Many of the men around here have a penchant for cards, and this man wasn't the first to be indebted to his vice.

"As soon as Hatch was on the plantation, he was given the option of remaining or going north as a free man. He was so grateful to Papa, he agreed to stay on as horse handler. The idea of being free to leave at any time was enough for him."

With each story, Maggie's respect for the Polks flourished. The extent to which they'd gone to ensure the safety of their workers as well as assisting others was astounding. Their operation was as delicate as the gears of a clock, each intricate piece working together to function as a whole. Any small glitch and the entire workings would screech to a halt.

Despite her admiration, Maggie didn't want to get too

attached to the Polks for fear she'd be forced to flee again should her uncle discover her whereabouts.

LATER IN THE AFTERNOON, Maggie took a walk. The sun massaged her shoulders in warmth as a flock of pelicans soared overhead and a soft breeze caressed her cheek. The serenity was shattered when she heard a blood-curdling scream nearby. Stepping up to a run, she hurried toward the sound. When she reached the clearing near the huge old oak, she was shocked to find Elora swinging back and forth like a pendulum at the end of a rope with a board affixed at the bottom. Initially, her squeals of delight sounded more like a cry but now Maggie realized she was shrieking with delight as she flew through the air.

Seth was standing on the edge of the marsh laughing at her antics. With a mischievous grin, he looked her direction and hollered. "Hey Miss Milner, you're next!"

Although she longed to swing across the glimmering waters, Maggie didn't dare. Even though everyone had been gracious to her thus far, she still wasn't comfortable enough to engage in something so, uninhibited. Seth's casual smile gripped her heart, making her feel like a foolish schoolgirl instead of a young woman.

"No thank you, Mr. Daniels." With a slight curtsey, she continued on her way admonishing herself for being so stuffy. As the path curved, Maggie noticed a cottage nestled near the water's edge with a small dock jutting out over the water. It was a lovely location and she made a mental note to ask Elora who resided there.

A LITTLE WHILE LATER, Maggie headed back toward the house, stopping to take in the sprawling beauty before her. The breeze had loosened the makeshift swing from its mooring, taunting her to take a ride.

Looking around to insure no one was nearby; she reached for the rope, stepped onto the wobbling plank, and pushed off of the tree trunk. Maggie propelled over the water soothed by the salty winds rushing past as she sailed back and forth. Lost in the moment, she was startled when a voice called out.

"I see you like the swing, Miss Milner," Seth hollered, a smile wrinkling his face.

Maggie turned abruptly, causing her to falter and plummet into the marsh. With a resounding 'splash,' she bobbed up from beneath the water, her hair stringing around her shoulders in long strands.

Seth rushed into the water, apologizing as he reached for her hand. "I'm so sorry, I didn't mean to make you fall!"

"Mr. Daniels, I don't require your assistance. I'm perfectly capable of getting to shore," she snapped, shoving his hand away.

No sooner had the words crossed her lips she lost her footing in the slippery pluff mud and went tumbling forward into Seth. He caught her before she went under the water, helping her back on her feet. His eyes had darkened in the shifting light making them a deep indigo blue, his face a few inches from hers and the scar on his right cheek more prominent. Her stomach tumbled as she whispered, "Thank you, Mr. Daniels."

"You're welcome," he replied, his gaze locked onto hers.

She accepted his hand as he led her through the grassy tide. They emerged from the water dripping wet and soggy. Maggie glanced at her mud-soaked dress before looking at Seth who was shaking water from his curly locks like a wet dog. When their eyes met, they burst into laughter.

"I should head back to the house and change," she said, wringing water from her hair.

"Shall I walk with you?"

"I think you've helped enough for one afternoon," she responded, a hint of Irish curling her words.

He flashed her a sly smile as he rounded the bend to the cottage she'd noticed earlier. *So that's where he lives,* she thought, her blood pumping with the force of a tidal wave as she watched him walk away.

SETH JOINED them for a lively evening meal followed by time on the verandah. Shadowed in the dappled light of a setting sun, the expanse before them seemed almost mystical. Moss swayed gently from gnarled tree branches as a herd of deer grazed at the far corner of the front lawn. Somehow the conversation wavered from the condition of the cotton crop to childhood remembrances.

"She's been a pain in my neck for years now," Seth declared.

"Is that how you speak about your pirate queen?" Elora taunted, sticking out her tongue.

"You're a pirate queen that's a pain in my neck," he replied, a mischievous smile accentuating his playful tone.

Looking at Maggie, Elora grinned. "Poor Papa, we're always in some sort of mischief, but mostly Seth. Especially the time he let the pigs escape."

Maggie raised her eyebrows, curious about the incident. One thing was certain; Elora was blunt if nothing else. "Pigs?"

"According to what papa told me, Seth had been working here for a few weeks and was eager to make a good impression. After feeding the pigs, he went to the stables to help Hatch. Unbeknownst to him, he'd scooted out of the pigpen without securing the gate. No sooner had he started haying the horses, and the pigs were scampering about, squealing and rooting in mother's garden," Elora chuckled.

"Did you witness this?" Maggie asked, her eyes wide.

"I was in the tree swing nearby when I heard the commotion. I ran towards the sound to discover pigs scurrying all over the yard. Seth was frantically trying to herd them, but to no avail. The more he chased them, the more they ran around. It was rather funny, until they trampled mother's roses."

"I was terrified your father would dismiss me."

"Had it been anyone else he would have done so," she said, grabbing his hand and holding it. "Even then, he knew you were special,"

Seth shook his head. "He said that everyone makes mistakes. Didn't even hesitate, just sent me back to the barn and told me to be more careful in the future. That's when I knew I'd found my place."

Mesmerized, Maggie studied his sculpted features and the way his eyes glimmered when he laughed. Despite the ragged scar on the right side of his face, he was perfect in every way. But Maggie quickly dismissed the thought. The connection between him and Elora was evident.

Mrs. Polk stepped onto the porch, interrupting the moment.

"Elora, Maggie, we have an early morning."

"I guess that's our signal to retire for the evening," Elora said, rising from the rocker.

"Goodnight, ladies," Seth responded with a sly smile as he placed his hat upon his head and jaunted down the stairs into the night.

As Maggie followed Elora inside, she glanced over her shoulder, wondering about Seth's life before Rose Hall, and how to suppress the longing that lingered in her heart.

"How did Mr. Daniels come to be a part of Rose Hall?" Maggie asked when they reached the upstairs landing.

"That's his story to tell."

Elora's elusiveness on the topic was unexpected. She was generally straightforward about all subjects, further fueling Maggie's curiosity about Mr. Daniel's mysterious past.

26

The following morning, after breakfast, Dr. Polk asked to see Maggie in his office.

Chewing her lip, she fidgeted with her hands as she followed him, nervous that she may have done something wrong. The room exuded a masculine feel with a massive hearth, leather furnishings, and a substantial desk nestled within a windowed alcove framed by tartan draperies.

"Please have a seat," he said, motioning to one of the wing chairs as he sat on the leather settee across from her.

"I wanted to speak with you about your knowledge of herbal remedies."

"What would you like to know?"

"Everything."

Maggie informed him about the concoctions she'd mixed at the Milner's farm.

"Do you have any other medical experience?"

"Only which herbs treat certain rashes and illnesses. I learned how to mix the remedies at my..." She stopped, rubbing her sweaty palms against her skirt.

"Is something the matter?"

"I, um, don't know how much you've been told about me."

His smile was warm as he leaned forward.

"If you're referring to the unfortunate circumstances that brought you to us, then yes, I know something of your background. But I'm not asking you to tell me anything personal. Your references are impeccable and we're happy you're able to join us. I'm only asking about your knowledge so I can determine how to utilize your skills."

Maggie exhaled as she disclosed all of the things she'd learned from Willa and Letty. Every so often, Dr. Polk nodded as he listened to her list the different salves, ointments, and balms, along with their applications.

"Impressive," he said rubbing his neatly trimmed beard. "This is good news. Up to this point, I've done most of the work in this area so your skills will be a great asset. Heddy knows a lot, but mostly how to mix the things I've given her. When do you think you'd be ready to start?"

"As soon as you'd like me to do so."

"Splendid. I'll send word to Heddy that you'll be working with her. I know she'll be happy to have the help." Dr. Polk stood, a broad grin crinkling the edges of his eyes. "You can start tomorrow morning."

"Thank you, Dr. Polk for this opportunity," Maggie replied. "I'm thankful for your kindness."

He rested his hand on her shoulder. "We're happy to have you with us."

AT LUNCHTIME, Maggie meandered along the path toward the house when she came across Elora and Seth chasing each other. Hanging back, she watched Elora scampering across the lawn, her giggles echoing through the low-lying branches of the massive oaks as she chased Seth. Poor Seth zigged when he should have zagged but was able to pivot and run the opposite direction. However, in his quest to turn sharply, he lost his footing stumbling and spinning in a series of ridiculous bumbling moves until he rolled to the ground in a fit of laughter. Their unspoken affection for one another was obvious.

Although amused by their escapades, Maggie's heart ached. Despite the kindness and friendship that had been lavished upon her, she found she was rather lonely. The longing to be reunited with her da was suffocating. Furthermore, the emotional scars left by her uncle, not to mention being torn from the Milners, made her feel as if she would never truly be a part of anything again. How long would she be able to stay before she'd have to move on? After all, she was only being housed here until her uncle ceased his pursuits, which had no expiration date.

Nevertheless, she was determined to work hard for the Polks to prove her worth. At this point, the most dangerous thing she faced was an underlying affection for a man she could never have. A flush warmed her cheeks as she watched Seth with Elora, his sandy brown curls and broad smile tugging at her heart. She had to curtail her feelings, and the only way to do that was to keep her distance.

If only she could go home, back to the safety of her father's cottage, and erase all the awful things she'd endured. Yet, the idea of never seeing Seth again stabbed at her chest. Shaking the thought from her head, she concentrated on the situation at hand. There was important work to be done, and she hadn't time to wallow in self-pity and impossible dreams.

Elora's squeals pulled Maggie from her pool of self-despair. Seth managed to tag her as he raced for the fence, Elora fast on his heels. Maggie was amazed at her athletic prowess despite the long skirts and petticoats. A smile broke through Maggie's sorrow like sunrays following a rain storm. She watched as Seth broke stride and cleared the fence in one smooth leap, leaving

Elora standing in a breathless stance with her hands planted on her hips.

Moments later, Seth rejoined Elora as they walked side by side to the house, their cheeks flushed and chests heaving. They did make a handsome couple. Maggie wanted to be happy for them even though her heart was in tatters.

GRABBING a couple of jugs from the pottery shed, Maggie finished a remedy for bug bites. The mosquitos had been exceptionally troublesome this season and the workers were going through salve at an alarming rate. It was as if the marsh was breeding the gnarly creatures for the express purpose of making everyone miserable.

Once in the kitchen, she began mixing the powders and beeswax while Heddy whipped up another batch of lavender oil. The door of their workspace was propped open, allowing the salty marsh breezes to blow through the suffocating atmosphere when the scuffing of Elora's boots caught their attention.

"Maggie, I have a surprise for you!" Elora declared, popping her head in the door.

"What is it?"

"If I told you, it wouldn't be a surprise," she said, pursing her lips. "Put that stuff away. You've done enough work for the afternoon."

Maggie replaced the ingredients on their respective shelves, removed her apron, and rinsed her hands at the washstand.

"Can you at least tell me where we're going?"

Elora grinned sheepishly. "Nope."

Skittering along the path, Elora led Maggie to the main house. As they approached the porch, she grabbed Maggie's hand, tugged her up the brick stairs, through the entry, and into the dining room. When Maggie entered, Miss Olive, Miss

Bertie, Dr. and Mrs. Polk, and Seth hollered, "Happy Birthday!"

"How did you know it was my birthday?" she muttered, tears welling in her eyes.

"You mentioned it a few weeks ago," Elora replied.

Maggie's heart swelled at the love showered upon her from people she hardly knew.

Miss Heddy entered the room huffing. "My goodness that was a taxing walk in this heat."

The cake was cut and dispersed as everyone chattered and laughed making the atmosphere merry. Moments later, one of the stable hands rushed into the room, handing Seth a note.

"Please forgive me, but I need to attend to a matter of great importance. Placing his plate upon the mahogany table, Seth strode from the room without uttering a word.

Elora reached over and patted Maggie's hand. "Please don't take offence, he often leaves abruptly."

Maggie nodded, although his departure dampened her enthusiasm more than she wanted to admit.

SETH HURRIED to the stables where he found Phantom tacked and ready to go.

"Thanks Hatch," he called, taking the reins and swinging into the saddle. Spurring Phantom into action, he raced down the drive toward town.

The note told of a family traveling from Florida that was hiding in an abandoned shed outside of Savannah. One of the members was ill, the hunters were on their trail, and bad weather threatened to impede their escape. It was a trifecta of unfortunate circumstances demanding immediate intervention.

Phantom's pace mirrored the anxiety surging through Seth's

body. Turning down the road, Seth spied a modest two-story house with a porch spanning the front where Rudy Tindell lived with his wife, Rachell.

Seth dismounted, secured Phantom, and marched up the wooden stairs to the front door. Rudy greeted Seth with a handshake. Aside from his shrewd business acumen, Rudy was known for his antics, high spirits, and jovial countenance.

"I just received your note. What's the status of the family?"

"I fear it's grim. The hunters aren't far off and they're determined to bring this group to justice."

"Have you any idea where they're hiding?" Seth asked.

"Somewhere near Duncan Hall. The hunters have been tracking the area for several hours now. Capture seems inevitable."

"What's the problem?"

"One of their party, an older man, has succumbed to fever, complicating their escape. They won't leave him behind and he's too weak to travel. The only viable route is by way of the marsh."

The floorboards creaked beneath Seth's footfalls as he paced up and down the porch until a plan formulated.

"I'll try to divert the hunters. If someone can help the family make their way up river to Sanders' farm, we can hide them there until the old man is stronger and Dr. Polk can treat him."

"I'll send a scout to deliver the message."

"Thanks Rudy." Seth mounted his steed and headed back to Rose Hall at a full gallop.

The evening's events just became more complicated.

Elora and Maggie were sitting on the verandah when Seth galloped up.

Dismounting, he called out, "Elora, where's your father?"

"In his office."

Seth raced past her into the house.

"What's going on?" Maggie asked.

"I don't know, but when Seth gets like this it's usually something serious."

Moments later, Mrs. Polk appeared. "Maggie, please come with me."

Maggie followed her to the office at the back of the house where Dr. Polk sat with Seth.

"Maggie, please sit." Dr. Polk motioned toward the wing chair. She perched on the edge, her palms moistening.

"We have a situation in Georgia that requires immediate action. A traveler is ill and in need of attention. Mrs. Barnwall is in labor and there could be complications so my presence is needed there. Would you be willing to go with Seth and tend to the sick man?"

Looking back and forth between the two men, Maggie stammered. "I know how to mix and apply remedies but I haven't any medical training."

"There's nothing to fear. Your knowledge about which remedy to use is all that's needed. I don't know the reason for the fever, whether it's due to dehydration, insect bites, or a virus.

"Willa and Letty taught me all of that when they showed me how to mix the remedies."

"Perfect." Dr. Polk stood. "Maggie, how good are you on horseback?"

"I can ride well enough."

"Excellent. Fancy will be saddled and waiting at the barn." Looking at Seth, he continued. "You'll need to go by way of the old mill to avoid the hunters."

"Yes, sir."

"Good luck to you both."

Maggie followed Seth from the room, her stomach knotting at

the thought of assisting with such a complicated situation. Up to this point she'd helped indirectly but had never been involved with an actual rescue mission. Her body trembled with excitement and perspiration moistened her brow. While the situation was dangerous, she couldn't tell if her nerves were the result of the errand itself or the idea of working alongside Seth. Either way, she needed to focus on the task at hand. Lives depended on it.

She chose several small containers for everything from bee stings to poison ivy and stashed them in a leather satchel. She accompanied Seth to the stables where a dark bay mare pawed the ground, ready to go.

Maggie and Seth rode along sandy paths bordering the marsh. The serenity of the surroundings seemed incompatible with the dire nature of their errand. How could the world be so beautiful and yet filled with such cruelty?

As the sun began its descent, Seth slowed Phantom to a brisk walk. Turning to Maggie he put his finger to his lips. They rode a bit further before he dismounted and tied Phantom to a tree. Maggie did the same with Fancy and followed Seth a few hundred feet down the river's edge to a dilapidated shack.

Seth's gaze darted about as if an army were hiding behind every tree ready to ambush them. They approached the shanty with its rotting exterior and sunken roof. Seth knocked three times in a distinct rhythmic pattern. A similar knock echoed from within. The door opened, exhaling a rank odor. The stifling heat had baked in the odors of sweat and urine, making Maggie turn her head in disgust. It was reminiscent of the close quarters on the ship from Ireland.

A dozen people ranging from toddler to elderly filled the cramped space. In the far corner a spindly gent leaned against the wall, choking and sputtering.

"No need to worry, we're here to help," Seth whispered. With outstretched arms, the youngest of the group reached toward Seth, his mother crouching in the shadows. Seth scooped the child up as if it were his own, melting Maggie's heart at the tenderness of the scene.

"See if you can help the man over there," he whispered with a nod.

Stepping carefully around each person, Maggie made her way to the elderly fellow and knelt.

"I need to ask you a few questions."

He nodded. The old man's hunched stature, coupled with the dullness in his eyes, led her to believe his illness was progressing at an alarming rate. Maggie panicked. What if she couldn't help him?

"What are your symptoms?"

His words escaped in whispered breaths. "My head be achin' and my body feel weak. When I stand it feels like everything is spinnin'."

After listening to what he had to say, Maggie felt confident he was suffering from over exertion after traveling in the heat without enough fresh water. No doubt, he'd been drinking from the marsh and the salt water had depleted his energy. Reaching into her satchel, she removed a bottle and applied the contents to the man's forehead and chest. She took the canteen from her side and offered it to him, his eyes piercing her soul as he gulped it down. She started to rise when the man's long fingers wrapped around her hand, gratitude emanating from his stare.

"Thankee," he muttered.

"You're welcome. I pray you make it to your destination safely," she said, squeezing his hand.

Seth tapped her shoulder. "We need to be on our way."

"Surely, we're not going to leave them here to fend for themselves?" she whispered, her heart thudding at the idea.

"Reinforcements are on their way. We've done what we

came to do and need to leave. Our presence puts them in grave danger."

Maggie gazed at the group crammed in the cramped space. Her time at her uncle's seemed insignificant compared to what this family was risking for freedom. Seth touched her shoulder again.

"Maggie, let's go," he repeated vehemently.

She stepped from the confines of the darkened shack, drawing in a long breath of clean air. Guilt racked her mind as she mounted Fancy wondering if the group would make it to their destination or not.

"Will they make it?" Maggie queried as Fancy plodded along.

"Don't know."

"What about the old man? How will we know if he recovers?"

Seth halted Phantom, his stare chilling Maggie to the core despite the sticky atmosphere.

"You have to detach yourself. If we allow our emotions to take over, we become ineffective. The horrors you'll see and hear will destroy you otherwise. Rarely do we know the fate of those we seek to help."

The coldness of his words rattled her. How could someone so compassionate turn his feelings off so easily?

They arrived at Rose Hall well after midnight exhausted and hungry. Passing the main house, Maggie gazed upon its elaborate exterior and pristine features, considering the unfairness of those living so abundantly while others were holed up in dilapidated shacks with no food or water. She followed Seth to the stables where Hatch waited.

"Everything go OK?" he asked, holding Fancy as Maggie dismounted.

"As well as can be expected. If they can make it out of Georgia, they'll have a better chance," Seth replied. "Let's get back to the house. It's been a long day," he said to Maggie as Hatch led both horses down the aisle.

Maggie walked alongside Seth to the entrance of the kitchen house. Stepping inside, they followed the dancing shadows of an oil lamp to two plates of food and a note. "Eat some supper. I'll want a full report in the morning."

Seth looked at Maggie. "Care to join me?"

"If you don't mind, I'd rather go to bed."

"You did a good job this evening."

"Is it always so disheartening?"

"Tonight was mild compared to some of the things you'll encounter."

Maggie sighed. "Goodnight."

"I'll be here tomorrow morning. Dr. Polk will want to know what happened."

Seth sat at the table and began eating. Maggie traipsed up the back stairs of the main house, weariness weighting her legs. Helping others escape persecution was a euphoric experience, and despite her fatigue, she was happy to have been involved with something so meaningful. Yet a sense of unease haunted her well into the night.

27

A soft knock at the door stirred Maggie from her slumber. Elora popped her head inside and grinned. "How are you this morning?"

"A bit sore." Maggie sat up, her back and legs aching from the ride. It had been a while since she'd been on a horse.

Elora plopped on the edge of the bed. "Were you able to help them?"

"I think so. The entire thing was shocking."

"You should see what they're running from." Elora huffed. "The shacks they're forced to live in are deplorable not to mention the fear of being sold or beaten."

Maggie shook her head. "I just can't understand it."

Elora grasped Maggie's hand. "It doesn't get any easier, but our efforts are saving many. Get dressed and meet me downstairs. Miss Clara made pancakes for breakfast!"

Maggie admired Elora's ability to face the depressing nature of their work and still focus on pleasant things.

Following breakfast, Maggie joined Seth in Dr. Polk's office to discuss the events of the previous evening.

"Well done. I'd have drawn the same conclusion considering the symptoms," Dr. Polk replied with a grin.

"Thank you, sir."

When they finished their debriefing, Seth and Maggie stepped into the hallway. He rested his hand on her shoulder, her skin tingling beneath his touch.

"You did well yesterday." His steely blue eyes locked onto hers.

"Thank you. It was a bit overwhelming," she replied, her heart pounding against her ribcage.

"Wish I could say it gets easier," he sighed. "You're a great asset to us, Maggie." His smile pierced her heart, rendering her speechless. When she didn't respond, he flashed a smile and walked out the door.

Maggie rubbed her shoulder in an effort to still her quivering flesh where his hand had rested. *He must think me a fool*, she thought, feeling like a mindless schoolgirl with a crush. Chewing her lower lip, Maggie pondered how much longer she could harness her feelings, and what their next adventure would entail.

MAGGIE SPENT most of the morning with Miss Heddy before returning to the house for lunch. Dr. Polk was checking on a patient at the Bellamy Plantation, leaving only the women at Rose Hall for the midday meal.

"Elora, I need you to deliver something to Mr. Tindell," Mrs. Polk announced when the meal was over. "Take Maggie with you, she'll enjoy the ride to town."

Hatch brought the carriage around and helped the two ladies inside.

"Who is Mr. Tindell?" Maggie asked, as they tottered down the dirt drive.

"He's a stockholder in the Railroad."

"A stockholder?" Maggie asked.

"A financial benefactor," Elora replied. "He also owns *The Home Hearth* publication. He advertises messages for the Railroad."

"I thought it was all secret."

"Everything is done in code and listed in the personal pages, allowing messages to be sent clandestinely to our agents in other states." Elora gazed out the window, a smile creeping across her face. "He's a fascinating fellow with quite a reputation."

"Tell me more."

"Rudy is always tinkering with old, discarded things and has a knack for refurbishing carriages. The English funeral carriage he brought over after his last excursion to Europe is exquisite."

"He conducts funerals too?"

"No, he just liked the look of it. It's rather ornate and catches the eye. I can't tell you how many times I've watched people stop and lower their heads when he rolls past thinking he's transporting the departed. Mostly he's carrying a few barrels of whiskey."

"He sounds like an interesting man."

"You'll not forget him; I can assure you of that."

The carriage tottered back and forth, while Elora chatted about Rudy's escapades and his contributions to the Railroad.

"Supposedly, Rudy came from humble beginnings in Kentucky. He grew up working in his father's hardware store, which is probably where he learned to fix things."

"How did he end up here?" Maggie asked.

"My brother William moved to Atlanta with his wife years ago to set up his law practice. He met Rudy through a mutual acquaintance at a soiree. Rudy was intrigued by my brother's stories of the Lowcountry. He'd just married Rachell and they decided to honeymoon here. Needless to say, they fell in love with the area. When Rudy discovered our lack of a reliable news source, he sold his Atlanta news enterprise and started *The Home Hearth* here," Elora said with a grin.

The carriage rattled down the drive and stopped in front of a clapboard house with a sweeping front porch. Rudy strode toward them, his relaxed demeanor and sparkling blue eyes putting Maggie at ease. His snowy mustache curled as he approached the carriage.

"Good afternoon, Miss Polk. How are you this fine day?"

"Quite well, thank you. May I introduce my friend, Maggie Milner? She's come to stay with us for a while."

"Nice to meet you, Miss Milner. What do you think of the Lowcountry so far?"

"Positively mesmerizing."

"She'll fit in just fine," he said with a wink.

"Mother asked this to be posted in the next issue," Elora said, handing him the parcel.

"I'll make sure it is," he responded with a bow before heading up the path and into the house.

"He seems quite the gentleman," Maggie said, looking out the window.

"That he is, and much more," Elora giggled. "Remind me later and I'll share some of his more notable escapades. His wife Rachell is delightful and makes the most delectable peach pie. Her painted porcelains are some of the finest in the county."

ONCE THEY RETURNED to Rose Hall, Maggie went about her duties, as did Elora. The sun hovered in the late afternoon sky as she shelved the last jar of salve. Maggie bid Miss Heddy adieu and made her way back to the house to wash up for dinner. The evening meal was uneventful. Dr. Polk told Seth about the new team of horses he'd acquired, while the ladies discussed the latest fashion trends from Paris.

After dinner, Maggie, Seth, and Elora retired to the front parlor. Elora plopped onto the settee beside Seth, leaned against him, a sheepish grin lifting the corners of her mouth. Their comfortable acquaintance made Maggie's chest tighten.

Stop it, she thought. *You're being foolish.*

"Maggie met Rudy today," Elora declared.

"What did you think of him?" Seth asked, his lips curling.

"I liked him," Maggie replied not meeting Seth's gaze.

"Have you told her about the cannon incident?" Seth asked.

Elora shook her head with a chuckle. "Not yet."

"Cannon?" Maggie arched her eyebrows.

"As I said, Rudy can get into some mischief. But Seth tells the story much better than I do," Elora said.

"A few years ago, Rudy acquired a working cannon," Seth began, leaning forward.

"Whatever for?" Maggie asked.

"Because he could," Seth replied. "Rudy doesn't need a reason to do things. Anyway, Mr. Houston had whipped one of his slaves on the courthouse steps for a minor infraction. He did it to send a warning to other slaves of the consequences for disobedience."

Maggie's stomach churned at the thought. "Who are the Houstons, again?"

"The most wretched group of people you'll ever meet. They own Belmont Plantation at the edge of town," Elora said with a scowl.

Seth nodded before returning to the tale. "When Rudy learned what had happened, he decided to have a little fun with them."

"How?"

"He figured it was a good time to test the firing distance of his cannon by placing it at the edge of the Houston's property," Seth replied.

"He fired a cannon at them? Wasn't he concerned he might

injure someone?" Maggie asked, her eyes growing to the size of quarters.

"Rudy is smarter than that," Seth said, a slight smile curling his lips. "He has a way with figures and calculated the distance and powder content needed to hit their cotton barn. He aimed it accordingly, hitting the target without error."

"What happened?" Maggie gasped.

"The cannon ball cut through the roof of the cotton shed, lighting the place up like a candle and destroying an entire season's worth of cotton. Houston was outraged. When he heard who was behind it, he stormed into town and confronted Rudy, blustering about restitution. Rudy just grinned, wrote him a check, and apologized for any inconvenience."

"Mr. Houston didn't challenge him?" Maggie asked.

"That's the benefit of being a newspaper man. Rudy knows a lot of things that go on around here. Most people don't cross him for fear their secrets could be revealed in print," Seth said, bobbing his eyebrows.

"What could possibly intimidate Mr. Houston?"

"The sort of thing he wouldn't want his wife to learn about," Elora giggled, her cheeks coloring.

Seth's eyebrows arched. "Why Miss Polk, you shouldn't speak of such things. Perhaps we should talk to your mother about instilling some decorum to prevent further gossip."

"If my mother were concerned about decorum, she'd surely deny me access to a rascal like you," she said, nudging him with her shoulder.

Maggie watched as the two bantered back and forth, envying their comfortable relationship. Her situation was complicated. Throughout her life, her father had filled her head with dreams of attending University. Instead, she found herself in a foreign country hiding from an abusive uncle, wondering what had become of her father, and longing for a man who belonged to another. Now more than anything, she longed to escape her turmoil and be the one who held Seth's heart.

Once Seth left, Maggie and Elora climbed the winding staircase to the second floor and bid each other goodnight. Maggie nestled beneath the covers, resting her head against the feather pillow, and closed her eyes. But slumber evaded her. She repositioned herself several times, tried counting to one hundred, and even resorted to reciting childhood fairy tales in her head. Despite her exhaustion, Maggie couldn't sleep. She lit the oil lamp and leaned against the headboard to read. An hour later her eyes began to flutter when a strange noise from the first floor caught her attention. Sliding from bed, she grabbed the oil lamp, and ventured downstairs to investigate.

In the quietude of night, Maggie padded across the entryway careful not to wake anyone. An uncomfortable silence shrouded the atmosphere as she ambled across the darkened corridor, a foreboding feeling bristling the hairs on the back of her neck. Gathering all her courage, she turned around only to find the space empty. She quickened her steps, bolting back up the spiral staircase, the lamplight bouncing with each footfall. When she reached the second-floor landing, Maggie heard a rustling sound emanating from below. She leaned over the railing and caught a glimpse of a misty form stirring in the shadows. Her body tensed as she focused her eyes in the direction of the movement but nothing materialized.

It's only shadows, there's nothing there.

She wandered down the hall to her room gently closing the door behind her. Setting the oil lamp on the night table, she crawled into bed, her muscles stiff from the tension. She hadn't been that spooked since she was a wee little thing and feared the banshees would find her hiding beneath the covers. Her father reassured her there was nothing to fear, but being a sensitive child, she'd always felt as if a presence lingered nearby. In an effort to ease her trepidation she used to tell herself it was the spirit of her mother watching over her.

She left the oil lamp burning and snuggled beneath the covers. With her eyes squeezed shut, Maggie ruminated over the work to be done the following day, hoping to chase away the jitters rattling her nerves. Eventually her efforts were successful as reality fogged into slumber.

The following morning after breakfast, Maggie mentioned the previous night's experience to Elora.

"Did you hear a noise last night?" Maggie asked.

"What noise?"

"Never mind," Maggie replied, shaking her head. "I'm sure it was just my imagination,"

"What happened?" Elora sat straighter.

"I heard someone downstairs and went to check, but nothing was there. When I reached the top of the staircase, I could have sworn I saw something move."

Elora chuckled. "That's our ghost. She's harmless."

"You have a ghost roaming through your house at night?"

"All plantation houses have spirits." Elora took another sip of tea as if having a ghost was as normal as breathing.

"So, you're telling me this house is haunted?"

"The South is known for many things, especially its ghosts. Didn't you have spirits in Ireland?"

"Well yes, but it's not something we readily embraced. Ours are rather frightening." Maggie shuddered at the thought of the screeching banshees discussed in Ireland folklore.

"Around here everyone has some sort of ghost. No self-respecting plantation would be without one. It's practically a requirement."

"Do you know the identity of your ghost or is it just legend?"

Placing the cup on the table, Elora leaned forward with eyes blazing. Her voice took on a dramatic flair as she began the tale.

"We don't know much about her except what the coach driver told us. Apparently, the young woman fell ill during her journey south to visit family. By the time the coach arrived, she was unconscious."

"Who was she?"

"We never found out. As I said, she was incoherent when she arrived. The driver knew father was a physician and came here straightaway when the woman's condition grew worse. But father was away that week. We took her in and cared for her but she succumbed to her fever a couple of days later."

"How sad," Maggie sighed.

"We knew nothing about her, not her name or who she was going to visit. We gave her a proper burial in our graveyard, and had Rudy place an ad in the paper but never received a response." Elora sipped her tea.

"How do you know she's the one haunting the place?"

"Who else could it be? Some of the maids have seen her. They describe her as a slender figure in a grayish dress. She's not harmful but will scare the life out of you when you don't expect it."

"Have you ever seen her?" Maggie asked.

"Once. I nearly tumbled down the stairs it frightened me so. She seems harmless so we've adjusted to her presence."

"Do you truly believe it?" Maggie squinted, leery of the tale.

"If I hadn't seen it with my own eyes, I may have been more skeptical. As it is, she's as real to me as you are. You should feel privileged, she doesn't make her presence known to everybody, only the people who call this place home."

Maggie wasn't sure this was the kind of welcome she desired. However, being accepted as part of the family was appealing, even if the acceptance came by way of the spectral sort.

28

Rain fell in torrents making travel precarious, even on plantation grounds. Maggie sat in the bay window listening to the rhythmic staccato of droplets pelting the copper roof in a harmonic summer serenade. Breathlessly, Elora dashed into the room.

"My gracious Elora, what's the matter?"

"Mrs. Reese tripped into the hearth. Her skirt caught fire and she has burns on her left leg. Father is out on another call and she needs immediate attention. Father sent word asking if you'd be willing to help?"

"Of course," Maggie said, rising from her seat.

"Seth will take you in the carriage."

"Why not Hatch?"

"Because Papa wants Seth to escort you."

Maggie's chest tightened. At least she'd be riding inside the carriage and wouldn't have to sit next to him. Her heart palpitated at the thought. She started upstairs to change into something more suitable for the damp weather when Elora grabbed her hand.

"There's something else," Elora declared.

"What?"

"Mrs. Reese is not a gracious lady. She's ill mannered. Always has been."

"I'm sure I'll be fine," Maggie said, starting up the stairs but Elora stopped her again.

"She's trouble, Maggie. Do what's needed and leave." Elora's expression was stern as her eyes locked on Maggie's.

"She can't be all that bad."

"Don't underestimate her. She looks like a sweet old woman but she's meaner than a rattlesnake. When she taught school, she used a ruler to smack the hands of children who sneezed in class."

"Why would she hit a child for sneezing?"

"Because she could." Elora rolled her eyes. "Oh, did I mention she's also the aunt of Curtis and Coyle Houston?"

"The infamous Houstons I've heard so much about?"

"Same ones. That's why I'm telling you to be cautious. She comes across as a kind, helpless old woman but she'll do everything she can to cause trouble, not to mention the problems you'll encounter if her idiot nephews are around. That's why Papa is sending Seth with you. I'd go myself but I have to deliver a notice to Mr. Tindell and father feels you've more experience treating burns."

Maggie nodded and trotted up the winding staircase. After she changed into a work dress, she scurried down the back stairs, grabbed a jar of aloe salve from the shelf, and slipped it into her satchel. Seth burst through the backdoor with water trickling from his hat, his soggy curls soaking the shoulders of his shirt.

"You ready?" he asked breathlessly as the rain thundered against the roof.

"Yes."

They scooted out the back door beneath a waterfall of rain. Seth helped Maggie into the carriage before climbing to the driver's seat. The carriage lunged forward as the horse's hooves sloshed in the gullies created by the downpour. Maggie looked through the window but everything was a blurred mess.

After a harrowing drive where the carriage almost capsized a couple of times, they turned down the long drive to the Houston's place, Belmont Plantation. The lane was masqueraded by storm debris consisting of large branches and mounds of Spanish moss.

Belmont loomed from the watery shadows like a sandcastle rising from the sea with ivy crawling up the tabby walls in spider-like tendrils. The shutters were faded, and two rockers pitched to and fro in the wind gusts. Maggie couldn't tell if it was the unkempt nature of the place or her preconceived notion of the Houstons that made her skin crawl with unease. The structure's uninviting facade mirrored that of her uncle's farm, making her insides jitter at the sight.

Seth helped Maggie from the carriage, the warmth of his hand on her arm easing her discomfort. Escorting her to the front door, he banged the brass knocker, a hollow echo resonating from within. A spindly, colored woman donning a simple black dress and plain white cap greeted them.

"Good afternoon. Dr. Polk sent us to see Mrs. Reese," Seth announced.

"Thank you for comin' so quick. Mrs. Reese be in de back parlor."

The storm encapsulated the entryway in a shadowy darkness lending to the somber atmosphere. They followed the tiny woman to a sumptuously decorated room bedecked with a myriad of paintings, silk curtains, and mahogany furnishings. Trinkets and souvenirs littered shelves and tabletops, alluding to a well-travelled lady. A petite gray-headed woman with pale blue eyes sat in a wing chair with one leg propped on a needlepoint footstool. Elora was correct; her appearance was that of a frail, elderly woman. She seemed harmless enough.

"Mrs. Reese, dese people is here to see you."

"What took you so long? And where is Dr. Polk?" she barked, the scowl on her face wrinkling her eyes and mouth.

"He's tending to another patient," Seth replied, seemingly indignant of her haughty attitude.

"I'm not surprised he's helping some insignificant piece of chaff instead of me. As if I should be neglected for the lower echelon of this community." Looking Maggie up and down, Mrs. Reese scoffed. "This is all Dr. Polk has to offer?"

Maggie was astonished at her condescending demeanor while Seth took it in stride.

"Mrs. Reese, I'm sorry you're unhappy, but Miss Milner is quite capable of dressing the wound."

"I assure you I've had a great deal of experience treating burns," Maggie said, her voice soft, revealing her trepidation.

"I don't know that I want *your kind* touching me."

"My kind?" Maggie tilted her head unsure of Mrs. Reese's meaning.

"You're Irish, are you not?"

"What makes you think that?"

"I'm well-traveled and recognize the hint in your accent," she sneered.

Maggie was dumbfounded. *Be kind,* she thought, *a confrontation will only bring shame to the Polks.*

"My apologies, ma'am. Would you like for me to send someone else?"

"Absolutely not!" she wailed. "I'm in agony and don't wish to wait for another petty subordinate!" She slammed her withered fist on the arm of the chair.

Maggie swallowed hard, conjuring as much compassion as possible. Glancing back at Seth, Maggie noted the grimace masking his normally jovial countenance. She walked across the room and knelt beside her patient to check the extent of the burn.

"Are you clean? You haven't any lice, have you?" Mrs. Reese grumbled.

Before Maggie could respond, Seth spoke up.

"Mrs. Reese, one more derogatory remark and I'll take Miss Milner away and you'll have to wait until Dr. Polk is available. I assure you he'll not be pleased to hear that you treated someone he holds in high regard so poorly."

"Very well. She can treat the wound, but if anything goes awry tell Dr. Polk I'll deal with him in the severest manner," she declared, pursing her lips.

Maggie glanced nervously at Seth who gave a nod of reassurance as she started to lift the woman's petticoats.

"Mr. Daniels, please leave," Mrs. Reese squawked. "I'm not a harlot who wishes to expose her bare flesh to a man with whom she has no connection."

"I'm Miss Milner's escort and intend to stay right here."

"It's alright, Mr. Daniels. A lady must maintain her modesty in these situations," Maggie replied.

Mrs. Reese lifted her chin in triumph as Seth left the room and took a seat in the hallway.

Maggie proceeded to cleanse and dress the wound. Once she completed wrapping the leg, she handed a jar of salve to Mrs. Reese with instructions for its use.

"This should help with the healing and sooth any discomfort or blistering."

"Blistering?" Mrs. Reese exclaimed.

"It's part of the healing process. Clean and redress the wound each morning and again before bed. And keep your leg elevated to avoid any swelling." Maggie flashed a smile hoping to capture Mrs. Reese's approval.

"Clean and dress the wound?" she clamored, sitting a bit straighter. "You don't expect *me* to perform medical procedures? That's what I pay Dr. Polk to do."

"I'm sure one of the servants can help if necessary."

"Humph," she snorted. "As if I'd let a darkie attend to something medical."

"There's no need to fret, it's quite simple if you wish to care for it yourself." Maggie held back her urge to scream at the cruel old woman.

"So you say, but be warned, if any permanent scaring occurs I'll have you locked up for maiming me!"

"If you follow my instructions you should heal without any lasting reminders of the injury," Maggie said as she stood and gathered her things.

"If there *are* any issues it will be due to your incompetence!" she screeched.

"Not if you follow Miss Milner's instructions!" Seth hollered from his seat outside the door.

Maggie bit her lower lip to harness the grin threatening to form at Seth's declaration. Fighting to maintain her serious expression, she placed the jar of salve on the table. Mrs. Reese's lips formed a hard line of disgust as she turned her head away.

Without another word, they left the house. Seth helped Maggie into the carriage, climbed to the top, and started for home. Sunlight shimmered on the puddles as the carriage splashed down the drive. Maggie leaned back against the tufted seat and sighed, glad to be leaving such a wretched place.

The next few days were worrisome for Maggie as she feared Mrs. Reese would lodge some sort of complaint with Dr. Polk. When none came, Maggie decided to check on her patient's progress. She was determined to develop some sort of rapport with Mrs. Reese in case she ever had to treat her again.

Humming as she went, Maggie roamed the wooded path to Belmont. Moss danced in the breezes while tall grasses swayed to the rhythm of marsh life. Despite the vast differences from the Irish landscape, Maggie was falling in love with the Lowcountry. It's mystique and general splendor soothed her soul.

Much to her relief, Maggie found Mrs. Reese rocking on the front verandah, taking in the fresh air.

"Good morning, Mrs. Reese. I've come to check on your progress," Maggie said, scampering up the stairs.

A smile creased the old woman's visage, easing Maggie's trepidation. She seemed much kinder this time. Perhaps her ill temperament on the previous visit had been a result of the pain.

"Dr. Polk better not bill me for this visit. I didn't request it," she scowled, her smile fading, letting Maggie know it was all a ruse.

"I came of my own volition to check on you," Maggie replied; regret churning in her stomach over the decision to return.

"Ah, doubting your capabilities. Just as I suspected, you *are* incompetent."

Maggie sucked in her lip in an effort to suppress the sharp retort clamoring to escape.

"I've brought another balm to help reduce scarring. Apply it three times daily for the next four weeks," Maggie said, digging the jar from her satchel.

Mrs. Reese looked away when Maggie offered the container. Realizing Mrs. Reese wasn't going to accept it, she set it on the ground by her rocker and stepped back.

"What're you waiting for?" Mrs. Reese barked.

"Nothing," Maggie muttered. "I hope you have a pleasant day."

"I will once *you* leave."

Mrs. Reese's antipathy pierced Maggie with the searing pain of a sword. At that moment, she recognized there was no point trying to communicate with such a bitter, narrow-minded old woman.

"I'm sorry to have troubled you ma'am."

With a quick curtsey, Maggie descended the brick steps,

and hurried down the lane, thankful she'd put forth an effort even if it didn't soften Mrs. Reese's attitude.

As Maggie disappeared across the yard, Mrs. Reese tossed the jar of salve into the bushes. "Wretched Irish tart."

MAGGIE MADE her way down the dirt path, relieved to be done with that horrible woman. Traipsing through the woods, she basked in the glorious beauty of the day to the tune of birdsong and whispering trees. She began humming a favorite Irish melody when the sound of footsteps joined the woodland symphony. All of a sudden, a feeling of unease fingered her spine as if a predator was ready to pounce. It was the same sensation she used to get whenever her uncle entered a room.

She quickened her pace but the footsteps matched her speed. Her heart rate doubled as she broke into a jog, sunrays flashing through the dense canopy of trees. The toe of her boot caught on a root, catapulting her to the ground. Maggie gasped when a hand reached down and helped her up.

"Thank you," she said, brushing debris from her skirt. She looked at the young man who'd come to her aid. Although clean-shaven, he had a menacing appearance with a broad girth and a crooked smile.

"Didn't mean to startle you," he said, his gaze like that of a hungry tiger. "Saw you leave our house and wanted to make sure you made it through the woods safely. It can be dangerous out here for a woman." His smile broadened, revealing a couple of missing teeth.

Maggie exhaled. "You're related to Mrs. Reese?"

"I'm her nephew, Coyle," he replied, his eyes traveling up and down her body.

"I appreciate your concern but I'm on my way to see another patient," she announced, shocked at the ease with which the lie flowed from her lips. Something in his demeanor evoked a strong need to get away. Maggie gave a nod and as she turned, he grabbed her arm with such force she yelped.

"Is that anyway to respond when a gentleman offers his assistance?" he purred, his eyes narrowing into slits.

At that moment, Maggie recognized the seriousness of her predicament. Her palms moistened as panic pounded against her ribcage.

"I really must be on my way. They're expecting me and I'm already running late." She attempted to extract her arm from his clutch but his grip tightened with the strength of a boa constrictor.

"I think a little appreciation for my chivalry is due," he said, stepping closer.

Maggie tried to pull away but his hold on her arm was firm, preventing her from wrenching free. His other hand grabbed her chin and jerked it toward his face as he lowered his lips toward hers, his foul breath hot against her skin. Paralyzed by panic, she felt her knees begin to falter when a gunshot shattered the quietude. Coyle lurched backwards, releasing her arm and falling to the ground.

"Maggie?" Seth called out as Coyle scrambled to his feet.

"Seth, I'm so glad to see you," she replied, trying to steady her quavering voice.

Dismounting, he walked over to them. "What's going on here?" he asked, his tone stern.

"Just offering to escort this lovely lady to her destination as any good gentleman would do," Coyle responded, straightening his shirt and regaining his balance. He altered his expression and raised his eyebrows in what appeared to be an attempt at chivalry.

"No need. I'm her escort," Seth replied, draping his arm around Maggie's shoulders.

A twinge of electricity surged through her body at his touch.

"So, I see," Coyle sneered. Without another word, he turned and disappeared into the woods.

"Are you alright?" Seth asked, his blue eyes narrowing as they met her gaze.

Maggie nodded, unable to form words for fear she might cry instead. Her skin crawled where Coyle had touched her. Now that she'd encountered him, she understood why he had such an unfavorable reputation.

"Let's go home," Seth said, helping Maggie onto the saddle before swinging up behind her.

Her body melted against his as Phantom started toward Rose Hall, his gait as smooth as silk. Thankfully, Seth didn't question why she was in the woods near Belmont as they rode along in silence.

When they arrived at Rose Hall, Elora was on the front porch rocking in one of the rockers. Seth vaulted to the ground and helped Maggie dismount.

"Maggie, where have you been?" Elora asked. "I was worried about you."

"I went to check on someone," she mumbled, diverting her gaze.

Elora stood, tilted her head, and rested her hands on her hips. "Please tell me you didn't go see Mrs. Reese."

"I wanted to make sure she was alright," Maggie replied, her cheeks coloring. "I thought if I put forth an effort..."

"What were you thinking? I already told you, there's no reasoning with her. She's sick to the core of her soul. Stay away from her, Maggie. She's trouble."

Turning to Seth, Elora scowled. "How could you let her go there? You know how horrid that woman can be."

Before Seth could respond, Maggie chimed in. "He didn't know I was going. He found me in the woods after I'd lost my way."

"I'm just thankful I was there to help," he said stiffly. "If you ladies will excuse me." Seth remounted Phantom and trotted off without another word.

Seth's abrupt departure rattled Maggie, making her question whether she'd said something wrong. "I hope I didn't offend him."

"Why would you think such a thing?" Elora asked as Maggie took a seat beside her.

Maggie blew out a breath as she rocked. "I had a little incident with Coyle Houston."

Elora stopped rocking, her posture straightening. "What sort of incident?"

"He got fresh with me. But Seth rode up before anything serious happened." Chills bumped across Maggie's skin as she considered what could have occurred. "Nevertheless, I think I may have upset Seth. I hope he didn't think I instigated the situation."

"You didn't upset him, Coyle did. He knows you'd never do something so unseemly," Elora replied, grasping Maggie's hand. "Curtis and Coyle have a reputation for taking advantage of women. This isn't the first time Seth has had to intervene on a lady's behalf."

"Why doesn't someone stop them?"

"Because the Houston's have a lot of power and influence in this area. They instill fear in most, and pay off the rest. Father is one of the few people they don't cross. With all of Curtis and Coyle's bumbling acts and injuries, they can't afford to offend my father. They need his medical services," Elora said, the right side of her mouth curling.

29

The next morning, Mrs. Polk sent for Maggie and Elora. The girls entered the room where Mrs. Polk spoke in hushed tones to a curvy, well-dressed woman whose eyes were swollen from sorrow.

"Maggie, I want you to meet one of my oldest and dearest friends, Mrs. Elaine Bartlett. Elaine, this is Maggie Milner, she's come to stay with us for a while."

"It's nice to meet you," Maggie responded with a curtsey.

"Likewise," Mrs. Bartlett sniffled.

Elora leaned over and kissed the cheek of her mother's friend. "It's good to see you, Mrs. Bartlett."

"My goodness Elora, you get prettier every time I see you," she replied, squeezing Elora's hand. "The ladies at church are still raving about the hymn you sang last Sunday. You have the voice of an angel."

"Thank you, Mrs. Bartlett," she replied, her cheeks coloring as she took a seat next to Maggie.

"Girls, I asked you here because Mrs. Bartlett needs our assistance with a delicate matter. What she's about to share is not to be repeated. Understood?"

Both girls nodded.

"Go ahead Elaine."

Wringing her hankie into a twisted wad of linen, Mrs. Bartlett spoke.

"I've come to ask you to help my maid, Celia, and her family. My husband, George, has owned Celia since she was an adolescent. As much as I love him, we have our differences. He believes slavery to be an acceptable practice, whilst I feel differently. No one should own another person. It's not right.

"Years ago, in an effort to appease me, he promised to free our slaves when we died. Since I haven't the authority to release them, I took comfort knowing they'd be free someday. Celia is so dear to me. She's more family to me than my own offspring, and a much kinder soul.

"Lately George has been on edge and short tempered. I did a bit of prying and discovered that he's been gambling and his debts are rather substantial. When the money ran out, he used our property as collateral. He has two options for redemption, parcel off the farm or sell the slaves."

Mrs. Bartlett took in a deep breath before continuing.

"He won't part with the land. Instead, he's decided to sell some of the slaves, starting with our beloved Celia and her family. He means to separate them because it will bring a higher price!" The wadded hankie made its way to her lips, masking a sob. "I can't allow this transaction to take place."

"What do you intend to do?" Mrs. Polk asked.

"I want to send Celia and her family north. I've heard there are ways to do this but haven't any idea where to begin. I didn't' know where else to turn. You're my dearest friend, Diane. Even when we were children, you always knew what to do."

"I'm not sure how I can help but I'll certainly try. I think it's best we all agree not to share this with anyone outside this room, even Dr. Polk."

Both girls nodded.

"Mr. Bartlett left for business in Charleston this morning. He'll be gone for at least a week," Mrs. Bartlett muttered.

Mrs. Polk ruminated for a moment before turning to her best friend. "I cannot impress upon you the seriousness of this endeavor and your need to keep it a secret, even from your sister."

Mrs. Bartlett's chest heaved as she glanced out the window.

"I need your assurance on this, Elaine. We could all hang for helping slaves run away."

"I promise I'll never breath a word of it to another living soul," she said softly.

Mrs. Polk grasped her friend's hand. "Make plans to bring Celia and her family here this evening."

"What do you intend to do?"

"I'll figure something out. I have the girls to help me," she smiled knowingly at Elora and Maggie.

"Alright," she sighed. "I should get back to the house and tell Celia to ready her family."

She bid the girls goodbye and followed Mrs. Polk from the room. Maggie and Elora gazed out the window, watching Mrs. Bartlett climb into her carriage and careen down the drive.

"Mother, is it safe for Mrs. Bartlett to know what we do?" Elora asked as soon as her mother returned to the parlor.

"She has no idea what goes on here."

"But we're helping her free her slaves."

"She came to me in shambles over what was happening with Celia and asked if I would help. Elaine is as dear to me as a sister and I couldn't say no, especially on a subject such as this," she said. "I told her I'd need some help and convinced her that you two would be willing participants. She's terrified of being caught but more frightened of what will happen to Celia. I dare say she loves her more than her own sons."

"What will we do once she brings them here?" Elora asked.

"I'll tell her that I'm going to drive them to the next county so they can make their way north on their own."

"Are you really not going to tell father?"

"Of course, I'll tell him but I couldn't let her know that," Mrs. Polk replied. "She believes this scheme is between the three of us and I intend to keep it that way. We'll make arrangements for Celia's family to travel to Oak Point and from there they'll be conducted north."

"What can we do to help?" Maggie asked.

"I have a list of items we need to pack for their journey. If you girls could gather those things, it would be a great help."

A feeling of unease slithered across Maggie's skin as if the scenario was bound to fail. Regardless of her doubts, Maggie was determined to do her duty and help in any manner possible.

NIGHTFALL BROUGHT the clattering of wagon wheels to the back of the mansion, announcing Mrs. Bartlett's arrival. Mrs. Polk, Elora, and Maggie met them at the back of the house with the items they'd prepared for the journey.

Celia and her husband disembarked, grabbing their children and a few belongings.

"I'll miss you Celia," Mrs. Bartlett said, clasping the young woman's hand.

"I be missing you too, Miss Elaine. You bin awful good to me."

The two embraced as Celia's husband, Jonah, stood by, his countenance as rigid as a stone wall.

"Don't you want to say goodbye?" Celia whispered to him.

"Gots nothing to say to nobody who be holding my family in bondage."

"But she freeing us," Celia said, tears streaking down her

cheeks. "She ain't got no say in dese things. She a woman and been like a mother to me."

"Still don't make it right."

Celia turned back to Mrs. Bartlett. "Thank you for dis. I pray God blesses you."

Mrs. Bartlett nodded; her words choked by the sorrow of saying goodbye to one of the most beloved people in her life.

Celia and her family waited by the river's edge with Elora and Maggie while Mrs. Polk walked Elaine back to her wagon, their voices carrying on the night breezes.

"I know how much you love Celia. You're giving her the greatest gift possible, her freedom," Mrs. Polk said, draping her arm about her friend's shoulders.

"Thank you for your help. When George returns, I know he'll search for them. At least they'll be far from here. I only hope Celia will be happy wherever she ends up." Wiping a tear from her cheek, Mrs. Bartlett gave a weak smile. "I'd better get back to the farm."

"Would you like me to send someone with you? You shouldn't travel alone at night."

"Nonsense, I've been traveling these trails for more than forty years. I might not be able to see as well as I did, but I can find my way through these woods blindfolded."

"Please be careful. Come for tea next Tuesday?"

"That sounds lovely," she responded. Tears flooded her eyes as she glanced back at Celia before climbing to the wagon seat. She clicked the horses into action and disappeared into the darkness.

Maggie watched Mrs. Bartlett drive out of sight, a sense of dread lingering in her chest. The plan had worked flawlessly thus far, but she knew there was a long way to go before Celia's family would be safe. Mrs. Polk rejoined the group.

"Celia, Mr. Daniels will be here in a moment to transport your family to Oak Point Plantation outside of Charleston.

Arrangements have been made for you to travel by ship to a northern port. You'll be traveling with the ship's cargo so it won't be comfortable but the end result will be worth it." Mrs. Polk said. "When you reach Philadelphia a gentleman by the name of Stills will meet you. He'll provide transport to a free state with new names for you and your family,"

"Thank you, Mrs. Polk. We's thankful you be doin' all dis for us," Celia replied before glancing at her husband who gave a nod.

The clattering of wagon wheels and hoof beats broke through the stillness of the night as Seth drove up.

"You all ready?" he asked.

"Yes sir, we is," Jonah replied.

Seth pulled back a tarp in the bed of the wagon revealing piles of straw. "I apologize for the uncomfortable accommodations but it's the only way to travel safely. I need you to hide in the straw and I'll cover it with the tarp."

Celia and Jonah looked at their children whose eyes were wide with fear. They helped the kids into the back of the wagon and joined them, camouflaging themselves beneath the straw. Once they were hidden, Seth pulled the tarp across the wagon and climbed onto the bench seat. With a tip of his hat, he smiled before launching the horses forward, rattling into the night.

"I'm surprised they can travel by ship," Maggie commented, watching the wagon disintegrate into the darkness.

"We have several captains who stow passengers for an extra fee," Mrs. Polk said.

"I hope they make it," Maggie muttered.

"As do I," she replied.

30

Several days had passed since the Bartlett slaves set off on the road to freedom, and thus far no word of capture had been reported. Of course, their journey would be a long one fraught with danger and no guarantee of success. After an extremely busy day, Maggie and Elora relaxed on the front porch. Spanish moss waltzed with the breezes against a jewel-toned backdrop as evening set in. The night promised to be uneventful as no passengers were expected.

"This is a lovely end to a tiresome but productive day," Maggie said, swaying in the wooden rocker, her russet locks cascading across her shoulders. "I managed to make several batches of salve for mosquito bites as well as ointment for sore muscles. I might need some of it myself. My shoulders are aching."

"Pretty bad when you have to use your own concoction on sore muscles that you got from creating it," Elora chuckled as the rungs of her rocker creaked against the porch floor.

They rocked steadily to the serenade of cicadas as twilight painted its farewell in shades of purple and orange across the horizon. Hoof beats pounded down the lane, interrupting the symphony of nightfall.

Elora rose as Seth dismounted and strode up the brick walkway.

"Your timing is perfect," Elora called out. "Won't you join us?"

Seth sprinted up the brick stairs, his hair wild from riding.

"Is your father at home?"

"He's in his office. What's the matter?"

Seth rushed through the double front doors. "We've got shadows in the moss," he called out.

Maggie looked at Elora. "Shadows?"

"Escapees who have set out on their own without benefit of the Railroad."

Moments later, Seth reappeared with Dr. Polk.

"Ladies, we have a serious situation. Five children are hiding in the marsh at the edge of our property."

"Children? How were they able to get here on their own?" Elora asked.

"They didn't start that way," Seth replied. "They were running with their mother who died last night. I found them when I went down to check the crab pots behind my cottage."

"How are we to send five children on their way with no adult supervision?" Maggie asked, flabbergasted at the idea of children making the journey without adult protection.

"We're making arrangements but it will be a few hours before we can get everything in place. Our only hope is that the marsh can mask their scent from the hunters' dogs until we get them somewhere safe."

"Hunters are searching for them?"

"That's what the eldest told me after I convinced them I wasn't going to hurt them," Seth replied.

"We can't expect children to hide quietly in the marsh for hours," Elora declared.

"We'll do the best we can. If you ladies would help Miss Olive prepare some food, Seth is going to ride out and deter anyone who may be searching for them."

Maggie and Elora hurried to Miss Olive's cabin where they found her rushing about the kitchen preparing biscuits and ham for the little ones. They fell into a graceful rhythm alongside her, packing a basket of food, a jug of clean water, and some clothes.

"We'll take these for the littlest ones," Miss Olive said, pulling three scrap dolls from the cupboard and adding them to the basket. "They'll be needing something to comfort 'em."

Once everything was packed, Maggie, Elora, and Miss Olive rushed along the edge of the marsh beneath a crescent moon. Nearing the spot that Seth had indicated, they looked around to ensure no one was about before making their way through the thick underbrush to the river's edge. As the tree branches parted, Maggie caught a glimpse of movement and made her way closer. She slipped through a cluster of moss-laden oaks, where she found the children wide eyed with fear, yet silent as death. Surprisingly, they hadn't made a sound, even the youngest, who looked to be no more than three years old.

"It's ok, we're here to help you," she said reassuringly.

The oldest nodded, clutching the toddler a bit tighter. The little girl struggled to break free from her sister's grasp as Miss Olive handed out the dolls.

"My name is Maggie and this is Elora and Miss Olive."

"I's Minnie and dis here my brothers Jack and Charlie, and my sisters Sissy and Little Eliza."

Poor Sissy looked as if she was about to faint, her eyes darting about at every little sound.

"What's the matter?" Maggie asked.

"She be scared of monsters," Minnie whispered.

"What monsters?"

"Mama tell us we have to stay quiet or de moss monsters

come and take us back to de massa," Sissy said, her lips quivering.

Maggie sat down with them as Elora and Miss Olive stood nearby.

"There's nothing to fear," Maggie replied. "You're safe here."

"But dere be monsters in de marshes. I see dem moving," one of the boys responded.

"There are no monsters, I promise."

The marsh was teeming with bugs and critters while the water and trees made eerie noises leading vivid imaginations astray. Maggie was amazed at the self-discipline exhibited by such young children. Minnie appeared to be about twelve although her resolve was more like that of a thirty-year old. Their fear was palpable, breaking Maggie's heart. Her need to scoop them up and protect them was strong. Fireflies twinkled against the velvety backdrop of the night sky, sparking an idea. She remembered a tale her father used to tell when she was afraid of the dark. She'd have to make a few alterations to the story, but hoped it would lessen their discomfort.

"Do you see those itty-bitty lights flashing over the water's edge?" Maggie asked, pointing to the blinking points of light.

"Dem be fireflies, Miss," Minnie said proudly.

"Actually, they're fairies. Small creatures with beady eyes and shimmering wings that flit about in the night sky."

"How you know dis?" Charlie asked, cocking his head.

"Because I know the legend. Long ago, a terrible ogre prowled the countryside. He liked to steal little children and eat them for supper. No matter how strong the lock on the door, the mean old ogre would slip through the window after dark and take the children as they slept."

"What be an ogre, Miss?" Jack asked.

"It's a horrible creature with sagging skin and sharp teeth."

"Dere be ogres in de marshes?" Sissy asked, her eyes wide as she scanned her surroundings.

"Not at all, we have fairies to keep them away."

"Oh," she nodded, apparently not convinced that small winged creatures flying about could keep them safe from a slovenly monster that feasted on children.

"Hush! Let her tell de story 'fore you go interruptin' again." Charlie scolded.

"The parents in the village didn't know what to do so they called upon the fairies. Their pleas touched the fairies' hearts and they agreed to help them. After nightfall, beneath a shadowy crescent moon, the fairies spun locks of their long wavy hair into magic moss. They flew above the treetops, lacing the shimmering strands through the branches. Fairy hair is delicate to the touch, but strong as iron.

"Later that night, the ogre crawled through one of the cottage windows, snatched a sleeping child from his bed, and made his way to the forest nearby. The moss was translucent in the light of the moon and he became entangled in the wiry tufts. The little fairies twinkled in the sky as they watched him fight to free himself. But the harder he fought, the more entangled he became, causing him to drop the slumbering child. The fairies scooped up the child and carried him home."

"What happened to de ogre?" Minnie asked.

"Hate oozed from his fangs as he fought to break free. Little did he know that hate doesn't mingle well with fairy magic, causing the strands to get tighter and tighter until he turned to dust. And ever since, fairy moss hangs from the trees to protect children from nasty old ogres."

"Is dis fur true?" Jack asked, scrunching up his face.

"Of course."

"Is de ogre we massa?" Sissy queried.

"Yes, my dear."

"And de moss keep us safe from de massa?" Charley asked.

"That's why you're hiding here. Remember, you're safer in the moss."

"You talk funny," Minnie said.

"Do I?"

"Where you from?" she asked.

"A faraway place called Ireland."

"Is it a magic place?" Sissy said, her eyes widening.

"Yes, it is," Maggie replied. Moisture gathered in her eyes at the memory of home.

"With lots of fairies?"

Maggie chuckled. "Yes, with lots of fairies. Enough questions, you all need to eat something." Maggie helped Miss Olive distribute the biscuits and ham while Elora offered the jug of water. The children devoured every morsel as if they hadn't eaten in days.

"Miss Maggie, can you stay wid us?" Minnie asked, her eyes pleading.

"I suppose I can stay until the wagon arrives."

"Can you tell us more stories of de fairy land you comes from?" Jack asked, sitting straighter.

"Yes, I'll tell you more."

In the quietude of night, a soft breeze rustled through the trees while Maggie filled their heads with legends from the rolling hills of the Irish countryside. Once the tales ended and the bellies of the children were filled, Maggie started singing an old Irish lullaby. Minnie squirmed beneath little Eliza's weight as the toddler shifted in her sister's arms.

"Eliza, why don't you sit in my lap for a while?" Maggie suggested.

Her pudgy little hands reached for Maggie, who scooped the toddler into her lap. Minnie's relief was apparent as she exhaled and slumped against a tree trunk.

Maggie hummed the lullaby while rocking Eliza, her tiny hand spinning a strand of Maggie's red hair between her fingers. The others gathered round Maggie like kittens to their mother. As the night wore on, the moon shifted and the sound of hoof beats and wagon wheels caught Maggie's attention.

A wagon emerged from the shadowy darkness and halted at the edge of the marsh. Rising stiffly, Maggie cradled Eliza and whispered to Minnie to gather her siblings and get into the wagon. Elora helped them into the bed of the cart and covered them with straw, instructing them to stay hidden. Once they were settled, Seth issued another warning.

"I know it's uncomfortable, but I need you to stay quiet. We don't want the bad men to find you."

A muffled, "Yes sir" was heard from under the hay.

Still holding a slumbering Eliza, Maggie looked at Seth with concern.

"We can't expect her to travel like this. She's too young and doesn't understand that she needs to stay silent."

"We don't have a choice. She'll have to stay quiet," Seth replied. "If she carries on, we risk being discovered."

"Perhaps she could keep still if her mother were here, but not like this," Maggie said.

Eliza's eyes fluttered and she began to whine when Maggie handed her to Minnie.

"Miss Maggie, can you come wid us?" Minnie pleaded.

"No, my darling."

"Why?" Minnie asked, trying to comfort Eliza who was now squirming against her grasp.

Looking at Seth, Maggie gave a questioning glance.

"I suppose there's no harm in your coming along, especially if it keeps her quiet."

"Be safe," Elora said, giving Maggie a quick hug.

Careful not to sit upon the buried children, Maggie settled in the tufts of hay with Eliza in her arms as the wagon lunged forward into the darkness.

Because of the danger, they were forced to travel back roads, which were poorly kept. Bouncing and jostling made the journey more uncomfortable, especially for the children who stirred and squirmed in the itchy discomfort. It hurt Maggie to see them like this, but it was the only way to get them to safety.

Several hours later, they arrived at a thickly wooded expanse along the marsh's edge. Eliza was still slumbering in Maggie's arms.

"This is where we're leaving them?" Maggie asked.

"It's where we're meeting the transport." Seth responded, alighting from the wagon bench.

Holding out his arms, he took Eliza and waited for Maggie to disembark before handing the child back to her. The other children remained in the wagon. As if understanding the gravity of their situation, they didn't question where they were or if they could get out.

Moments later, a dim light bounced in tandem with wagon wheels.

"Good evening," a gruff voice called out.

Maggie watched as Seth walked over and spoke to the man in hushed tones. Seth returned and called for the children to climb down from the wagon. Like sprouts after a spring rain, each of their little heads bobbed from beneath the layers of straw. Amazingly, the children followed Seth without hesitation. Maggie handed Eliza to Minnie.

"Thank you, Miss. We's glad for all you done for us," Minnie said with a broad smile.

Maggie leaned over and whispered.

"May you have warm words on a cold evening, a full moon on a dark night, and a smooth road to your dreams."

"Where you hear dat?" Minnie asked.

"It's something my father used to say to me. It's a blessing of sorts."

Minnie smiled as she joined her siblings at the other wagon. Once the children were settled, the wagon rattled away. Maggie's chest tightened at their predicament. The road ahead would be treacherous for these orphans, with only the shadows to shelter them.

Seth helped Maggie to the bench seat, her skin warming at his touch. He climbed up next to her and sent the horses forward.

"What are the chances of five orphans making it to safety?" Maggie asked, wanting reassurance that the children would be safe.

"Depends upon how badly the hunters want to capture them. Most of the Underground Railroad conductors are pretty creative in situations like this and will find a way to transport them as stealthily as possible."

They traveled back in silence; Maggie's mind too distracted by the fate of the children to worry about how close she was to Seth. She envied his ability to switch his emotions on and off, and wondered if she'd ever be able to do the same. Her arms still felt the weight of little Eliza's slumbering figure, bringing a tear to her eye. She said a silent prayer that the five orphans would be successful in their journey to freedom.

31

Maggie arose the following morning feeling good about what had transpired the night before, although she wondered if the children would make it to their destination without interference. She went about her daily duties with Miss Heddy, humming as she mixed a liniment for sore muscles. After shelving the last jar, Maggie hung her apron on the hook and started back to the house.

She slipped through the side door and heard Mrs. Polk chatting with someone in the ladies' parlor. *Elora and Mrs. Polk must be having tea*, Maggie thought, a grin lifting her lips.

Teatime was a favored respite on the rare days when she finished her work early. Retrieving a cup and saucer from the china cabinet in the dining room, she padded toward the ladies' parlor. As she approached, she realized the other voice in the room was not Elora, but Mrs. Polk's friend, Mrs. Bartlett. Not wanting to interrupt, Maggie started to turn away when Mrs. Bartlett's words caught her attention.

"It's even worse than I thought," Mrs. Bartlett declared. "My husband's *business* trip was actually another card game with a group of men from Pennsylvania. His losses were substantial. Since he hadn't the means to pay, one of the men accompanied him back to the house to collect."

"What did this man intend on getting?" Mrs. Polk asked.

"My Celia," Mrs. Bartlett's voice cracked. "He promised this Mr. Stevenson he could take her in payment for his debt. The scoundrel!"

At the mention of her uncle's name, Maggie's heart seized and her body tensed.

"Mr. Stevenson is a brute, ordering me around as if I were a servant. He has no manners whatsoever, and he won't leave until he has something of value. Even worse, once George realized Celia and her family were gone, he enlisted the services of Houston and Blakely to go after them. I'm terrified of the consequences should they be found," Mrs. Bartlett sobbed.

The cup dropped from Maggie's hand, shattering to the floor as her knees gave out. Mrs. Polk rushed to the hall where Maggie stooped, hurriedly plucking up shards of glass.

"I'm so sorry about the cup, I'll clean it up, I promise, I'm so sorry, I really didn't mean to..." Maggie prattled, her body trembling.

Mrs. Polk patted Maggie's shoulder while Mrs. Bartlett looked on from the doorway.

"My dear, it's only a cup, there's no need to fret."

Maggie's eyes were wild as she stared at Mrs. Polk, revealing the terror racing through her body.

"Clara," Mrs. Polk called out, "I need your help!"

Within seconds, Clara appeared. "What can I do ma'am?"

"Please clean up this glass and bring Miss Milner a shot of brandy. I fear she's had a shock."

"Yes ma'am," Clara replied, hurrying down the hall.

Mrs. Polk helped Maggie from the floor, guiding her to the settee.

Mrs. Bartlett touched her best friend's shoulder. "I'd better get back before George gives away everything in the house." Then looking at Maggie with the kindness of a mother, she caressed her flushed cheek. "My poor girl, whatever has upset you, I pray you find peace."

"I didn't mean to interrupt. Please don't leave on my account," Maggie said, her voice quaking.

"Don't be silly, our conversation was finished." Mrs. Bartlett gave a nod to Mrs. Polk and sashayed from the room.

Mrs. Polk sat next to Maggie, grasping her trembling hand. "Now tell me what has you in such a state."

"I didn't mean to eavesdrop, but I overheard you speaking with Mrs. Bartlett about the guest in her home."

"There's no need to worry. Celia and her family are far from here by now. Houston and his companions aren't likely to discover their location, especially with those dimwitted sons of his," Mrs. Polk said reassuringly.

"That isn't what upset me." Maggie gulped air between sobs. "The man from Pennsylvania, did she say his name was Stevenson?"

"She did."

Maggie gasped, "That's my uncle." Her tears flowed freely, and her entire body shook as Mrs. Polk held her close in an effort to calm her.

Clara entered and placed a glass of brandy on the table. "May I be of assistance?"

"Please send for Dr. Polk."

Moments later the doctor arrived, taking a seat on the chair nearest his wife.

"I'm so sorry to make such a fuss," Maggie muttered, wiping her eyes with the back of her hands.

"Drink this, it'll help settle your nerves and then we can discuss the situation," Mrs. Polk said, handing her the glass of brandy.

Maggie emptied the contents, coughing as she handed the glass back to Mrs. Polk.

Dr. Polk studied Maggie, waiting for her to settle before speaking. "What's going on?" he finally asked.

"I overheard Mrs. Bartlett say something about a man from Pennsylvania by the name of Stevenson who's staying at their house."

"And you know this man?"

"He's my uncle," Maggie said, her body shaking violently.

Dr. Polk's eyebrows furrowed as he rubbed his beard.

"Are you certain?"

Maggie nodded, tears trickling across her flushed cheeks. "I've got to leave. If he finds me...."

The doctor leaned forward and took Maggie's hands. "Listen to me. I need you to stay calm and trust me to handle things. Can you do that?"

Maggie nodded, sucking in a sob.

"Go upstairs and lie down for a bit. I've got an idea, but I'll need to make a few inquiries. When you come down to supper, I should have some answers. Most importantly, I need you to remain inside."

Maggie's legs wobbled as she stood and traipsed to the doorway, her ears ringing. Turning back, she muttered, "Thank you both. I'm sorry to have caused so much trouble."

"I'll not hear another apology out of you. You're part of our family and we adore you," Mrs. Polk replied sternly.

"Yes ma'am," Maggie said, ducking her head.

Maggie trudged up the stairs feeling as if she'd run a hundred miles, her legs heavy and her chest tight. All she wanted was to feel her Da's arms around her and hear his baritone voice whisper that all would be well. "Where are you Da?" she whispered as she slipped into her room and flung herself onto the bed. Whether it was the shock of the day's events or the brandy, she could barely hold her eyes open. Curling into a fetal position beneath the covers, she fell asleep as soon as her head touched the pillow.

AFTER SUPPER, Dr. Polk invited Maggie and Seth to join him in his office. The little she'd eaten rumbled around her stomach. Dr. Polk closed the door and motioned for her to take a seat.

"I've come up with a plan but I need you to seriously consider it before committing."

Maggie nodded, fresh tears clinging to her lashes. She took in a deep breath, trying to calm her nerves. The last thing she wanted was to appear weak in front of Seth.

"Seth is leaving on a mission to Ohio day after tomorrow. I think it would be prudent for you to accompany him."

A sob escaped her lips. She was being sent to another family.

"Whom will I be living with?" she gasped.

"You're only helping to transport escapees. Once they're safe with Mr. Coffin in Ohio, you and Seth will return."

Maggie glanced back and forth between the two of them, trepidation squeezing her lungs. Her mouth was dry as she spoke. "My most complex mission so far was with Miss Taylor, and that was only to deliver papers and money, not people. This one seems much more intense, and dangerous. Do you truly feel I'm ready for something of this magnitude?"

"I believe you are," Dr. Polk replied. "Keep in mind, this will also get you away from your uncle."

"Maggie, everything will be alright," Seth said gently, reaching for her hand.

"How can you say that?" she hollered, recoiling from his touch. "I'll never be free of that wretched man!"

She buried her face in her hands, her body quivering as she cried.

"We'll take care of the situation so he never searches for you again," Dr. Polk said.

"He won't stop until he kills me," she murmured, swiping the tears from her face.

"Not when we explain that you're already dead."

"What?" Maggie mumbled, sitting straighter.

"We'll pay a visit to the Bartlett's plantation and hopefully make contact with Mr. Stevenson. I'll broach the subject of unwelcome guests and say a young woman arrived by stagecoach with a raging fever. Despite our efforts, she succumbed to the illness without a clue as to her identity or that of her family."

"That sounds like the story…."

"Of our own ghostly lady, yes. It's time we resurrected her existence to save a life," Dr. Polk said.

The idea sounded like something out of a novel but crazy enough to work. Maggie's heart began to steady and her breathing slowed.

"You really believe this will work?"

"Perhaps. Nevertheless, until you leave, I need you to stay inside," Dr. Polk replied. "The less visible you are, the safer you'll be."

"But I need to help with preparations."

"We can handle all of that," he replied in a tone that warned not to dispute anything further.

Maggie sighed heavily, her shoulders slumping.

"Get some rest. This won't be an easy mission," Dr. Polk said.

She glanced at Seth whose steely eyes cut through her terror straight to her heart. The determination in his gaze dissolved the fear holding her hostage. She inhaled deeply. If she could be rid of her uncle forever, she could live in safety. Although the trip ahead was daunting, she was motivated to get away. The sooner they completed the mission, the sooner she could return unfettered by the manacles of her uncle's wrath.

Elora waited in the corridor outside her father's office when Maggie emerged.

"Want to talk about it?" she asked, looping her arm through Maggie's.

Maggie nodded, smiling weakly. "Come with me. I need to pack."

The two plodded up the back stairs to Maggie's room where she sorted through dresses and undergarments.

"It's only temporary," Elora whispered, plunking onto the bed. Her eyes glistened, betraying the wave of emotions swirling through her chest.

"I know." Tears stung the back of Maggie's eyes, threatening to flood her cheeks once more. "You know about the plan?"

"Father told me earlier. He wanted to finalize everything before speaking with you."

Maggie placed several items in a small travel bag. She stopped abruptly and looked toward the window. "I can't stand the thought of leaving again. I love you all and the work I've been doing here has been the most meaningful of my life."

"You're still doing the work," Elora said, reaching for Maggie's hand and giving it a squeeze.

"It feels like this is more about me than the escapees. I loathe my uncle. He's destroyed everything I've ever held dear and continues to do so. I'm beginning to believe I'll never escape him!" she declared, her eyes blazing.

"You're absolutely correct. This is about you. Your safety is just as important as those you're helping. There's nothing wrong with that."

"What if something goes wrong? What if I lose my nerve or my uncle doesn't believe your father? Then what? The passengers could be captured because of *me*."

"Seth will be nearby, the transport will be a success, and

you'll be too preoccupied with the safety of the passengers to think about your uncle."

Elora stood and embraced Maggie.

"I know it's frightening but all will be well. When the escapees are safe and your uncle gives up his search, you can come home."

Pulling back from Elora, she closed her eyes and took in a breath. "What if he comes here and discovers what we do?"

"Don't worry about that. My father's been dealing with the Houstons for years and they've yet to figure it out. If he can keep them at bay, he can handle the likes of your uncle. Hatred makes you careless and stupid, so fooling your uncle should be as easy as chasing a squirrel up a tree." Elora walked to the door. "I'm going to help Miss Heddy with preparations. I'll see you later."

With a nod, Maggie resumed her packing, letting Elora's words pour over her like syrup on pancakes. She knew her friend was trying to comfort her, and it was working.

BREAKFAST WAS SUBDUED with the upcoming journey plaguing everyone's minds. Elora moved the food around on her plate, her somber demeanor mirroring the tension hovering in the room. Maggie was wired with nervous energy, partly because her uncle was only a few miles away, and partly because she'd have to travel alongside Seth for an undisclosed period of time. The thought of embarking on such a serious endeavor was intimidating when she hadn't much experience. Most of her missions, aside from the one that brought her to Rose Hall, had been one-day excursions. Despite Dr. Polk's statements regarding her abilities, she felt his words were meant to pacify her frazzled emotions rather than boost her confidence.

When the morning meal was over, Maggie resumed her preparations for the mission. Dr. Polk had given her a gun for the journey. As she fingered the cold steel barrel, an image of Sellers' lifeless expression in a halo of crimson flashed through her mind, sending a chill bumping across her skin. He died protecting her and his sacrifice gave her the strength to face what lay ahead. Risking her safety seemed inconsequential compared to the horrors the escapees faced on a daily basis. She slipped the wooden heart Sellers had given her into the pocket of her dress, but left the silver locket with her parent's hair and the garnet brooch from Annalissa in her night table drawer. She'd learned that traveling with anything valuable was dangerous and she'd not risk losing such precious mementos.

Sleep was a stranger to Maggie that night, her mind refusing to settle. She and Seth were set to leave shortly before midnight the following evening. Maggie would drive the wagon while Seth rode Phantom. The family they were conducting consisted of a husband and wife with three children, one of which was a baby, making stealth travel precarious. Eventually, Maggie's mind drifted to sleep where an angry uncle and failed missions haunted her dreams.

32

The next night, Maggie sat in the front parlor gazing through the open jib window as summer breezes caressed her cheek. She'd spent the day pacing the floors and rechecking her packing to be sure she had everything that was needed for the journey. She'd known nothing but peace here and found the mystical beauty of the Lowcountry had taken root in her soul. Even though this was a temporary displacement, she feared she'd be forever separated from the Polks. In such a short time, Maggie had come to love and trust them. It wrenched her heart to leave the sanctuary she'd found at Rose Hall.

The sound of Dr. Polk's footsteps caught her attention, making her stomach flop. Determined not to lose her dinner, she swallowed hard as he approached.

"Maggie, it's time," he said, placing his hand on her shoulder.

Picking up her satchel, she followed him out back where Mrs. Polk and Elora waited.

"I'll miss you," Elora whispered, embracing her friend.

A lump lodged in Maggie's throat, blocking her words as

she squeezed Elora tightly. Flashing a halfhearted grin, Maggie pulled away and turned to Mrs. Polk.

"Thank you, for everything."

Mrs. Polk cradled Maggie's face in her hands.

'Don't look so glum. You'll be home before you know it. God bless you and keep you safe," she said, her eyes glistening in the lantern light.

Maggie's chest was heavy as she walked down the dirt path with Dr. Polk to the stables where Seth waited with Phantom. Hatch held a team of horses hitched to a wagon specially constructed for transporting passengers.

"Keep a light hand wid dese two. Dey's good horses but dey don' like you to get hold of dey mouths," Hatch instructed.

With a nod, she boarded the wagon, settled onto the seat, and took up the reins.

"Good luck, Maggie. We'll see you soon," Dr. Polk said.

She gave a weak smile, her eyes swimming.

"You ready?" Seth asked.

Maggie nodded and clucked the horses into action. Seth tipped his hat to Dr. Polk and nudged Phantom into a trot as they started down the sandy drive. He rode ahead for well over an hour until they reached Oak Point where they were to pick up their cargo.

Part of Maggie was exhilarated by the endeavor, while another part worried about all the things that could go wrong. This wasn't like the short stints down the road; it was a full out mission. No matter how much planning had been done, the unpredictable shifts in weather, impassable roads and detours, not to mention scheming hunters, would mean she'd have to remain alert at all times. With several hundred miles ahead, she knew the prospect of making the trip without delays or unexpected interference was unlikely.

The road glowed beneath a bright moon as the wagon careened northward. It was well past midnight when they made the turn down an avenue of oaks leading to Oak Point Plantation. She followed Seth towards the cotton dock at the edge of the marsh and stopped the carriage.

Maggie disembarked, taking in the mystique of her surroundings. The discordant croaking of bullfrogs, in harmony with the screeching crickets muffled the drumming of her heart. A lantern bounced toward them in the darkness as a gentleman came into view.

"Good evening, Mr. Daniels," he said, tipping his hat. "You must be Miss Milner. I'm Mr. Sams, the overseer here."

Mr. Sams was an exceptionally tall black man with broad shoulders and a warm smile. If she'd met him under different circumstances, she may have been intimidated by his large stature but in this context, he was reassuring.

"It's good to meet you," she replied.

"We need to go over a few things before you head out."

Maggie and Seth followed Mr. Sams listening to the plans for transport, alternate routes, and the stops that were prepared for their arrival.

"This here's a list of safe houses and friends who can help along the way, as well as places to avoid. Everything's in code just in case you encounter wolves," he said, handing her a note.

"The passengers have been prepped on what's expected of them. The missus is dressed in men's clothing so it looks like you're traveling with two men. The slave hunters are eager to get their hands on them, so you got to stay alert."

Maggie glanced at Seth who gave her a nod and a half smile, letting her know she'd be fine.

"The youngest children will ride in the bed of the wagon with their papa. Here's a bit of laudanum if the little one gets fussy."

"I understand." Maggie slipped the papers and the bottle of laudanum into her coat pocket.

"Here's some cash, ownership papers for your cargo, and a gun in case you need it. It's dangerous out there."

Maggie chuckled. "I've already got one." She pulled back her shawl to reveal a pistol snuggled in the waistline of her dress.

"Don't hurt to have a spare," he said over his shoulder as he turned.

Mr. Sams disappeared into the night to get their passengers.

Moments later, the silhouette of the family emerged from the darkness. They'd traveled from Louisiana and had been rerouted several times due to weather and slave hunters. There was a hefty bounty on their heads, and several groups wanted to collect. Because the hunters were searching for a family of five, the little girl was going to ride with Seth. Hopefully, the change in appearance and the alteration in number would throw off their pursuers. The bed of the wagon was fitted with a compartment where the father and the children could travel should things get precarious along the way.

Once everyone was settled, the little ones carefully hidden amongst the loose straw with their father, the mother, dressed as a man, climbed onto the bench next to Maggie.

They planned to take a route that wound along a back road rarely traveled because it was potted and difficult to traverse. Seth would ride on a nearby trail. Maggie took comfort that he'd be close by, even if he wasn't right beside her. He was the first person she'd ever completely trusted with her life, aside from her Da. The thought of her father made her twinge. It seemed an eternity since she'd heard his deep laugh and inhaled his special blend of pipe tobacco. But now was not the time for reminiscing and melancholia.

"Ready?" Seth asked with the little girl snuggled on the saddle in front of him.

"Let's go," she replied.

Maggie smacked the reins against the horse's haunches,

sending the wagon lurching forward. Once they reached the main road and the horses were moving at a steady pace, Maggie turned to the woman sitting beside her.

"I'm Maggie."

The woman was convincing as a man, wearing a baggy tweed coat and cotton trousers that camouflaged her curves. Her hair was pinned beneath an old straw hat, giving her a masculine appearance.

"I's Bea."

"Nice to meet you."

"Thankee for helpin' us."

Maggie glanced at her charge and grinned, "I'm honored to be of service."

They rode for some time without a word passing between them. An hour into the trip, Maggie's back was beginning to stiffen and weariness toyed with her eyelids. Despite her afternoon nap, she was battling to keep her eyes open. In an effort to wake her dulling senses, she sat as straight as she could and spoke to Bea.

"Tell me about yourself."

"Ain't much to tell. I's married and gots three little 'uns. Been a slave my whole life."

"I'm sorry for that. But soon you'll be free."

"Humph. We's a long way from freedom. Ain't gonna believe it till I reach de promise land."

Maggie reached over and took Bea's hand. "We're going to make sure you and your family get there."

Bea turned to Maggie, their eyes locking.

"How you come to do this?" Bea asked.

"It's a long story."

"We gots nothin' but time."

Maggie blew out a breath. She talked about her work with the Polks but left out everything prior to that. The less Bea knew about her past, the safer they'd all be.

"What made you decide to take such a risk?" Maggie asked.

"De master was gonna take my babies and sell dem off. Dey took me from my mama, and I's not gonna let no one do dat to my young'uns. I'll die before dey takes 'em from me."

Maggie's skin crawled at the thought of families being torn apart. She'd learned about these practices during her time with the Railroad, but to hear it firsthand was heart wrenching.

They traveled through the night unhindered, reaching their first destination before the sun announced a new day. Thankfully, this stop was equipped with a cellar for Bea and her family to hide, while Maggie was provided a room on the third floor of the house. Seth stayed in the barn. The accommodations were modest, but welcome after bouncing around in a wagon all night. Shortly after Maggie's head rested upon the pillow, sleep handed her to dreamland where all experienced freedom and everlasting joy.

OVER THE COURSE of several days, Bea shared stories of her troubled life. Maggie's skin crawled as Bea spoke about being torn from her mother at the age of five. At age twelve, she was beaten for dropping a water pitcher in the main house for which she was banished to the cotton fields. When she fought off the master's advances at thirteen, she was sent to the auction house where she was chained and demeaned as men inspected her from head to toe.

"I thought my life was over. De men be looking in my mouth and inspecting my privates. I never felt so shamed in all my days. When dey done lookin' me over, de man on de block say I's a healthy specimen for hard labor and breeding. I's scared when Mr. Johnson buy me cause I don' know what he do to me. I's sad when he make me pick cotton, until I met my Solomon. My heart be pounding de first time I see him smile.

He a good man, always treat me special. He even bring me wildflowers he pick in de woods."

"And then you were married?"

"It be a slave marriage, but dat all we can have."

"What do you mean?"

"Ain't no preacher, just one of de other slaves make a speech and say we married. We knows we's married and that all dat matters. It be a secret cause de master don't like de slaves to get married. Makes it harder to sell we off if we's attached."

"But you had children," Maggie said, surprised that being pregnant hadn't alerted others to their marriage.

"Mr. Johnson's overseer didn't pay no mind to Solomon and me. All he care 'bout is de work. We's hard workers and don't cause no trouble. I work up to de day I give birth, and then back to work de day after. So long as de cotton get picked, he leave us be. Things pretty good for us until Mr. Johnson fall on hard times. When he say he gonna sell off my babies, dat's when I knows we gots to run."

They made another stop for a few hours of rest and a hot meal. Afterwards, Maggie and her charges boarded the wagon with prayers from the hosting family for a safe trip to their destination. Seth rode ahead, leaving the girl to travel with her family in the wagon where she'd be more comfortable.

The moon rose, casting an eerie glow that illuminated the road. The horses seemed exceptionally skittish, pricking their ears at every little sound and stepping a bit higher than usual. Cicadas sang as an owl screeched from a treetop nearby. The underlying energy was unsettling.

"Were you able to rest earlier?" Maggie asked, hoping the conversation would help settle the unease sticking to her skin.

"Can't rest till we's on de other side of de border. We ain't safe until dat time."

"At least it's a nice night for travel."

"You think dis is good?" Bea shook her head. "Dis not a good moon, dere's danger in de shadows, I can feel it."

Maggie's stomach knotted up at Bea's words. She told herself to stop fretting; Seth was somewhere out there and wouldn't let anything happen to them. It was only natural that Bea would be skeptical. Regardless of her attempts at self-assurance, Maggie felt something wasn't quite right. The air was heavy and the atmosphere stagnant, in spite of the movement and wildlife stirring in their wake. Nevertheless, they'd have to keep going and face whatever obstacles lurked ahead.

33

Dr. and Mrs. Polk traveled to the Bartlett's plantation where Elaine Bartlett waited on the front porch to welcome them. The strain of her situation was evident in her sallow complexion and shadowed eyes.

"I'm so glad you've come," Mrs. Bartlett said as she embraced her best friend and whispered in her ear. "I didn't realize Dr. Polk was coming with you."

"I hope it's not an imposition," Mrs. Polk replied, arching her eyebrows.

"Of course not, you're both always welcome here."

The two friends walked inside while Dr. Polk spoke with the carriage driver.

"I'm worried about you Elaine. You look peaked," Mrs. Polk said.

"I'm not certain how much more I can endure," Mrs. Bartlett replied in a hushed tone. "Last evening that horrid Mr. Stevenson brought some friends with him and engaged George in another round of poker. Now the debt is worse than before! It would seem they swindle unknowing victims by pretending to play poorly until they win it all. Since we've nothing to give, they're demanding George travel with them until his debt is paid. Apparently, this is how they recruit their members."

Mrs. Polk took her friend's hand. "I had no idea the situation was as bad as all this. I don't know how you've been able to tolerate such behavior, especially in your own home," Mrs. Polk sighed.

"My husband will be forced to align himself with these ingrates who cheat at cards. I can hardly stand the thought," she sniffled. "Mr. Stevenson is the worst of them all. I don't believe the man has a conscience. He orders me about like a slave."

Mrs. Bartlett raised a hankie to her lips, stifling a sob when Dr. Polk entered. "Why *is* Dr. Polk with you?" she asked, an expression of worry clouding her pale features.

"He knew you had unsavory guests and insisted on accompanying me."

"Does he know about the cards?" she queried, her brow furrowing.

"I mentioned it to him but don't worry, he'll not repeat a word of it. He's a man of discretion."

"Do you think he'd be willing to speak with George, maybe give him some guidance, man to man?" A spark of hope glinted in her puffy eyes.

"I think that's a grand idea." Turning to her husband, Mrs. Polk clasped his hand. "Dearest, perhaps you'd like to join Mr. Bartlett and his guests in the gentleman's parlor while Mrs. Bartlett and I chat?"

"A splendid idea," he said with a bow before walking down the hall to the gentlemen's parlor.

Momentarily, Dr. Polk listened to the muffled exchange of voices before rapping on the door. Mr. Bartlett opened the door, an expression of relief brightening his gray pallor and sunken eyes at the sight of his friend.

"Dr. Polk, how wonderful to see you. Won't you join us for a brandy?" He stepped back, allowing the doctor to enter. "This is Mr. Archibald Stevenson from Pennsylvania, a new business associate of mine," he said, clearing his throat.

"Nice to meet you, Mr. Stevenson," the doctor said, shaking his hand. "Are you enjoying your time in the Lowcountry?"

"Not exactly," he grumbled.

"I'm sorry to hear it. What brings you here?" Dr. Polk took a seat next to him. The man's tense stature and sour countenance alluded to a troubled soul.

"Business," Mr. Stevenson growled, casting a look of disdain toward Mr. Bartlett.

Seemingly uncomfortable, Mr. Bartlett excused himself. "Gentleman, if you'll pardon me for a moment, I need to get another bottle of brandy."

Once Mr. Bartlett was out of earshot, Dr. Polk initiated a conversation.

"Have you any family Mr. Stevenson?" Dr. Polk asked.

"None worthy of acknowledging. Had a son, but he died of the fever. Left me with a miserable wife and a worthless daughter. Granted, the daughter is no longer a burden. I was able to pawn her off as a governess." A sneer wrinkled his lip as he gazed out the window. "Women serve but two purposes, neither of which is worth the trouble they inflict. Aside from performing wifely duties and maintaining a household, they have nothing to offer."

The man's obvious disdain toward women was unsettling, but Dr. Polk played along in hopes of getting to the subject of Maggie. If this was going to work, he had to convince Mr. Stevenson that she'd arrived here and died.

"I understand completely. Since you've broached the subject of silly women so eloquently, I must admit I have more important things to do than accompany my wife on her social endeavors. However, southern manners require a gentleman to do his duty." Dr. Polk smirked and took a sip of brandy.

"It would seem you and I share similar views," Mr. Stevenson said, raising his glass to Dr. Polk. "Most men abandon all sound judgment for a pretty face and the promise of marital bliss. As if a man can't get what he needs without the chains of marriage."

"Indeed. My son left to practice law in Atlanta a few years ago, leaving me with my wife and daughter. If that wasn't bad enough, recently an anonymous young woman was dumped on my doorstep, adding to the overabundance of sniveling females in my home."

"I understand your predicament. Being surrounded by frivolous women is enough to drive a man to lose his bearings," Mr. Stevenson huffed. "Have you resolved the issue with the unwelcome visitor?"

"It resolved itself when she died. A stagecoach driver brought the woman to our house because she was delirious with fever. Apparently, he knew I was a physician. By the time they arrived she was unconscious, so my wife settled her in one of the rooms on the second floor and tended to her," Dr. Polk said. "Sadly, I was out of town at the time and when I returned it was too late to save her. The fever had taken its toll."

"And you never discovered her identity?"

"The only thing the driver knew was that she was traveling from Pennsylvania to visit family here. No names were given. We made several attempts to locate her relatives by placing ads, but to no avail. Her appearance was rather distinctive, long red hair, fair skin, green eyes."

Mr. Stevenson straightened in his chair, his face contorting. "Describe her again."

Dr. Polk inhaled. It was working. "A young woman in her late teens or early twenties, about 5' 4", medium build with red hair, green eyes, and very pale skin. Of course, her pallor could have been a result of the illness."

"That sounds like my wretched niece," he blustered. "Been

searching for her since she ran away! She left a mound of debt in her wake after I was kind enough to take her in. You say this woman came from Pennsylvania?"

"That's what we were told. I believe the driver mentioned somewhere just outside of Philadelphia. Are you from that area?"

"I am." Mr. Stevenson's lips formed a thin line as he considered the news, his fingers thrumming the table beside him.

"Have you any way of identifying her?" Dr. Polk asked.

"She fits the description you've given, right down to the green eyes and that disgusting red hair."

"My goodness, what are the odds that we should meet like this? It would seem fate wants to put your mind at ease," Dr. Polk said with a sly grin.

"At ease? I'm glad to be rid of her! I only hope her death was one of discomfort and suffering."

"I assure you she received the finest care possible and a proper burial, all of which set us back a few dollars," Dr. Polk replied, raising his eyebrows.

"Surely you're not suggesting I owe for medical expenses and a burial?"

Mr. Bartlett reentered the room, holding a full bottle of brandy. He refilled his guest's glasses and took his seat while Dr. Polk continued the conversation.

"I'm certain we can work something out. Perhaps I could get in on this business deal you have with Mr. Bartlett?" Dr. Polk leaned forward in his chair, resting his elbows on his knees. "I'm always looking for a sound investment."

"I don't think you'd be interested in our business dealings, Dr. Polk. It's of a sensitive nature," Mr. Bartlett sighed.

"What he's trying to say is that he owes me money," Stevenson grumbled.

"It seems you and I share that dilemma, don't we?" Dr. Polk smiled, relishing the added component to the scheme.

"So it would seem," Mr. Stevenson scowled.

"Maybe we can work out a trade, say Mr. Bartlett's debt in exchange for yours?"

"What kind of fool are you? Why trade my debt for his? You'd not benefit at all!" Mr. Stevenson exclaimed.

"I'm certain Mr. Bartlett can settle his debt with me. He has a stallion I've had my eye on for some time."

Mr. Bartlett lowered his gaze, his complexion reddening, apparently embarrassed by his current situation.

Mr. Stevenson sneered. "Have you any proof of your claims?"

"Only that the young woman buried on our property fits the description of your niece, right down to the bright red hair. I don't believe in coincidences, Mr. Stevenson and neither would my good friend Judge Humphries should he learn of my financial burden."

"Even dead she's still costing me money," Stevenson declared, bolting upright with his fists clenched at his sides. "You say she's buried on your property? I want to see her grave!"

"You're welcome to ride to our plantation and pay your respects."

"Very well. I'll be there in an hour."

"I look forward to putting this unpleasant business behind us. Until then." Dr. Polk rose from his chair with a slight bow and left the room.

On the trip back to Rose Hall, Dr. Polk shared with his wife what had transpired, and the pending visit from Mr. Stevenson.

"He fell for it. We need to make sure everything is in order. If all goes as planned, Maggie will finally be free of that man forever," Dr. Polk said with a mischievous smile.

~

ELORA WATCHED from the upstairs window as a gleaming carriage rounded the curve and stopped at the end of the walkway. A man emerged, his tall stature and rigid posture exuding authority. Something in the way he carried himself was staunch and unwelcoming, sending a shiver racing down her back. Yet curiosity got the best of her. She padded down the back stairs and hid in the corridor outside of her father's office where the men were seated. Stilling her breath, she listened to their conversation while peering through the small opening of the door.

"Good to see you again, Mr. Stevenson. I've drawn up some papers so we can make the transaction official."

"Being rid of that filthy wretch is worth any price," he grumbled, signing the papers and sliding them across the desk. "Now take me to her grave. I'd like to see what I paid for."

"Of course. Follow me."

Elora scurried back to the shadows of the hall as Dr. Polk waved Mr. Stevenson from the room. She longed to follow but fear of being discovered made her pause. Hesitating for a moment, Elora mustered all her courage and slipped out the door. She'd grown up on this land and knew every inch of the terrain. She could follow without being discovered if she took care to tread lightly.

It didn't take long for her to catch up to her father and Mr. Stevenson as they trudged along the path by the marsh toward the oyster shed. They stopped at a simple wooden cross with wildflowers sprouting from the mound of dirt. To avoid being seen, Elora huddled behind a large oak and listened intently as her father spoke.

"My daughter felt badly that the young woman died without her family so she planted the wildflowers."

"Hope you don't plan to charge me for that," Mr. Stevenson huffed.

"It was our pleasure to honor her in this way, even if we didn't know who she was."

"She was a vile, lazy creature who cost more than she was worth," he said, spitting on her grave. "I'm only sorry I didn't have the pleasure of watching her gasp out her last breath with my hands wrapped around her throat."

Elora bit her lip to prevent a retort from crossing her lips. He was truly a despicable man.

"I want to be clear; we're done with this business. You're not going to come after me for more money in the future?"

"I'm a man of my word. So long as you uphold your part of the deal and release any further claims against Mr. Bartlett, we need never see each other again."

"Very well," Mr. Stevenson replied. "Being rid of my wretched niece is worth more than what Bartlett owes."

Mr. Stevenson and Dr. Polk started for the house. Elora waited a few moments before following them, making sure to keep a safe distance. Once the men reached the house, Elora stood at the far corner near the side entrance. She watched Mr. Stevenson climb into his carriage and the driver launch the horses forward. Materializing from the shadows, Elora walked over to her father and looped her hand through his arm.

"Everything is settled?" she asked.

"So it would seem. He believed the fake grave and the story of Maggie's demise."

Elora giggled, "Aren't you glad I made you bury my donkey, Willie?"

The right side of his mouth curled, "Yes, my dear, I am. That blasted donkey just saved a woman's life. I'll not argue the next time you want to bury a beloved pet."

"Shall we have some tea?"

"Tea is a splendid idea," he replied.

They entered the house hand-in-hand; pleased they were able to save another soul from the bondage of hate.

34

After a week of traveling by night and hiding by day, Maggie and Bea had developed a bond through conversation and mutual respect. Maggie was amazed at how well Solomon and the children were able to travel quietly in such uncomfortable accommodations. Even the baby stayed silent except when the wheel of the carriage had dislodged, sending Solomon rolling to the edge where the baby bumped her head. Thus far, it was the only time they'd had to use the laudanum to quiet her. One night, they traveled along a rutted back road beneath a glowing moon. The air was thick and the silence unnerving.

"Why you risking all dis for us?" Bea asked.

"Because it's the right thing to do."

"Dat no reason," Bea shrugged. "Is it dat Mr. Daniels? I see de way you looks at him."

With a sideways glance, Maggie swallowed, her throat suddenly dry.

"I don't know what you're talking about. Mr. Daniels is nothing more than an acquaintance."

Bea pursed her lips. "If dat de story you want to tell, go ahead but I 'spect it's more than dat."

"Bea, I believe your imagination has run away with you."

Shaking her head, Bea grinned at Maggie's feeble attempt to hide what was so obvious to others. "You can tell yourself all de stories you want, but de truth is de truth and you is going to have to face it one day."

"There's nothing to face, I promise," Maggie said halfheartedly.

"Chil' you gots it bad. Why don' you just tell him?"

"Because Mr. Daniels is already spoken for."

"Hmm, dat be a problem. Is she ugly?"

"Bea!"

"Well, is she? Cause if she is, you could catch his eye and steer him your way."

"She's a lovely woman of whom I'm quite fond. I'd never do anything to hurt her."

"Never is a long time," Bea replied, shaking her head.

Maggie grinned at Bea's attempts to intervene with her love life. "Besides, my life is too complicated for love."

Bea's dark skin shimmered in the moonlight as she fixed her gaze on Maggie.

"Ain't nothing in life more important than love and freedom. Don' miss out 'cause you waitin' for life to be just right, 'cause it ain't never gonna happen."

Bea's wisdom settled hard on Maggie's heart. She'd been chained by fear of her uncle for so long she'd almost forgotten what it was like just to be. When the baby began to fuss, Bea reached back and took the squirming figure into her arms and snuggled the whining bundle. Amidst the moonbeams, Bea gazed upon her daughter, her eyes sparkling as she began to sing a soft lullaby. Her soulful voice carried the rhythm of love in each word until the baby drifted to dreamland.

Maggie was relieved for the quiet night and the opportunity

to breathe a bit. They were nearing their destination and she desperately hoped they'd be able to get there unencumbered by any more delays. As they bumped along beneath a spray of stars, Maggie's mind drifted to dark places, wondering if her uncle was still hunting for her or if the Polk's had successfully sent him away for good. And what about her Da? Was he alive and if so, where was he?

After more than an hour of somber ruminations and bumpy roads, Maggie's back began to ache when Seth rode up.

"We need to change course. Got some hunters on the route we're headed on."

"I thought this trail was virtually unknown."

"It may have been in the past, but the bounty on this family is steep and somehow the hunters have found their way here. I need to head them off. You take the next road to the left. Follow it until it forks to the right. There's an old cabin down that way where you can stay until I can find a safer route."

He spurred Phantom into a gallop, disappearing into the night.

"Dis gonna take more time, ain't it?" Bea asked, the sparkle fading from her eyes.

"I'm afraid so."

Bea sucked in her breath, her body tensing. Apparently, all of the route changes and delays were beginning to distress her.

Maggie's nerves were raw despite her trust in Seth's abilities and experience. She knew the cabin was safe but would feel better once Seth returned. They were so close to their destination that the delay taunted her, raising her anxiety to a higher level. There was so much that could go wrong. Maggie took in a deep breath in an effort to squelch the suffocating dread filling her chest.

A grove of tall pines sheltered the cabin from the path as moonbeams traversed the yard. Maggie slung her satchel across her shoulder, unharnessed the horses, and put them in a paddock next to the cabin while Bea and Solomon helped the children from the wagon. The atmosphere percolated with nervous energy making Maggie more aware of every sound and shadow.

Stale air assaulted Maggie's nose as she shoved open the door and stepped into the dilapidated space. Bea, Solomon, and the children followed her inside. She lit a few oil lamps that spit and sputtered to life illuminating the dingy interior with its sagging floors and water-stained ceiling. Setting her satchel and gun on the table by the front door, Maggie joined Bea and the children in the back room while Solomon spied through a rift in the curtains.

Bea settled in a chair with the baby in her arms and Elijah at her feet. Maggie and Hannah sat across from her near a tall cupboard filled with dishes and a few chipped mugs. Obviously, this had been the area for food preparation. On the other side of Bea was a small table with a few pots and pans and a couple of rusted knives.

"Solomon, it's much more comfortable back here. Why don't you join us?" Maggie asked, worried about his agitated state as he peered out the window, shifting around as if he was ready to bolt.

"Can't relax, needs to keep watch," he replied without looking her direction.

"Don' mind him. He not one to sit still," Bea replied, rocking the baby in her arms as two-year-old Elijah sat on the floor tugging at his toes. His contented prattling and broad grin warmed Maggie's heart. Within a few days, he'd never know the slash of the whip or the sting of slavery.

"Once we's free, I's gonna make us a feast to celebrate," Bea announced proudly. "Den we's gonna find work and learn de youngins to read and write. Dey's gonna have everything we didn't."

Seeing Bea's smile and sparkling eyes was worth all the

hardship and long hours of travel they'd endured. Even though the journey had been fraught with several route changes, Seth's skills had outsmarted the hunters at every opportunity. The expedition was nearly complete. Yet, something niggled at Maggie's nerves, like winds before a storm alluding to impending doom.

The baby drifted off, hushing the conversation to a series of whispers. Hannah fiddled with her skirt when Solomon cried out.

"Someone be here!"

"It's probably Seth," Maggie replied, standing.

"It not Mr. Seth, it be hunters! Bea get de youngins outta here," Solomon yelled. Bea snatched a large knife from the small table with one hand while holding the now squalling baby on her hip.

"Bea put that down, they may not be who you think they are," Maggie said. Her fortitude was beginning to waver as her chest constricted. This place had to be safe, otherwise Seth wouldn't have told her to come here.

"Don' care Miss Maggie. We ain't going back. Ain't no way my youngins going to be slaves no more."

The front door crashed open followed by a gunshot and a barrage of shouting. Maggie fell to the floor, her heart pounding so hard she couldn't catch her breath. Men's voices echoed through the space, letting Maggie know that Solomon had been correct. The hunters had arrived. Across the room, Bea screamed as the baby wailed. Maggie reached for her gun when she realized she'd left it in the front room.

Stupid, she thought. Regret pounded her ribcage as she tried to figure out how to stop the insanity unfolding in the next room. On her hands and knees, Maggie crawled to the far corner where she spied Hannah cowering behind the cupboard a few feet away, the whites of her eyes as bright as the full moon. Maggie managed to slip into the space between the cupboard and the wall and waved Hannah over. The child hesitated, looking towards her mother, younger brother, and baby sister on the other side of the room, and then back at Maggie. Hurriedly, she scooted toward Maggie who scooped her up and held her tight. Her tiny body quaked in Maggie's arms as the shouting and screams intensified.

Chaos ensued as men barked orders and Bea screeched out threats while Solomon's voice escalated as he argued with the intruders. In the meantime, Maggie clung to Hannah, whispering in her ear to stay quiet. The child did as she was told, pressing her head into Maggie's chest. She was shocked at the child's ability to stay silent in the midst of the melee until she felt the scars of past punishments through the thin cotton fabric of Hannah's dress. No wonder she was soundless, she'd been taught harshly. Holding Hannah, Maggie chewed her lower lip, hoping Seth was close by and could salvage the situation before anyone was hurt.

A thunderous boom resonated through the cabin followed by a volley of gunfire. Maggie squeezed her eyes shut but all she could see was Sellers lying in a pool of his own blood, his eyes empty and his smile gone. She couldn't let anyone else die, not again, but panic pulsed through her veins rendering her motionless. Bea's cries and the baby's wailing broke through Maggie's thoughts.

"We's not going back to dat place. Ifin' you comes closer, I'll cut you," Bea screamed as the hunters cornered her.

Maggie sucked in a breath, simultaneously tightening her grip on Hannah. She prayed the hunters didn't come far enough into the room to find them.

"Stupid darkie, you're only making this more fun," one of the men growled, placing his gun on the table. "I'll take you on," he said, lunging at her with arms spread wide. He yelped as Bea swiped the knife, slicing his upper arm.

"Miserable wench cut me!" he exclaimed, blood trickling from the tear in his shirt.

"You're gonna regret that," another man grumbled, bouncing back and forth as Bea slashed the knife through the air. When he lurched toward her, the knife pierced his shoulder.

"She stabbed me!" he yelled, backing up.

"I told you we ain't going back. My babies gonna be free one way or 'nother!"

A third voice joined the fray, telling the two men to grab Bea without causing too much damage since the reward depended on how many they brought back alive. Bea's screams coupled with the baby's squalls, sounded like the banshees Maggie had heard about in her youth. The sound ripped through her soul, wounding the last remnant of her innocence.

"Don't you do it!" one of them yelled.

The discord was punctured by a guttural yelp, and the infant's wailing ceased.

"Stupid darkie! What're you doing?"

"Stop her before she does it again! These animals have no sense!" the other man hollered.

Bea's screams and Elijah's cries intermingled with the shuffling of feet and furniture being knocked around.

"There's one more! Where is she?" the man demanded of Bea.

"She run off when you come bustin' in," Bea replied defiantly.

"Find her," he commanded one of the other men, "Little darkie can't be too far."

"What about my arm?" the man squalled.

"Stop your cryin' and find that darkie! We've already lost money on two of 'em. When you catch her, meet us at the river but don't take too long, we ain't gonna wait all night."

The sounds of shuffling feet and Elijah's cries disintegrated into the night as the two men took their captives away.

Worn floorboards creaked beneath the remaining hunter's feet, curdling Maggie's stomach. The only thing blocking them from view was the cupboard. If the hunter stepped a few feet closer, he'd catch sight of her. She felt as if he could hear the rise and fall of her chest and feared he'd discover them. Hannah's body shook with the force of fallen leaves in an autumn wind, her tears soaking through Maggie's bodice. Maggie leaned hard against the wall desperately wanting to disappear into the corner. *Where was Seth? He'd always arrived when they needed him most.*

The hunter's footsteps faded as he exited the cabin. Unable to move, Maggie clung to Hannah. They stayed in that position for what seemed like hours when the sound of footfalls at the front door squeezed Maggie's lungs. The hunter had come back. The floorboards groaned beneath his footfalls, ratcheting Maggie's heart rate up with each step when a familiar voice called out.

"Maggie?"

Still clutching Hannah, Maggie tried to stand but her legs were numb from squatting in one spot for so long.

"Over here," she croaked, her mouth as dry as the desert.

Seth rushed to her side and grasped her upper arms, his crystal blue eyes cutting through her fear. "Are you alright?"

She nodded.

"What happened?"

Maggie shook her head, tears cresting in her eyes. "I don't know. We were chatting when Solomon yelled that the hunters had arrived. They broke through the door followed by gunshots and then Bea was screaming..." All of Maggie's pent-up agony gushed out in a sob.

"We need to get out of here," Seth said in a hushed tone, his eyes darting around the space.

"What about Solomon and..." her words trailed off when Seth gave her a stern look and shook his head.

"We can't worry about that now." Seth exhaled. "Hannah, I need you to let me carry you, but you have to keep your eyes closed, OK?" he said, reaching for her.

Hannah nodded and let go of Maggie, falling into Seth's embrace. "Now close your eyes and don't open them until I tell you." She nodded as she leaned her head against his chest and squeezed her eyes shut. Seth looked at Maggie. "You ready?"

Maggie bobbed her head and fell into step behind him. She swallowed the scream hovering at her lips as they passed Bea's baby lying in a pool of blood, her throat cut. Stepping around Solomon's body, Maggie shuddered, blinking away the image of Sellers' face where Solomon's once was. Blood streaked the door jam and speckled the walls. She grabbed her satchel from the floor and followed Seth out of the cabin.

Maggie inhaled the fresh night air as Seth lowered Hannah to the ground. "You can open your eyes now," he whispered.

Hannah looked around, her gaze fixating on the wagon that was engulfed in flames.

"Now what?" Maggie asked, trying to swipe the bloody images from her mind.

"I'm going after Bea and Elijah. They can't be too far off. Did you hear the men say where they were heading?"

Closing her eyes, she concentrated, trying to remember anything aside from the screams and gunshots.

"One of the men said something about meeting at a river," she muttered. "And another one was going to search for Hannah in the woods."

"I know where they're going," Seth said, looking off.

"What about Solomon and the baby?"

"We haven't time to bury them. You and Hannah take the horses and stay on the main trail until it jogs to the right. Follow the path until you see an old shed. I'll meet you there."

"Can't we go with you?" Maggie asked, grabbing his forearm. She didn't want to be separated from him again.

"It's too dangerous," he said. "Where's your pistol?"

She nodded toward the cabin, "I think Solomon used it to shoot at the men."

Seth ran back inside, retrieved the gun, and handed it to Maggie.

"When I get to the shed, I'll knock three times, otherwise shoot anyone who walks through the door."

Too weary to resist, Maggie took the gun.

"What if the other hunter finds us?" she asked.

"Shoot him."

Maggie nodded, fear fingering her throat as she watched Seth swing onto Phantom and disappear into the night, all of her courage going with him. She gathered the two horses, adapted the harnesses, placed Hannah on one and mounted the other.

"Let's go," Maggie said, with a weak smile.

They plodded along the darkened trails, following the gleam of the full moon until they reached the shack. They tied the horses to a tree branch and entered the ramshackle structure, the scent of dirt and decay permeating the air. At least it was safe, or so she hoped.

Settling on the far side of the space, Maggie sat on the moist ground facing the door with pistol in hand.

"Is we safe here, Miss Maggie?"

"As safe as we can be," she replied.

"Is my mama gonna be ok?"

"Mr. Daniels will do his best to save her and your brother. Try to get some sleep. We've got a long journey tomorrow."

"What about my papa and my sissy?"

"I'm so sorry Hannah. They're gone."

"At least they is free," she whispered. Even a child understood that death was better than bondage.

Hannah's frail frame curled against Maggie and within minutes she was sound asleep, her steady breathing keeping time with the chirping cicadas.

When Maggie closed her eyes visions of Solomon, Sellers, and the baby flooded her thoughts. Guilt and shame cascaded down her face for hiding instead of helping Bea. Two more people were dead because of her cowardice. How could she face Seth and the Polks after all this? Leaning her head back against the wall, she cried into the night for all the pain and suffering she'd inflicted on so many innocent people. It seemed no matter what she did, heartache followed.

35

At some point, Maggie drifted off to sleep until the reverberation of hoof beats coaxed her from slumber. Her breath caught and her body stiffened for fear the hunters had found them. Hannah was still sound asleep, her head now resting in Maggie's lap. In that moment, she contemplated waking Hannah and trying to escape except there was only one door. They were trapped. Mustering all her fortitude, she aimed the pistol at the door, her hands shaking so badly she was more likely to hit a wall than anyone who entered.

Maggie swallowed hard, tried to steady her hands, and rested her finger on the trigger. Tension blew through her lips when she heard *knock, knock, knock*. Seth stepped inside and seeing that Hannah was asleep, held his finger to his lips before slumping on the ground next to Maggie. Relief washed over her until she realized he was alone. Then again, he may have taken Bea and Elijah elsewhere while he came back for them.

"What happened?" Maggie whispered.

Seth took in a deep breath. "I made it to the river and saw two men in a boat with Bea and Elijah. Elijah was wailing and the men were telling Bea to shut him up. I was getting ready to take a shot when Bea tossed herself overboard with Elijah."

Maggie's spirit lifted. "They got away?"

Seth stared at the ground. "Don't think so. She looked like she was shackled with Elijah in her lap. I watched for signs of her in the water but didn't see anything. One guy hung over the side of the boat searching while the other fired a few shots into the water. It was so dark I couldn't see much. If she was alive, I wanted to give her a chance to get away so I fired at the boat. I hit one of the men and he tumbled into the water hollering for help. The other guy screamed that he didn't know how to swim. I took aim, hit the hull of the boat, and watched them go under. I searched the water for signs of Bea and Elijah but never found them."

Without uttering another word, he leaned his head back and closed his eyes. Bea had said repeatedly that she'd not return to bondage and neither would her children. At least they were finally free. Not wanting to wake Hannah, Maggie decided to take advantage of the quietude and the comfort of Seth's presence. Shutting her eyes, she resumed her troubled sleep.

They rose with the sun and prepared to leave. Normally they wouldn't travel by day, but with the family's number greatly reduced, Seth felt it was better to keep moving. Hunters weren't likely to stop a white man and woman with a Negro child.

Hannah sat up, her eyes puffy from crying.

"Good morning, Hannah. How are you feeling?" Maggie asked.

"Hungry," she mumbled, rubbing her eyes.

"Let's move on and find something to eat," Seth offered.

"Will the bad men catch us?" she whimpered.

Seth grinned. "No chance of that."

An hour later, they arrived at a small farmhouse where friends of the Railroad resided. Once they'd eaten and washed up, they rested until nightfall. Beneath the cloak of darkness, they made the final leg of the trip to Mr. Coffin's establishment without incident. While it wasn't the results they'd hoped for, at least they'd saved Hannah. Bea would be happy to know one of her children would experience the freedom she gave her life to achieve. With all that had transpired in the past twenty-four hours, Maggie was emotionally drained. She and Seth were set to leave at dawn. As she rested her head upon the pillow, she wondered whether the Polk's had been successful in permanently banishing her uncle from her life.

SUNRISE DISSOLVED the darkness like sugar in a teacup as Maggie and Seth prepared for the long trip home.

"Will I ever see you again?" Hannah asked, gripping Maggie's hand.

"Probably not. You'll be in Canada and I'll be..." Maggie paused. She'd no idea if her uncle's efforts had been thwarted or if he was still searching for her.

At that moment, Maggie realized she and Hannah were both on their own in the world, and she'd never felt so forlorn. Maggie reached into her pocket, removed the wooden heart, and placed it in Hannah's palm. "Take this. A dear friend gave it to me and now I'm giving it to you. Whenever you look at it, remember you're not alone and will always be in my heart."

Hannah ran her finger over the intricate carvings as she studied the treasure.

"He gave you his heart," she replied with a smile.

"More than that, he gave me his life," Maggie said, her vision misting.

"Thank you for saving me."

"I'm sorry I couldn't save the rest of your family."

Hannah stepped closer and squeezed Maggie's hand. "It's

not your fault. Mama and Papa knows you did your best. Besides, they know you had to save me."

Maggie bit her lower lip to prevent a sob from escaping. How could someone so young be so wise? She scooped Hannah into a snug embrace. "You're going to have a wonderful life, Hannah. Make your parents proud."

Hannah pulled away and smiled. "Bye, Miss Maggie."

She watched Hannah scurry into the Coffin's house and shut the door. The weight of the past few days strained Maggie's breathing and dampened her spirits. In such a short period of time, she'd come to love Bea and her family. Even though Hannah was safe, Maggie carried the guilt of not doing more to protect the rest of them.

Somberness permeated the early morning air, making it difficult to concentrate as Maggie drove the wagon with Seth riding alongside. For miles, the only sound was the clattering of wagon wheels and the beating of horses' hooves against the ground. The shifting and jostling of the wagon kept Maggie alert although she was exhausted from the events of the previous few days. Hours later, they stopped at a farm on the other side of the Kentucky border to rest the horses and eat. A meal of steaming coffee and roast chicken revived them both before they set out again.

The journey was going much faster without all of the route changes for which Maggie was thankful. The sooner they returned to Rose Hall, the happier she'd be. Lost in her thoughts, she considered whether her uncle was finally gone from her life or if she'd be forced to relocate. And if so, where would she go? The thought of never seeing Seth again made her stomach flop. Even though he belonged to Elora, she wanted to be near him.

All her jumbled thoughts were making the trip feel as if it would go on forever. She'd never been one to dream of marriage, only University. And then her mind drifted back to

Bea and Solomon. They'd been in love and had a family but still couldn't live in peace. Maggie's eyes stung at the unfairness of it all.

At that moment, all she wanted was to go home, back to her father and the farm. Even that was lost to her. The further they traveled, the lower she sank into a realm of despair.

After several days and a few stops, they finally crossed the South Carolina border as the sun bowed to evening in ribbons of gold and pink. When the front wheel of the wagon began to squeal, Seth circled back to her.

"That doesn't sound good. Follow me over to that field so I can take a look at it."

As they pulled into the open space, the wagon shifted to the left with a violent thump, nearly catapulting Maggie from the bench. Seth halted Phantom and was instantly at her side, helping her to the ground.

Examining the damage, Seth shook his head. "Looks like one of the bolts has come loose. It's getting too dark to work on the repair. I'm afraid we'll have to camp here until morning."

Maggie scanned the pasture as the sun made its final descent in shimmering hues of orange and purple. Seth started a fire while Maggie grabbed supplies and food from the wagon. She spread blankets on the ground and pulled cured ham and biscuits from the basket. Once Seth settled the horses, he sat down beside her, his close proximity radiating warmth through the core of her body. Now more than ever, she was determined to rebuff the pining reverberating through her soul.

When the meal was done and everything was put away, Maggie pulled her knees to her chest, wrapped her arms about her legs, and gazed toward the heavens, taking in the spectacular display of stars and the halo rounding the moon.

"Tis beautiful," she muttered, her words tinged in her native brogue.

"Well, listen to that," Seth teased, "If it ain't the real Maggie Milner come for a visit."

A blush heated her cheeks as she turned away.

Sitting straighter, his tone softened, "I'm sorry, I didn't mean to embarrass you, but I never hear the real you. You're always trying to hide it."

"My Da told me to keep my Irish under control. I never understood why until I came to this country. Sometimes I forget myself and let it slip out."

"Don't apologize for who you are, Maggie. There's enough falsehood in this world without you pretending to be someone else."

Maggie exhaled. Since arriving in America, she'd lived in three places, changed occupations several times, and altered her name. She didn't know who she was anymore.

"Since we've got nothing but time on our hands, tell me more about how you came to this country," Seth said.

"Let's talk about you instead. How did you come to help with the Railroad?" Maggie replied, anxious to divert the conversation from her past.

His expression tightened as he leaned back on his elbows and clenched his jaw.

"I'll give you the abridged version. My father was an abusive jerk who made everyone around him miserable, especially his slaves."

Maggie sucked in a breath.

A sly grin crossed Seth's face. "Yup, the Daniels owned slaves. I hated the institution from childhood, as did my mother. Spent most of my early years either hiding from my father's abuse or trying to stop it. One day my father came home reeking of whisky when my mom confronted him about one of the slaves. Her accusations were like gas to a flame. He threw her to the ground, straddled her, and started pummeling her face.

"I managed to wrestle him off of her and started slamming his head against the floor. That's when he knocked me out with a whiskey bottle."

Seth swallowed hard before continuing. "My mother didn't survive. Annie, one of the house slaves, tended to her wounds but the damage was too severe. Her face was completely bludgeoned and she never regained consciousness. My good-for-nothing father wouldn't let us call for the doctor."

"How terrible," Maggie muttered.

"Annie was the closest thing I had to family, outside of my mother. She was one of the kindest most beautiful women I knew." His words broke off in a whisper. "A few months after my mother's death, Annie gave birth..." Seth stopped, sat up straight, and placed his finger on his lips.

"What's the matter?" Maggie muttered, looking about, alarm squeezing her lungs like a lemon.

"Someone's coming," he whispered, cocking his head to listen. "Do you trust me?"

"With my life."

"I apologize for what I'm about to do but I need you to follow my lead."

Maggie's heart pounded as the sound of hoof beats drew closer. Without warning, Seth pulled Maggie to him and pressed his lips against hers. Instinctively, she pulled back but his grasp tightened preventing her from moving. The scent of fireside smoke and leather filled her senses as days of his unshaved travel pricked her chin. Seconds later, a man on horseback cleared his throat. Embarrassment colored Maggie's cheeks as Seth jumped to his feet and strutted toward the man. They spoke in hushed tones with Seth occasionally nodding her direction and snickering. The man threw his head back with a laugh, tipped his hat, and rode off.

"What was that about?" she asked as Seth approached.

"I'm not sure you want to know," he said, sitting beside her, stretching out his legs and folding his arms behind his head.

Maggie nudged him, "Now I really want to know."

"He was returning from a neighboring farm and asked why we were on his property. I told him this was the only place we could find where my wife and her friends wouldn't discover our little tryst. He told me to have a good night."

Maggie's jaw dropped. "Seth Daniels that's a terrible thing to imply! That man thinks I'm some sort of floozy!"

"Maybe so, but he didn't question our presence any further. We're safe for the night," he snickered, raising an eyebrow. "You're welcome."

"Thank you for ruining my reputation with such an indecent innuendo," she retorted.

"You'll never see this guy again, and he doesn't know who we are anyway," he yawned. "It's getting late and we need to get some rest."

"What if he comes back to, you know, watch or something?"

"Now who's being indecent? Trust me, he won't be back," Seth chuckled.

"How do you know?"

"Because I know how men are," he said, raising his eyebrows. "You sleep in the wagon and I'll sleep here."

"Exiling me to the wagon, eh? Afraid I'll take advantage of you in the middle of the night?" she scoffed, getting to her feet.

"You don't have the courage," he replied, shifting his hat over his face.

Maggie crawled into the back of the wagon and curled up on a mattress of hay. She felt badly that Seth was sleeping on the hard ground but also realized this was probably a common occurrence for him. Closing her eyes, she tried to shift her thoughts from the memory of Seth's lips pressed against hers, but to no avail. Although the kiss was without passion, it had stirred the longing rooted in the depths of her heart. She shifted on the hay and stared at the twinkling canopy above wondering what her Da was doing at that very moment. The weight of the day's travels fluttered her lashes until slumber ushered her to a land of troubled dreams and wicked uncles.

MAGGIE SLIPPED into a dreamscape where she padded down the aisle of the cattle barn as the cows rustled on straw bedding awaiting their morning feed. A deathly chill gripped the morning air, biting at her skin like hounds devouring their prey. Her heart pounded as she looked around for Sellers who should have been wheeling the hay cart down the aisle by this time of the morning. A foreboding feeling slithered through her soul making her hair stand on end. All of a sudden, she spied the hay cart parked in front of her. Looking around, she searched for Sellers, her eyes scanning the area when the quietude was shattered by Mr. Stevenson's voice shouting her name.

"Maggie McFarland, you worthless coward! Come here this instant!"

She willed herself to flee but her legs refused to move. Her uncle's footfalls amplified the anger stewing within him.

"Stupid Irish tramp, where are you?"

Terror strangled her words and weighted her legs, preventing her from running away. She managed to slip behind a wall of hay bales as her uncle entered the barn blustering for her to reveal her location. His words rang out with the force of a trumpet, and despite the hay bales separating them, she could feel the heat of his breath on her neck.

"You can't hide from me! I'll kill you when I find you!"

Maggie tried to breathe but her lungs wouldn't take in air. He was only inches from her when she heard him whisper, "I won't kill you but I will destroy your soul. Say goodbye to him..."

The sound of the hammer being cocked loosened her muscles, allowing her to step out from her hiding place as he pulled the trigger. She was too late, again. Kneeling by the body, she cradled Seller's bloodied head in her hands. But instead of Sellers' face, it was Seth's.

A scream erupted from Maggie's lips as she bolted upright, her limbs quivering and her eyes blurred with tears. Seth stood at the side of the wagon with the gun clutched in his hand and the right side of his hair rumpled from sleep.

"What's the matter?" he asked breathlessly, his eyes darting around.

Grasping her chest, Maggie gulped in the fresh air as her mind adjusted to wakefulness.

"I'm so sorry for waking you. It was just a bad dream."

His shoulders relaxed as he replaced the gun in its holster.

"You going to be OK?" His words were soft, melting the tension holding her muscles hostage.

"I'm fine now. Sometimes the nightmares get the better of me," she said, rubbing her arms. "I'm sorry for disturbing you."

"No need to apologize, we all have ghosts. Do you want to talk about it?"

"No, thank you anyway," she mumbled, shaking her head.

"Try to get some sleep."

The right side of Seth's mouth curled, sending a flutter through Maggie's stomach. He returned to his spot on the ground while Maggie snuggled against the straw, unable to close her eyes for fear the gruesome images would return. Although Seth could keep her safe from an angry uncle, he couldn't protect her from the guilt of her cowardice and the pain she'd caused so many.

PART III

36

The grass of the pasture glowed in the early morning sun while Maggie watched Seth make repairs to the wagon wheel. Brushing the dust from his knees, Seth stood declaring the wagon was safe for travel.

They sat on the ground eating the remainder of the biscuits and ham amongst a flurry of birdsong. From the corner of her eye, Maggie watched as a soft breeze ruffled the curls at the bottom of Seth's hair. Something in his countenance exuded comfort, making her feel at ease.

"Did you get any sleep last night?" he finally asked.

"Not much," she said, fidgeting with a loose button on the bodice of her dress. "But I haven't slept well since arriving in America."

"Why not?"

Shaking her head, she shrugged her shoulders and looked away. Seth moved closer and touched her hand.

"Sometimes it helps to share it with a friend."

Maggie inhaled, trying to figure out what to say without revealing too much. She didn't want to taint Seth's opinion of her.

"Maybe you can explain why people in this country hate the Irish?"

He huffed. "People hate what they don't understand and can't control. I don't think they're opposed to your culture, it's fear that things might change. Look at the Negroes. They're human beings and pose no threat, yet people treat them worse than animals."

"But you don't feel that way."

"My mother raised me better than that." He picked up a small stick and traced circles in the dirt. "My mother was an intelligent, compassionate woman who raised me to think for myself and to consider the feelings of others."

His jaw clenched as he tossed the stick into a patch of tall grass several feet away. "My father was a drunken brute who hated everyone and everything that he deemed a threat to his authority. With each slap and every punch my father inflicted on me, I grew more determined to hold on to the wisdom of my mother. His need to beat her teachings out of me only made me stronger and more resolute in my effort to defy his ways.

"I suppose that's why I love the Polks, they have the same values as my mother." A smile creased his eyes. "And Elora has the innocence and integrity of a child, yet she's not afraid to stand up for others. Her lighthearted nature touches everyone. When I'm with her, I forget about the horrors of my childhood."

Maggie forced her lips to curl. "You sound like you adore her."

Seth's smile broadened and his eyes sparkled. "I love her."

His declaration crushed her chest like an anvil. She could no longer deny her suspicions regarding his attachment to Elora or the reality that he would never be anything more than a close friend. All of a sudden, Maggie longed to be on the road and escape the lingering whisper of Seth's kiss from the night before and the burgeoning of her heart for a man she could never have.

They finished their meal and prepped the horses for travel. Shortly thereafter, they were back on the road, much to Maggie's delight. Although the danger had passed, the failure of the mission along with her longing for Seth weighed heavily on her mind making the journey to Rose Hall feel like an eternity. As the wagon rocked back and forth, Maggie's thoughts swirled from the gruesome scene in the cabin to the guilt of kissing Seth. Technically, they'd done nothing wrong. After all, it was only a ruse to prevent trouble with a stranger, except Maggie's feelings were genuine.

Maggie's thoughts kept her company as they plodded along the main road, Seth riding ahead of the wagon. It seemed her life had gone from difficult to complicated to impossible. When he did ride alongside her, she tried not to focus on the curve of his jaw, the deep blue of his eyes, or the crown of sandy curls furrowing from beneath his hat. Heat radiated through her body at the thought of him, rising to her cheeks like a beacon to all who saw her. It was nothing more than an infatuation, she told herself because of the kindness he'd shown her. She was determined to quell her affections and see Seth the same way he saw her, as nothing more than a friend.

A familiar line of trees rose from the horizon, guiding them to the entrance of Rose Hall. At the sight of the towering roofline, Maggie's shoulders released the tension holding them captive. It was good to be back. She felt as if she'd lived a hundred lives in the weeks they'd been away. As they trotted up to the stables, Hatch emerged, a broad smile wrinkling his face.

"Welcome home!"

"It's good to be home," Seth replied, vaulting to the ground and leading Phantom into the barn.

Hatch helped Maggie down from the bench seat.

"Miss Maggie, I can drive you to the house, if you want," Hatch offered.

"No, thank you. I'd like to walk and get the blood flowing in my legs," she said, grabbing her satchel.

He gave a nod and began unhitching the horses. Maggie trudged along the sandy path, her limbs weary, her joints aching, and her heart in tatters. She hoped to slip into the house unnoticed so she could gather her wits before having to answer questions and face Elora.

Maggie entered through the back door, closing it gently behind her. Tiptoeing up the back stairs, she held her breath and listened for sounds of activity. When she reached the second floor, she exhaled and hurried to her room. Once inside, she scanned the elegant space with all the luxuries a person could desire; a comfortable bed, a beautiful view, fresh water in the pitcher, and the freedom to come and go as she pleased. Her chest tightened, squeezing tears from her eyes.

How could she enjoy these things when others suffered so horribly? Bea's face haunted her. She'd endured so much, being sold from place to place, beaten, mistreated, and overlooked as a human being. Maggie cried for the unfairness of it all and the hopes and dreams that drowned with her that night. At least Hannah had a chance for a better life.

When her tears ran dry, Maggie washed her face, changed into a clean dress, and rested on the bed for a bit, reading a few pages of Byron to settle her troubled soul. When she felt strong enough to face questions about the journey, she made her way down the winding staircase to the front parlor where Elora and Mrs. Polk chatted.

"Maggie! You're back!" Elora squealed, wrapping Maggie in a tight embrace. "When did you get home?"

"A short while ago. I wanted to make myself presentable before coming down."

"Where's Seth?"

"He was at the stables when I last saw him."

"Well, let's take a walk and find him, shall we?"

"Elora, perhaps Maggie wants to rest a bit," Mrs. Polk said. "She's just returned from a long journey."

"I'm sorry, I wasn't thinking."

"I'd enjoy a stroll." Maggie hoped Elora's exuberance would wash away her sorrow. No doubt, Dr. Polk would want a full report of the excursion. The idea of reliving it took her breath away.

Arm in arm the two made their way out the front door when Seth approached. Elora bolted down the stairs, wrapping her arms around him as he lifted her from the ground in a bear hug.

"I'm so glad you're home!" she squealed with delight.

He kissed the top of her head, glancing toward Maggie who shifted her gaze to the porch floor. Seth draped his arm about Elora's shoulder as they climbed the stairs. Elora broke free and hurried into the house to tell her mother Seth had arrived.

Touching Maggie's arm, he whispered, "Let's not say anything about last night."

She nodded, her throat tightening and her heart thumping. At that moment, Maggie wanted to escape. She padded down the porch steps to continue her walk.

"Wait for me!" Elora hollered, catching up with Maggie.

"Where's Seth?"

"He needed to speak with Father about the trip."

"Of course," Maggie replied, looking out over the marsh as they strolled along the sandy path. "Does your father need to speak with me as well?"

"If he does, he'll send for you."

They strolled in silence when Maggie gathered her courage to ask about what had transpired in her absence.

"What happened with my uncle?"

"The plan worked splendidly. He actually believed you were dead."

Maggie's knees gave way as Elora tightened her grip on Maggie's arm steadying her.

"Are you alright?"

"Just overwhelmed. I never thought I'd ever be free of him. Tell me what happened."

"Father went to the Bartlett's and told them about a young woman matching your description that had died at our house after traveling from Pennsylvania. Your uncle believed the story and came to see your grave."

"My grave?" Maggie declared, stopping to look at her friend. "What grave?"

Elora giggled and started walking again. "Actually, it's Willie's grave, my pet donkey."

"You buried a donkey?"

"He was my favorite pet when I was little. When he died I insisted he be buried. I even planted flowers on his grave."

"And my uncle believed I was buried there?"

"Why would he question it? There's a cross with no identifying names and a patch of flowers."

"Are you certain he's not coming back?"

"I doubt he'll ever set foot on our property again. He was as callous as you described. When father charged him for your expenses and the cost of burying you, he wanted nothing more to do with this place."

"I can't believe my uncle paid anything."

"He didn't pay exactly. Father negotiated your expenses in exchange for the gambling debt Mr. Bartlett had incurred. So, you see, the plan benefited everyone involved."

Maggie filled her lungs with the pungent scent of the marsh trying to accept her newfound freedom. Perhaps she could have enjoyed the moment more if she weren't burdened by the failed mission and her burgeoning feelings for Seth.

AFTER MEETING WITH DR. POLK, Seth headed toward the stables when he saw Elora speaking with Maggie. They looked so serious he decided to lighten the mood. Grabbing a stick, he ran up to Elora, swatting the back of her skirt.

"Aye me princess, have ye seen me ship?" he clamored in a gruff voice.

"Of course not, you wretched marauder!"

A series of giggles followed as Seth chased Elora about with his makeshift sword. Maggie watched the two bantering, their obvious affection weighting her heart like an anchor.

Without warning, Seth ran for Maggie, lifting her in his arms and dashing for the marsh. He stopped at the edge with her teetering over the water.

"Princess Polk, shall I throw this stowaway overboard or make her walk the plank?"

The strength of Seth's arms made Maggie feel secure, despite his threats to toss her into the water. At this angle, she could see the specks of gold in his blue eyes and the depth of the scar rippling down his right cheek. *Stop staring,* she thought as Elora scurried toward them.

"Let's make her swab the deck!"

Seth looked at Maggie, his face only inches from hers. "What'll it be for you, m'lady? A swim in the river or cleaning up behind the messiest princess to sail the seven seas?"

Maggie's tongue stuck to the roof of her mouth. Staring at him, she was certain he could feel the thumping of her heart and the blood rushing through her veins.

"If she refuses to speak, she must be a spy!" Elora hollered.

Jolting from her trance, Maggie's playfulness emerged.

"I don't believe this pirate has the courage to throw me overboard. He looks a wee bit yellow to me!" her words rolled out in an Irish brogue.

With a chuckle, Seth's eyebrows raised as he hoisted Maggie closer, "So ye thinks I be a scared mite does ya? Let's just see about that!"

At that moment, it occurred to Maggie that he'd accepted her challenge.

"No Seth, I was only joking! Don't you dare..."

Seth hurled Maggie forward over the embankment into the salty marsh waters with a splash.

Elora squealed, backing away as Seth rushed toward her. But her efforts failed as he lifted her effortlessly over his shoulder discarding her in the same fashion, leaving the two friends on a throne of sticky pluff mud. Strands of dampened hair clung to their faces while Seth stood on the shore raising his pretend sword to the skies in triumph.

"Captain Daniels has defeated the lady pirateers and now declares this shore off limits to all scalawags of the female pursuasion!"

Maggie looked at Elora with a sly smile, "Shall we?"

"Oh my, yes," she replied.

The two emerged from the water, walking side by side to the edge as Seth began to back away.

"Ladies, we're just having some fun. No need for retaliation."

Maggie whispered, "On three, you go left and I'll go right."

Elora nodded.

"Three!"

Seth started to run but tumbled to the ground when the toe of his boot caught on a tree root. The girls converged, each grabbing an arm, lifting him to his feet and dragging him toward the water's edge. They started to catapult him into the water, but before they could release their grip, he twisted his hands and grasped their wrists, pulling them in with him. With a splash, the three sat, soaked and muddy laughing hysterically when Miss Heddy walked past. Stopping, she looked at them, shook her head, and went on her way.

After splashing about in the water, they emerged, sodden and muddy but filled with playful exhilaration. With a deep bow, Seth bid them adieu, salt water dripping from his soaked ringlets as he walked to his cottage. Elora and Maggie headed for the house.

"What are you thinking about?" Elora asked as they sloshed along.

"How wonderful it is to be free."

Elora wrapped her arm about Maggie's waist, rested her head upon her shoulder, and whispered, "Missed you."

"Missed you too."

"Last one to the house has to launder these wet dresses," Elora declared, breaking into a run.

Maggie took off in close pursuit. With skirts flying, the two raced up the brick stairs, tagging the double front doors simultaneously.

"And who washes the dresses in the event of a tie?" Maggie asked.

"Last one to reach the second floor!"

Elora slipped in the door and bolted up the sweeping staircase two steps at a time, leaving Maggie in her wake.

"I suppose I've got some laundering to do," Maggie gasped as she reached the top of the stairs.

"Normally, I'd hold you to that deal but being I've missed you so, I shall forego the penalty and agree we wash our own clothes."

"Fair enough."

The two girls retired to their bedchambers to change. The following morning, they scrubbed and rinsed the dresses, hanging them from tree branches to dry in the sweet summer breezes.

37

Weeks had passed since their return and Seth was scheduled to leave that day on another mission to Virginia. Lured by the aroma of coffee, Maggie dressed and made her way to the dining room. When she arrived, she found Elora and Seth side by side with their heads bowed together in what appeared to be an intimate conversation.

"Please forgive me. I didn't mean to interrupt," Maggie said, turning around, a flush coloring her cheeks.

"Don't be silly," Elora replied, straightening up. "I'm certain Seth would be happy to share." Elora nudged Seth who shifted in his seat.

Seth's cheeks reddened as he looked away, obviously not wanting to discuss their personal exchange.

"I only came for a cup of coffee. I've some things to do before breakfast," Maggie muttered before rushing from the room.

In her urgency to escape the awkward situation, she forgot the coffee. *What's wrong with you?* she thought, scurrying to the top of the stairs. There was no reason to be embarrassed. It wasn't as if they were in a passionate embrace, they were merely speaking in a confidential manner. So why were her palms sweating and her heart racing? Not wanting to return so soon after departing, Maggie decided to straighten her room before joining the family for breakfast.

When Maggie finally returned to the dining room, Dr. and Mrs. Polk had joined the two paramours. Seth and Elora were engaged in a lively conversation as Maggie slipped into her spot at the table. Elora reached for Maggie's hand.

"My apologies for earlier. I hope I didn't make you uncomfortable."

"Not at all," Maggie replied, trying to appear nonchalant. "I forgot something in my room and needed to take care of it." Maggie silently scolded herself for such a lame response. Thankfully, Elora didn't query further.

When the morning meal was over, Elora and Maggie followed Seth to the porch where Phantom waited.

"Don't go stirring up trouble while I'm away," he said, sweeping Elora into a strong embrace.

"The only trouble I get into is with you," she said, tousling his hair.

"Miss Milner, I expect you to be a good example to Elora and don't fall prey to her antics," he commanded, placing his hat upon his head.

"I'll do my best, Captain Daniels," Maggie replied with a salute, sending Elora into a fit of giggles. His gaze locked onto hers cutting through her heart like a warm knife through butter.

Seth mounted Phantom, touched the brim of his hat, and rode off. A part of Maggie wanted to accompany him, although she wasn't sure if the reason was to be of assistance or just to be near him. Elora sniffled, catching Maggie's attention.

"Are you alright?" Maggie asked.

"I miss him when he's away. This is a complicated endeavor

and while I know he's resourceful, I worry all the same." Wiping the moisture from the corners of her eyes, Elora brightened. "Of course, you're here which makes his absence bearable."

A pang of guilt dampened Maggie's spirits at the memory of her interaction with Seth in the farmer's field. Her longing for him only made matters worse. It seemed the more she fought to sever her feelings, the stronger they grew. Thankfully, there was plenty of work to distract her while he was away, and she intended to take full advantage of the diversion.

SETH HAD BEEN GONE for nearly a week when Dr. Polk sent for Maggie. She hurried along the water's edge from Miss Heddy's as seagulls drifted and dipped in a brilliant blue sky. Going in the side entry, she rapped on the doorframe of Dr. Polk's office.

"Come in," he called.

Breezes wafted through open windows caressing Maggie's cheek as she stepped into the room.

"Thank you for coming so quickly. I need you to run an errand for me."

"Of course."

"I'd ask Elora but she's with her mother visiting Mrs. Bartlett. Please take this note to Mr. Tindell. It's imperative he post this in the morning edition. Hatch will have Fancy ready to go," he said, handing her the envelope.

Intrigued by the urgency of Dr. Polk's directive, Maggie considered asking about the contents but thought better of it; instead, she walked to the barn where she found Fancy tacked and waiting.

"Hello Hatch," Maggie smiled.

"Hey Miss Maggie. Be sure to check dat saddle. You know how Fancy like to blow up her belly so the saddle slide off when you puts your foot in the stirrup."

"Thanks for the reminder," Maggie said with a wink. Tightening the girth, she mounted up, bid Hatch goodbye, and made her way to town.

Fancy trotted along while Maggie took in the splendor of skittering squirrels and soaring pelicans as trees whispered their secrets in the late summer breeze. Although she enjoyed her work, she was thankful for a break from the regular routine.

Trotting down the dirt roadway, she steered Fancy to the Tindell residence, dismounted, and knocked on the door. She listened to the echo of footfalls before the door swung open and Rudy appeared with a broad smile, his blue eyes twinkling.

"Good afternoon, Miss Milner. What can I do for you today?"

"Dr. Polk sent me. He needs you to place an ad in tomorrow's publication," she said, handing him the note.

He unfolded it, his jovial countenance dissolving into concern. "I'll get this published directly."

"Is everything alright?"

"It will be," he said, although his obvious unease suggested otherwise.

"Is there something I can do?" she asked.

"Not at this time. It's probably best you head back to Rose Hall," he replied, staring at the note as he stepped inside.

"Thank you, Mr. Tindell," Maggie called out as the door closed.

Maggie rode back to the plantation as clouds clustered overhead. Something about Mr. Tindell's reaction rankled her nerves. For a fleeting moment, her mind drifted to her uncle. *Was it possible he'd discovered the Polk's deception? Is that why everyone was acting so secretive?*

Shaking off the thought, Maggie chastised herself for worrying. She was safe now and had meaningful employment. Her Da would be so proud. Her eyes misted at the thought of her beloved father and the fact she'd not spoken with him in what seemed an eternity. She nudged Fancy along as the wind picked up and a soft drizzle began to stipple the roadway.

DIAMOND-SIZED DROPS PELTED the ground as Maggie rode up to the barn. Leaving Fancy with Hatch, she hurried back to the house, the rain intensifying. A chill bumped across her damp skin as a strong breeze accompanied her through the back door. Once inside she traipsed to the front parlor where she found Elora pacing, her eyes puffy and her demeanor melancholy.

"My dear Maggie, I'm so glad you're back. I was worried you'd get caught in the storm."

"What's wrong?"

Elora inhaled deeply. "It's Seth. He missed the first checkpoint and we've not heard from him. Even worse, the route he was supposed to take has been compromised."

Maggie's breath caught at the idea that Seth was in danger. "Has he gone silent before?"

"Once, but it was a completely different situation," she said, wiping away a tear. "He'd sent a notice to a paper and somehow they failed to print his message. It was a harrowing few days, but not a situation likely to repeat itself."

"Perhaps he's staying quiet for safety reasons to protect his cargo. I'm certain he's just being cautious to keep everyone safe."

Like the rain falling from the clouds outside, tears soaked Elora's reddened cheeks.

"Forgive me but I need to lie down. My head is pounding." Elora hurried from the room leaving Maggie jittery with anxiety.

The idea that Seth could be hurt, or worse, plagued her. Maggie stared at the sheets of water cascading down the windowpanes trying not to let her imagination run wild with images of Seth injured or lying in a ditch. Chewing her lower lip, she reminded herself that Dr. Polk would do everything possible to see his daughter's beau home safely. Nevertheless, worry wrapped its sinewy fingers around her heart. Unable to settle, she walked down the hall and knocked on Dr. Polk's office door.

"Maggie, I'm glad you made it home before the rain got too heavy. Won't you come in?" he said, motioning for Maggie to take a seat.

"Forgive my interruption, but have you heard from Seth?"

"I see you've spoken with Elora," he sighed, sitting on the chair across from Maggie. "I suppose you've deduced the message I sent to be published in tomorrow's Home Hearth is for Seth. Please don't worry, he's a resourceful man. This isn't the first time we've had a lapse of communication, but the situation is a delicate one. It's better he not reveal his location by communicating with us. All the same, when he sees the message, he'll know what to do."

"How can I help?" Maggie asked, a sense of helplessness dissolving her fortitude.

Dr. Polk leaned forward, resting his elbows on his thighs.

"Keep my daughter calm. She can be overly sensitive when it comes to Seth."

"I'll do my best."

Maggie left his office, worry weighting her shoulders as she climbed the back stairs. While she appreciated the doctor's encouraging words, she could see the concern in his eyes. Obviously, he was worried or he wouldn't have placed the ad. All the same, Maggie would do her best to sooth Elora's frazzled nerves while trying to keep her own worries at bay.

~

THE FOLLOWING day an ad appeared in the personal section of a Virginia paper.

$1,000 reward offered for runaway slave from Bluffton, SC. Last seen traveling toward Virginia border with three horses. If seen, please send correspondence to the Baltimore Herald, care of Rudolf Tindell.

The notice was code, informing Seth to avoid the Virginia border where hunters were searching for the missing slave woman and her three children. Disquiet shrouded Rose Hall. Seth was well past the time allotted for the transport and he'd not sent any communication. Hopefully, he would see the message, take an alternate route, and get the passengers to safety.

FOLLOWING weeks of heightened nerves and wringing hands, the sound of the front door opening and closing accompanied by Elora's squeal of Seth's name sent chills bumping across Maggie's skin. She hesitated before going downstairs, debating whether or not to join their reunion. Shaking off her trepidation, she scampered down the winding staircase stopping momentarily to check her reflection in the pier mirror. She straightened her bodice and swept back a few loose wisps of hair before mentally scolding herself for being so vain. Voices emanated from the front parlor where Elora sat next to Seth, her head resting on his shoulder while he spoke with Dr. Polk about the journey.

Although his appearance was slightly disheveled and he'd lost a few pounds, his demeanor was the same sturdy Seth they all adored.

"So glad you've arrived safely," Maggie said, secretly wishing she could sit where Elora was.

"It's good to be back," he replied with a smile.

His baritone voice strummed Maggie's heart like a

mandolin, sending a flutter through her chest. The conversation took several turns before arriving at the recent mission.

"Were you able to get the passengers to safety?" Dr. Polk asked.

"I was able to help the woman, and two of the children..." Seth looked down, a hush suffocating the excitement of his return.

Dr. Polk took in a deep breath. "What happened?"

"I picked up Miss Patsy and her three children at the designated location and we made our way through North Carolina. When I heard barking in the distance, I realized we'd have to take a detour. I remembered a family in the vicinity who'd helped us once before and took refuge there. The next morning, we found the infant to be with fever, making her extremely fussy. We didn't want to risk her health or being caught, so we decided to leave the baby with the family. I assured Patsy we would do our best to reunite them at a later date.

"The following night, we started out again but only made it as far as the neighboring village. A group of hunters was searching carriages passing through the area. Fortunately, I was able to turn around without notice but we couldn't go back the way we'd traveled so I took an alternate route.

"I found an abandoned farmhouse along the way where we stayed the night. The little ones started hollering for something to eat but I had nothing to offer. I feared their wailing would reveal our location so we moved on. By daylight they'd fallen asleep, exhausted from their crying. I picked up the Baltimore Herald and saw the message and went a different direction. I managed to get the family to the next station but somehow the hunters were able to keep up. It's almost as if they knew where we were going. The crying children were jeopardizing the mission so I tried to convince her to leave them behind with one of the stationmasters, again promising to reunite them later, but she refused.

"That's when I decided we needed to go straight to Ohio and forego any other stops. It took three extra days and two alternate routes to get to Mr. Coffin's house. It's no wonder the hunters were steadfast in their efforts with a $2500 reward offered.

"Were you able to get the baby back to her?" Elora asked, her eyes locked on Seth as her hand entwined his.

Shaking his head, he responded sullenly.

"The family caring for the infant was captured two days after we left them. The woman went to town for supplies and the merchant thought it strange when she purchased items for a baby when her children were much older. Apparently, the hunters stopped at the mercantile and convinced the shopkeeper to give them information."

Elora gasped, "What happened to the family sheltering the baby?"

Seth rolled his lips and stared at the ground when Dr. Polk intervened.

"I'm sure Mr. Daniels is weary from his journey. Why don't you and Maggie see about helping Miss Olive? She's had a great deal to do these past few days."

Elora kissed Seth's cheek before scurrying from the room with Maggie on her heels. As they walked out the door, Maggie's imagination ran wild with horrible visions of what had happened to the family who'd risked everything to help strangers. It seemed there was always some sort of interference or dilemma. She was tired of all the effort and risk, only to be thwarted by flesh pedaling savages. For a moment, the fiery temper she knew as a small child resurfaced but she squelched it. Hotheadedness wouldn't help the situation. If she was going to contribute to this organization, she must remain calm and think clearly.

"It can't have ended well if Father is sending us away," Elora said.

"What do you mean?"

"He thinks I'm too fragile to know what really goes on. But I'm not. I can handle the things he seeks to shield me from."

"Elora, let your father protect you from the miseries of this world as long as he can. There's no need to experience too much before you're ready."

She stopped and looked at Maggie. "Just because I'm female doesn't mean I'm fragile. I can handle anything a man can."

"I think there's more to it than your gender," Maggie huffed.

"Well, if you think it's my age that shouldn't matter either. I'm not much younger than you and I've already assisted with several missions."

"How dangerous were they?"

Elora shrugged. "Not terribly dangerous, but transporting escapees is always risky."

Maggie draped her arm over Elora's shoulder and pulled her close. "It's hard for a father to release his daughter into a cruel world. Let him shield you as long as he can. You'll be under the shelter of another soon enough."

"I suppose you're right," she sighed.

When they reached the cottage, Miss Olive welcomed them with her usual satirical greeting and put them straight to work.

38

When the last plate was cleared from the dinner table, Seth grabbed Maggie's hand and led her to the front porch. Resting his hands on her shoulders, he stood before her, his lips curling into a smile as the breeze tousled his hair.

"I didn't get a chance to tell you earlier about the good news."

"Good news?" Maggie tried to focus on his face and not the warmth spreading through her body at his touch.

"While I was with Mr. Coffin, he told me that Bea and Elijah were reunited with Hannah."

"But how?" she gasped, clutching her chest. "I thought she and Elijah drowned."

"Apparently, she knew how to swim and managed to get to shore. She remembered what we'd discussed about our route and made her way to Mr. Coffin's home. She's one smart woman."

"I can't believe she was strong enough to swim through the Ohio River at night with her son!"

"Never underestimate the power of a mother's love," he said with a smile.

"Are they still with Mr. Coffin?"

"They were safely transported across the Canadian border."

Maggie's hand rested on her lips as an overwhelming sense of joy pooled in her eyes. *They'd made it. Bea's dream of freedom had come to fruition.*

"Are you ok?"

She nodded, too overcome with emotion to speak. Before she could compose herself, Elora stepped through the front door, her exuberance filling the air with electricity.

"I turn my back for one second and you two run off without me!" she declared playfully until she noticed Maggie's tears. Her eyes formed slits as she planted her hands on her hips. "Seth Daniels, what did you say to make her cry?"

"Nothing terrible, he gave me some good news," she replied, wiping tears from her cheeks.

"Then I shan't scold you for ungentlemanly behavior," Elora said with her nose in the air.

Seth cleared his throat. "I believe you owe me an apology for assuming I'd said something unsuitable to Maggie," he stated matter-of-factly.

"Very well, I'm sorry for misinterpreting the situation."

Maggie chuckled at their antics when Mrs. Polk popped her head out the door. "Ladies, Seth, I'm afraid your leisurely evening has come to a close."

"Is everything alright?" Elora asked.

"We have stragglers. Your father is speaking with them now."

They walked inside where Dr. Polk met them in the entryway, his countenance one of a serious nature.

"We have two escapees who were separated from two others when they heard dogs and ran. The last they saw of their party was at the border of the Houston's place. I've alerted Hatch who is preparing a wagon. It's getting dark, which will work in our favor. Maggie, you already know how to drive the team and Elora knows the trails. Seth will scout ahead of you and hopefully find the men safe. It's imperative you do as Seth instructs you. This is an extremely precarious situation and we cannot risk anyone following you. Do I make myself clear?"

"Yes sir," they chimed in unison.

"Seth will meet you at the stables. I have a few things to discuss with him first."

"Do we need to take anything in case of injuries?" Maggie queried.

"There's no time for that. As I said, this is a delicate situation. I'm not in favor of sending either of you but we haven't a choice."

Elora and Maggie hurried to the barn where the horse drawn wagon waited. Hatch helped them onto the bench seat and handed Maggie the reins.

"Keep a steady hand with dese two. Remember, dey can be skittish in de dark."

"I'll do my best," she replied, taking the reins. Seth approached and spoke with Hatch for a few moments before retrieving Phantom from the barn.

Maggie and Elora waited quietly in the wagon as the last bit of light faded from the sky. The moon shimmered across the glassy water, giving the atmosphere an eerie feel. The moss was still as death and even the crickets seemed mute.

Seth emerged from the barn, leading Phantom who seemed exceptionally alert, his ears twitching and his eyes wild. Hatch held the ebony steed who pawed the ground as Seth vaulted to the saddle in one graceful move.

"Ready?" he asked.

Maggie nodded and cued the horses forward. Seth trotted alongside, issuing directions.

"We're going to take the old cotton road along the marsh to

the south of the Houston's property. I'll ride ahead and search for the men. Once I find them, I'll bring them back to you and we'll stow them below the planks in the wagon bed. Under no circumstances are you to follow me or come looking for me, no matter how long I take. Understood?"

Elora nodded as Maggie stared at Seth. She'd never seen him so serious before, not even on the mission to Ohio. *He must be worried about Elora*, she thought. No doubt he felt a strong need to keep her safe.

"Maggie, did you bring a pistol?" he asked.

"No, we went straight to the barn."

Seth reached into his pocket and removed a small gun and handed it to her. "Keep this in case you need it. I only hope the Houstons aren't aware of these men. I'm sure there's a reward offered and they never miss an opportunity to make a buck."

Maggie slipped the gun into her pocket and drove the horses forward as Seth moved a short distance ahead of them. They left the main road onto an old trail littered with fallen limbs, ruts, and underbrush making passage difficult. The noise from the wagon's rattling planks seemed to echo through the woods like a trumpet announcing their arrival. As the trail curved toward the river, Seth held his hand out to stop them. Voices and barking echoed in the distance.

"The wagon's making too much noise. You stay here," he said, dismounting. "If anyone tries to harm either of you, shoot them. And under no circumstances are you to leave this spot until I come back."

"Maybe I should go with you," Maggie offered. "What if one of the men is injured?"

Seth's jaw tightened as he stepped toward her, his eyes blazing in the moonlight.

"Do not follow me. If there are any injuries, I'll handle it." His words tumbled from his lips in a growl. He draped Phantom's reins over a low hanging branch and made his way toward the commotion.

"Have you ever seen him like this?" Maggie whispered.

"No, but I'm sure he's just being cautious," Elora replied.

Maggie shifted on the seat, her senses on high alert as every little sound sent her heart racing. Even Elora's bubbly personality was subdued.

Time passed at a turtle's pace making Maggie antsy. The hair on her neck bristled as voices escalated amidst the barking. Visions of Sellers body sprawled on the floor of the cattle barn and the carnage in the cabin in Ohio taunted her.

"Stay here," she said, handing the reins to Elora and climbing down from the seat.

"Where are you going?" she muttered, alarm tinting her words. "Seth said to stay here."

"Trust me, I know what I'm doing. Don't leave the wagon, I won't be long."

Maggie crept along the trail careful not to make too much noise. As she navigated through clumps of underbrush and across tree stumps, she spied Seth crouched under a massive live oak. His eyes widened when he saw her approaching.

"What are you doing?" he said, gritting his teeth.

"I couldn't stay behind and do nothing."

"Go back to Elora this instant!" he demanded.

"She's fine. I'm here to help."

"This is no time to try to prove yourself. Go back." His eyes narrowed into slits and his cheeks colored.

"I'm not trying to prove..."

Seth put his finger to his lips as the barking intensified.

"Stay here and do *not* move," he instructed.

He scaled the tree to a branch several feet up. His ability to climb without making a sound reinforced his nickname of the Ghost.

Maggie squatted at the base of the tree with the pistol in her hand should she need it. Her knees began to ache and her feet tingled but she didn't dare move for fear the dogs would hear. She watched as Seth stretched along the branch on his stomach.

From her vantage point, she could see a group of men armed with shotguns accompanied by several hounds circling the escapees. Mr. Blakely, overseer for the Houston's plantation, led the group. Adrenaline pulsed through Maggie's body as Seth climbed back down the tree.

"It's not good. There are about eight men and several dogs surrounding the runaways."

Maggie started to rise when Seth yanked her back.

"Where do you think you're going?"

"We can't just sit here."

"There are two of us and eight of them."

"We have to help."

His grip tightened, radiating pain through her arm.

"They have rifles and we have two pistols. Elora has nothing. If we move in now, you'll get us all killed."

Maggie shrank beneath the sharpness of his gaze. She hadn't thought about the fact she had the gun and Elora had nothing. Her foolishness had put her friend in danger.

"I'm sorry," she muttered.

"Don't be. This was doomed from the start."

"What do we do?"

He exhaled. "We wait."

"What about Elora?"

He shook his head. "We need to stay here until they take the men captive and are out of earshot. Then we can make our way back."

Maggie fought to extinguish the anguish burning in her chest. Knowing what the escapees would endure when they returned to their master was disheartening. Her ruminations were interrupted when a voice cut through the night air.

"You darkies think you can just pick up and leave without a farewell party?" Blakely hollered at the quivering men.

"No sir," one man responded. "We don' mean no harm sir, we jes got lost in de dark. We don' want no trouble," he said, his eyes bulging with fear.

"Fellas, you reckon these darkies are telling the truth?" Blakely hollered.

"Not likely," one yelled, punctuating the phrase with a wad of spittle, his scraggly mustache and beard camouflaging several rotting teeth. He lifted his gun and aimed it at the two runaways, making one man wet himself.

With arms raised in front of their faces and terror pooling in their eyes, one escapee pleaded, "Sir, we's willin' to go back wid you and never go out after dark again, promise."

"You boys hear that? They want to go home." Blakely's head rolled back, a laugh exploding from his lips. "You say you won't run again but how can we believe you?"

"We ain't runnin sir, we's jus lost."

"Now that we can agree on. You *are* lost." Blakely raised his gun, the other men following suit.

"We's sorry sir, honest! We's sorry! Please don' shoot us, we go back wid you!" the other man pleaded, his arms shaking like tree branches in a storm.

"Since you asked nicely, I reckon we won't shoot you." A sinister grin wrinkled Blakely's upper lip as he glanced at his comrades. "You heard the darkie, he don't want us to shoot him." The men laughed as the two escapees stood wide-eyed and quivering.

"We can't have other slaves thinkin' they can run away. And don't tell me you're lost. If a darkie's lips are moving, he's lyin'," Blakely huffed. "We need to make an example of you two so others don't fall into the same situation. Don't you want to help your kind avoid what you're facing right now?"

"Yes sir!" they replied in unison.

"As a man of my word, I won't shoot you," Blakely said with a smile.

The two runaways lowered their arms, apparently relieved they'd been spared.

Maggie's body stiffened as she watched the exchange, helplessness knotting her stomach. No doubt, Blakely had some sort of sinister plan for the runaways that probably involved whipping them within an inch of their lives. Seth's countenance was one of disgust, his lips taut and his breathing labored. She could tell he was upset about the inability to intervene, not to mention that Elora was alone.

"What do you think we should do fellas?" Blakely asked. "These darkies ain't worth much and no reward's been offered."

"Ain't but one thing to do," one man replied with a sly grin.

"What's that?" another asked.

"Release the hounds!" Blakely bellowed.

In a chorus of snarls and barks, the dogs descended on the terrified men. Maggie squeezed her eyes shut and cupped her hands over her ears. The sound of flesh being torn from bone intermingled with the escapees' screams as the dogs attacked without resignation. The melee rose in volume with each bite and every plea. Laughter erupted from Blakely and his men as the escapees begged for their lives, their cries for mercy gurgling away as their throats were ripped from their necks.

Obviously pleased with themselves, Blakely and his cold-hearted cohorts stood in the torchlight cheering on the blood-thirsty beasts as the hounds made game of the escapees. When the runaways were reduced to dismembered piles of flesh and bone, Blakely and the others called the dogs back. The blood-splattered canines panted and wagged their tails triumphantly as they rejoined their masters. At that moment, a refrain of victorious shouts and rifle fire echoed through the woods, the murderers sauntering away rejoicing in their kill.

The entire episode felt like an eternity. A sickening hush

eclipsed the fetid atmosphere. Maggie couldn't move, her muscles frozen and her breath shallow. Seth rose to his feet and peered around the trunk of the tree, his head slumping forward at the sight.

Tapping Maggie's shoulder, he muttered, "You need to get back to Elora."

"We can't leave them like this," she mumbled, refusing to accept what had transpired. "We have to get them to Dr. Polk so he can..."

"They're gone."

"How do you know?" her voice cracked as she stood on wobbling knees. Seth grabbed her shoulders.

"Take Elora home. I'll take care of the bodies and meet you when I'm done."

"But you don't have the tools..." she replied, tears blurring her vision.

"I'll figure something out. Just go."

Maggie traipsed back to the wagon while Seth made his way to the bodies. Nausea gripped Maggie's stomach, wringing it like a wet rag until she lost her last meal.

Wiping her mouth, Maggie straightened up and hurried back to Elora, who was wide-eyed and silent.

"Let's go," she said, climbing up to the wagon seat.

"What happened?" Elora murmured.

"We'll talk about it later."

"Where's Seth?"

"He's taking care of...things. He'll be along shortly."

Maggie's body felt like rubber and her heart pounded so hard she couldn't catch her breath. She slapped the reins against the horses' haunches and turned them toward home. As they rattled through the woods, she tried desperately to push the images from her mind but the savageness of what she'd witnessed screeched through her thoughts like banshees.

Based on Elora's solemn nature, Maggie suspected she'd

heard it all. When they arrived at the mansion, Maggie stopped the wagon at the front steps. Dr. and Mrs. Polk hurried down the porch stairs to greet them. One look at their daughter and it was obvious they knew something had gone terribly wrong. Dr. Polk helped Elora to the ground and handed her into Mrs. Polk's embrace. Elora leaned against her mother sobbing as they walked up the brick stairs into the house.

"Where's Seth?" Dr. Polk asked.

"He's cleaning up..." Maggie's gaze dropped to the ground.

"What happened?"

"They didn't make it."

Dr. Polk rested his hand on her arm. "Take the wagon to the barn. Seth can fill me in when he returns."

"Yes, sir."

Maggie drove to the stables where Hatch waited.

"Everything Ok, Miss Maggie?" he asked, helping her down.

"I don't think anything will ever be OK again," she muttered, her eyes downcast.

"You want me to give you a ride back to the house?"

"No, thank you. I'd rather walk."

She trudged along the dirt path, the toes of her boots kicking up sand as she went. Stopping at the edge of the marsh, she looked out over the sparkling water as a slight breeze wafted through the trees rustling the leaves. Maggie crumpled to her knees gasping out sobs so hard she could barely breath. Her mind's eyes filled in all the gore and heinousness of what had transpired. Blakely and his men made her uncle seem like a saint.

Her stomach finally gave up the remainder of its contents, leaving her weak and shivering on the ground even though it was the middle of summer. Why was there so much hate in the world? And how had she lived so long without knowing it?

Maggie dipped her hands in the cool water and splashed the heat from her cheeks. Now more than ever, she longed to be back in her native Ireland with her Da and the baying of sheep where the horrors of slavery, hunters, and merciless uncles didn't exist. Standing on quavering legs, she trudged back to the mansion.

When Maggie arrived at the house, Dr. Polk was sitting in the parlor with Seth.

"Where's Elora?" she asked, looking around.

"Her mother took her upstairs. Seth was getting ready to tell me what happened," Dr. Polk said, compassion radiating in his gaze. "Would you like to join us?"

Maggie inhaled and sat. Seth's shoulders were rounded and his eyes were rimmed in red. He ran his fingers through his hair and sighed.

"It was bad from the start. Apparently, Blakely got hold of the runaways and brought them to the woods."

As Seth shared what had happened, Maggie fought back the urge to run from the room. It was like reliving it all over again, every scream and every plea echoing through the sound of dogs ripping flesh from bones. All the while, evil men stood by taunting and laughing at the victims. Bile rose in Maggie's throat. She swallowed hard and bit her lower lip, trying not to appear weak.

When Seth finished, he leaned back against the chair.

"How much did Elora hear?" her father asked.

"Not sure, she wasn't with us."

Dr. Polk turned to Maggie his eyebrows arched. "Maggie?"

"Judging by her quiet demeanor on the trip home, she may have heard everything."

Dr. Polk's fists tightened and his mouth formed a thin line.

"One of these days those monsters are going to get what they deserve. I only hope it's sooner than later." He stood up his hands still shaking. "If you'll excuse me, I'm going to check on my daughter."

"Dr. Polk," Maggie said, standing as he passed. "What about the two escapees that came here earlier?"

"They're on their way to another safe house. We'd hoped to arrange transport for the others tomorrow," he said, clenching his jaw. "I'll see you both in the morning."

Dr. Polk left Seth and Maggie in the parlor with only the sound of crickets chirping through the open windows.

"I want to apologize for my behavior this evening. I don't know what prompted me to behave so recklessly." Tears streamed down her cheeks. "I'm just so sick of it all! The death, the torture, the cruelty..." her words trailed off as a sob stuck in her throat.

Seth walked over and brushed a loose strand of hair from her forehead.

"Your heart is bigger than your head," he said, his eyes locking on hers. "The more you do this, the better you'll get at reading the scenario. I'm sorry you had to go through it."

Indignation rushed through her body. "Sorry for me? What about those poor men? They're the ones who suffered! And why can't we prosecute those lousy beasts? They murdered two men tonight! Doesn't that matter?" Her voice rose with each declaration until the anger came out in hiccups.

Seth pulled her close, holding her to his chest until her body relaxed into his and the pent up rage gushed from her lips in sobs.

He kissed the top of her head and whispered in her ear, "It doesn't get easier but you will get stronger. You're going to do great things, Maggie. You already have. And we both know that no justice can come to the Houstons. The law favors them and views Negroes as nothing more than property."

His words brought her blood to a boil as she pushed back and stared at him.

"I hate this, all of it," she declared and ran from the room up the winding staircase. She stopped at Elora's room and rapped on the door.

"It's Maggie. May I come in?"

Elora opened the door but didn't meet Maggie's gaze. Her complexion was waxy and her eyes puffy.

"Would you like me to sit with you for a while?" Maggie asked.

"That would be nice, thank you," she said, stepping back for Maggie to enter.

"Do you want to talk about it?"

"There's nothing to say. Innocent people lost their lives this evening and for no other reason than hate and greed. Sometimes, I want to strangle those fiends with my bare hands. They infuriate me so!" she growled, clenching her fists and shaking them in the air.

Wiping a tear from her cheek, Elora leaned against Maggie in a torrent of sobs. When her tears ran dry, she slumped onto the bed, drained from the experience. Maggie sat on the edge, stroking Elora's coffee brown tresses until she slid into the comforting embrace of sleep.

Maggie traipsed to her room and looked out the window, her body numb with anger and despair. Staring at the marsh, she wondered how many others were hiding in swamps, being bitten by mosquitoes and ticks or trying to escape gators or dogs. Physically and emotionally spent, she crawled into bed and stared at the ceiling. For the first time in her life, she felt the pang of hate thumping in her chest. One thing was certain; she'd do everything in her power to stop anything like this from happening again, no matter the cost.

39

Maggie couldn't sleep. She descended the winding staircase and made her way to the ladies' parlor. Sitting in the darkness, she stared out the bay window at the moss swaying gently in snippets of light from the waning moon. A few hours had passed since the gruesome event in the woods, yet it seemed like only minutes. Her stomach lurched at the memory, threatening to heave once again.

She hadn't realized how long she'd been sitting until a lonely chime rang out from the grandfather clock in the main hall accompanied by the sound of footsteps. Maggie turned to see Elora wander into the room, her countenance forlorn.

"You couldn't sleep either?" she asked, taking a seat next to Maggie.

"No."

"Sometimes I wish we had nothing to do with the Railroad. It's almost too much to bear."

"Aye, 'tis a terrible thing you experienced tonight," Maggie muttered, her words tinted in Irish.

Looking at Maggie, Elora sat straighter. "Don't lament over

me. My life is blessed. I have a beautiful home and a loving family. Most importantly, I'm free to travel, marry whom I choose, anything I desire. I have no fear of being ripped from my home and sold off. I cannot, I will not, allow my emotions to thwart what must be done," Elora said firmly, clenching her jaw. "We cannot save them all, but I'll do my best to help as many as I'm able."

The two sat in silence trying to cope with the horrors of the evening.

"Perhaps we should go to bed. It's getting late and we have an early morning," Maggie suggested with a yawn.

Elora nodded as they stood, walked through the grand entry, and climbed the stairs hand in hand. When they reached the second-floor landing, Elora embraced Maggie.

"My dear Maggie, I'm ever so grateful you're here."

"I'm glad to be here."

Elora released her friend and traipsed down the hall to her room. Maggie stepped into her chambers and plunked down on the bed. Burying her face in the pillow, she cried for the two men who died that evening. She cried for Bea and Solomon. She cried for Sellers. And she cried for all those who would lose their lives trying to gain their freedom.

SETH SAT ON THE EMBANKMENT, tossing stone after stone into the water creating a series of luminescent ripples. Moonlight glimmered overhead, giving the marsh an ethereal feel. His blood boiled over Blakely's savagery, not to mention the trauma Elora had endured. While he wanted to confront Blakely and his cohorts, he knew he couldn't reveal what he'd witnessed. Too much was at stake. When his arm began to cramp, Seth marched down the pathway to his cottage accompanied by indignation and a thirst for revenge.

MAGGIE AWOKE THE NEXT MORNING, determination pulsing through her veins. After what she'd endured the night before, she resolved to be prepared if she ever encountered Blakely and his comrades torturing runaways again. With a pistol and ammunition, she trudged into the woods and constructed a target with fallen branches and piles of moss. For nearly an hour she shot at the clump of debris until she was able to consistently hit center mass. She didn't even startle when Seth sauntered up beside her.

"What are you doing?"

"Practicing," she replied, taking another shot.

"For what?"

Lowering the gun, she looked at him with a steely stare, "The next time I encounter the Houstons."

"Maggie, you can't go around shooting people."

"Don't plan on it," she replied with a lift of her chin. "But at least I'll be prepared if I have to defend an escapee."

Seth huffed, the right side of his mouth curling as he shook his head and walked away.

Maggie raised the gun and continued firing until she was out of ammunition. Pleased with her progress, she meandered back to the house with her ears ringing, her arm stiff, and confidence in her step.

40

An autumn sun dangled in a deep blue sky, sending light dancing across fallen leaves. Maggie delighted in the crisp breezes filtering through the open windows as she sat in the parlor sewing. A group from Georgia was scheduled to arrive later in the evening. Although there'd been no signs of pursuers, Dr. Polk had scouts monitoring escape routes, keeping him apprised of any unwanted movement by hunters. Seth would be conducting the passengers northward after nightfall. Elora was with Miss Olive working on food preparations for them.

Mrs. Polk entered the room and announced, "Maggie, luncheon is ready."

"Thank you, but I want to finish these last few stitches."

"Very well, I'll have Clara bring you a sandwich and some lemonade."

"That would be lovely."

Stitching as fast as she could, Maggie yelped in pain when the needle stabbed her finger, a pearl of blood beading at the tip. She wiped it away and resumed her sewing. Clara stepped into the room carrying a silver tray with a sandwich and a tall glass with lemon slices floating at the top like water lilies on a pond.

"Here's your lunch, Miss Maggie," she smiled, setting it on the table.

"Thank you, Clara."

Maggie sipped the cool drink and nibbled the sandwich when Elora dashed into the room, her smile full and her eyes sparkling with excitement.

"Hatch just got back with sacks full of oysters! We'll be feasting tonight!" she declared.

"Oysters? I don't know that I've ever eaten oysters without stew, but I'm willing to try."

"Good gracious, you've not lived until you've had oysters fresh from the marsh. Duke roasts them, Miss Heddy bakes corn muffins, and Seth tries to eat them all," she giggled.

At the mention of Seth's name, Maggie decided it was best to forego the gathering. With each passing day, it was getting more difficult to curtail her longing for him.

"I've still got some sewing to finish," Maggie said.

Stepping closer, Elora gently touched her arm. "You really must take some time or you'll wither away beneath the weight of it all. It's an important thing we do here but we must care for our well-being, otherwise we're of no use to anyone."

"But there's so much to be..."

"Nonsense. You're coming to the oyster roast this evening. Don't make me talk to Papa or you'll get the scolding of your life," she said, her cheeks glowing as she lifted her eyebrows.

"Very well, I shan't suffer the wrath of Dr. Polk," Maggie smirked.

"Scoff if you will, but Papa can be stern when need be, you mark my words!" Elora said, scurrying from the room.

. . .

As afternoon yielded to early evening, Maggie placed the needle and thread in the sewing box, her back stiff as she headed upstairs to change. Although not as frigid as northern temperatures, long sleeves would be necessary to ward off the chill from the swampy breath of the marsh not to mention the swarming mosquitoes that made meals of the flesh.

She slipped on a homespun dress in hues of blue and burgundy, draped a deep blue shawl about her shoulders, and headed down the back stairs at the same time Elora popped inside.

"Are you ready to attend your first oyster roast?"

"Tis good a time as any," she replied in her native brogue.

Elora linked her arm through Maggie's as the two strode down the path to the shed beside the barn. Smoke filtered through the autumn sky as a crowd of workers gathered. Dr. Polk chatted with Miss Heddy who placed a large tray of corn muffins and biscuits on a roughly hewn wooden table.

At that moment, Hatch walked past them, dumping a huge pot of oysters across the table in an avalanche of steam. Everyone gathered round and began to pry the shells open. Elora led Maggie to an open spot and picked up a knife.

"Let me show you how it's done."

Jiggling the knife into a crevice of the shell, she pried it open to reveal a sloppy lump swimming in a small pool of liquid. Elora used the same knife to scoop the grayish mess out and pop it into her mouth. Closing her eyes, she savored the moment.

"Mmm, tastes like home," she said, opening her eyes and handing the knife to Maggie. "You try it."

Unsure as to the appeal of something that appeared so disgusting, Maggie hesitated when a voice boomed from behind.

"May I have the honor of serving you your first oyster, Miss Milner?"

Maggie turned to find Seth grinning at her.

"I'm sure I can do this," she said grabbing the knife from Elora, determined to show him she was capable of a task as simple as prying open an oyster. Grasping the elongated shell, she forced the blade of the knife into the hairline crevice. In her overzealous attempt the knife slipped, cutting the edge of her hand. The slice was clean, causing little pain as blood trickled across her palm and dripped onto the ground.

"Oh Maggie, you're bleeding!" Elora declared.

Seth pulled a handkerchief from his shirt pocket, grabbed her hand, and wrapped the wound. Hearing the commotion, Dr. Polk made his way over to them.

"Let me see." He unwrapped the bloody cloth and looked at the cut. "This is minor, but you'll need to wash and bandage it. Perhaps you should let Elora open the oysters for you."

"I'm happy to help," Seth responded like an eager schoolboy.

"Very well. Maggie, I leave you in very capable hands."

Elora went with Maggie to help her clean the wound and bandage it properly. When they returned to the table, Seth had taken the liberty of opening several shells for Maggie. She gazed at the oysters swimming in a half shell of oozing mucus.

Great, Maggie thought, *now I have to ingest these disgusting little balls of slime*. Her heart palpitated as Seth watched her, a smile creeping across his lips as he waited for her reaction to one of the Lowcountry's greatest delicacies.

Maggie inhaled as she lifted the elongated shell to her lips, hoping she'd be able to get the oyster down without gagging. She was embarrassed enough about slicing her hand not to mention having to rely on Seth to manage her supper.

With eyes closed, she thrust the oyster in her mouth and swallowed. Much to her surprise it wasn't as disgusting as she feared it would be. The flavor of the salty marsh ran across her tongue in layers.

"Well, what do you think?" Elora asked.

"It's rather good."

"Why are you so surprised?" Seth queried.

"Because they look so...awful."

Seth and Elora erupted in laughter.

"It's better not to look at them. And whatever you do, don't ever cut one open or you'll never touch the things again," Elora said.

Seth and Elora took turns prying open shells for Maggie, all of them eating oysters and laughing as if they'd been the closest of friends their entire lives. A mountain of empty shells grew at the end of the table as the harvest dwindled. When the sun hovered over the horizon, Seth helped Hatch and Duke clean up the discarded shells. They filled the pots and hauled them to the marsh, dumping the contents over the edge. Once everything was cleaned up, Seth joined Maggie and Elora around a smoldering fire, the logs sputtering and spitting sparks into the darkening night sky. A slight breeze wafted in from the marsh sending goose bumps across Maggie's skin. Then again, it may have been her close proximity to Seth.

"It's been a lovely evening," Elora said, a contented grin lifting her cheeks.

"Indeed, it has but I should probably head back to the house." Maggie replied, anxious to distance herself from Seth.

"You can't leave me unchaperoned with this scandalous creature," Elora declared.

"Who you calling scandalous?" Seth retorted, furrowing his brow. He sat before the fire with his legs stretched out before him, his curls falling haphazardly to his shoulders. "Maggie, you need to stay and protect me from this little scamp."

"Very well. I'll chaperone both of you."

"Splendid," Elora declared. "Seth can tell us a ghost story."

"A ghost story?" Maggie asked.

"It's tradition. After oyster roasts, we gather round the fire and tell scary stories."

"So, Mr. Daniels, you're a storyteller too? Is there anything you *don't* do?" she asked, studying Seth's eyes as they glinted in the firelight.

Cocking his head, he stared at the sky, his lips pursed. "Not that comes to mind. I guess you could say I'm a full-fledged renaissance man."

Elora tossed a stone at him. "Such a modest gent!"

"Hey now, no need to get violent. Do you want to hear a story or not?"

"Of course!" Elora replied, sitting straighter.

Seth leaned forward and rested his elbows on his knees, his eyes glinting as if he were about to reveal a dark secret.

"It was a dark and stormy night..."

"Why do your stories always start with a dark and stormy night?" Elora asked, scrunching her lips.

"Who's telling this story?" Seth replied, arching his eyebrows.

Elora gave a sideways glance and a huff in response.

"As I was saying, it was a dark and stormy night when Esmeralda, lady of Hamilton Manor arrived home after a long journey. She was weary from travel and her body ached. Stepping into the darkened hall of her home, she was unaware that something otherworldly waited in the shadows."

Maggie hung on his every word, enthralled by Seth's intonations and facial expressions as he spoke. His flair for the dramatic captivated her, intensifying her internal battle of wanting to be with him but staying true to her friend.

For the next hour, the three shared ghostly tales until the fire fizzled into nothing more than glowing embers, much like Maggie's heart.

Seth got up and shoveled sand on the fire smothering its last light.

"Well ladies, I have to ride out in a few hours, so let me escort you back to the house."

Seth positioned himself between the two women, looping his arms through theirs as they walked along the path.

"How long will you be away?" Elora asked, disappointment tainting her words.

"If all goes as planned, a few days, two weeks at the most."

Maggie's heart thumped harder. She knew all too well how plans could go astray depending on the cargo and the fortitude of hunters.

"Promise to be back in time for the Rucker's dance?"

"I'll do my best," he said with a sheepish grin.

They'd reached the back entrance of the house when Seth released Maggie's arm as Elora leaned and whispered, "I'll miss you."

Taking the hint that Elora wanted to be alone with Seth, Maggie bid goodnight and hurried in the back door. As she headed up the back stairs, her skin tingled where Seth's arm had looped through hers. How could something that felt so natural be so wrong? Misery escorted her to her room where she fell into bed, conflict pitting her mind against her heart in a battle that couldn't be won.

41

Seth had been gone for a couple of weeks. Maggie immersed herself in her work to escape her underlying worry for her father. Not a day passed when she didn't ponder where or what he was doing. But she knew him to be a strong and resourceful man, and convinced herself he was working somewhere with enough food to survive.

More troubling was the daily struggle to suppress her feelings for Seth. If only she could find some peace. She pummeled her frustrations away on mint leaves when Miss Heddy gave a sideways glance.

"What wrong with you?"

"Huh?"

"You mashing them things up like they's your worst enemy."

Stopping, Maggie looked into the mortar at the obliterated leaves.

"Nothing's wrong, my mind was just wandering."

"I feels sorry for whoever be occupying your mind like that," she replied, shaking her head.

The right side of Maggie's mouth curled as she gave a little chuckle. She dumped the leaves and started with fresh.

"If you ever needs to talk, I's happy to listen," Heddy offered.

"I appreciate it but there's nothing to discuss," she said, resuming her task with a little less aggression.

When the salves were mixed and shelved, Maggie made her way back to the house. Elora waited on the front porch, a smile dazzling her porcelain complexion.

"My goodness, what has you in such a good mood?" Maggie asked.

"Seth got back today," she replied, tottering in the rocker.

"I'm glad he's home safe."

"Even better, he'll be able to escort us to the barn dance at the Rucker's Plantation this Saturday night.

"Is this the one you two were speaking about before he left?"

"The same one. You'll have a wonderful time," she declared, hopping up from the rocker and twirling about the porch on her tiptoes. "Oh, how I love to waltz."

Maggie's gaze shifted to the floor as she chewed her lower lip. Somehow, she needed to find an excuse to get out of this. The idea of being so close to Seth made her flush.

"What's the matter? Don't tell me you've never danced before," Elora said.

"I know how to dance, but I don't have anything suitable to wear."

"It's not a fancy ball. Wear what you would to church. Besides, Seth doesn't care what we wear so long as we dance with him."

"I doubt he'll want to dance with me," Maggie said, fidgeting with her fingers.

"Don't be silly, there'll be plenty of dances for both of us, I assure you," Elora said with a sparkle in her eye.

. . .

Maggie rose early, skipped breakfast, and went straight to Miss Heddy's. She'd tossed and turned throughout the night, worried about the upcoming dance. The idea of dancing with Seth weighed heavily on her. It was hard enough being around him every day and suppressing her feelings without having to dance alongside him. One thing she'd learned, the more time she spent immersed in her work, the less opportunity she had for her mind and her heart to wander.

At midday, Maggie headed toward the house when she heard voices blustering from the front lawn. Starting in that direction, she saw Elora shoving a note into Clara's hand.

"Take this to Mr. Tindell quickly," Elora muttered. With a nod, Clara scurried down the stairs to the path by the marsh, and out of sight.

"Elora, what's going on?"

"I haven't the time," she said, running to the front.

Maggie walked to the edge of the porch where she saw Blakely, the Houston boys, and another man on horseback. At the end of the brick walk, Mrs. Polk stood her ground as Mr. Blakely hurled commands from atop his horse.

"I know Mr. Houston's runaway slave came this way. I want to see each and every one of your slaves right here, right now!"

"Mr. Blakely, I assure you there have been no sightings of runaways here. My staff would have alerted me if it were so."

"You may have deluded yourself into seeing your *staff* as people, but they're nothing more than beasts. Heck, my horse has more sense than they do," he grumbled, spitting on the ground. "I insist you gather your slaves and bring them here so I can question them. If they're hiding Mr. Houston's slave, I can have them arrested and hung for sheltering stolen property!"

Elora stood at her mother's side while Maggie lingered a few feet back watching the rowdy scene. Flashbacks of Blakely and his men's savagery in the woods weighted her legs and cemented her feet to the ground. Now these same men were threatening Mrs. Polk and Elora. With a few deep breaths, Maggie steadied her nerves and turned to go for help when a voice called out.

"Where d'you think you're going Missy?" Coyle Houston shouted, directing his rifle at her.

"I was going back inside," she muttered, her blood racing through her veins making her limbs quiver.

"I wouldn't do that, unless you's going to get them darkies."

Maggie wanted to scream that he was a worthless wretch and had no right terrorizing them, but she held her tongue knowing her indignation would only aggravate the situation. The last time she spoke out of anger had ended in a beating by her uncle and she'd not let her Irish pride endanger the Polks.

SETH RODE PHANTOM along the trail that meandered toward the back of the house, taking in the splendor of the day. Out of nowhere, Clara bolted from a clump of trees, her skirts flying as she ran down the path.

"Clara, where are you off to in such a hurry?" Seth asked, halting Phantom.

She stopped, her words coming in gasps as she spoke. "It be bad, Mr. Daniels. They be at the house causin' a ruckus with de missus, sayin' all sort of terrible things."

"Clara, slow down. Who's at the house and what's happening with Mrs. Polk?"

"Somethin' about a runaway. Miss Elora gave me this note to take to Mr. Tindell."

Clara handed the crumpled paper to Seth. Reading the message, he returned it to her.

"Listen carefully, don't go to town yet. Dr. Polk is over at the Meade's place. Go there first and tell him I'm heading to the house. Then take the note to Mr. Tindell."

With a nod, she dashed away, disappearing into the thicket.

Seth spurred Phantom forward, racing towards Rose Hall with the immediacy of a fire brigade.

Instead of arriving by way of the main entrance, he continued along the marsh's edge to the back of the house where Blakely's threats echoed. Everyone knew of Blakely's indifference toward females, but to apply that crass disregard to the wife of another man was unconscionable. Seth peeked from behind the privy where he had full view of the standoff. When Curtis Houston started for Elora, Seth spurred Phantom forward. He galloped into the group of riders, startling their horses. Blakely bobbled in his saddle, scrambling to stay seated while Curtis tumbled backwards into a rose bush, yelping as the thorns caught his backside.

"Good afternoon, Mrs. Polk. I see I'm not the only one who's come for tea," Seth said mockingly.

"Mr. Daniels, I'm glad you've arrived so promptly. I fear Dr. Polk is running behind his time," she replied, taking in a deep breath, apparently glad for Seth's sudden arrival.

"Curtis you oaf, get back on your horse!" Blakely hollered.

"Care to join us Blakely?" Seth taunted.

"We've got more important things to do than flit about having *tea*." Turning back to Mrs. Polk he growled, "Tell your husband if I find out your darkies had anything to do with Mr. Houston's missing property, there'll be a high price to pay."

"Perhaps you'd like to deliver the message to me directly," Dr. Polk said, stepping from the house. "Is there a problem, Mr. Blakely?"

"Your wife can explain everything."

"I believe it's customary for men to discuss things between each other, not rely on women to convey messages."

"I was told one of Mr. Houston's slaves was spotted near here. When I asked your wife about it, she was uncooperative."

"Haven't we always worked together on these things?"

"I suppose," he grumbled.

"Then why are you questioning my wife?" Dr. Polk asked sternly.

Muttering something under his breath, Blakely glanced from Seth to Dr. Polk before harkening his group to depart the premises.

"Let's go. Ain't no one here going to help us." He reined his horse around, spurring him forward with the others galloping behind in a cloud of dust.

Dr. Polk approached his wife.

"What's going on?" he asked.

"Those imbeciles are on the hunt for a slave who took flight from their blasted plantation," she replied between clenched teeth.

"Mother!" Elora declared, shocked at her mother's strong language.

"I'm sorry, but I've little tolerance for those bullies. They're belligerent and cruel. It wouldn't bother me if they never showed their faces here again, and I don't mind saying so in front of others!" She turned on her heels and marched into the house, punctuating her exit with a slam of the front door.

A sly grin creased Dr. Polk's face, revealing his admiration for his wife's spirit.

"Seth, I want to thank you for getting here so quickly. Clara told me about your swift response."

"Glad I could help."

"Papa, aren't you going to do something? You can't let them speak to us like that!"

Dr. Polk's expression softened.

"My dear, I could inform the sheriff of their behavior but they've broken no laws and the end result would be vengeance on their part. These are the most arrogant and ignorant of men, an extremely volatile combination. I'm often gone from the premises and will not put you, or your mother, in harm's way to feed my prideful ego."

"After everything they've done, we're going to stand by and let them get away with it *again*?"

"Suppose I was to ride to their plantation and threaten them. What do you think would happen?

She shrugged her shoulders.

"They'd respond in kind. Even worse, they already suspect their runaway is in the area and that our workers have a hand in his escape. If they came back after dark and discovered what we really do..." His eyebrows arched as he looked upon his daughter, hoping she'd understand.

Gazing toward the marsh, Elora replied, "They could discover our operation."

"Exactly my point. The safety of others far outweighs my need to vindicate insulting words toward my family. My arrival was enough to put them on notice."

"Do you really believe that?"

"Consider it an unspoken understanding between men."

Elora was visibly rattled as she traipsed up the walkway, Maggie trailing behind.

"She's struggling with all of this," Seth said, watching Elora disappear into the house.

"Life's lessons aren't easy. She must learn to suppress her own feelings for the greater good, or she'll jeopardize all we do."

Seth grimaced, indignation percolating in his gut.

"Care to come inside?" Dr. Polk offered.

"No, thank you, sir. I've got some business to attend to."

Dr. Polk gave a nod before heading into the house. He listened to Phantom's hoof beats pounding down the drive knowing Seth was troubled over the encounter, but that his actions would be stealth.

. . .

Seth rode to town, his mind steeped in rage. Blakely and his entourage were out of control, and getting more dangerous with each incident. He'd not allow the Polks to be harassed in such a manner. One thing was certain, he knew just the man to help with the situation. Trotting up to the clapboard house, Seth dismounted and took the porch stairs two at a time. Before he could knock on the front door, Rudy emerged from within.

"Mr. Daniels, I just sent Clara home."

"There's an issue with the Houstons."

"When is there not an issue with those imbeciles?" Rudy shrugged in disgust as he led Seth inside.

"Seems one of his slaves has taken flight. Apparently, Houston got word the runaway might be in the area of Rose Hall and sent Blakely to find his man. His treatment of the ladies was inexcusable."

"Nothing from those witless fools surprises me anymore," Rudy replied, straightening his coat.

"Whether they believed the slave was there or just wanted to stir up trouble, we can't have them poking around."

"Come with me," Rudy said, placing a silk top hat upon his snowy hair.

Seth raised one eyebrow as the corner of Rudy's mouth curled mischievously. He hadn't noticed until now that Rudy was donning a black frock coat and trousers. They walked out the back door to the wooden structure that housed Rudy's extensive collection of coaches, including the ornately clad funeral carriage. Two gleaming ebony horses were hitched to it, pawing the ground impatiently, their harnesses jangling as they tossed their heads.

"Are you conducting a funeral?" Seth queried.

"Not exactly," he said, raising his eyebrows as he climbed to the bench. "But I am transporting precious *cargo*."

"This cargo wouldn't be heading north, would it?" Seth asked with a sly grin.

"By way of the rails," Rudy smiled.

Seth shook his head with a chuckle. "Very creative. And your cargo had no objections to riding in a casket?"

"Life after death will be a blessing for this particular soul. Now if you don't mind, I must be on my way." Rudy tipped his hat and cued the horses forward. "Can't keep the mourners waiting."

Seth rode Phantom to the edge of town watching the hearse travel the main roads to the outskirts of the township. The best part was seeing Houston and his men sitting atop their horses with hats over their hearts as Rudy trotted past with their runaway slave stashed within the glassed compartment.

WHEN SETH ARRIVED at Rose Hall, he went straight to the doctor's office.

"Where have you been all afternoon?" Dr. Polk asked, rising from his desk.

"Got caught up in a funeral procession."

"For whom?"

"Let's just say Houston's search for his runaway slave is dead and buried."

Doctor Polk stepped from behind the desk, folding his arms across his chest. "Now this is a story I want to hear."

"It involves Rudy and that fancy funeral carriage of his."

"In that case, let's have a brandy while you fill me in."

Seth relayed the entire story to the doctor who laughed at the irony of Houston and his band of idiots watching the runaway being transported right under their noses. When Seth finished the tale, Dr. Polk raised his glass, toasting their good friend Rudy, and his creative ingenuity.

42

A slight breeze ruffled the moss dangling in the light of a full moon. Maggie adjusted the front of her green cotton frock, her auburn tresses neatly rolled at the nape of her neck. She patted the bodice of her dress where the garnet brooch from Annalissa was affixed to the neckline of her chemise. Elora loaned her a lovely lace cap with deep green silk ribbons cascading down the sides. Maggie affixed the cap to her head and scrutinized her appearance in the full-length mirror. She dreaded the evening and pondered whether she should feign illness to avoid having to attend. Granted, if she did, Elora would make a fuss and Dr. Polk would likely discover her deceit. How could she possibly explain her only ailment was an aching heart?

Stepping into the hallway, Maggie met Elora. She donned a gown of deep blue silk with her coffee brown hair cascading in ringlets from a spray of silk roses. A strand of pearls accentuated the fine lines of her neck and shoulders.

"You're stunning," Elora announced. "Every gentleman will be clamoring for a turn about the floor with you. Poor Seth will be so jealous." The right side of Elora's mouth curled as she winked.

Maggie looked away, her cheeks coloring. She didn't care if the other gentlemen noticed her. Seth was the only man whose attention she desired.

"I didn't mean to embarrass you, but you really are beautiful," Elora said, squeezing Maggie's hand.

"You look lovely too."

"Thank you," Elora replied, a smile lifting her rosy cheeks. "Let's not keep the carriage waiting."

Elora scuttled down the staircase ahead of Maggie as Dr. and Mrs. Polk watched from below.

"My goodness, you two are the epitome of elegance and grace. You'll be the most beautiful ladies at the dance," Dr. Polk said, taking his daughter's hand and planting a kiss on her cheek. He repeated the gesture with Maggie. Warmth spread across Maggie's cheeks. He treated her like part of their family and it was grand. If only her Da could be here, the evening would be almost perfect.

Elora and Maggie would be traveling to the dance in Dr. Polk's carriage. He and Mrs. Polk had decided to enjoy a quiet evening at home while the girls danced the night away. Seth would meet them there.

Dr. and Mrs. Polk stood on the porch as the driver helped Elora and Maggie into the carriage, secured the door, and climbed to the bench seat. With a cluck of his teeth and a tap of the reins, he launched the horses forward. Elora waved as the carriage tottered down the drive, her parents shrinking from sight. As they jostled along, Elora chatted about the hospitality and elegant gardens of the Ruckers who were hosting the dance.

"Mrs. Rucker refuses any help with her flowers. She plants and tends them all by herself. I've never seen such amazing roses!" Elora said. "But don't say anything to Mother about that;

she works so hard to grow the finest roses. I fear it would wound her pride."

When they arrived, the barn-turned-dance-hall was swarming with a company of ladies clad in a rainbow of colorful dresses, most in search of husbands. The space had been lusciously decorated with candle stands, potted plants, and an army of chairs lining the outer walls. With all of the finery, one could almost forget that on any given day the structure housed farm equipment. The atmosphere crackled with excitement.

Standing on her tiptoes, Elora scanned the space until her gaze rested on Seth who stood on the other side of the room leaning against the wall.

"There he is," Elora declared, dragging Maggie by the hand.

Seth was dressed in a white cotton shirt, navy blue waistcoat, and tan trousers. His hair was slicked back, the tips of his curls resting on his broad shoulders as his blue eyes glimmered in the flickering candlelight. The sight of him squeezed Maggie's heart like a lemon.

"Took you long enough to get here. I was beginning to think you'd abandoned me and left me to dance with old Mrs. Ferndale from the bakery," he said, teasingly, his smile broadening.

Before Elora could respond, the screeching and moaning of instruments being tuned shifted the conversation in the room to a low murmur. Everyone watched with anticipation, obviously ready to dance. When the ensemble began playing a reel, Elora grabbed Seth's hand.

"Shall we?" she said, her eyes fixed on his.

With a smile, he whirled her onto the dance floor where they joined a small group for the Virginia Reel.

Maggie watched as Seth and Elora twirled arm-in-arm and sashayed with other couples to the vibrant notes of the band. Each step and sideways glance of the paramours felt like a hammer pounding nails into the coffin of her heart. If only she could be the one dancing and swirling with Seth's arms around her, his gaze communicating the depth of his adoration. After months of admiring him from afar, Maggie's ability to mask her true feelings was beginning to crumble.

Two dances later, the happy couple made their way over to Maggie, Elora puffing as perspiration sparkled against her skin in the flickering lights. "It's your turn," she declared, fanning herself.

A blush colored Maggie's cheek as she opened her mouth to protest but nothing came out.

Sensing her hesitation, Seth held out his hand. "You know she won't let it go until we have at least one dance."

His baritone voice and steely blue eyes captivated her as Maggie placed her hand into his, a tingle resonating up her arm at his touch.

The ensemble strummed an upbeat tune as old man Holden called the steps for the Patty-cake polka. Seth was smooth on the dance floor, leading Maggie in a series of shuffles and turns in sync with the other couples. The dance had several exchanges with other partners, leaving Maggie somewhat disappointed that she didn't get Seth all to herself. Then again, it was probably for the best. She didn't need to inadvertently expose the adoration she harbored in her heart for him. When the dance ended, Maggie curtseyed to Seth's bow.

Seth escorted Maggie to a chair as the ensemble began to play a waltz. Turning to Elora, he offered his hand and swept her into the fray of dancers. Maggie watched as they glided back and forth, Elora beaming up at Seth as he gazed down at her affectionately. Maggie's chest tightened. They whispered and giggled as they twirled, their fondness for each other evident to all who looked on.

After the waltz, the band took a brief respite. The atmosphere was buzzing with excitement as guests conversed and giggled in the wavering candlelight. All eyes drifted across the room when Curtis and Coyle Houston sauntered through the barn door, instantly making Maggie's stomach turn. Without doubt, they were two of the most repugnant creatures she'd ever encountered. The crowd's attention shifted when a series of notes floated through the air as the band tuned their instruments and began another reel.

Seth offered his hand to Maggie. Although she longed to accept, she declined, instead fidgeting with the tips of her gloves.

"I was going to step outside for some air. It's getting a bit warm in here," Maggie said. If she didn't distance herself from him, she feared her heart would burst.

"I'll come with you," Elora offered.

"Go on and dance. I won't be long," Maggie said.

She started across the room, glancing over her shoulder as the fiddle warbled an upbeat tune. Watching Seth and Elora fall into step with a group of dancers, Maggie blew out a breath, envy squeezing her chest. A sweaty, slovenly Coyle slithered up to Maggie, the right side of his mouth lifting.

"Hey Red, why don't we take a spin with the others?" he said, sandwiching Maggie between his bulging torso and the wall.

"No, thank you," she replied, repulsed by the idea of touching him.

"Your loss," he sneered before slinking across the room.

Maggie sauntered outside taking in the crisp autumn air. She gazed at the field of stars twinkling in the moonlight and exhaled. The night was reminiscent of the one in the farmer's field when Seth had kissed her. Tears crested in her eyes when an unexpected voice made her jump.

"What's a pretty little thing like you doing out here by yourself?" Curtis asked, sidling up beside her.

Taking in a deep breath to calm her racing heart, Maggie

conjured all her wits to respond with as much decency as she could muster.

"I came out to get some air," she replied curtly.

"Nice girl like you shouldn't be alone on a moonlit night," he said, stroking her cheek.

"Don't touch me," she blurted out, slapping his hand away.

"That's not very ladylike," he replied, clutching her wrist. He leaned in pinning her against the tree.

Maggie wriggled against his weight, his foul breath making her skin writhe in disgust.

"You're playing hard to get but I don't give up so easily. I know what you want," he muttered, moving his face closer. "Come on and give me a little kiss."

His hands locked around her face and drew her closer. She pushed against him but to no avail. The fullness of his girth trapped her against the large oak as his lips pressed against hers, his hands now holding her arms. Horrified, she bit down on his lower lip, sending him jerking back with a yelp. Taking advantage of his momentary lapse, Maggie kicked his shin and then stomped his foot, sending him crumpling to the ground. Before he could recover, she landed several more kicks to his ribs and gut. Anger shook her frame as she continued the assault until Seth grabbed her by the waist and pulled her away. Curled in a fetal position, Curtis squalled from the attack.

Maggie's chest heaved as she pulled forward in an effort to break free and resume her attack. Seth tightened his grip around her waist, lifting her from the ground as she thrashed to get free.

"Maggie, it's ok. You've made your point," he muttered in her ear.

Several people had gathered watching Coyle rush to his brother's side.

"What the heck is going on?" he asked, helping Curtis to his feet.

"Tripped over a tree root," Curtis mumbled, clutching his ribs as he stood, a spot of blood on his lip.

Maggie clenched her teeth and started to respond when Seth squeezed her shoulder and whispered, "Why don't we go back in?"

She shot him a fiery look before wrenching her shoulder from his grasp and marching inside. Seth caught up to her and grabbed her arm. "Are you ok?" he asked.

"No, I am not," she responded through gritted teeth. "That fiend tried to force himself on me!"

Seth chuckled and shook his head.

"What's so funny?" Maggie asked, fury thumping in her chest.

"He didn't have a chance against you," Seth stated, the right side of his lip curling.

"What's going on?" Elora asked, ambling up to Maggie. "You look flushed."

Anger smoldered within her like lava rising from a volcano. She feared she'd erupt if she tried to speak. Before she could respond, an Irish tune floated through the air. What better way to extinguish the antipathy pulsing through her limbs than to dance?

"Would you like to learn an Irish dance?" Maggie asked, wanting to move on from the incident.

"I'd love to," Elora replied, taking Maggie's arm. The two took to the floor prancing about in an Irish jig, Elora following Maggie's fanciful footwork. When the last note was played the two stood breathless.

"What a dance," Elora declared, her smile as broad as the river.

"I've not danced like that since I left home," Maggie responded, wiping pearls of sweat from her brow. The two made their way to the punch bowl for some refreshment when Seth joined them.

"Are you going to forgive me?" he asked.

Maggie pursed her lips. "There's nothing to forgive," she replied, taking a sip from the crystal cup.

Elora looked back and forth between them. "What's going on?"

"I'll tell you later," Maggie said, placing the cup on the table.

Over the course of the evening, Seth took turns dancing with Elora and Maggie. While he seemed to enjoy himself, it was apparent his efforts were more for Elora's pleasure than his own. As Seth and Elora sauntered from the dance floor, the tempo slowed.

"Oh, another waltz," Elora said. "Seth, you must dance this one with Maggie."

"I don't think that's a good idea," Maggie stammered.

"Why ever not?"

"Because I, um, I'm not very good at waltzing."

"Not to worry, Seth is a wonderful lead," she said, pushing the two of them toward the dance floor.

Maggie stopped. "Wouldn't you rather dance this one?"

"My feet are aching," Elora responded, exhaling as she plunked into a chair.

Maggie drew in a breath and accepted Seth's outstretched hand as he led her to the dance floor. He wrapped his arm about her waist drawing her to him, their bodies fitting together like pieces of a puzzle. Being this close to him was intoxicating. His eyes locked onto hers as they swirled and swayed, each step drawing Maggie further from reality until the rest of the world ceased to exist. Despite his tall build, he was graceful as he guided her to and fro, his gaze never shifting from hers and the strength of his hands as soft as a feather. For the first time in her life, Maggie felt complete. Each step seemed to draw them closer until their noses were almost touching. Lost in the moment, she was oblivious that the music had stopped until Seth released his hold and gave a slight bow.

"Thank you for the dance, Miss Milner," he murmured.

"It was my pleasure, Mr. Daniels," Maggie replied with a quick bob. The glint in his steely eyes and the subtle manner in which his lips curled turned Maggie's insides to jelly. Something in his gaze plucked at her heart.

Elora approached and looped her hand through Maggie's arm.

"That was the last dance of the evening," she announced, leading Maggie into the cool night air with Seth trailing behind. Her skin still tingling from his touch, Maggie could feel the heat rising from her core, flushing her complexion. *Stop it*, she thought, *he belongs to someone else*. Yet, she'd seen something in his eyes tonight, something more than what she'd seen the night he kissed her in the farmer's field. Perhaps he was feeling something as well. Her emotions battled between love and loyalty, neither of which would result in complete victory. In spite of her complaints of aching feet, Elora's step was lively as they made their way to the awaiting carriage.

Seth handed the ladies into the carriage and peeked inside.

"Until tomorrow m'ladies," he said, placing his hat upon his sandy curls.

"Thank you for a splendid evening," Elora chimed with a broad smile.

"Indeed, it was a lovely evening," Maggie added.

Seth shut the carriage door and sent the driver on.

It was well past midnight when they arrived at Rose Hall. Elora had grown quiet, obviously worn out from an evening of dancing and socializing. Hardly a word was spoken as they disembarked from the carriage. Weariness saturated Maggie's body as she climbed the stairs behind Elora.

"Did you enjoy yourself tonight?" Elora asked.

"I did. It reminded me of the dances I used to attend in our village."

With a nod, Elora muttered, "It's late and my feet are throbbing. I fear I'll be soaking them most of tomorrow. See you in the morning."

"Goodnight."

Maggie stepped into her room and shut the door. Leaning against it, she closed her eyes envisioning Seth's tender expression and gentle touch. Her only hope of redemption was to avoid him, which wouldn't be easy considering the circumstances at the plantation. But she'd try. No more sideways glances or lingering in a room for a few moments just to be near him. She was certain he loved Elora, and she'd not do anything to interfere.

Inhaling deeply, Maggie changed for bed, slipped beneath the covers, and fretted herself to sleep. She needed to change the course of her heart before it collided with her disappointed hopes over a man whose affections belonged to another.

43

Breezes billowed across the marsh, expelling the crisp breath of autumn through the open door of the cottage as Miss Heddy and Maggie worked. The season for coughs and sore throats was fast approaching and they were hustling to get the shelves stocked with needed remedies, in addition to the standard treatments for bug bites and sore muscles.

Maggie was absorbed in her work when Elora popped her head in the door.

"I'm heading to town to take some food to the Greenes. Do you need anything while I'm out?"

Miss Heddy shook her head.

"Nothing I can think of." Maggie said, looking up from her task. "How is Mrs. Greene's arm?"

"Father says he'll be able to remove the splint next week. I know the children will be happy. I've heard Mr. Greene isn't a very proficient cook."

Heddy and Maggie giggled at the statement.

"I should be back by lunchtime," Elora said.

"See you then," Maggie replied.

She resumed her work, pounding the pestle into the aloe and honey concoction for mosquito bites before treating the eucalyptus leaves she needed for the sore muscle salve.

Rubbing the stiffness from her right shoulder, Maggie decided to take a break and go to the house before the midday meal. She hung her apron on the hook, bid Heddy goodbye, and traipsed down the sandy path, watching the marsh grasses billow in the breezes. Her stomach rumbled as she darted up the stairs through the back door.

The house was eerily subdued when a muffled voice resonated from the back hall. Making her way toward the hushed declarations, she noticed a man's figure sandwiching Clara between his body and the bead-board wall. Maggie sheltered in the far corner, trying to make out his words when she recognized the voice.

"You worthless simpleton, tell me what you know or I'll beat the life out of you," Blakely grumbled.

"Don' know nothin' bout Mr. Houston's man." Clara's voice was steady beneath the shadow of his threats.

How Blakely had made his way into the house without an invitation was a mystery. And why was he interrogating Clara? A foreboding feeling constricted Maggie's chest, hastening her heartbeat.

"I know something's going on here. I can feel it," Blakely said. "Give him up or *you'll* be the one hanging from a tree. Hiding runaways is a crime 'round here. I'm beginning to suspect the *good doctor* isn't as stalwart in his view of slavery as he ought to be."

Terror trickled through Maggie's veins. If Blakely suspected the Polk's worked with the Railroad, things could get deadly. A protective force took hold as the image of Sellers' lifeless form saturated her thoughts. She'd not let anyone else die because of her trepidation. Stealthily, she crept to the hunt room where Dr. Polk housed his hunting rifles. Pulling the latch on the cabinet, she removed a black powder rifle, loaded it, and padded through the dining room to the butler's pantry where she could get a better angle on Blakely.

By now, he had a pistol pressed against Clara's temple.

"Stupid little darkie, tell me what you know or I'll blow a hole in your empty skull."

Clara's body stiffened and her hands shook. The situation was getting out of control, leaving Maggie little time to think. Taking aim, she snuggled the butt of the rifle against her right shoulder. She could feel the rush of blood pulsing through her limbs as she fought to hold the gun steady.

"Step away from her!" she hollered.

With a start, Blakely turned, his eyes creasing into slits.

"How dare you threaten me, you miserable little wench! I know y'all are housing Mr. Houston's man! I'll have this place searched and seized by sundown tonight!" he hollered, stepping toward Maggie with pistol drawn. His hand was as steady as an anvil.

"Lower your gun and leave, Mr. Blakely. You haven't any business in this house!" Maggie tried to sound forceful but her voice wavered as she issued the threat. The thumping of her heart echoed through her ears, making it difficult to think as she poised her finger on the trigger.

Stepping closer, Blakely had a gleam in his eyes that exuded a sense of power and a lack of conscience. A snarl curled his upper lip, dissolving Maggie's fortitude. Nevertheless, she stood firm in her bluff, hoping it would drive him from the house.

"Stupid little Irish whore, who do you think you're dealing with?"

Time slowed to a standstill as he cocked the pistol and aimed it at her. An explosion rattled Maggie's body, slamming her against the wall as she sank to the floor, her shoulder throbbing as if a thousand bees had stung her.

The gravity of the situation registered when Maggie's eyes

rested on the puddle of blood spreading across the floor. A few feet away Mr. Blakely's body lay face down in a river of his own blood, with parts of his skull splattered about.

"Miss Maggie, is you alright?" Clara asked, kneeling at her side.

"I think so," was all she could mutter, her lips dry as toast. Although she was unscathed, the lifeless body before her was a different matter. Her dress and face were splashed with crimson droplets and her mind was muddled as she tried to process the scene.

Looking about, Clara spoke again.

"Miss Maggie, I don' mean no disrespect, but we gots to do something 'fore anyone discovers what happened. Someone was bound to hear that shot."

Clara's calm demeanor anchored Maggie. She was right. There wasn't time to ruminate on what had transpired. There'd be plenty of time for that later.

Maggie struggled to her feet, her legs quivering as her heel slid in the blood, nearly toppling her back to the floor. Grasping the newel post of the back stairs, she steadied herself.

The sound of the front door opening and closing echoed through the house followed by footsteps. Mrs. Polk appeared, shock veiling her expression when she peered at the dead body sprawled across the floor. Her hand flew to her mouth stifling a scream.

"What happened?" she asked, breathlessly. "I heard the shot while I was in the rose garden."

"Mr. Blakely threatened Miss Clara," Maggie muttered, still trying to regain her equilibrium.

"It weren't jus' that, Mrs. Polk. He said he knew what we's doing here and he was gonna tell everyone. Then he pointed a gun at my head. If Miss Maggie hadn't got the rifle, I'd be dead and everybody would know about the runaways."

The revulsion in Mrs. Polk's expression rattled Maggie's fortitude. Her recklessness had caused more harm than good.

Without hesitation, Mrs. Polk took charge. "We need to dispose of him before anyone discovers what happened." As if reading Maggie's mind, Mrs. Polk spoke with conviction. "No matter the reason, you'll hang for this."

"Where we gonna take him?" Clara asked

"I don't know but we need to remove the body and clean up this mess. It's imperative we keep everyone away from this part of the house. The fewer who know about it, the better," Mrs. Polk said resolutely. "Clara, go to the kitchen house and delay the midday meal. Tell them we've had a change of plans and will be dining elsewhere. I'll get Dr. Polk."

Maggie stared at the lifeless form on the floor. She'd killed a man. Never in her wildest dreams did she imagine she'd be capable of doing such a thing. It felt as if a hundred pounds of grain was sitting on her chest. Her shoulder throbbed and her legs felt like lead. Her mind couldn't process her role in the bloody scene, despite what her eyes beheld. What would the Polk's do? And worse, how would Seth react?

Time seemed to stand still until Dr. and Mrs. Polk bolted in the back door along with Seth. Moments later, Clara returned.

"Dr. Polk, I'm so sorry for this..." Maggie whimpered.

"No need for apologies. We haven't time to discuss it now." Unmoved by the gruesome display, Dr. Polk's quick thinking strengthened her resolve. Obviously, years of medical emergencies had made him impervious to a grisly scene such as this. His presence of mind was stalwart as he issued orders.

"Clara, gather cleaning supplies along with extra rags. Maggie, you help her."

A look of disgust shrouded Seth's countenance as he glanced around the space. His anger was apparent, wrenching Maggie's heart. *He must despise her for killing a man and putting the Polks at risk.* Granted, this wasn't the time to consider his opinion of her, or the affairs of her heart.

"Mrs. Polk, have Hatch bring the wagon and shovels around back. Seth, I need you to help Hatch dispose of the body."

"Where's Elora?" Seth asked.

"In town," Dr. Polk replied.

"Thank goodness," Seth sighed. "Where do you want us to bury him?"

Dr. Polk pondered for a moment before responding, "Put him in Willie's grave. No one will think to question the burial plot of a donkey."

With a nod, Seth raced out the door. Dr. Polk gently grasped Maggie's arm. "We'll discuss this later, but right now I need you to stay strong and help Clara clean up."

Maggie nodded and joined Clara in the back room gathering rags and bleach. Dr. Polk snatched the rifle and disappeared down the hall. Once inside his office, he pried up the floorboard nearest the mantle, slipped the rifle into the darkness, and replaced the board.

An hour and a half later, all evidence of Mr. Blakely's visit to Rose Hall had been wiped away. Although shaken by her deed, Maggie knew he would have killed Clara had she not taken action. Yet, she felt badly for the trouble she'd caused the Polks. The entire scenario rattled the foundation she'd worked so hard to achieve at Rose Hall. It seemed no matter what she did, it was always wrong. Whether being too timid or overreacting, her presence brought trouble to those she cared about.

Once everything was done, Maggie lumbered up the back stairs to change from her blood-spattered clothes. She stripped down to her chemise and scrubbed her face and hands in an effort to remove the evidence of her transgression. Slipping into a fresh frock, she crumpled the sullied one and tossed it into the hearth, watching as it disintegrated into ash.

Maggie skipped the evening meal, instead choosing to stay

in her room. She wasn't ready to face anybody. Even though she'd taken a life, she felt indifferent and it bothered her. A knock on her door startled her from her ruminations.

"May I come in?" Elora called.

Maggie opened the door and stepped back as Elora entered and plopped down on the bed.

"Would you like to talk about what happened?" she asked, adjusting her skirts.

"I can't believe I did this," Maggie said, sitting beside her.

"You did the right thing and saved Clara's life."

"Are you certain this was the right thing?" Maggie fixed her gaze on Elora's soft features with her sympathetic eyes and porcelain skin.

"How can you possibly doubt your motives? You're not a murderer."

Maggie looked away, again grappling with the day's events and the lack of remorse she felt. Elora squeezed her hand.

"Sometimes we have to make hard decisions, like taking one life to save others. He was trespassing and wielding a pistol with a threat to kill Clara, and possibly you too. Your instincts, and your aim from what I hear, were impeccable."

"By the way, who told you?"

"Mother. She's worried about you."

Maggie wiped the regret streaming across her cheeks. "I've caused your parents so much pain..."

"Nonsense! They adore you."

Maggie sighed. "I don't know what's worse, killing a man or the fact I feel no regret for it."

"Why don't you come downstairs? You'll feel better being around people, not cooped up in your room alone. Besides, you need to eat something."

"Alright," Maggie sighed.

They traipsed down the stairs and started toward the dining room when Dr. Polk appeared.

"Maggie, may I see you in my office?"

"Papa, I was just getting Maggie something to eat."

"I need to speak with her first."

Maggie's insides churned as she followed him. He was probably going to send her away, not that she could blame him. Wringing her hands, she sat in the wing chair across from him.

"I want you to know I hold no ill will toward you for what transpired today. In fact, I'm relieved you were here and had the sense to arm yourself. Blakely was a dangerous man and would have fulfilled his threats."

"You've spoken with Clara?" Maggie asked, her insides quaking.

"I have. She's forever grateful for your quick thinking. She owes you her life."

"But I killed a man," Maggie blurted out with a sob. Her shoulders shook as she buried her face in her hands. She was no different than her uncle who'd killed Sellers without forethought or conscience. The idea that she could be so similar to a man she loathed was more than she could bear.

"You did so in defense of another. Would you rather Blakely had killed Clara?"

"Of course not," Maggie sniffled. "What if someone discovers what happened?"

"No one will be the wiser. Seth helped Hatch bury the body in the same grave as the donkey. That burial site saved you from your uncle and it's saving you again now. Then Seth took Blakely's horse to the edge of the Houston's property and released it. No doubt, we'll hear of search parties for the next week or so, but I don't believe anyone will make the connection. As you know the Houstons aren't the brightest family when it comes to intellectual capabilities."

Maggie took a few deep breaths.

"What's still troubling you?" Dr. Polk asked, his gaze as gentle as a fawn.

"I murdered a man and I don't feel any...shame."

Dr. Polk folded his hands. "Maggie, I'm not trying to minimize what happened but I will tell you this. Blakely was a man who killed and tortured people for years. He'd have done the same to Clara, and you, given the chance. What you did wasn't murder, it was self-defense."

Maggie knew what the doctor said was true, yet she couldn't reconcile her actions with her conscience. "But I've placed you and your family in a terrible situation."

"Blakely did that, not you," he replied, his voice firm.

"I appreciate your kindness in this matter, but I'd understand if you need to send me away," she muttered, her chest aching at the thought.

Dr. Polk leaned forward, fixing his gaze on her. "You're part of this family and we are indebted to you. We have no intentions of sending you anywhere. This is your home."

"Thank you, sir," Maggie replied, wiping her eyes. "May I be excused? I'm feeling a bit tired all of a sudden."

"Get some rest. If you need anything, just ask."

She flashed a quick smile, hurrying from the room and up the back staircase, hoping to avoid Elora and everyone else. Her appetite was gone and she didn't have the energy to discuss the subject further. Once in her room, Maggie changed into her nightgown and slid beneath the covers, her shoulder throbbing where the rifle had struck.

Memories of the shotgun blast rang through her head followed by the gruesome scene with Blakely's body sprawled in a pool of his own blood. Maggie shivered at the thought. Panic began to finger her lungs when the doctor's words echoed in her head. *What you did wasn't murder, it was self-defense.* He was right.

Conflicted, Maggie couldn't reconcile her actions with the trouble she'd created for the Polk's, even though she knew she'd done the right thing. How had she gone from an innocent sheep farmer's daughter to a cold-blooded killer? Then again, it wasn't as if she'd walked up to Blakely in the street and shot him. He was threatening to kill Clara, what other choice *did* she have?

Maggie's eyes fluttered and her head ached. The more she pondered the day's events the more she longed for the solace of sleep. If only she could clear her conscience and move on to more pleasant thoughts. Finally, her eyes closed and she drifted off to dreamland where the Irish countryside awaited and the only sounds were the baying of sheep and her father's voice calling her home.

THE NEXT DAY, Mr. Houston and his small band of miscreants arrived, searching for information about Mr. Blakely's whereabouts. An unfamiliar gent with an air of depravity rode with them. His black eyes were devoid of feeling and the bend of his nose showed signs of having been broken at some point in his life. His skin was potted and scarred as if he'd run through a field of briars head first.

Houston dismounted and grabbed one of the workers who happened to be walking past. Shoving him against the porch baluster, he demanded to know if he'd seen Mr. Blakely. Despite the Negro's insistence that he was ignorant of Mr. Blakely's location, Mr. Houston continued his interrogation while the other men watched.

From the front parlor, Elora saw the confrontation and ran to fetch her father. Dr. Polk rushed to the front porch, Elora watching from inside. He started to speak but was quickly interrupted.

"Dr. Polk, I'm lookin' for Mr. Blakely," Houston yelled.

With the demeanor of a lamb, Dr. Polk responded. "Mr. Houston, will you kindly release my man?"

Indignation flushed Houston's countenance as he pushed the man and stepped back.

"My apologies, Dr. Polk. I meant no disrespect."

"What seems to be the problem?"

"My overseer, Blakely, was last seen riding toward your plantation. His horse was found at our barn last evening without him."

"Was he in need of medical attention?"

"No."

"Then why was he coming here?"

"He was investigating a new lead on my runaway slave. Obviously, I'm eager to know his whereabouts. It's bad enough I've lost money on that ungrateful darkie, but Mr. Blakely had a considerable sum of money with him to fund the search."

"Haven't we already discussed this?"

"I've lost a slave and now my overseer," he huffed. "Certainly, you can understand my need to recoup my losses."

Dr. Polk glanced toward the mysterious stranger.

"I don't believe we know each other. I'm Dr. Richard Polk. And you are?"

"Mitchell Ingram."

"And your business here?"

"To help with the recovery of his runaway slave."

Turning from Mr. Ingram, Dr. Polk addressed Houston.

"If Mr. Blakely was here, I'd be aware of it. Next time you have questions please see me about it, not my slaves. They've plenty of work to keep them busy, and you know how ineffective they can be when rattled."

"Ain't that so!" he laughed. "Worthless creatures, all of 'em. They're lucky we treat 'em as good as we do. Forgive me for stormin' in like we did. Blakely's a good man and I can't afford to lose him. He knows how to keep the darkies under control."

The corner of Houston's lip curled while Mitchell Ingram

sat stone faced. His soulless eyes glared at Dr. Polk as if he knew the entire scenario was a charade.

"If I hear anything, I'll send word immediately. Please excuse me, I must return to my work."

It vexed Dr. Polk to refer to the workers as slaves but it was imperative to blend in, thus making it a necessary evil. Fortunately, Houston believed the good doctor to be like-minded, and didn't question him further.

The posse of ingrates wheeled their horses around and galloped down the drive. Dr. Polk inhaled deeply, obviously grateful he was able to ward them off, and that Maggie's secret was buried and holding firm, at least for now.

THINGS QUIETED after the visit from Houston and his new accomplice, Mitchell Ingram. Word about town was that Blakely must have fallen in the river and drowned. When his horse returned to the barn without its rider, it was the only logical conclusion, especially since everyone knew he couldn't swim.

With each passing day, Maggie's life became more like a puppet show. She engaged mindlessly in the same routines, stifling any emotions that tried to surface. Her only regret was the odd feeling she got when Seth was close by, as if his opinion of her had altered. He'd never said anything to her about what had happened, for which she was thankful. Self-loathing saturated her every thought, making her feel as if she could never be cleansed from the sin of her ways. She'd left too many bodies in her wake.

44

Buds freckled tree branches while birds flew about singing of spring's revival. It had been nearly two years since Maggie had left the lush country of her birth and she felt as if she'd lived ten lifetimes. She'd survived abuse, missing her Da, Sellers' death, a murder, and coping with a deep-seated love that would never be reciprocated. Since killing Blakely, she'd yet to regain any semblance of her old self and wondered if she'd ever feel whole again. At least she had her work for the Railroad to keep her mind occupied and make amends for her sins.

Perhaps it was time to move on and find work elsewhere so she could save enough money for passage home. Then again, she had no home in Ireland, not anymore. Her Da was her home and she'd no idea where he was. She'd sent several letters since leaving her uncle's farm but had yet to receive a response.

Even if she returned to Ireland, it wouldn't be far enough to sever the attraction she felt toward Seth Daniels. The idea of never seeing his blue eyes, sandy locks, or mischievous smile again was unbearable. Granted, her feelings were a moot point.

Seth belonged to Elora, there was no denying it. It seemed they were always huddled close together in hushed whispers or engaged in playful amusements. Maggie's emotions swirled like a tornado. Whatever her decision, it would be saturated in doubt with a strong dash of sorrow.

MRS. POLK SAT across from Mrs. Bartlett, sipping tea while they chatted.

"I'm sorry to come without an invitation but I couldn't keep the news to myself," Mrs. Bartlett said with a broad smile.

"You're always welcome here with or without an invitation. So tell me, what is this exciting news?"

"I overheard George speaking with one of his old poker buddies."

"I thought he no longer engaged in such things."

"Thankfully, he doesn't. But sometimes those heathens come by in hopes of dragging him back to that wretched game," she huffed. "The other day, one of them visited and asked him to join their traveling group."

"Whatever for?"

"To replace one of their members." Mrs. Bartlett leaned forward. "Do you remember that horrid man, Mr. Stevenson, who came to our house demanding reparation for George's losses? Well, it seems he went mad, shot his wife, and then turned the gun on himself!"

Mrs. Polk gasped. "Are you certain?"

"Quite. George never liked him and was relieved he's no longer a threat. He always feared Mr. Stevenson would rescind their agreement."

Mrs. Polk took a sip of her tea, the cup quivering in her hand.

"Are you alright, Diane?"

"Just a bit overwhelmed. My schedule is full today."

"I do apologize for coming unannounced. After everything Dr. Polk did for us, I felt compelled to let you know. We're forever indebted to you both." Placing her cup on the table, Mrs. Bartlett smiled. "I should let you get back to your duties."

"Please stay and finish your tea. I always have time for my dearest friend."

Thirty minutes later, Mrs. Polk stood at the end of the front walk watching her best friend's carriage totter down the drive when Elora ambled up beside her.

"Was that Mrs. Bartlett?" she asked.

"Indeed, it was. Where's Maggie?"

"With Miss Heddy."

"Please tell her to come to the house immediately."

Mrs. Polk walked inside to speak with her husband while Elora ran down the sandy path to the cottages.

SCAMPERING up the stairs of Miss Heddy's, Elora peeked in the door.

"Maggie, Mother needs you to come to the house," she said breathlessly

"Right now?"

"Yes!"

"Whatever for?"

"I don't know, but she was adamant you come straight away."

"Don't keep her waitin'," Miss Heddy said. "I can take care of this batch."

Maggie removed her apron and followed Elora to the house where Dr. and Mrs. Polk waited in the front parlor. Mrs. Polk waived Maggie over and grasped her hands.

"Sit down, I have something to tell you that may come as a shock."

Perplexed by Mrs. Polk's serious state, Maggie did as she was told, Elora joining them on the settee.

"I've received some disturbing news regarding your uncle."

Maggie's breath caught and her insides began to churn. He was back and now they were sending her away.

"I'm sorry to tell you this, but he's dead."

The words reverberated in Maggie's ears. He was dead.

"How?" she asked, taking in a deep breath.

"According to my source, he went mad. He shot your aunt and then killed himself."

"My aunt is gone too?"

Mrs. Polk nodded.

"What about my cousin, Susannah?"

"There was no mention of her."

"I know I should be angry with her but I can't help feeling concerned. She never really had a chance in a family like that."

Silence pervaded the atmosphere as Maggie processed the news. Her uncle's death meant she was no longer bound by the fear of discovery. She was finally free of him, although the memory of his cruel acts would enslave her forever.

"Are you OK?" Dr. Polk asked. "It's perfectly understandable if you feel sorrow over the loss."

"I'm not certain what I'm feeling. I never wished him dead yet I'm relieved he's gone. Poor Susannah. At least she's inherited the farm and any assets that went along with it." Maggie stood. "Maybe a walk will help me sort through it all."

"Would you like some company?" Elora asked.

"No, thank you. I need to be alone."

Maggie left the room, her emotions swirling as she slipped out the back door. Taking a deep breath, she held her hand to her chest when she felt the bar of the garnet brooch press against her skin. Tired of hiding it, she removed it from her chemise and affixed it to the neckline of her dress. If anyone asked about it, she'd say it was a gift from an old friend.

She started down the path along the river's edge, humming as she went. While sorrowful for the grisly manner of her aunt and uncle's death, Maggie was happy to be free. Reality took hold, livening her steps. As she bounced along the trail, her humming morphed into words.

"Come thou fount of every blessing..."

"You have a beautiful voice."

Stunned, Maggie turned. Seth leaned against an ancient oak tossing stones in the water, a broad smile lifting the corners of his mouth. Her cheeks colored, partly from the compliment and partly from embarrassment that he'd overheard her singing.

"You startled me."

"My apologies, I didn't mean to scare you," he said, the breeze ruffling his hair as his eyes sparkled in the afternoon sun. "You look positively radiant. What has you in such a good mood?"

"Freedom," she replied.

"It suits you," he said, walking up to her.

Her gaze locked onto his, silencing the world around her except for the echo of her pulse thumping in her ears. He leaned down, his lips softly brushing hers. Her eyes closed as he circled his arm around her waist, his kiss intensifying.

No, she thought, pushing back, her fingers resting on her lips as she tried to steady her breathing. Without thought, her hand landed hard across his cheek with a slap.

"How could you do such a thing?" she cried out, upset with herself for succumbing to the brazenness of his actions. She turned to walk away when he reached for her arm.

"Maggie, wait."

Hesitating, Maggie turned back, her mind screaming for her to flee before temptation overpowered her restraint. His gaze implored her to stay until his eyes traveled to the neckline of her bodice.

"Where did you get that?" he demanded, lines creasing his forehead.

"What?"

"That," he pointed at the brooch.

"A friend gave it to me."

"What *friend*?" he barked.

"A very dear one." Indignation colored Maggie's cheeks. *How dare he question her in such a manner?*

Seth grabbed her upper arms. "Tell me who gave it to you," he said, displeasure tinting his words.

"You're hurting me!" she shouted.

Twisting from his grasp, she turned and ran toward the house as Seth threw his hat to the ground, his teeth clenched as he plowed his fingers through his sandy locks.

Winded, Maggie rushed through the front door toward the stairs.

"Maggie," Elora called, stepping from the parlor.

Stopping at the foot of the staircase, Maggie froze, trying to conceal the despair trickling down her face.

"Won't you join us for tea?" Elora asked.

"I'm unwell and need to lie down," she replied before scurrying up the steps at a rabbit's pace.

Inside the confines of her room, Maggie crumpled to her bed and cried. The whisper of Seth's kiss lingered on her lips, wringing her heart like a wet rag. Everything she did was wrong and now her feelings for Seth seemed to be pulling him away from Elora. She'd done right by refusing any further advances, but she'd crossed a line by hitting him. Sitting up, she unfastened the brooch and gazed at the faceted gems, wondering what had made Seth react so aggressively. Perhaps he thought it was a gift from an admirer. With a long sigh, she slumped back to the bed with the brooch clutched to her chest. *If only he weren't' promised to Elora.*

Maggie skipped the evening meal, her appetite as barren as

her heart. She stared out the window of her room, fingering the brooch in her hand. Apologizing to Seth and explaining where she got the brooch would be a good start. At this point, there was no reason to hide her past now that her uncle was dead.

She affixed the brooch to her collar, scurried down the back stairs, and out the door where she collided with Seth. Regaining her balance, she met his gaze, the deep blue of his eyes piercing her heart.

"I came to apologize for my behavior earlier. It was unacceptable," Maggie muttered, her heart racing.

"I'm sorry too," Seth replied. "If you'd permit me to explain, I think you'll understand why I behaved in such a severe manner."

He and Maggie walked side by side along the edge of the marsh.

"I've told you a few things about my past, but not all of it." He took in a deep breath before continuing. "That brooch belonged to my mother."

Maggie gasped, stopping in her tracks.

"Please, let me finish," he said, offering his arm, which she accepted hesitantly.

"I already told you my mother died after one of my father's tirades. They'd fought because my mother discovered one of the slaves, Annie, was pregnant by my father."

"How awful. She must have been devastated by your father's indiscretion."

"She wasn't angry about that. She was furious he'd forced himself on Annie. She loved Annie like family. Anyway, my mother wore that brooch every day. It was a gift from her father when she turned sixteen. After my mother died, I gave it to Annie so my father couldn't pawn it.

"It wasn't until Annie had her baby that I learned the reason behind my parent's argument. I'd no idea Annie's duties involved meeting my father's needs. Despite the manner of conception, Annie adored her little girl. She named her Elizabeth in honor of my mother. That child gave her hope and a purpose.

"By the time Elizabeth was three, my father was struggling financially and poor Annie was pregnant again. Since my father couldn't afford another mouth to feed, he decided to sell the child. Annie was beside herself with grief. I'd had enough of my father's abuse and suggested we run away. She wouldn't agree at first but when I explained we'd head north and get married, she acquiesced. The child was fair skinned and could pass as mine."

"Did you love her?"

"Yes, although not in a romantic way. I figured the only way to keep her safe was to marry her. I owed her that much after the years of cruelty my father had inflicted on her. At least she and my half-sister would be free.

"When the day arrived, I spiked my father's whiskey with something to knock him out so we could escape. Once he was unconscious, we made our way to the woods and from there northward. Annie was wearing the brooch on her collar when we left. A few days later, we came across a group of escapees and joined forces with them.

"After several days in the woods, we were hungry and tired. I left the group by the river to search for food. As a white man, it was easier for me to get around. I was only gone for an hour," he swallowed hard before continuing. "When I returned, everyone was gone, except Annie."

"Was she...?"

"There wasn't much left of her. She'd been strangled and her body mutilated. I buried her and searched for the others but never found them, leading me to believe they'd been captured. Since the brooch was gone, I assumed whoever killed her had taken it."

Maggie's heart seized. She removed the brooch from her

collar and held it in her palm, the stones glimmering in the setting sun.

"What did you do?" she muttered, her stomach constricting.

"I didn't know what to do so I headed back to my father's farm. I found that good-for-nothing bum attacking another slave. She wasn't much older than Annie had been when he forced himself on her. I pulled him off and started pummeling him. What I didn't see was the knife in his hand. He slashed my face before stumbling from the house. I wrapped a shirt around my head to stop the bleeding and left. Knowing my father, he'd come back with a gun and kill me. I rode as far as I could until the loss of blood was too much.

"I woke up here. Apparently, one of the conductors found me in the woods near Rose Hall. After Dr. Polk heard my story, he put me to work," Seth said, exhaling. "I harbored so much anger toward my father and the monsters that murdered Annie, I spent much of my time sabotaging the slave hunters' efforts. I was pretty good at it and well, you know the rest."

They stood in silence. Maggie turned the brooch over in her hand, contemplating everything Seth had shared.

"I don't know how your friend came to have that brooch, but chances are he's one of the men that murdered Annie."

"You said she was wearing this when you ran away together?"

"Yes. I know you're trying to protect this person, Maggie, but I *need* to know who gave it to you."

"How long ago was that?"

"About twelve years."

"And the child was three when you ran away?"

"Yes."

"I don't know how to say this," Maggie mumbled.

"Tell me, please."

"A dear friend gave this to me to wear until we were reunited. But it's not what you think. She's like a sister to me."

"You got this from a woman?" Shock resonated in his voice.

"A young lady. She's the adopted daughter of the Milners, the family that saved me when I ran from my uncle and was starving."

"Did she say how she came to be in possession of it?"

Maggie nodded, gathering the courage to tell him about Annalissa.

"According to the Milners, a group of escapees brought Annalissa to them. Supposedly, Annalissa's mother went to the river for a drink when she heard horses approaching. She implored the others to take her daughter and run as fast and far as they could while she distracted whoever was coming. She fastened the brooch to her daughter's dress before they ran. The Milners arranged transport for the escapees but kept Annalissa because she was too sick to travel. They fell in love with her and adopted her as their daughter."

"Are you telling me your friend might be Annie's daughter? My sister?" Seth asked, hope animating his face.

"I think it's possible. She had the brooch, she's the right age, and there's no doubt she's mixed race."

"I've got to meet her. If I see her, I'll know."

"She's in Pennsylvania." Maggie smiled. "I'll write to her parents and let them know you'd like to visit."

"If they agree, would you accompany me?"

Maggie shook her head and took a step back. "You need to make this trip on your own."

"I can't travel to see a woman I don't know, especially with news as sensitive as this. Considering the circumstances, she may not want to know me."

"Of course, she would," Maggie replied, touching his arm. "I'm certain of it."

"She might be more receptive if you were with me." The pleading in his eyes melted Maggie's resolve. How could she possibly turn him down? Then again, how could she agree to accompany him? Perhaps Elora could come along with them.

"Very well, I'll go." A smile crept across her face when she realized there was no reason to avoid Pennsylvania any longer, and if Elora could come it would create a buffer between them. "I'll send a letter in the morning's post."

"Thank you," he replied, exhaling.

"Do you want the brooch?" Maggie asked, holding it out. "It's rightfully yours."

"Keep it. You have a pact with Annalissa and I'll not interfere with that. If she's truly Annie's daughter, it belongs to her." Seth paused. "You said their last name is Milner?"

"Yes."

"Same as yours?"

Maggie glanced at the ground. With her uncle's demise, there was no need to maintain a false identity. "My name is Maggie McFarland. I took the name Milner to thwart my uncle's efforts in locating me."

"Maggie McFarland," he said with a sly smile. "Definitely more fitting."

"I'm truly sorry for slapping you earlier," Maggie said.

"And I'm sorry for my actions." Seth removed his hat and scratched his head. "I suppose I should speak with Dr. Polk."

When they reached the house, Seth went to Dr. Polk's office to discuss the situation and what would hopefully be an upcoming trip north. Maggie traipsed up the back staircase to her room and closed the door.

What were the odds that Annalissa was Seth's half-sister, and that she would be the one to bring them together after all this time? Sitting at the small desk in the corner of her room, Maggie retrieved a piece of parchment, dipped the nib in the inkpot, and began scripting one of the most sensitive letters of her life. She dipped and wrote until her nails were stained and her hand cramped. First thing in the morning, she'd post the letter and hopefully reunite a brother and sister.

45

The Milners responded quickly to Maggie's request with great enthusiasm. They discussed it with Annalissa who was excited to learn if in fact Seth was her brother. Dr. Polk approved of the decision to travel and offered to send them in his carriage. However, Elora adamantly refused to accompany them, claiming she had pressing engagements that couldn't be rescheduled.

The day before they were to depart, Elora plopped on the bed as Maggie pulled dresses from her wardrobe to pack.

Elora shook her head. "It's beyond belief, like a novel or something. What are the odds he would find her after all this time?"

"It's quite a story."

"And you were the one to bring them together. How extraordinary," Elora sighed, her hands clasped in her lap as she stared out the window.

"I don't know that I'd call it extraordinary, but I'd be honored to know I brought two people together who'd been separated for so long."

"My dear Maggie, you're so practical," Elora teased.

The two chatted while Maggie completed her packing to include a couple of books and some knitting to occupy her time in the carriage, anything to distract her from being so close to Seth.

AT DAWN, Seth and Maggie boarded the carriage and set off on the long trek to Pennsylvania. Maggie's nerves jittered with excitement over the prospect of seeing the Milners again, although being so close to Seth for an extended period of time would prove arduous. Hopefully, reading and knitting would distract the yearning plucking at her heart.

Seth watched as Maggie read a book of poetry by Shelley. The weight of his gaze brought a flush of color to her cheeks and a half smile to her lips.

"Is it interesting?" he asked.

Looking up, she stared at his strong jawline, tanned skin, and shimmering blue eyes, the scar on his right cheek highlighted by the sun filtering through the window.

"If you enjoy poetry. Shelley was something of a radical for his time and a great influence for my favorite poet, Byron."

"So, you like poetry?"

"Indeed. My Da and I read to each other every evening and most of our choices were poets. Some of our favorites were Keats, Wordsworth, and Burns. I'd not read Shelley in a long time and found this volume in the Polk's library."

"You've never told me much about your past. What else did you do in Ireland?"

Maggie took in a deep breath and closed the book setting it on the tufted seat beside her. "Mostly I studied. Da was adamant about my lessons. My mother made him promise to educate me so I'd have opportunities and not be bound by societal restrictions."

"What happened to your mother?"

"She died a few months after giving birth to me."

"I'm sorry."

"According to my father's accounts, she was a beautiful, kind, and intelligent woman. They read poetry every night and he continued that tradition with me. I have a well-worn copy of Byron's poetry he gave me the evening before I sailed to America. I read it every night."

"That's a nice tradition," he said with a grin.

"Do you enjoy reading?" Maggie asked.

He shrugged. "Most of my reading revolves around notices in the newspapers."

An awkward pause stifled the atmosphere as Maggie stared at her hands, unsure what to say next.

"Would you read one of the poems to me?" he asked, a slight smile wrinkling his cheeks.

Maggie began reading, conscious of Seth watching her as she enunciated each word. When she finished the poem, she lifted her eyes to meet his.

"What do you think?"

"It sounds as if he's pursuing perfect love and freedom."

"That's exactly what I thought."

They discussed the poem further before Maggie read another.

"Do you believe in perfect love?" he asked, his gaze fixed on hers.

Tension fogged her mind, making it difficult to think. In her eyes, he was her perfect love except he wasn't free to commit. The irony of the situation wasn't lost on her.

"Perhaps. But I think that's highly unlikely for me."

"Why?"

"My life is...complicated," Maggie said.

"In what way?"

"I can't explain it," she sighed, shaking her head. "I've caused so much grief, I'm not sure I deserve to be happy."

Seth leaned forward, resting his elbows on his knees. "What could be so horrible you believe you're unworthy of love?"

"Some things are meant to be locked away because bringing them to light would shatter the heart like a crystal goblet," she whispered, looking out the window. Sellers' death continued to plague her spirit. Living a loveless life would be penitence for her actions, or lack thereof, and she accepted her fate freely. Her affection for Seth and his inability to reciprocate seemed adequate punishment.

"Things that remain in the dark fester and rot," Seth replied. "Bringing it to light prevents unwarranted decay."

"Your logic sounds poetic."

"Regardless, I don't believe you've done anything as terrible as you imply."

Maggie paused, uncertain how to respond without revealing too much.

"We've been through a lot together. I hope you'd trust me enough to tell me anything," Seth prodded, his gaze piercing her heart like cupid's arrow.

Maggie swallowed hard. She wanted to tell someone, anyone, about her past indiscretions and unburden the guilt that had held her captive for so long. With a sigh, she began.

"When I was at my uncle's farm, he sent me to work at the cattle barn. I became close with one of the workers, Sellers. He was my dearest friend," she whispered, fidgeting with her hands. "After I discovered my uncle had been keeping my father's letters from me, I made the mistake of confronting him."

Seth sat quietly, waiting for her to continue.

"I thought he was going to beat me to death," she paused, stifling a sob. "That's when I realized I needed to escape. I packed my things and hid in the hayloft of the cattle barn. My plan was to leave before sunrise so I'd be far away when my uncle discovered I was gone.

"Unfortunately, I overslept. Before I could sneak out, my uncle came searching for me. Sellers saw me hiding. Despite my uncle's threats, he claimed ignorance of my whereabouts." Maggie wiped a tear from her eye. "That's when my uncle shot him."

"Surely, this Sellers person didn't blame you."

"He couldn't. He's dead."

Seth sat back against the cushioned seat, furrowing his brow.

"What does this have to do with you being unworthy of love?"

"Sellers died because I didn't come forward," Maggie replied, her voice quavering.

"And?"

"He's dead because of me!" she declared, tears trickling down her cheeks.

"No, he's dead because your uncle killed him."

"If I'd given myself up, Sellers would still be alive."

"Would he?" Seth queried, leaning forward. "How do you know your uncle wouldn't have shot you? And if he's as cold-blooded as you say, he probably would've killed Sellers to silence him."

"My weakness cost Sellers his life."

"It's not weakness when you're staring down the barrel of a gun, it's survival."

"It's not that simple."

"I believe it is. You're blaming yourself for the acts of a crazy man. Sellers is dead because of your uncle, not you."

Maggie pondered Seth's words. It mirrored what Dr. Polk told her after Blakely's death. Maybe she wasn't to blame. In her mind she was beginning to see the wisdom of Dr. Polk's and Seth's words, yet she couldn't dismiss her role in Sellers' demise.

"Maggie, did you hear what I said? It wasn't your fault."

She stared out the window of the carriage watching the landscape whizz past. Despite the fact she was beginning to accept what he'd said, guilt still held her in its grasp like a hawk with a rat refusing to release it from its talons.

Seth brushed a tear from her cheek, drawing her gaze to his steely stare. How could she resist such a compassionate soul? Then again, she'd be forsaking her relationship with Elora if she gave in to her desires. She'd not allow her selfishness to destroy another friend's future.

"I didn't mean to burden you with my troubles," she mumbled.

"You didn't burden me, I asked you to tell me," he replied with arched eyebrows. His cheeks creased in a smile. "Will you read some more?"

Maggie grinned and continued reading. It was easy being with Seth. He was always so accommodating and made her feel comfortable, no matter the circumstances.

THANKFULLY, the remainder of the trip was uneventful. The weather was glorious and the roads well maintained. Several days later, the carriage tottered down the bumpy drive to the stone house where the Milner's resided. As the carriage came to a halt, joy lifted Maggie's cheeks when she saw Annalissa step outside.

"There she is," she said, pointing to her old friend.

Maggie watched as Seth stared at Annalissa, his eyes misting and a smile curling his lips.

"My goodness, it's like looking at a fair-skinned Annie," he said under his breath.

Maggie hopped from the carriage and rushed to greet Annalissa in a warm embrace.

"My dear Maggie, it's ever so good to see you again!"

Pulling back, Maggie smiled, her heart pounding as tears clung to her lashes.

"I've missed you terribly and cannot wait to hear all that's happened since I left." Looking around, Maggie asked, "Where are your parents?"

"They went to town but will be back soon. They wanted to give me some time alone with my brother."

Seth stood by the carriage with his hat in his hands watching their reunion.

"Is that him?" Annalissa whispered, glancing his direction.

"It is. Are you ready to meet him?"

Annalissa nodded.

"Seth," Maggie called, waving him over.

He walked toward them; his eyes fixed on the ground. Maggie had seen Seth in so many harrowing situations with danger lurking in every shadow, but never had she seen him as subdued as he was now.

"Seth Daniels, may I introduce Miss Annalissa Milner."

"Nice to meet you," he said with a slight bow, his gaze meeting Annalissa's.

"I'm delighted to make your acquaintance," she replied with a curtsey. "Shall we go inside?"

Annalissa escorted Maggie and Seth into the formal parlor where a tray of tea and biscuits waited. Maggie was astounded at how changed her friend was. Womanhood was taking hold, creating a refined, beautiful lady.

Annalissa poured tea and handed them each a cup as they sat down. Maggie removed the brooch from her collar.

"This belongs to you," she said, handing it to Annalissa.

"I always knew we'd meet again," she replied, studying the trinket as it sparkled in her hand. Affixing it to her bodice, she addressed Seth.

"Tell me about my mother's brooch."

"It was a gift to my mother from her father on her sixteenth birthday. When she died, I gave it to Annie, your mother, for taking such good care of her."

"And my father?"

Seth looked down, apparently uncomfortable explaining his father's atrocities.

"Mr. Daniels, please don't be shy about my history. I'm aware that my mother was enslaved by your family."

"My father was the one that owned her, my mother loathed the institution of slavery. She loved Annie. When she learned of Annie's condition and that it was my father's doing, she lost control. Not over the betrayal to their marriage, but because of what he'd done to your mother."

He paused, taking in a deep breath.

"Mr. Daniels, if this is too painful, we need not discuss it," she said softly.

"I'm fine, and please call me Seth."

Annalissa's dimples reappeared as she lifted the teacup to her lips.

"My father was a brute and didn't take kindly to my mother's outburst. In his rage, he pummeled her until she was bruised and bloody. Every time I intervened, he'd turn on me. I wasn't very strong then and couldn't match his rage, especially when he'd been in the whiskey. Annie nursed my mother day and night until she succumbed to her injuries several days later."

Annalissa gasped. "Was your father charged?"

Seth huffed. "The sheriff was one of my father's drinking buddies. Even if I had reported him, nothing would have come of it."

"I'm sorry for your loss."

Maggie sat quietly listening to Seth's account, moisture welling in her eyes for all he'd suffered.

"When you were about three years old, your mother was

pregnant again. By that time, my father's drinking was out of control and he wasn't making much money from the farm, so he decided to sell you. Your mother was devastated. She and I had grown rather close over the years. She always tended to my black eyes or busted lips following my father's tirades. She even set my arm once when he broke it.

"I convinced her to run away with me. Once everything was planned, we took off. Along the way, we met another group of runaways and joined forces with them. They'd heard about the Railroad and were hoping to find one of the stops.

"We went days with hardly anything to eat which weakened your mother considerably. I left to search for food. I was only gone for about an hour. When I returned..." Seth inhaled deeply.

"Go on," Annalissa said, shifting in her seat with her hands clasped in her lap.

"Annie was dead and everyone else was gone. I didn't know what to do. I buried your mother and searched the area for you and the others. When I didn't find anyone, I assumed they'd been captured. I was desperate to find you. You were the most important thing in the world to Annie and I couldn't let her down again."

Annalissa stared at her lap, tears trickling across her cheeks.

"Mr. Daniels, Seth, you didn't let my mother down. She gave her life to save me. What you didn't know was that hunters were tracking the group you were traveling with. When they heard the horses coming, my mother insisted the others take me and run. According to what the runaways told my parents, my mother was going to distract whoever was coming and hopefully rejoin the group later. As we both know, that didn't happen."

"I never knew about that until recently, but it sounds like

something she'd do. You were her life." Seth ran his hand through his curly locks as he exhaled. "She was a brave woman. Living with my father's constant assaults and cruelty would have broken anyone else, but not Annie. She gathered her strength from you. Her only wish was for you to have a better life than she did."

"Her wish was granted. My life is charmed. I have the most wonderful, loving parents a person could have. I'm educated and live in a safe home. Most importantly, I'm free."

Seth nodded. "I'm thankful to know it."

Annalissa sniffled and wiped her cheeks as a smile reappeared. "So, you're my half-brother?"

"Yes."

Annalissa rose from her chair and walked over to Seth.

"It's nice to know you, brother."

Seth stood and gazed down at her.

"It's good to see you again."

As the two embraced, Maggie smiled, her heart full. After all these years, brother and sister were reunited in a most unexpected way.

The clattering of carriage wheels interrupted the moment. Annalissa peered out the front window. "My parents have arrived!" she said, scurrying to the front door.

Maggie grinned at Seth. "What do you think?"

"She's even better than you described. I can't get over how much she resembles her mother. I only wish Annie could have been here for this moment."

The room seemed to brighten as Reverend and Mrs. Milner entered.

"My dear Maggie, it's ever so good to have you home," Mrs. Milner said, pulling Maggie into a firm embrace.

"I've missed you," Maggie replied, fresh tears clinging to her eyelids. She released Mrs. Milner and hugged the Reverend.

"Welcome back, Maggie," he said.

"Mama, Papa, I'd like you to meet my brother, Seth Daniels." Annalissa smiled. "These are my parents, Rev. and Mrs. Milner.

Seth shook the Reverend's hand before bowing to his wife.

"I'm grateful for all you've done for Annalissa. Her mother would be grateful too."

"We're happy things worked out as they did. We couldn't have asked for a sweeter more beautiful daughter," Mrs. Milner replied, her eyes glistening as she clutched her daughter's hand.

Dinner was a joyous gathering. The conversation percolated like a fresh pot of coffee with the topic bubbling from the irony of the reunion between siblings, to the joy of having Maggie back at the farm, to the workings of the Railroad. When the dishes were cleared and yawns filtered through the room, everyone bid goodnight and retired to their quarters. Maggie was staying with Annalissa while Seth slept in Maggie's old room.

After changing into her cotton gown, Maggie slipped into bed next to her friend.

"Are you happy?" Maggie asked.

"I am. My brother seems like a wonderful man."

"He's the best of men," Maggie muttered, her heart quickening.

"I can see you like him."

Maggie huffed, her cheeks warming.

"Tell me about your relationship," Annalissa said with a giggle.

"We're good friends. Sometimes we work together..."

"That's not what I'm talking about. How long have you two been attached?"

"Why would you say such a thing?" Maggie gasped.

"Any dullard can see the way you look at each other."

"It's complicated," Maggie sighed.

"I'm good at complicated."

Maggie shared how they met and all that had transpired between them up to the discovery of the brooch and its connection.

"He has an understanding with Elora, so you see there's nothing romantic between us."

"He might have an understanding with her but it's obvious his heart belongs to you."

"You're being melodramatic. Seth and I are nothing more than friends," she said, picking a thread from the quilt. Not wanting to discuss it further, Maggie changed the subject. "Enough about me, I want to hear all about you."

Annalissa giggled and spoke about her studies and her ongoing desire to attend Oberlin College. They chatted and chuckled late into the night like old times until exhaustion swept them off to sleep.

For the next two days, Annalissa and Seth spent time getting aquainted while Maggie reminisced and shared stories with Mrs. Milner and Darla about all that had transpired since she'd left. While not happy to hear her aunt and uncle were dead, they were relieved he could never harm her again.

Days later, their visit was cut short when Seth received word through a cryptic message in the paper that he needed to go to Mr. Still's office in Philadelphia. Early next morning, the Milners gathered at the front of the house as Maggie and Seth prepared to leave.

"It was good seeing you again," Annalissa said, hugging Maggie close.

"I'm glad everything worked out between you and Seth."

"Speaking of which..." Annalissa leaned in and whispered in Maggie's ear, "Don't wait too long to let him know how you feel."

"There's nothing between us," she replied, pulling away. "I already told you, he's spoken for."

"Perhaps, but I dare say it won't be a happy match with you around. There's definitely something brewing between you two. If you recall, I have a sense for these things. And I'm never wrong," she said, squeezing Maggie's hand.

46

The carriage rocked down the drive, Maggie's thoughts swirling over what Annalissa had said. Her heart ached at the idea that the connection between she and Seth was so obvious to others. What if Elora noticed?

Then again, Elora was so trusting she'd never conceive that two people she cared about could do anything deceitful. Once they got back to Rose Hall, she'd search for a job elsewhere. Now that her uncle was gone, Maggie was free to go where she pleased. She needed to earn some money so she could go home and search for her Da.

"You want to talk about it?" Seth asked.

"About what?"

"Whatever's troubling you? You haven't said a word for miles. Elora wouldn't have made it to the end of the drive without starting a conversation." The sparkle in his deep blue eyes made Maggie's stomach flutter. The mention of Elora's name reminded her she needed to curtail her affections and leave Rose Hall as soon as possible.

"I was just thinking about our time with the Milners. I've missed them terribly yet I found myself missing the Polks too."

"I suppose you and I are lucky in that respect. We share two families."

"So, what did you think of your sister?"

He exhaled, shaking his head. "She's amazing, just like her mother. And just as pretty. She has the same dimples and twinkle in her eyes."

"Did you tell her that?"

"She wanted to know everything. I told her about her mother's kindness and how proud she'd be to know her daughter's future included going to Oberlin College."

His voice broke when he said college and tears crested in the corners of his eyes. Instinctively, Maggie laid her hand upon his. A tingle radiated through her fingertips, causing her to withdraw them quickly as if she'd been burned.

"She wouldn't have had these opportunities had I married her mother," Seth said. "It's almost as if she's better off this way."

"There's nothing wrong with being happy about her good fortune. It doesn't mean you loved her mother any less."

"You're a wise woman, Maggie McFarland," he said, the right side of his mouth curling. Sunlight filtered through the carriage window, illuminating the contours of his jawline and the highlights of the sandy curls framing his visage.

Looking away, Maggie tried to conjure up the strength to keep her feelings at bay. The detour meant additional time alone with him, adding an extra element to her struggle. She swallowed hard in an effort to still the thrumming of her heart as they jounced down the long road towards Philadelphia.

THE CITY WAS alive with the hustle and bustle of wagons, carriages, and pedestrians. They halted at the back of a brick structure where Seth disembarked.

"Wait here, I won't be long."

Maggie gazed out the window watching people pass; some dressed in glorious silks whilst others carried the day's load of produce or laundry when one figure in particular caught her eye. There was something in her manner of walking, almost a waddle, as she hauled a large basket of linens down the alleyway. Maggie's heart beat faster as recognition flooded her mind. Throwing open the carriage door, Maggie called out,

"Willa!"

The woman stopped and gazed at her, a smile plumping her cheeks. Maggie leapt out and ran across the road, throwing her arms about the woman, nearly knocking the basket to the ground.

"Miss Maggie is that really you?" she asked, tears streaming across her face.

"Willa, what are you doing here?"

"I's the washer woman for Mr. Harmon now. Letty and the rest of us had to find work after Mr. Stevenson," she hesitated, "when we gots new owners at the farm," she said quietly, placing the basket on the ground.

"I know about my uncle," Maggie said flatly.

Willa's eyes grew to the size of half dollars. "How'd you find out?"

"That's not important. It was a terrible tragedy."

"That it was. Didn't take long for them bankers to come seize the place and then we's all homeless."

"Where's Letty?"

"She cookin' for Mr. Shanklin. They treats her real good."

Willa looked tired; her jovial countenance greatly altered. Lines creased her eyes and a curve bent her once stout stature. Her cotton dress was worn but neat, and sprigs of her once black hair were beginning to fade to a soft gray.

"Where you been all this time?" she asked.

"It's a rather long story, but I was able to find refuge with some wonderful people."

"Here in the city?" Willa's eyes grew wide.

"Down south, actually."

"We was worried when you and Sellers run off," she said, shaking her head.

A pang knotted Maggie's stomach at the sound of Sellers' name. "Sellers isn't with me."

"Then where is he?"

Tears flowed across Maggie's cheeks as her mind drifted back to the image of Sellers lying in a pool of blood. "Mr. Stevenson killed him."

"He killed Sellers?" Willa muttered, her mahogany eyes filling with sorrow.

"Shot him dead like an animal." Maggie replied as a sob burst from her lips, shaking her body.

Willa wrapped her arms around Maggie and held her tight.

"I's sorry 'bout that. I knows you loved him. We all did. Sellers was like a son to me and Letty." Willa sniffled as Maggie cried on her shoulder.

"He must have removed his body after I ran," Maggie mumbled, pulling back. "What about Susannah?"

"She got sent off to a man here in Philly a few days after you run away. She supposed to be a nanny to his children. Ain't seen her since."

Maggie exhaled, relieved that Susannah was safe. If she'd been at home, she might have been killed too. Despite their last encounter, Maggie held no ill will towards her cousin. After all, Susannah had never known anything but animosity, so how could she possibly behave any other way? Da always said the actions of others were usually the result of their environment, not necessarily the person inside.

Maggie wiped away her tears. "Are you happy here?"

"It not like it was at your uncle's farm. I know he was a bad man, but he left us be. We had good houses and all the food we need. Long as we did our work and mind our business our lives was good."

"Is Mr. Harmon a cruel man?"

"He not a bad man, but he don't pay much." Willa clasped the small of her back with her left hand. "Don't know how much longer I can do this launderin'. I miss makin' remedies. If my back give out, I be livin' in the streets, sure enough."

"Come with me," Maggie said, an idea blossoming.

"Where we going?"

"Trust me."

Maggie grabbed the basket and ran across the road with Willa waddling behind.

"Wait here, I'll be right back," Maggie said, placing the basket on the ground before bolting in the door she'd seen Seth use earlier. The interior of the building was clean and well-kept with offices lining a long hall. Seth stood at the other end of the space shaking hands with a well-dressed colored man.

"Mr. Daniels, I need to speak with you please," Maggie called out.

Seth walked down the hall and leaned over, concern masking his face. "What's the matter?"

"We have a situation."

Straightening up, he grabbed her hand and lead her down the hall. "Mr. Stills, this is Maggie Mil...McFarland."

"Nice to meet you," he said with a nod. "I overheard you say there's a situation. How can I be of service?" He wore a crisp white shirt, neatly confined in a brocade waistcoat, and dark trousers. His dark eyes were kind but serious, giving her a sense that he could, and would, provide whatever help was needed.

Maggie told them about Willa and her plight after Mr. Stevenson's farm was sold. "She's getting older and won't be able to do heavy lifting much longer. I cannot abandon her." Maggie's throat constricted as she spoke.

"What do you have in mind?" Seth asked.

"Maybe we could take her back with us. She's the one who taught me about herbal remedies. She'd be an asset to Rose Hall."

"You say she has knowledge of remedies?" Mr. Stills queried.

"Extensive knowledge of ointments, salves, and liniments."

"Where is she?" he asked.

"In the back alley."

"Please, bring her in."

Maggie ran down the hall and motioned for Willa to join them. She lumbered up the stairs with the overflowing basket, huffing as she stepped inside. Maggie took the basket and placed it on the floor. "Follow me."

Willa looked up and down the walls, taking in the atmosphere as she followed Maggie.

"Mr. Stills, this is Willa, the woman I spoke of."

"It's very nice to meet you, Willa," he said with a slight bow. "Your friend has informed me you have knowledge of medicinal treatments."

"Yes sir, I does." Pride straightened her posture and lifted her chin as she spoke.

"It just so happens I know a physician in need of someone with your capabilities."

"You think he want a colored woman workin' for him?" she asked, arching her eyebrows.

Mr. Stills chuckled. "It's not a man, and yes *she'd* be happy to employ a colored woman. Dr. Towne is an abolitionist."

"Abo what?" Willa asked, tilting her head as she scrunched her face.

"Abolitionist," he said, his eyes twinkling. "It's a person who opposes slavery."

"Well, I'll be. Never heard of no one like that, or a female doctor either."

"Would you be willing to speak with her?" Mr. Stills queried, his eyebrows raised in anticipation.

Willa glanced at Maggie. "You be here with me?"

"Of course," she replied, squeezing her old friend's hand.

"I'll send word. Can you wait a bit?"

Willa looked down the hall at the basket of laundry. "I suppose the washin' can wait, but not too long or I be up till midnight."

With a smile, Mr. Stills disappeared into his office, wrote a note, and sent it by way of his currier.

Seth waited with Willa and Maggie in a large room furnished with a set of parlor chairs, a silk covered settee, and framed maps of the east coast decorating the walls. Seth and Maggie sat down. Willa remained standing.

"Have a seat Willa," Maggie said, motioning to the spot next to her on the settee.

Willa hesitated, her brows furrowing.

"Not used to sitting on the good furniture," she said, gazing around the space.

"You're a guest here and allowed to sit on the furniture. Honest," Maggie said softly, encouraging her friend to sit.

"How he get all this?" Willa asked, lowering her ample figure onto the settee.

"Mr. Stills is very successful." Seth smiled, obviously endeared by Willa's wonderment as she studied her surroundings.

"What he do?" Willa asked.

"He's in the business of helping people," Seth replied.

Before Willa could ask another question, an attractive woman walked into Mr. Stills' office wearing a well-tailored dress of blue broadcloth, her dark hair pulled into a tight bun. Moments later Mr. Stills entered the room and made introductions.

"Miss Willa, this is Dr. Laura Towne."

"Please, Mr. Stills, Miss Towne is sufficient." Her no-nonsense manner warmed the atmosphere as she sat in the chair next to Willa.

"I understand you're well versed in herbal mixtures," she said gently.

"Yes ma'am, I is."

"Tell me more."

Maggie watched Willa's guarded demeanor soften as the conversation between the two women progressed. Dr. Towne was an intelligent, yet kind soul who seemed intrigued by Willa's talents. By the time the conversation came to a close, Dr. Towne was giving Willa the address where she was to report the following morning. She'd send a carriage to pick Willa up and move her into her establishment where she'd have a room and fair pay for her duties.

"Forgive me ladies but I must return to the clinic. Until tomorrow, Miss Willa," Dr. Towne said with a nod of her head. "Safe travels to you Miss McFarland, and you Mr. Daniels."

"Thank you, Miss Towne. This means the world to me," Maggie said, extending her hand. "I hope we meet again someday."

"If you ever return to Philadelphia, please call on me. It's not likely I'll ever travel south," she replied, returning the handshake.

Overjoyed by the outcome, and Willa's improved prospects, Maggie watched Dr. Towne saunter down the hall and out the back door.

"Thank you, Miss Maggie. I owes you for this. You's a good girl and I loves you," Willa said, tears welling in her eyes as she clutched Maggie's hands in hers.

"I love you too, Willa. And consider this repayment for saving my life. I wouldn't have survived without you and Letty. All the things you taught me have served me well and helped so many others."

Seth and Maggie escorted Willa to the end of the hall. Grabbing the basket, Seth looked at Willa. "Where are you heading?"

"I can't let you haul that!" Willa said with hands on her hips.

"You don't have a choice. Either I carry it for you or it stays right here," he said, his jaw set.

"Humph. If you's gonna be stubborn, I reckon I ain't got no choice."

Seth raised an eyebrow as he glanced at Maggie before following Willa down the street to the washhouse.

AFTER SPENDING much of the day with Mr. Stills, they made arrangements for the night at a hotel in the center of town. Anxious about the trip home, Maggie rose early the next morning, dressed, and stood at the front of the hotel watching carriages and wagons rattle past as clouds of dust swirled from the dry roads. It would be another hour before they left, enough time for her to take a quick stroll.

Lovely brick houses laden with trelliswork and bordered by picket fences lined the street. Wanting to escape the dust from the main thoroughfare, Maggie jaunted down a side street where the scenery altered to ramshackle homes and derelict cottages. Her heart skipped when she noticed a young woman across the road clutching a child to her chest. She watched as the woman turned, her face registering immediately with Maggie, despite its sallow hue.

"Susannah!" Maggie hollered, running across the street and nearly colliding with a man on horseback.

As Maggie approached, she noticed Susannah's shadowed eyes, sickly pallor, and ragged clothing.

"What do you want?" Susannah grumbled, a sneer wrinkling her upper lip.

"Susannah, I'm so happy to find you," she said, reaching for her cousin's hand.

Recoiling from her touch, Susannah readjusted the child resting on her hip.

"I've been concerned for you since I heard about your parents," Maggie declared.

"A pathetic thing to say considering you're the reason they're dead."

Maggie sucked in a breath at the accusation.

"How can you say such a thing?"

"Because Father was right about you. You've brought nothing but shame and disgrace to our family." Her words were punctuated by a cough. Regaining her breath, she continued her tirade. "You ruined my life and I'll never forgive you for it!"

"I've been gone for a long time. How could I have done anything to harm you?"

Susannah stepped closer, her eyes narrowing as she hissed, "You were the one that was supposed to serve Mr. Farris, not me. Instead, you ran off leaving Father no choice but to send me in your place."

"I was told you were a nanny."

"Ha! You're as stupid as ever! You never did see the world for what it truly is. I was sent as a nanny, but had other *duties* to perform for the man of the house."

Maggie swallowed the lump rising in her throat. "I'm so sorry, Susannah, I had no idea of your father's plans..."

"You're sorry? Do you have any idea what it's like to be sent away under the pretense of caring for children only to discover there was more to the position than you thought? Do you know the horror of being awakened in the middle of the night with a hand pressed over your mouth while he climbs on top of you and does as he pleases?"

Susannah clenched her jaw, bouncing the child who began to squirm in her grasp. Turning back to her cousin, she growled, "Every time he climbed on top of me, I closed my eyes and thought about how much I loathed you for putting me there!"

Maggie gulped at Susannah's declarations.

"It's not my fault, Susannah."

"Yes, it is. You ran away, you coward. What else could my father do but send me?"

"Susannah, I know you're upset but your anger is misdirected. I knew nothing of this arrangement, and you of all people can understand why I ran away. My life was in danger. If you knew what your father had done..."

"Don't you dare blame my father!"

The child began to fuss as Susannah steadied her breathing.

"Susannah, I can help you now. Take the child back to her parents, pack your things, and leave that dreadful man."

"Parents? I'm her mother! After using me for his own pleasure, that miserable wretch threw me out into the streets because of my *condition.* My parents were too ashamed to take me in, so I lived like a beggar until I found a way to survive. It may not be dignified but it's the only skill I possess and men are always in search of it."

A wave of nausea traveled from Maggie's stomach to her throat rendering her speechless. Mr. Stevenson was truly a monster. Despite Susannah's wrongful accusations, Maggie couldn't bring herself to hate someone who'd endured so much suffering.

"You must know that my leaving had nothing to do with what happened to you."

"What I do know is that no one would give a second thought about an Irish whore, but a lady such as myself," a cough interrupted her vitriolic outburst.

"Come with me Susannah, you and your daughter. I can get you respectable work."

"How dare you pity me after your selfishness made me what I am? When my mother learned of my condition, she wouldn't even look at me. At least my father had the good sense to put them both out of their misery. I'd rather die than take charity from Irish filth." With her last statement, she spat on Maggie and strode up the walkway into the dilapidated house behind her.

Stunned, Maggie wiped the spittle from her face and glanced around trying to process what Susannah had said. Anguish squeezed her lungs making it hard to breathe as she hurried back to the hotel. She was ready to head home, far from the torment of her past and Susannah's unfounded accusations. She longed to help Susannah but her cousin's hatred thwarted any chance of reconciliation between the two of them.

When she reached the hotel, she was breathless and defeated. Seth leaned against the front of the building with one foot propped on the wall and his hat corralling his unruly curls.

"You OK?" he asked as Maggie approached.

"Not really. How soon can we leave?"

"As soon as we call for the carriage. What happened?"

"I'll explain once we're on our way. I want to leave this place and never come back," she muttered, hurrying to her room to get her things.

When she reemerged from the hotel, Seth was standing by the carriage. He helped her in and took the seat across from her and secured the door. Maggie settled on the tufted seat as the carriage lurched forward.

"Tell me why you're in such a rush to leave."

Maggie released a long breath.

"I ran into my cousin this morning."

"And?"

"It wasn't a pleasant reunion."

"What happened?"

Maggie told him everything that had transpired and the

miserable circumstances in which Susannah now found herself.

Seth let out a whistle. "That's pretty bad."

Maggie nodded, looking out the window as the landscape whizzed past in ribbons of color.

"I can't help but wonder, if I hadn't run..."

Seth grabbed her hand. "If you hadn't run, you'd be the one that man took advantage of. How would that have helped the situation?"

"Perhaps he was attracted to Susannah and wouldn't have done such things to me."

Seth released her hand and sat back with a huff. "Trust me, men like that don't care about women. He'd have used you the same way and tossed you to the street. Be thankful you got away when you did."

"I'm thankful but feel terrible about Susannah. She has a point..."

"Stop it, Maggie, it's not your fault. You offered to help her and she turned you away. She's an adult and capable of making her own choices. She could have gone home if she chose."

"She tried. Her father sent her away because of her condition."

"Still not your fault."

Maggie knew Seth was right but it didn't sooth the sting of Susannah's words. It seemed everyone would have been better off if she'd never come to this country. The bulk of it all weighted her chest as her mind wandered to her Da. Would she ever see him again? A cloud of despair hovered over Maggie as she closed her eyes and rested her head against the cushioned seat, thankful to be galloping towards home.

47

They traveled for several hours, stopping occasionally to rest the horses. A light rain began to fall, dampening the roads and reducing the dust. Maggie's body rocked with the rhythm of the carriage as she and Seth talked about Annalissa and her biological mother, Annie.

"Is Annalissa a lot like her mother?"

Seth hesitated before responding. "In a sense, she is."

He glanced down at his hands.

"I know how much you loved Annie."

"I did care for her. Mostly, I wanted to do right by her, make up for all the horrible things my father had done. But honestly, there's only one woman I've ever truly loved." His voice trailed off and his eyes shifted toward the window.

Maggie could see the longing in his expression as the clattering of carriage wheels and hoof beats drowned out the whispers of her heart. With all her soul, she wished she could be the object of his affections even though she knew Elora was the only one who could fill that role.

"Tell me more about your friend Willa," he said, his jovial

countenance chasing the shadows of the past from his expression.

Maggie shared how Willa and Letty had taken her under their tutelage and treated her like family. "If it hadn't been for them, I don't think I could have survived, well them, and Sellers."

Maggie swallowed the lump in her throat and fidgeted with her fingers.

"I didn't mean to stir up unhappy memories," Seth said. "How about you read some more poetry?"

His smile sent a warmth spreading through her chest, melting away her remorse. Maggie's heart pounded as she reached for the book and opened it. She felt a flush spread up her neck as she read each stanza beneath Seth's gaze.

They stopped in Virginia to deliver the papers for Mr. Stills before resuming their journey, each night staying with various friends of the Railroad. The last part of the trip was inundated with rain, slowing their travel and forcing them to seek shelter with another family acquainted with the Railroad. Fortunately, the family wasn't housing any passengers at the time and was more than happy to take Maggie, Seth, and the carriage driver in for the night.

After a filling supper and casual conversation, everyone retired to their quarters. Once in her room, Maggie slipped into her cotton gown and slid between the sheets as warm breezes flapped the gauzy curtains in steady rhythm with the rain. When the droplets pelting the windowsill increased, she padded across the wood floor and yanked the sash down slamming her finger in the process. A yelp flew from her lips as blood trickled from the wound, a dull pain radiating up her hand. She'd need a proper bandage and felt certain she could find something downstairs. Pulling a hankie from her travel bag, she wrapped the finger, grabbed a candle, and stepped into the hallway. Seth peeked his head out from the room across the hall, his rumpled curls and bare shoulders making her knees weak.

"Everything ok? I heard you holler."

"I slammed my finger in the window and need to bandage it."

"Let me help you." He disappeared into his room as the door creaked open, giving Maggie a glimpse of the muscular framework of his back while he slipped on a shirt. She turned away abruptly, her heart pounding and a blush heating her cheeks. Closing the door behind him, Seth took her candle leading her down the stairs and out the back door toward the kitchen house. Rain extinguished the candle as their feet splashed across the yard. Once inside the kitchen, Seth lit two candles and rifled through the pantry for bandages. Droplets beaded the tips of his hair, soaking the top of his shirt. Even in his unkempt state, he was handsome. Maggie inhaled, her heart and her finger throbbing.

"You seem to know your way around here," she said.

"Been here a few times before. The Covingtons do a lot for us."

He motioned for Maggie to sit at the table where he joined her and moved the candle closer. In the flickering light, his blue eyes danced and his wet hair began curling into ringlets.

"Give me your hand," he said softly, unwrapping the crimson-stained cloth. His touch sent goose bumps crawling up her arm.

She watched as he gingerly wrapped her finger and secured the bandage.

"That should hold till morning," he murmured, looking up.

"Thank you," she replied, her mouth suddenly dry.

The rain intensified, pelting the tin roof with stone-sized hail followed by a loud thump. They darted to the window looking for the source of the noise.

"Over there, a limb fell," Maggie said, pointing to the right.

"We might need to wait a bit before heading back," Seth suggested, turning around and bumping into Maggie.

"Sorry, I wasn't paying attention," he mumbled, gazing down at her.

The candlelight cast shadows across her face, illuminating her fair skin and green eyes. Seth reached out and fingered a length of her auburn locks that had come loose. Maggie couldn't think for the sound of her heartbeat pounding in her ears, silencing her internal cries to step away.

Gently, Seth cupped her cheeks and pulled her close, his kiss as gentle as the petals of a rose. As his hands made their way down her back, she melted into his form, the warmth of his body chasing away the chill from her damp clothes. She didn't care what her inner voice was saying; all she knew was that somehow this was right. In that moment, she forgot everything as the kiss washed away her guilt and sorrows.

Another kiss brushed her cheek as he whispered, "I love you, Maggie McFarland." His lips returned to hers this time with more passion.

"I can't do this," she said, stepping away. Her entire frame quivered as tears sprang to her eyes, her hand covering her mouth. "This is wrong."

"How can this be wrong?" he muttered, grasping her upper arms, his eyes pleading with her. "If you don't love me, tell me now and I'll never bring it up again."

Wrenching free, she bolted out the door, her bare feet splashing across the puddled ground. When she reached the house, she burst through the door and ran up the stairs to her room where she slammed the door and crumpled to the floor, her tears mingling with the drops of rain streaming from her hair. The hem of her nightdress was stained with mud and her heart ached. The interaction with Seth left no doubt that something was developing between them, something she had to stop before things went too far. Maggie couldn't let her selfish ambitions ruin Elora's future with Seth.

The sound of footfalls on the stairs alerted Maggie that Seth was coming.

With a quiet rap on her door, he whispered, "Maggie, I'm sorry. Please open up and let me explain."

"Leave me be," she sobbed.

When she heard his door close across the hall, Maggie rose from the floor, her knees trembling. She changed into a dry nightgown, plunked down on the bed, and wept. She loved everything about him; the way his eyes glimmered when he was up to something mischievous, and how his hair cascaded in waves from beneath his tattered hat. She loved the gentleness in his touch and the softness of his lips. Wiping the tears away, Maggie rested her head against the pillow, listening to the rain pitter-patter against the windowpanes. With this latest accidental tryst, she pondered how she'd be able to face Elora again, not to mention endure the long journey home with Seth.

48

Morning brought to light the shame Maggie was feeling from the previous night's transgression. Seth's refusal to meet her gaze during breakfast told her he felt the same. After the morning meal, with hardly a word passing between the two of them, they prepared for the final leg of the journey. Once they bid goodbye to the Covingtons, Seth escorted Maggie to the carriage and opened the door for her.

"About last night..." he muttered.

"We need never speak of it again," she replied, keeping her back to him while fighting back the need to cry out that she loved him too. "Let's just go home."

Seth handed her into the carriage and started to close the door.

"Where are you going?" she called out.

"I thought it best if I rode up top."

Maggie nodded. With a weak smile and a battered heart, she slumped against the seat as Seth secured the door and alighted to the bench seat beside the driver.

Maggie's mind wandered to her future plans. Now more

than ever, she needed to find employment elsewhere. The agony of knowing Seth might reciprocate her feelings was more than she could bear, especially when she'd have to watch him marry someone else. And he would marry Elora, he was too decent to go back on a promise.

Sighing, Maggie closed her eyes and ruminated on the previous evening's encounter. No doubt, their slip was a mistake spawned by Maggie's deep-seated affection for him. As the carriage jostled her about, she tried desperately to erase the feel of his arms around her waist and the soft brush of his lips against hers.

The journey seemed to last forever while Maggie stewed over her hopeless situation until the gothic arches of Rose Hall came into view. Maggie's eyes moistened. She adored the fairy-tale mansion and all the people who resided there. The trip had been pure misery. She felt guilt for Seth's predicament and remorse for her role in it. Convinced she'd unintentionally sent some sort of signal to cause him to behave in such a manner, Maggie hoped it wouldn't deter him from his commitment to Elora. After all, Elora was the victim in all of this. Perhaps Maggie was the conniving person her uncle and cousin had accused her of being.

Maggie practically leapt from the carriage when it halted in front of the mansion. Elora rushed down the porch stairs as the carriage pulled away.

"Welcome home!" she declared, embracing her friend. "I've missed you so!"

"It's good to be back," Maggie replied, forcing a smile.

"Where's Seth?" Elora looked around, her shoulders slumping.

"He must've gone to help with the horses," Maggie replied, glancing over her shoulder as the carriage tottered down the trail.

Elora shrugged and looped her hand through Maggie's arm. "Let's go inside, tea is ready."

As they walked into the house, Maggie inhaled taking in the delicate scent of freshly cut roses soaking in a porcelain vase by the door. The splendor of the place she'd come to call home with its ancestral portraits lining the walls and shards of sunlight dappling the floor bathed her in comfort. Her heart wrenched at the thought of having to leave it all. But what other choice did she have? She couldn't risk succumbing to her desires and leading Seth astray. First thing tomorrow, she'd have a discussion with Dr. Polk about relocating. The sooner she left, the better. With her thoughts racing, Maggie suddenly felt bone tired.

"Maggie, are you coming?" Elora asked, pausing in the doorway of the parlor.

"If you don't mind, I'm rather weary from the trip. I'd like to lie down for a bit."

Elora's lips sank into a frown. "One cup of tea will refresh you, I promise." She declared with a sparkle in her eye.

"I suppose one cup won't hurt," Maggie replied, following her friend to the parlor.

Maggie halted at the doorway, her knees weakening as her breath caught. She grabbed the doorjamb with her right hand while Elora steadied her on the left. Her eyes blurred as she locked onto the figure standing by the front window.

"Da!" she screamed, dashing across the room into his open arms. She held him with all her strength while sobbing into his shoulder, the scent of pipe tobacco tickling her nose. Minutes passed before the tears slowed to a trickle and Maggie lifted her head to make sure he was really there.

"I can't believe it," she whimpered as her body trembled.

"Aye. Stop all this carryin' on. Ain't nothin' but your ole Da."

"How did you, I mean when did you...?" She hugged him once more before plopping onto the settee next to him. At that moment, she realized the Polks were in the room, Mrs. Polk's eyes wet with joy while Dr. Polk looked on, his mustache curled in a smile.

Maggie waived off the cup of tea that Elora offered, too excited to drink.

"How did you get here?"

"It weren't easy. Wasn't long after you left that I lost the farm. So, I sold the herd and set out to find work. Did that for a few months and then fell ill. Nice lady in Dublin took me in and nursed me back to health. When I recovered, she put me to work making repairs to her house. When things started getting worse, I set out again but this time found solid work that paid well. I saved what I earned, bought passage on the next ship for America, and sailed to Pennsylvania," he grinned. "Only problem was when I got there, I learned your uncle was dead and no one knew where to find you. It took some doin' and a bit of cash here and there, but eventually I stumbled across a real nice lady who remembered seeing a girl matching your description. She suggested I place an ad in the paper and a few weeks later found my way here."

"When did you arrive?"

"About a week after you left. These folks were kind enough to let me stay until you came home."

Maggie hugged him again, her muscles releasing years of pent-up tension while a fresh trail of tears streamed across her cheeks.

THE EVENING WAS FILLED with laughter and chatter and no sign of Seth. With her Da by her side, Maggie was too overjoyed to dwell on his absence. After dinner everyone retired to the front verandah where they rocked and sipped sherry.

"Tis a beautiful place here. It's like nothing I've ever seen my entire life." His Irish brogue stained each phrase.

"I agree Da, it's magical." Maggie looked around. Everything seemed lovelier than it had ever been.

"Maggie, how was the trip?" Elora asked, apparently eager to hear all the details of their journey. "Did Seth and his sister like one another?".

"They got on very well but I think Seth should tell the story." Maggie didn't feel like discussing anything about Seth.

Thankfully, Elora didn't query further.

When the sherry glasses ran dry and yawns swept through like a dust storm, everyone decided it was time to retire. Maggie's father was staying in one of the cottages and kissed her forehead as he stood.

"G'night, my sweet Maggie."

"Goodnight, Da. I love you."

"Love you back."

She watched as he strode down the walk and disappeared into the night.

Elora and Maggie trudged up the stairs, Maggie's body aching from days of travel and the adrenaline rush from being reunited with her Da. She was content and exhausted at the same time while the woefulness of her relationship with Seth dampened her enthusiasm. When they reached the upstairs landing, Elora grabbed Maggie's hand.

"May I join you for a bit? We've not had a chance to chat privately since you returned."

"I'm not sure how long I'll last," Maggie announced, hoping to keep their conversation brief. "I'm exhausted"

"I completely understand," Elora replied, following her into the room.

They sat on the bed facing each other as Maggie adjusted her skirts, avoiding Elora's gaze.

"Did you have a nice time with Seth?" Elora asked, tilting her head, the right side of her mouth curling.

Guilt jolted through Maggie's body, straightening her stature. "What do you mean?"

A broad grin lifted Elora's flushed cheeks. "I was just wondering if anything happened between you two on the trip? After all, you were cooped up *alone* in that carriage for days." She drew out the word 'alone' like a heartsick schoolgirl.

"Why would you ask such a thing?" Maggie declared, jumping up, the color draining from her face. "Of course, nothing happened."

Elora's shoulders slumped. "Oh, it seems my hopes were in vain."

"Why would you want something to happen between Seth and me when he belongs to you?" Shock raised Maggie's voice an octave.

Elora's mouth gaped open as a full belly laugh tumbled across her lips.

"Me? And Seth? Where did you get such a ridiculous notion?"

"It's obvious how you feel about one another. You spend a great deal of time in each other's company and you're always whispering in such an intimate manner."

"Seth is like a big brother to me. And the only thing we whisper about is you! He's smitten with you."

The force of Elora's declaration knocked the wind from Maggie's lungs as she plunked onto the bed. Her mind raced from the way he'd held her at the dance to the kiss in the kitchen house to his profession of love. Not only had she misunderstood his intentions, but she'd turned him away more than once.

"He must hate me," she muttered, burying her face in her hands.

"Oh Maggie, what have you done?" Elora asked, resting her hand on her friend's shoulder.

"Nothing that can't be undone," she declared, taking in a deep breath.

A streak of boldness shot through Maggie's body, awakening a determination she'd never experienced. She'd spent too much of her life cowering and second-guessing herself. And that would stop this minute.

Maggie jumped to her feet, kissed Elora's cheek, and started for the door.

"Where are you going?" Elora hollered.

"To take control of my life."

"At this hour?"

"Why not?" A surge of courage pulsed through Maggie's veins. She was fed up with being meek. This was a time for action, not timidity.

Maggie marched down the back stairs into the sultry night air to the tune of chirping crickets and trilling cicadas. As she rushed along the river's edge, beneath a spray of glittering stars, Maggie's heartbeat quickened with each step, strengthening her resolve. She rounded the corner and noticed a light shimmering in the window of Seth's cottage. Thank goodness, he was still awake.

Stepping up to the door, she knocked, her heart thrumming at the sound of approaching footsteps. Seth opened the door and stood in the glow of lamplight his shirt untucked and his jaw set as he gazed down at her.

"Is everything ok," he asked curtly.

"May I come in?"

He diverted his eyes from hers as he stepped back, allowing her to enter.

Maggie took in the neat and orderly space as shadows pirouetted against the walls from the oil lamp on the center table. Her nerves jittered while she tried to find the words to express her feelings.

"Why are you here Maggie? You've made it abundantly clear how you feel about me."

"No, I haven't," she said, looking at the defeat veiling his demeanor, his lips furled in a frown. Her Irish spirit ruffled her heart as she cupped his face in her hands.

"I love you, Seth Daniels."

Pulling him closer, her body molded against his like it had the previous night. She kissed him with all the passion she'd withheld for so long, the wall of doubt tumbling down taking her inhibitions with it. He returned the kiss before pulling back, his eyes wild with delight.

"I don't understand," he said, a smile crimping his cheeks. "Last night you..."

"Last night I thought you belonged to Elora. Today I know differently."

"Why would you think such a thing?" he chuckled, his eyes regaining their familiar sparkle.

"It's a long story."

Brushing a lock of hair from her cheek, he grinned, "We've got nothing but time."

He took her hand and led her to the settee.

"Tell me what made you believe Elora and I were attached."

"You were always huddled in intimate conversations and seemed so...close. I just assumed you were promised to one another."

"Our conversations revolved around you," he said with a huff. "Elora was the first to notice my attraction to you and asked me about it. We've known each other a long time and share almost everything. She kept encouraging me to say something, but I'm uncomfortable sharing my feelings," he said, his lips forming a thin line. "I learned at an early age that feelings could be used against you."

There was an edge to his words as unpleasant memories

drifted behind his sea blue eyes. Maggie took his hand and drew him back to the present.

"When Elora told me the truth this evening I couldn't wait until morning. I had to see you tonight."

"All this time I thought you didn't like me," he replied with a chuckle that made Maggie's insides quiver.

She rested her hand against his cheek and met his gaze. "I liked you the first time I met you, but I've loved you all my life."

He leaned over and kissed her again, this time longer and harder. It seemed as if her world was finally coming together. All of a sudden, she pulled back.

"Is everything alright?" Seth shifted in his seat, his furrowed brow and apprehensive expression suggesting he feared he'd been too bold.

"Things couldn't be better, but there's something else I need to tell you."

"What?"

"I found my father."

"You're kidding?" Seth asked. "Where is he?"

"Here. He's been in America for months searching for me. Eventually he got a lead that brought him to Rose Hall. He arrived while we were up north."

"That's amazing! I know how much you've missed him." He caressed her cheek and leaned in for another kiss when he stopped and jumped up.

"What's the matter?" she asked, puzzled by the fear shrouding his expression.

"You should probably get back to the house."

"Why?"

"I don't want your father to get the wrong impression."

"He's already in bed for the night," she chortled. "Besides, he's going to love you."

"Not if he catches us alone." Seth's eyes were as big as marbles.

"He trusts me and knows I wouldn't do anything *improper*," she said, raising an eyebrow.

"Well, I'm not going to take that chance. I'm sending you to your room, Maggie McFarland before you put me on bad terms with your father."

Maggie rose to her feet planting her hands on her hips. "A gentleman wouldn't send a lady home in the dark without an escort."

"What makes you think I'm a gentleman?" he asked, pulling her to him.

Swallowing hard, Maggie's eyes scanned his face. "A dear friend told me."

Seth released her with a low bow, his arm sweeping the air.

"Shall I take you to the palace, m'lady?"

"Indeed," she replied, slipping her arm through his.

They took their time plodding along the path by the marsh, stopping once at the large oak to confirm their affection once more. When they reached the back door, Seth leaned over and left a whisper of a kiss on Maggie's lips.

"Until tomorrow, Miss McFarland."

"Until then," she whispered before slipping in the house and up the stairs to her room where she flung herself onto the bed in a fit of giggles.

After years of turmoil and doubt, Maggie was immersed in a state of euphoria. Her Da was alive, Seth was free to return her affections, and she had meaningful employment. She felt her heart would explode with the sheer exultation of her circumstances, and for the first time since coming to this country, her sleep was sweet.

49

Maggie rose with the sun, rejuvenated by the previous day's events. The excitement of Seth's affirmation sparked something deep within her. She felt freer and more confident. Like the poetry she'd read throughout her life, the day seemed brighter and more fulfilling. Even the air smelled sweeter.

When she entered the dining room, her father was already sitting with the Polks sipping coffee and chatting. Elora rushed to Maggie's side.

"How are you this morning?" she purred, leaning into Maggie, her expression one of anticipation.

"Better than I've ever been."

"What happened last night?"

Maggie winked. "Caught me a handsome buccaneer."

"You'll have to tell me everything after breakfast," she said, squeezing Maggie's hand as they joined the others at the table.

The conversation buzzed over coffee and eggs like a hive of bees when Seth walked in.

"Good morning, Seth," Mrs. Polk declared, a broad smile

lifting her cheeks. "We're glad you're able to join us. How was the trip?"

"Rewarding," he said, glancing at Maggie. He fixed a plate of food and a cup of coffee and took the seat next to Elora. Maggie made introductions.

"Seth, I'd like to introduce you to my father, Gerald McFarland. Da, this is Seth Daniels."

The two men stood and shook hands.

"Tell us about your sister, Seth," Dr. Polk said, taking a bite of eggs.

"She's as delightful as Maggie described. I'm hoping to see her the next time I travel north." Seth flashed a smile at Maggie, sending a flush of color to her cheeks.

The conversation continued as everyone had another round of coffee or tea while discussing the shocking revelation of Seth finding his sister after so many years. Finally, Mr. McFarland sat back in his chair, rubbing his chin, his change in demeanor catching Maggie's attention.

"Da, is everything alright?"

"I believe things are quite well by the looks of my lassie. Tell me Mr. Daniels, how long have you and my daughter been involved?" he asked, with a sideways glance, his lips pursed.

Elora nearly dropped her cup, tea sloshing over the sides as a murmur bubbled through the room in an effervescent fizz. Seth's face colored and Maggie fidgeted.

"What makes you think such a thing, Da?"

"I'm no fool. I can tell when two people are enamored with one another. How long has this been going on?"

Mrs. Polk's eyes widened as she perched on the edge of her seat while Elora blotted at the puddle of tea spreading across the table linen.

Maggie glanced at Seth, uncertain how to respond.

Seth sat up straighter, inhaled, and looked at Mr. McFarland.

"Sir, I've had feelings for your daughter for some time, but only recently discovered that she returns those feelings." Smiling, he gazed across the table at the halo forming around Maggie's head as sunrays filtered through the windows behind her.

Elora gasped at his declaration as Mrs. Polk declared, "Well, it's about time."

Mr. McFarland stood, walked around the table to his daughter, and pulled her into a bear hug like he had when she was little. "Seems my lassie is growing up and won't be needing her ole Da anymore."

Returning his embrace, she snuggled her head on his shoulder and whispered, "I'll always need my Da."

He kissed her forehead and turned to Seth. "I'm glad to know such a fine fellow has captured my Maggie's heart."

"With all due respect, sir, you don't even know me," Seth said with a puzzled expression.

"I know my Maggie," he replied, raising his chin. "If she's set her heart on you, that's good enough for me."

The right side of Seth's mouth curled as he gave a nod. "Thank you for your confidence."

When the morning meal came to a close, Maggie and Elora scurried off to their daily duties while Seth and Mr. McFarland lingered on the front porch. They stared at the sprawling field of green as a gentle breeze wafted in from the marsh, carrying the pungent aroma of the Lowcountry.

"You'll be good to my lassie?" Mr. McFarland asked.

Seth inhaled deeply. "I'll take good care of her and never let her come to any harm. I love her more than I've ever loved anyone."

Their eyes met briefly as Mr. McFarland gave a nod, letting Seth know he approved. Seth tipped his hat and strode down the brick walkway towards the barn, a swagger to his gait. Seth and Mr. McFarland, or Gerald as he insisted on being addressed, bonded quickly, each pleased to hold a special place in Maggie's heart.

Over the next few months, Maggie accompanied Seth on several missions. They made a formidable team when conducting cargo northward and their journeys home never seemed long enough. Each had traveled painful roads on their way to each other and they reveled in their good fortune.

Maggie wrote Annalissa about the reunion with her Da and the turn of events with Seth. Weeks later, she sat on the front porch chuckling as she read Annalissa's response.

Dearest Maggie,

How wondrous that you are finally reunited with your father and in love with my brother. I'm overjoyed at your good fortune which you greatly deserve. I love you and cannot wait to see you again.

Forever yours,

Annalissa Milner

PS. I told you I had a feeling about this, and I'm so glad I was right.

As am I dear friend, as am I, Maggie thought, swaying in the rocker with the letter resting in her lap as a herd of deer sprinted across the lawn in the late afternoon shadows.

50

OCTOBER 1850

The morning air hummed with excitement as Maggie woke to her wedding day. She was going to wear the emerald green frock she'd worn to the barn dance the previous autumn that highlighted her eyes and accentuated her auburn hair. More importantly, she'd be surrounded by all of her family members, both near and far, including the Milners who had arrived days earlier for the special event. Every aspect of the ceremony was steeped in meaning from the Rev. Milner presiding over the nuptials, to her Da walking her down the aisle, to Elora and Annalissa standing at her side. The best part was the amazing man she was about to marry. As she sat before the vanity mirror, she secured the crown of flowers with its sweeping train of lace to the crest of her auburn locks. She pondered all that had happened to bring her to this point; some bad, some good, but all had coalesced in a harmonic composition for this day.

A chill blew through the room, shuddering her body as if someone had left a window open in the dead of winter. Her lungs constricted when she noticed a shadowy figure in the looking glass materialize behind her. His dark lanky stature and broad smile tugged at her heart.

"Sellers," she whispered, turning to gaze at her old friend.

With a nod, he winked before vanishing as quickly as he'd appeared. A deep-seated peace enveloped Maggie for the first time since his death. After years of blaming herself for his demise, she realized it had all been in vain. Seth had told her repeatedly that his murder wasn't her fault, and although her mind accepted it, her heart never had. And now on the happiest day of her life, Sellers' spirit had paid a visit, and she was glad.

A knock broke the trance as Elora popped her head in the door, a wreath of tiny roses laced in her upswept hair.

"Are you ready?"

"Indeed, I am."

With one last glance in the mirror, Maggie stood, her spirit lightened and her regrets dispelled. The guilt she'd harbored for so long had sailed away, freeing her from years of anguish and self-doubt. Whatever had transpired in the past was nothing more than shadows in the moss.

Elora reached over to readjust the lace veil cascading down Maggie's back as they started out the door and down the stairs where Mr. McFarland waited. His eyes misted at the sight of his daughter descending the winding staircase.

"Always knew you'd be the prettiest bride in the world," he said, kissing her cheek as he tucked Maggie's hand into the crook of his arm. "I love you, sweet Maggie."

"Love you too, Da."

"Shall we?"

She nodded, tears tickling her lashes. Elora and Annalissa walked ahead of her onto the porch.

Maggie took in a sharp breath when her eyes rested on Seth. He was dressed in a suit, his wavy hair slicked back and his smile as broad as the river. The adoration emanating from his gaze grabbed hold of Maggie's heart, momentarily taking her breath away. The guests looked on in a series of grins and tears, as Maggie promenaded down the brick walk with her father to the grassy area beneath one of the towering oaks. Her Da kissed her cheek and placed her hand in Seth's before stepping back and joining the other onlookers.

Rudy and Dr. Polk stood at Seth's side, beaming as if it were their own daughter being given in marriage. When everyone was in place, the Reverend began the ceremony.

"Welcome honored guests as we come together to witness the bonding of two very special people in holy matrimony."

The rest of the world went silent, except for the Reverend's words, as Maggie gazed into Seth's deep blue eyes, her chest swelling and her knees quaking. They recited their vows and sealed the union with a soft kiss to an eruption of applause.

She was married. They walked into the crowd of well-wishers, overjoyed by the outpouring of love shared by all. Throughout childhood, Maggie's focus had been helping her father with the sheep, studying her lessons, and hoping someday to attend University. Although she'd always wanted a family, it hadn't been a priority at the time. Now she couldn't imagine anything else. Her trajectory had taken a sharp turn, giving her purpose, fortitude, and a man she cherished.

A four-piece ensemble started playing a waltz as Seth led his bride from the crowd and scooped her into his embrace. By the second stanza others joined in, whirling across the lawn in a rainbow of taffeta. All in all, it was one of the most magical moments of Maggie's life.

"Well, m'lady, I hope ye be happy with this old scalawag," Seth said in his best pirate voice.

"Indeed, I am," she replied, her eyes fixed on his.

. . .

Days later, everyone gathered on the front porch to bid farewell to the Milners as they prepared for the long journey north. Maggie's Da gave the reverend's hand a forceful shake.

"Thanks for saving my Maggie. I'm forever indebted to you."

"She's family and we were happy to have her with us."

Annalissa and Maggie embraced. "We're really sisters now," Annalissa said, tears streaking her cheeks.

"Indeed, we are."

After a series of hugs and promises to write, and a few more tears, Maggie and Seth stood arm in arm watching the Milner's carriage disappear down the drive in a cloud of dust.

51

Over the course of a year, Maggie and Seth went on several more missions until Maggie's girth began to expand, leading her to halt her trips for a while, as did Seth.

May brought spring showers and budding trees with soft breezes carrying the scent of jasmine across the porch. Maggie swayed back and forth in the rocker, her mind wandering back to the day she told Seth he was going to be a father. Exuberance flashed in his eyes and broadened his smile. Without speaking a word, his demeanor said everything as he swept her into his arms and held her tightly to his chest. His heart pounded against her cheek reminding her of the tiny heartbeat pounding in her womb. The moment still resonated in her heart.

By the ninth month, Maggie wobbled more than walked and she'd not caught sight of her feet in weeks. The baby was constantly shifting, keeping her awake at night. Seth was beginning to get anxious with all of her restlessness despite her reassurance that everything she was experiencing was normal.

As the sun peeked over the horizon, a sharp pain followed by another, woke Maggie. Seth stirred and rolled over.

"Everything OK?" he muttered.

"I think the baby is coming," she replied with a groan as she grasped her swollen belly.

Within seconds, Seth was out of bed, pulling on his pants and boots and running out the door to fetch the midwife. By the time Vera arrived, Maggie was pacing the floor, her skin beginning to glisten with sweat as apprehension withered her expression.

"Take a deep breath, we gots a baby to bring into dis world."

Seth left Maggie in the capable hands of Vera while he alerted the Polk's and his father-in-law of the impending birth. On several occasions, Mr. McFarland had expressed anxiety about his daughter's safety but Dr. Polk reassured him Vera was the best midwife in the county and had delivered dozens of babies without incident. Seth clung to the doctor's words in an effort to ward off his nervousness about the delivery. At least he'd have his father-in-law keeping him company while they waited for the baby to arrive.

The sticky Lowcountry heat shrouded the atmosphere inside the cottage. Mr. McFarland and Seth sat in the sauna-like parlor, tensing every time they heard Maggie's cries. Time moved at a turtle's pace, leaving Seth's nerves raw and his stomach in knots. Watching Mr. McFarland stare out the window, his jaw set and body tense, only added to the unease. It was obvious he was concerned. With his late wife having died from complications shortly after Maggie's birth, Seth could understand his trepidation. In order to maintain his sanity, Seth pushed those thoughts from his mind.

All of a sudden, Vera popped her head out of the door, her expression grim. "I need you to send for Dr. Polk."

Before he could ask why, she'd returned to the bedroom, shutting the door behind her.

"I'll go," Mr. McFarland offered.

Within minutes, Dr. Polk rushed through the front door and into the bedroom, leaving Seth and Mr. McFarland simmering with anxiety.

More than an hour passed when Maggie let out an ear shattering scream followed by the wailing of a baby, bringing exhales from Seth and his father-in-law.

Running his fingers through his hair, Seth breathed deeper than he had since the ordeal began at daybreak. Vera emerged from the bedroom cradling a small bundle swaddled in a blanket.

"Congratulations, Mr. Daniels. You gots a fine baby boy."

Seth took the infant in his arms and gazed at the tiny bundle, tears forming in his eyes as a smile wrinkled his cheeks. Love for his son filled his chest until he thought it would burst. Mr. McFarland walked over and tickled the baby's chin.

"How is Maggie?" Seth asked still staring at his son. When he looked up, Vera was gone.

Seth's mouth formed a thin line as a sense of dread wrapped around his chest like a boa constrictor.

"Don't worry, they'll let you see her shortly," Mr. McFarland said, patting Seth's arm. "They need to tidy things up before you go in there."

A slight grin lifted Seth's lips as he exhaled, comforted by his father-in-law's words. Seth padded back and forth across the small parlor, cradling his son. When the baby began to fuss, he knocked on the bedroom door. Without waiting for a response, he opened the door and peered inside only to catch a glimpse of the doctor working furiously as Vera sat at Maggie's head wiping her sweat soaked face with a cloth. Maggie's skin was pale and her expression glazed as if she were somewhere far away. Seth closed the door and held his son closer. Looking across the room, he met Mr. McFarland's gaze.

"What's wrong?" he asked, his brows furrowing.

Seth shook his head. Fear squeezed his throat, blocking any words from forming. He sat in the rocker and stared at his son trying to chase away the angst plucking at his heart. Mr. McFarland's relaxed demeanor shifted as he dropped onto a chair and rested his face in his hands.

Nearly an hour later, Dr. Polk emerged from the bedroom, his expression reserved and blood tinting the edges of his rolled-up sleeves.

"How is she?" Seth asked, rising from his seat.

"Not well. She's lost a great deal of blood."

"Can I see her?"

"In a moment. Let Vera clean things up."

A few minutes later, Vera stepped out and took the baby as Seth bolted into the room where Maggie lay still as death. Her face was devoid of color and her hair and body were drenched with sweat. The bed linens had been replaced; the bloody ones piled in the corner.

Seth pulled up a chair and lifted Maggie's motionless hand to his lips.

"Maggie," he whispered.

No response. The only sound was the beating of his heart in time with the ticking of the mantel clock.

"Maggie, it's me, Seth," he said, taking in a deep breath. "You did great. We have a beautiful, healthy son."

Stillness suffocated the room making him feel as if he'd go mad if she didn't respond.

"Maggie, please listen to me. I need you to fight." He squeezed her hand as tears flowed across his sculpted cheeks. He'd waited so long for her and he wasn't about to let her go now. "Our son needs his mother. We both need you."

Dr. Polk came in and stood at the foot of the bed.

"What's wrong with her?" Seth asked, his voice a whimper.

"Something went wrong during the delivery and she started

hemorrhaging. I managed to stop the bleeding for now but she's lost a lot of blood," Dr. Polk sighed.

"But she'll recover from it?" Hope lifted his eyebrows.

"At this point, I don't know how much damage has been done or if she's still bleeding internally. We'll keep her comfortable and do everything we can. I'm sorry but I can't give a more definitive answer than that."

Seth looked away, a river of tears dripping onto his shirt. She'd been fine this morning. They were so excited about the baby. How could something so blissful go wrong so quickly?

"I'll be back in a little while to check on her. Vera has the baby and will take good care of him."

"Thanks Doc," he replied, clutching Maggie's listless hand.

Dr. Polk turned to leave when Mr. McFarland entered. His watery eyes rested on his daughter as he swallowed hard. "If ye be needin' me to sit with ya, I'll gladly do so." His voice cracked as his stare fixed on Maggie.

"I'll send for you if anything changes."

Mr. McFarland gave a nod and left the cottage, leaving Seth in a state of agonizing disbelief and despair.

Elora arrived shortly thereafter with a basket of food. Rapping on the bedroom doorframe, she peeked in with a slight smile, careful to maintain a bright countenance.

"I brought you something to eat."

"Not hungry," he muttered.

"Seth, you have to eat something."

"I don't want to eat," he growled.

Elora stepped closer and draped her arm about his shoulders, speaking softly in his ear.

"I'll sit with her while you eat and get some rest. I promise I'll call for you if she wakes, but you must keep your strength up for the baby's sake, as well as for Maggie."

He turned to Elora, his eyes meeting hers with an unspoken recognition. They'd known each other for so long that communication was always a natural exchange between them, with or without words. He steadied himself as he rose from the chair, his legs numb from sitting for so long, and traipsed to the parlor.

Over the course of several days, Seth took breaks to eat and spend time with the baby while Elora sat with Maggie. Miss Clara was kind enough to bring a basket of food for the midday meals and dinners. The balmy days of May made the cottage stiflingly warm even with the windows open. Elora and Seth took turns washing Maggie's face and arms with a cool cloth and reading from her tattered copy of Byron. Birdsong drifted through the bedroom window as the sun sent slivers of light splattering across the wood floors.

With each passing hour, Maggie's frame seemed to shrink as frailness consumed her once healthy figure. Dr. Polk made frequent visits but kept his comments brief and to the point. She was fading slowly with little hope of recovery. Her father checked in periodically, hardly speaking a word when he was there. It was obvious the idea of losing his lassie was more than he could bear.

After a week of watching and waiting, Dr. Polk stood by the bed checking Maggie's pulse. He looked at Seth whose eyes were hollow, his once strong stature languishing in despair.

"Seth, it's nearly her time."

"No, I won't accept it. She's going to get better." His last sentence came out as a whisper.

"I'm going to ask her father to come in. He needs to take his leave of her."

Seth looked up at the doctor with red-rimmed eyes. "There must be something we can do."

"I'm afraid we've done everything medically possible. I

know it's hard, but you need to gather all your strength and focus on your son," he replied squeezing Seth's shoulder.

Seth stepped into the parlor with Dr. Polk where Mr. McFarland stood at the window. As he turned, grief shone in his eyes, shattering the last semblance of Seth's fortitude. Mr. McFarland had already been through this with his wife and now had to face it again with his beloved daughter.

"I'm sorry, Mr. McFarland. She's not got much time left. You need to say your goodbyes," Dr. Polk said quietly.

Standing in the doorway, Seth watched Mr. McFarland enter the room. He took in a deep breath as he looked at his daughter lying upon the bed, her burnished locks giving her pale skin a translucent appearance. He sat down and scooped up her hand.

"My beautiful lassie, listen to me. I need you to fight, wee one. You can't go out like your mum. She was a strong woman, but she hadn't the Irish spirit runnin' through her veins like you do. You got a son and a husband waitin' for ya and I'll not have ya giving up. Do ya here me?"

The only movement was the shallow rise and fall of her chest. His tears cascaded across her knuckles as he kissed her hand. "I love ya my sweet lassie."

With his jaw clenched, he walked past Seth and left the cottage.

Seth trudged across the room and sat by her side, studying the gaunt remnant of her body. Slumping over her, he rested his head on her chest and sobbed. He cried for everything they'd endured together, all the things they'd ever hoped for, and all the things that would never be.

The silence of the room was suffocating as he closed his eyes. All of a sudden, he felt her hand brush the curls from his forehead.

"Seth." Her voice was a mere whisper.

Opening his eyes, he gazed at the glowing aura surrounding her face, making her hair gleam a brilliant red.

"Maggie..." he muttered.

Seth bolted upright as the morning sun peeked through the curtains. His head drooped when he realized it was only a dream, until he felt her hand on his and heard the soft murmur of her voice.

"Seth."

"Maggie?"

Her eyes fluttered as she mumbled, "I'm thirsty."

"Hold on," he said, rushing to the dresser to pour a glass of water. He slid his arm behind her neck and propped her head up as he held the glass to her lips.

She took several shallow sips before asking, "Where's my baby?"

"With the midwife. She's taking good care of him."

"I want to see him," she said softly.

Seth swallowed hard. "You're weak Maggie and need to rest."

"Please, bring him to me."

He lowered her head against the pillow, her eyes fixed on him as he darted into the next room where Elora was reading.

"Maggie's asking for the baby."

Elora jumped to her feet. "She's awake?"

"Yes. Please hurry!" Seth exclaimed, returning to Maggie's side.

Moments later, Vera came in and handed the baby to Seth. Shortly after that, the doctor stormed into the room breathlessly, his eyes widening at the scene. Seth sat beside Maggie, one arm supporting her shoulders and the other helping her hold the baby. Her eyes sparkled from shadowed sockets as she gazed at her cooing son.

"Hello Maggie. How are you feeling?" the doctor asked with a grin.

"Tired. Thirsty," she replied, her voice barely audible.

"I would imagine so. Seth if you'd please take the baby out, I'd like to examine my patient."

Seth carried his son to the next room where he paced back and forth.

"How is she?" Seth asked when Dr. Polk entered the room.

"I can't explain it," the doctor said, shaking his head. "Her pulse is stronger and the fever has broken."

"She's going to be OK?"

"I can't say for sure, but this is a good sign."

A surge of hope puffed Seth's' chest bringing tears to his eyes. "May I go back in?"

"Of course. I'll have Clara prepare some broth."

Seth returned to Maggie's bedside with the baby, and reveled in the miraculous change in her condition.

"He's so beautiful," she whispered. "What's his name?"

Seth shrugged his shoulders. "I've been waiting on you."

Joy lifted the right side of Maggie's wan lips as her hollow eyes fixed on her child.

"I've always liked the name Joshua."

"It's a good name, a strong name, and I believe it suits him," Seth replied, his face beaming as he gazed upon his wife and son.

52

THREE YEARS LATER

Joshua was a sturdy child with curly red locks, crystal blue eyes, and a smile that brought joy to all. It had taken nearly a year for Maggie to recover from the delivery of what would be her only child. While she couldn't risk another pregnancy, per Dr. Polk's advice, she delighted in her son and was thankful she'd been given a chance to watch him grow.

Maggie's role as a mother superseded her availability to go on missions; however, she wasn't about to cease her work for the Railroad. She set up a crib in the kitchen where she and Heddy worked, allowing her to care for her son while mixing remedies. With his new role as father, Seth's outings were limited to ones closer to home.

Maggie and Heddy finished their work before lunch and called it quits. Summer baked the Lowcountry in a suffocating heat, forcing everyone to seek respite on porches or beneath the cool shade of sprawling oak branches. After luncheon, Maggie and Elora sat on the verandah of Rose Hall with little Joshua playing next to his mother. Their respite was interrupted when a coach caromed down the drive and stopped at the end of the walkway.

"That's odd. Was your father expecting guests?" Maggie asked.

"Not that I'm aware of."

Standing, Maggie and Elora watched the coach door swing open as a thin woman with a little girl stepped to the ground. Although greatly altered in appearance, Maggie recognized her instantly.

"Susannah," she whispered.

She hurried down the walk to greet her cousin with Elora trailing close behind.

"Susannah, what are you doing here?" Maggie asked, shocked to see her cousin.

"May I speak with you privately?" she said, a cough punctuating her statement.

"Of course. Elora, may I introduce my cousin, Susannah. This is Elora Polk."

"Nice to make your acquaintance," Susannah replied, her eyes eclipsed by dark shadows and her skin jaundiced.

"Is this your daughter?" Maggie asked.

A slight smile lifted Susannah's sunken cheeks. "This is Jane."

The little girl curtsied, bringing a smile to all. She was a smaller version of her mother; the same dark eyes and brown hair. She was nicely dressed in a pink frock with her curls corralled by a matching silk ribbon.

"Elora would you mind taking Jane inside for some tea while I speak with my cousin?"

"Come with me Jane. Maybe we'll get lucky and find some fresh baked cookies too."

The little girl smiled, grasping Elora's hand as they traipsed up the brick walk. Stopping midway, Jane turned and hollered, "Goodbye mama."

"Goodbye my sweet girl," Susannah replied tears welling in her bloodshot eyes.

Elora scooped up Joshua on the way into the house, leaving Maggie and Susannah alone.

Susannah looked away before speaking.

"I'm sorry to trouble you. You're the last person I ever wanted to ask for help but I have nowhere else to turn."

"What can I do?"

Susannah broke into a fit of coughing. Maggie reached for her arm to steady her but she yanked it away.

"I came to ask you to take my daughter. She's getting older and it's harder for me to hide what I do. She's the only good thing in my life and she deserves better than what I can provide."

Reaching into her purse, Susannah removed a few bills. "I have a small amount of money for her expenses and I'll send what I can as I earn it. She's no trouble at all. The only thing I ask is that you educate her. She's very bright."

"There's no need for financial support. I'm more than happy to care for her. Perhaps you could stay here with her. I could help you find a respectable occupation."

Another fit of coughing doubled Susannah over, a crimson stain spreading across the hankie she held to her mouth.

"Susannah, please come inside."

"The coach is waiting. I need to get back to Pennsylvania," she insisted.

"You traveled all this way to leave your daughter? What if I'd refused?"

Susannah's eyes met Maggie's with a hint of resignation. "I despise you from the depths of my soul but I knew you wouldn't turn her away. You're too kind for that, Maggie McFarland."

"Actually, it's Daniels. I'm married. That was my son you saw on the porch."

Susannah succumbed to another coughing fit that rattled her to the ground.

The coach driver hollered from his bench seat. "Ladies, I can't linger all day. I have passengers to deliver."

"Go on sir. The lady will be staying," Maggie called out, waving him on his way.

The coach driver snapped the reins against the horses' haunches and tottered down the dirt drive in a cloud of dust.

"What are you doing? I can't stay here. I need to get back..." Susannah coughed as she tried to stand.

"Don't be ridiculous. You need medical attention."

"I've already had medical attention," she sputtered. "How do you think I found you?"

Maggie kneeled beside her. "I don't understand."

"I met a doctor by the name of Towne. She said I was sick and needed to make arrangements for my daughter. That's when I saw the old Negro woman that used to work for my father. I asked if she knew where you were and she said to ask the doctor. Dr. Towne made some inquiries and was able to give me your location."

"Come with me to see Dr. Polk," Maggie said, trying to help Susannah to her feet.

"I don't want Jane to see me like this..." she gasped.

"Stay here, I'll be right back." Maggie ran around the side of the house to the back entrance of the doctor's office. Bursting through the door, she hollered breathlessly,

"Sir, I need your help."

The urgency in Maggie's tone imparted the seriousness of the situation to which Dr. Polk responded immediately. He followed Maggie out front where Susannah slumped against a tree trying to stifle another coughing fit.

"Can you stand?" he asked.

Shaking her head, Susannah muttered, "I don't think I can."

He scooped her up in his arms and hurried to his office,

leaving Maggie standing at the end of the walkway. She went inside and found Elora and Jane happily ensconced in the lady's parlor nibbling cookies and sipping tea. Joshua sat at Elora's feet with a half-eaten cookie in one hand and a wreath of crumbs on the floor around him.

"Please, join us Maggie," Elora said with a broad grin. "Jane was telling me all about her trip here in the coach. It sounds like quite the adventure."

"Are you the Miss McFarland my mama told me about?" Jane asked.

"I am, but please call me Maggie."

The little girl scrunched up her face. "I don't think mama would like that. She likes me to address people by their proper name."

"I believe she'd make an exception this one time."

Miss Clara popped her head into the room. "Dr. Polk would like to see you."

"I'll be right back," Maggie said before hurrying down the hall where Dr. Polk waited.

"How is she?"

"Not well. She's in the advanced stages of her illness." Dr. Polk's expression was grim, making Maggie's heart pound harder.

"What is her medical condition? Maybe I can mix something to help."

"It's affiliated with her line of work. There's nothing you can create that would cure this." The doctor's gaze was steady. "She'll not recover."

"How long does she have?"

"Weeks, maybe days."

"May I see her?" Maggie asked, a lump forming in her throat.

"Of course."

Maggie stepped into his office where Susannah was buttoning up her dress.

"Don't pity me Maggie," she said with a cough.

"I don't pity you, Susannah, but I would like to help you."

"Humph, I'll bet you would."

"Why are you so angry with me?" Maggie asked.

"Because of your self-righteous attitude with all that dribble about your wonderful life and *loving* father. You always acted as if you were better than everyone else. The only genuine person in my life is Jane. She's such a good girl..." her voice trailed off.

"She seems a very sweet little girl. Shall I bring her in?"

"No! I don't want her to remember me like this. I need to get on a coach to Philadelphia. That's what I told her would happen, no sense confusing her now."

"Does she know you intended to leave her here?"

"She cried a great deal when I told her, but I promised that her life would be so wonderful she'd soon forget about me."

"I'm certain she'd never forget you," Maggie said softly.

Dr. Polk knocked on the door and stepped into the room. "Miss Stevenson, I've had one of the cottages prepared for you."

Shaking her head, she held up a trembling hand. "I'm not staying here."

"I don't think you understand," the doctor said grimly, "You haven't a choice in the matter. You're much too ill to travel."

Susannah hunched over and closed her eyes. "Dr. Towne told me I had a few months."

"Her prognosis was probably accurate but the journey here may have weakened you. I'm afraid your disease is progressing at a rapid rate."

Susannah looked at him, her eyes swimming in tears. "How much time?" she muttered.

"Not long, I'm afraid. Maggie will take you to the cottage and get you settled in."

"I haven't any money..." she said, a sob shaking her frail frame.

Dr. Polk patted her shoulder. "There's no need to concern yourself with such things. You'll be well cared for, I assure you."

MAGGIE ESCORTED Susannah to a two-room cottage away from the main house. Once inside, Susannah collapsed against the pillow as Maggie helped her to bed.

"I don't need your charity, or your care," she muttered, turning her head away. "Just leave me be."

"You can object all you want, but I intend on nursing you."

Maggie's resolve won the battle. Too weak to protest, Susannah finally acquiesced. Per her request, they didn't reveal her location to Jane who believed her mother had returned to Pennsylvania by way of the coach.

Each day Maggie tended to her cousin. She left the front and back doors of the cottage open, allowing the marsh breezes to freshen the stale air of the sick chambers with summer's delectable scents of roses and honeysuckle.

As the time drew near, Susannah's complexion grew sallow and her manner altered to one Maggie had known before the world destroyed the small bit of kindness residing in her cousin's heart.

Susannah's brow was beaded in sweat and her body soaked with fever. Maggie blotted her forehead with a cool cloth before refreshing it in the basin and reapplying it.

"Why are you being so nice to me? I don't deserve it," she croaked.

"Because you're family."

"But I've been so cruel, just like my..." she closed her eyes.

"You're not like him, Susannah," Maggie said, brushing a sweaty lock of hair from her cousin's face.

"But the things I did to you."

"Are all forgiven."

"How can you possibly forgive me for what I've done?"

"Because I choose to do so," Maggie replied gently. "Hate only harms me. What good would it do if I shunned you? You'd die alone and Jane would be left to strangers. She's innocent and deserves a good life. And I intend to give it to her."

"No one but Jane ever loved me," she said, diverting her watery eyes from Maggie's gaze.

"I loved you once."

"And I destroyed it," Susannah muttered.

"There's still time."

"Not for me."

"As long as there's breath in your body, there's time for love. Please, let us be the family we were meant to be," Maggie said softly.

Susannah gasped out a sob that quickly erupted into a violent fit of coughing.

"Hush, dear cousin. Don't upset yourself," Maggie said, wiping the bloody spittle from her cousin's lips.

"I'm sorry for all the terrible things I've done or said to you," Susannah murmured.

A smile creased Maggie's cheeks as she stroked Susannah's hair. "I know."

"Promise me something."

"What?"

"Don't ever tell my Jane what I did to make money or how she was conceived." The look of desperation emanating from Susannah's sunken features squeezed Maggie's heart and moistened her eyes.

"I'll tell her that her mother was a dignified and educated lady who stitched the most beautiful embroidery I've ever seen. And I shall do my best to instruct her in the art, although I fear I'll fall short of your talent."

Susannah closed her eyes as a slight smile creased her hollowed cheeks.

"Sing to me, Maggie. You always had the loveliest voice," she said, her words a mere whisper.

Maggie swallowed the lump hovering in her throat and started singing.

"Come thou fount of every blessing..."

A cough arrested Susannah's chest, her life spewing out in a spray of scarlet. Maggie wiped her cousin's chin and held her hand as she hummed the tune. Susannah's breath came in labored gasps as her eyes fluttered shut. Tears leaked across her pallid cheeks, washing away years of repressed anger and bitterness until she breathed her last.

Leaning over, Maggie planted a kiss on Susannah's forehead. "Goodnight, dear cousin. I love you."

Maggie sat on the edge of the bed holding her cousin's lifeless hand. She wept for the years of abuse her cousin had endured, the anger she'd harbored, and the precious time she'd sacrificed in pursuit of revenge. But most importantly, Maggie wept at the love they'd shared in the end, and that Susannah was finally at peace.

SETH STOOD by Maggie's side as the pastor said a few words over Susannah's grave with Dr. and Mrs. Polk next to them. Elora stayed at the house with Jane and Joshua. The children were too young for a funeral service, and Jane was still under the impression her mother had returned north. When the pastor finished the prayers, he walked back toward the house with the Polks. Inhaling deeply, Maggie stepped forward and placed a single yellow rose on the freshly packed grave. Tears streamed across her cheeks as she stared at the simple headstone.

"Would you like some time alone?" Seth asked, draping his arm around Maggie's shoulders.

"No," she sniffled. "It's time to get back to the kids."

"What are you going to tell Jane?"

"Nothing yet. But I will soon. She's a bright child and she's already expressed concerns about her mother's health and the long journey back to Pennsylvania. Susannah's medical issues didn't go unnoticed by her daughter." Maggie wiped a tear from her eye. "Once Jane gets a bit more settled, I'll explain that her mother is gone. She deserves a chance to bond with our family before we permanently remove the only person she's ever known."

"You're a compassionate and clever woman, Maggie Daniels. I love you."

"I love you," Maggie smiled as Seth leaned in with a kiss.

He offered his arm, which Maggie gladly accepted. They strolled back to the house at a leisurely pace as soft breezes billowed in from the marsh fluttering the black ribbons flowing from Maggie's mourning bonnet. Her heart had finally healed. She'd endured abuse, the murder of a dear friend, guilt, regret, and fear. Despite it all, she'd survived and made amends with the ghosts from her past. It seemed as if all the horrors she'd encountered were nothing more than distant memories and she could finally face whatever the future held.

EPILOGUE

1859

Blood trickled from Maggie's nose as she rested her head on a pillow of hay and pulled the shawl tighter around her shivering frame. Cold air seeped through the boards of the hayloft, its icy fingers chilling her bruised cheek. The sound of cattle shifting in the stalls below comforted her racing thoughts. Hopefully, she could get some sleep and leave before dawn.

As her eyes fluttered shut, the echo of boots on the rungs of the ladder filtered through the space. Her breath caught as she leaned up on one elbow to see who was coming. In the darkness, her uncle appeared at the edge of the hayloft with a gun pointed directly at her. She opened her mouth to scream, but terror rendered her mute. His lips curled into a sneer, followed by a flash of light and a loud explosion. Then all went dark...

Maggie bolted upright in bed, her scream finally materializing. A hand touched her shoulder making her jump.

"Maggie," Seth whispered. "Are you alright?"

Her heart thudded against her chest with the force of a sledgehammer as she fought to shove the terrifying image from her mind. Steadying her breathing, she turned to see Seth sitting up, his gaze filled with concern. She exhaled when she realized she was at home.

"It was only a bad dream," she muttered, still shaking from the experience. Maggie hadn't had a nightmare about her uncle in years.

Seth brushed a wisp of auburn hair from her sweat-laden brow.

"Do you want to talk about it?" he asked, his hand guiding her head to his bare shoulder.

Maggie shook her head and buried her face into the crook of his neck.

"Whatever it was, you've got nothing to fear," he said softly. "You're safe and no one can hurt you anymore."

It was as if he knew what she'd dreamt. Relaxation took hold, her body melting into his. Even with the comfort of Seth's embrace, Maggie couldn't help but feel as if the dream was some sort of omen, warning of terrible things to come.

AUTHOR'S NOTES

The plight of Maggie McFarland and her need for family and love takes her from Ireland to America where she is faced with a series of trials that would destroy most people. But she perseveres and finds hope and purpose by helping the enslaved escape bondage. While all the intricacies of the Underground Railroad are not discussed in this book, the terms are accurate and similar situations did occur. After reading the memoirs of Levi Coffin and William Stills, I adapted many of the scenarios so the reader could get a broad view of how the Railroad functioned. The horrors faced by those seeking freedom were infinite. And yes, many would rather die along the route than return to bondage.

We tend to take our freedom in this country for granted but for many of the enslaved it was the most important thing in life. I hope this book encourages you to investigate the history of the Underground Railroad and its passengers more closely and to celebrate those who risked life and limb for freedom. Most importantly, we need to remember that we are all God's children and deserve love, dignity, freedom, kindness, and safety.

Glossary of Terms:

Stations, safe houses, or depots-hiding places in homes, churches, or schoolhouses for those traveling by way of the Underground Railroad

Passengers, cargo, or freight-escapees

Terminal, Heaven, or Promised Land-Canada or northern free states

Conductor-free individuals, both black and white, who helped escapees to freedom

Stationmasters-people who hid escapees in their homes

Stockholders-financial supporters who donated money for Railroad activities

ACKNOWLEDGMENTS

First and foremost, I want to give God all the glory for this story. Without him, this book would not exist.

To my loving husband, Darryl, who tolerates my long hours of writing, listens to the storyline again and again, and who supports my writing-I love you!

To my mom who reads, edits, rereads, and cheers me on-I love you! My mom is the one who cultivated my imagination and the belief I could do anything I put my mind to do.

To my other mother, Millie Boyce. Thanks for always believing in me and encouraging me. Love you!

To the greatest writing coach ever! Thank you Charlotte Rains Dixon-you are the best!

To Rena Violet-thank you for creating the gorgeous cover for Shadows of the Moss! You did an amazing job encapsulating the beauty and the meaning of the story!

To Susan Diamond Riley who offered to be my Beta reader-thank you for your encouragement, support, and your gracious words!

To my family and friends who have supported and encouraged me in my writing-Joan Jones, Christine Lanning, Jo Beaver, Diane Morrison, Kelly Taylor, Bernie Ladd, Lynn Bristow, Darlene Stokes, Sarah Hetzler, Janell McClure, Peggy Callahan, Richard Norris, Doreen Plyler, Charlotte Holmes, Jack and Becky Miller, and everyone who has read my books-I truly appreciate and love you all!

To those who have gone on to Heaven but remain in my heart: Harvey B. Oates, Catherine Oates, Michael Wiegel, Sam Poovey, Rachell Poovey Navratil, Mark Navratil, Phyllis Sooy, Cathy Benson, Dolly Nash, Pat Conroy, and Dorothea Benton Frank.

ABOUT THE AUTHOR

Kim Poovey is an author, storyteller, and living historian. She has traveled the Southeast for more than 20 years performing in period attire on 19th century fashion, mourning practices, sentimental hairwork, and other Victorian era topics. She is also a presenter for the OLLI program at USCB.

In 2011 she portrayed Mrs. Stanton, wife of Secretary of War Stanton (Kevin Kline), in the Robert Redford film, *The Conspirator*. Additional film projects include portraying the wife of a villainous husband in the Vook version of Jude Devereaux' novella *Promises* and the documentary *Beyond the Oaks, Lowcountry Plantations*.

Her published works include *Truer Words, Through Button Eyes: Memoirs of an Edwardian Teddy Bear, Dickens' Mice: The Tails Behind the Tale,* and *The Haunting of Monroe Manse.* In addition, Kim has written for several magazines to include Beaufort Lifestyles, Bluffton Breeze, Citizen's Companion, and the Civil War Times.

When not writing or performing, Kim works as a school psychologist. She lives in a haunted 1890s Victorian cottage in the South Carolina Lowcountry with her husband, Darryl, and their furry children.

CPSIA information can be obtained
at www.ICGtesting.com
Printed in the USA
LVHW041928260422
717290LV00006B/156